ROBBED

THE WINDS OF TRUTH

BOOK I

BY

LILLY MAE

AcuteByDesign, Publisher
Book Interior and E-book Design by AmitDey | amitdey2528@gmail.com

Map Design by Sammie Lam
Printed in the United States of America

Michele Thomas
Executive Publisher

For Baba.
This was always for you.

16 Kingdoms
Weatherhelm
D+F
Sumadine Woods
Paraoff
Tisara
Irnavai

CONTENTS

CHAPTER 1

Tara's breath made translucent white clouds in the icy air as she trekked up the hill on the way back to her house. The house was located in the quiet western outskirts of Jisara's bustling, dusty capital, on a hill that few visited and even fewer took the time to notice. Snowflakes fell and landed softly on her hair and shoulders, and she shivered from the numbing cold. She was returning from the marketplace, where her Aunt Beatrice, with whom she lived, had sent her to fetch some herbs and oils needed for cooking.

Aunt Beatrice loved to eat. She could eat huge amounts of food at a time, which was evident in a large physique that mirrored her intense personality. Delicacies of all kinds were whipped up in her house daily, and elaborate dinners, complete with four courses, were served every night. During the holidays, she loved to make extravagant meals that would leave her with days of leftovers. Dish after dish was made, until every pan in the house was dirty and not a teaspoon of flour was left in the flour jar.

But Aunt Bea never actually *did* any of the cooking, of course. No, that was Tara's job. As was everything else, it seemed.

Tara Florreson was beautiful, with a thicket of blonde curls and startlingly blue eyes. Uncommonly petite, she took after her short mother. She had been raised in a sophisticated environment by parents who taught her that being kind and ladylike was of utmost importance. Yet in her aunt's home, she was treated more like a slave than a lady.

Tara's parents were explorers for the King. They went to foreign lands and stayed for a time, exploring the new places and getting to know the people that lived there. When Tara was younger, their voyages were always short, and she stayed with her kindly Gramma Kate while they were away.

Some time ago, though, her parents had been called on by the King to *live* in a faraway jungle for several years. The mysterious land was called Paroaff.

Paroaff was a dangerous, wild land, filled with monstrous beings and unknown creatures. It was a sort of enchanted prison for the evils of the world, locked by magical barriers that contained the hellish things within. Humans did not dare settle there for fear of the unknown, instead naming it the Land of Hidden Monsters and avoiding it at all costs.

Four years back, griffins invaded Jisara and killed several people, one of whom was the first-born princess of the kingdom, leaving the kingdom without an heir. The attack instituted a widespread fear because the barriers of Paroaff were failing.

Tara, being a young girl, had overheard snatches and whispers of conversations about 'the protection' and 'stolen.' But no one ever told her anything more.

After that incident and the resulting death of his daughter, the King decided that he needed to know more. He sent Tara's parents to find the griffins' lair, learn more about them, and find out how they got into Jisara. As always, Tara's Gramma Kate cared for her while they were away.

However, a year into Tara's parents' mission, Gramma Kate got very sick and couldn't take care of Tara anymore. Kate was sent to a neighboring kingdom to receive medical care. A short time later, Tara received word that her Gramma Kate had died.

She had never imagined at the time of their final departure that she would never see her again.

Tara's parents came home to comfort her, but they had to return to Paroaff soon. They knew their daughter was too young to live alone, but they couldn't bring her into the Land of Hidden Monsters with them. So, they took her to Aunt Bea's house.

Aunt Bea agreed to look after Tara, but only if Tara followed all her rules. And Aunt Bea had a lot of rules. Eighty-seven of them exactly, each about not disturbing the household (meaning Aunt Bea), doing exactly as the household (Aunt Bea again) told her, and waiting hand and foot on the household (Aunt Bea one more time). Such tasks included cooking, cleaning, sewing, laundry, household repairs, gardening, and a myriad of other tasks that seemed almost arbitrary. Tara wasn't sure she could handle being a maid to her own aunt.

However, her mother, knowing how difficult Aunt Beatrice would be, asked Tara to make her a promise. "Be kind to her, Tara. Please. However hard it may become."

And ever since, Tara had forced herself to be kind all the time. She'd bit back rude remarks that she so longed to say to her aunt, all because she loved and respected her mother. She had promised to be kind, and Tara never broke her promises.

Tara sighed, lost in these thoughts, as the snow began to fall harder and her teeth began to chatter uncontrollably. The cold jarred her thoughts, and she remembered the holes in her tattered coat and her lack of proper boots or mittens—all of which was thanks to Aunt Bea's rule of "no fixing, making, or mending anything for yourself"—since it apparently wasted time that could be spent mending things for Aunt Beatrice. Tara quickened her stride, eager to get home and warm herself.

As she neared the house, she could hear Aunt Bea yelling. At whom or what she was yelling, Tara didn't even bother to wonder.

Aunt Bea was a strange woman. People tend to get attached to little hobbies, or things they love to do. Almost everyone has some sort of *something* they find very intriguing or enjoyable. Some find great pleasure in art or reading, others find pleasure in collecting little trinkets or crafting. Aunt Bea? She found great pleasure in yelling.

Aunt Beatrice yelled at everyone and everything. If she stubbed her toe on the leg of a chair, she would begin to scream at the chair for being in her way, and then at her foot for being so stupidly blind and running into the chair.

So when Tara heard her aunt's shrill, cracked voice echoing through the walls, hollering about who knows what, she decided to duck behind the house and slip quietly in through the back door to avoid getting lectured. However, the moment the door shut behind Tara, Aunt Bea was upon her, and—you guessed it—yelling.

"TARA FLORRESON!" Aunt Bea's voice thundered through the room and pierced any former silence right in the chest. "WHERE HAVE YOU BEEN?"

Tara crinkled her nose at the rancid stench of her aunt's breath in her face. "The marketplace, of course."

Her aunt grabbed Tara by the scarf and picked her up off the ground with one hand. "WHAT ON EARTH WERE YOU DOING THERE?" she screamed, spittle flying from her mouth.

"You told me to fetch some herbs and oils!"

"DID I TELL YOU WHEN TO DO IT? NO! YOU WERE SUPPOSED TO DO THAT THIS AFTERNOON! BUT YOU DIDN'T EVEN PAUSE TO HEAR ME ON YOUR WAY OUT! ARE YOU THAT EAGER TO GET AWAY, YOU WRETCHED, STUPID CHILD!?!"

"I'm not a child!" Tara squirmed in her aunt's grasp.

"HOW DARE YOU SPEAK TO ME!"

"Aunt Beatrice!" Tara shrieked.

Aunt Bea took a deep breath, calming herself. "You will address me as *Madam,* thank you very much," she said, her voice at a more reasonable volume now. Tara fell to the floor as she was roughly released.

Tara sat up and rubbed her elbow, wincing. "Since when?" she asked bitterly.

"Since now. I am making some new rules. You need some discipline around here! You're too lazy, too happy. You're living a splendid life, and a maid like you shouldn't have a splendid life. You don't deserve to have it as good as you do! Why, you're practically *living* on the couch!"

Tara's jaw nearly hit the floor. "Do you have any idea how much I do for—" Tara started angrily, cut short by her aunt.

"So, you shall prepare me *six*-course meals now, instead of four, and you shall not eat unless I allow you to."

"Six courses!" Tara cried in shock. Ignoring the outburst, her aunt spoke right over her.

"From now on, you shall make *every* bed in the house, instead of just mine and yours, and the kitchen needs a new coat of paint on the walls. And please, for goodness sake, pick a classier color this time. The yellow you picked last time made the kitchen the most hideous room in the house, next to your filthy excuse for a bedroom. You will not speak unless spoken to, and you shall style my hair each morning as well. Any questions?"

Aunt Bea took one look at Tara's disgusted face and burst out laughing; a screeching, horrible cackle of a laugh. "You look upset! My, don't you see? It's a great privilege, you stupid girl! I'm allowing you to wait on the fairest woman in all of Jisara. Some people would give their lives for that chance!"

Aunt Bea then strode out of the room, laughing to herself as Tara wearily got to her feet. Tara looked sadly down the hall at her aunt's retreating back. Out of earshot, she murmured, "It appears I've already given mine."

CHAPTER 2

Chase stood alone under a bridge, concealed in the shadows, his body pressed against the cool stone wall of the crossing overhead. From his hiding spot in the darkness, he had a perfect view of a group of girls sitting together and eating. They looked about his age, maybe a bit younger. They were laughing and talking together, and although their clothes were modest due to the cold, they were laced with expensive silks.

They were young. Unsuspecting. Perfect. Perfect, that is, for Chase, and how he lived.

So, let's start from the beginning. Chase was not quite your average teenaged boy. Despite his casual appearance and his ability to slip along completely unnoticed in a crowd, there was one thing that made him very different.

Chase did not remember his parents' faces. He did not remember his last name. He simply remembered waking up to find himself cold, alone, and hungry on the borders of Jisara's capital when he was little. He remembered nothing about his parents but one thing: their kindness. He remembered being loved, which was more a feeling than a tangible memory, by two people who had raised him up until that moment when he woke alone for the first time.

Chase had waited for his parents for days, never moving from his spot on the ground. He simply knew they wouldn't abandon him. Yet his hope nearly killed him. Since he refused to budge, he would have starved to death if not for a passing traveler who took pity on him and left him with some food and drink. The small meal, however, could only sustain him for so long.

After several days had passed and the sunrise of the coming day had begun to paint the sky gold, Chase finally accepted that his parents simply weren't coming for him. That they were dead.

So Chase had to take care of himself. He started off by picking apples and peaches from Jisara's public orchard and drawing water from the well at the center of the kingdom. But he soon found that he was getting very skinny and weak. There weren't enough nutrients in the fruit for him to live off them alone He needed to find another source of food.

One day, when he was extremely hungry, Chase discovered a new way of life. Winter had just begun, and the public orchards contained nothing more than rows of bare, frostbitten trees. Chase was starving, huddling in a vacant cave he used for shelter.

Coming up the road just beyond the mouth of the cave, he spotted a middle-aged woman carrying a fresh meat pie. The crust steamed in the cold air, the smell wafting into his cave and making his mouth water. He glanced around. One pie couldn't hurt. He would just grab it and run. Easy.

He leapt out at the woman as she passed by, eliciting a shriek of alarm as he frantically grabbed for the pie. They struggled back and forth in momentary tug-of-war of the pie before Chase's foot found the woman's shin. Her grip loosened, he snatched the pie from her hands, and he ran.

Chase stared at the food in wonder for several moments before eating it. He couldn't believe he'd gotten away.

And there he had it. His method of survival. Stealing.

Chase spent the rest of his childhood training himself through experiments. Some trials went well; others did not.

Some years later, Chase robbed a man of a sword that had jewels encrusted in the hilt, hoping to sell it for money. As soon as the theft was made, the victim and half a dozen other men with daggers began pursuing him. Chase, reasonably inexperienced with weapons, was backed into an ally, trapped and alone. Fear was mottling his thoughts, rendering him incapable of thinking straight. The first man swung his sword, and out of sheer desperation, Chase lifted the blade he'd stolen in defense.

It was then that something strange happened. The sword began to seemingly move entirely on its own. From Chase's completely unexperienced hand came slashes and parries that moved faster than should have been physically possible. He felt as though the sword was controlling him, rather than the other way around. His thoughts could not follow his actions fast enough to process what he was doing, but something in swinging the sword felt peculiarly familiar. He felt as though he had been fighting like this his entire life, despite never having touched a sword before.

By the time the men realized that there was no beating him, his arm was aching from the weight of a sword he shouldn't have even been able to lift. After the men retreated, Chase nearly collapsed.

The event certainly frightened him, but his fear was not enough to make him argue his odd ability. It had saved his life, and he soon began practicing with a sword constantly. Although the skill came naturally to him, he didn't yet have enough strength to move a heavy sword around. So, he took to practicing every day, getting stronger and more skilled as his thieving skills advanced with him.

After years and years of practicing and training and failing and trying again, he was an incredibly skilled master thief and swordsman. He found two methods of stealing that were amazingly successful. The first was fighting. He would grab whatever it was he wanted, scuffle a bit if necessary, and run for it. Using his sword in an actual theft was a rare situation. Chase was fast and quiet, which was always helpful in sneaking off with things, and he had a forgettable face. Of course, he fought people not only because it worked, but also because it was more fun than using his other secret—and that was his charm.

Chase was tall and strong from years of fighting and training, and the clothes he'd pilfered screamed danger. Much of what he wore was made of black leather, save the silver sword that hung in a black leather sheath at his hip.

Chase had deep caramel skin, deep brown eyes, and a thick mop of black hair. With all that and his smooth swagger, he could trick almost anyone into paying so much attention to him that he could swipe something right from their hands and walk away with it without them even noticing—a trick that he was just about to pull off.

Chase slowly sauntered towards the group of girls near the market, who sat with their shawls pulled tight to ward off the cold air. He approached, and put one foot up on the edge of a girl's stool, resting his elbow on his knee. The girls were silent, staring at him. Most of them looked slightly frightened and shifted away from him at first. He smiled, slow and mysterious, a smile that said, *I know something you don't.* A few girls smiled back, shy and small. Others just continued to stare.

"Good morning, ladies," he said in a friendly tone. "I was just passing through and was wondering if I might sit and chat with you."

And just like that, the girls smiled and shifted, making room for him at the table. *How easily bought,* Chase thought with mild surprise as he sat down. It was usually a little harder than that to gain such trust.

"What's your name?" several girls asked repeatedly.

Chase refused to give his name, but took the names of all the girls, talking to them and being friendly. Then he made his move. He sighed as if in great regret. "Goodness, ladies! Look at the time! I must be going now."

Cries of protest rose up, but Chase silenced them. "I will see you all again. I'll make sure of it." As he went around the group, politely kissing the hand of each girl, he snatched two of their purses and stuffed them quickly into a hidden pouch behind his sheath. He bid farewell to the rest of them, then walked casually away.

He rounded a corner, then immediately pulled the two satin purses out and emptied them into his palm, relishing the weight in his hand. He pocketed the coins and headed towards the northern borders of the city.

Reaching the gate that served as the pass between the capital and Peddler's Road took little more than a quarter hour. Most travelers and wagons came in and out that way, so it wasn't difficult for Chase to duck his head and slip silently past the king's guards while they were checking a cart. He walked on Peddler's Road for a couple dozen paces, then veered into the forest that marked the capital's northern border.

Once hidden deep in the trees, he unsheathed his sword and got to work. He lunged and slashed and spun around, fighting a fierce battle against a nonexistent opponent. As it always had, the sword seemed to move with instinct, not thought, but he now had much more control over his actions. He was stronger now, too, so his arms no longer hurt when he fought. He practiced for hours there, as he did every day, until his knuckles were stiff from gripping the sword for too long and he was drenched in sweat. When he was done, Chase sheathed his sword again, panting and hot despite the thin layer of snow that covered the ground.

He tiredly climbed up a tall tree, swinging from branch to branch until he found a comfortable cranny in the treetop. There he settled down with his back against the trunk. He unsheathed his beloved weapon and began polishing it with his shirt as he looked out over the city. His view provided him the marketplace, the castle…it was peaceful and serene. Beautiful, even.

From his perch in the tree, though, he saw something he'd never noticed before. It was a large house, standing all by itself on the top of a hill. He saw a speck of a figure moving slowly up the hill. The figure hurried around the side of the house, and Chase lost sight of the person. He began to wonder why that house was so far from all the others, and why he'd never noticed it before.

But he didn't have much time to think about it, because just then, a horrible scream pierced the air, and he seemed to be hit by an invisible force that sent him sprawling backwards towards the ground, his sword falling with him. The screaming continued shrilly as he tumbled through the air towards the thin layer of snow blanketing the ground, the wind whistling in his ears. He wasn't sure if the scream was from him or from someone else.

He hit the ground hard, his sword falling flat next to him. He tried to sit up, but that same invisible force flattened him against the snow. The screaming was so terrible and loud, the whole kingdom must have heard it, and he knew in that moment that it was not from his mouth. It felt like the sky was pushing down on him.

His mind filled with flashes of scenes he'd never seen before: a woman talking to a baby, a man guarding a door with a sword. A blinding light filled Chase's eyes, and the image changed.

He saw a cloaked man pushing the woman and her baby out the door, the guarding man following. He saw blinding flashes of swords clashing. He saw a man fall, and the same woman, now with a toddler at her side, kneeling over him, weeping. The man tried to get up, but was pushed back by a heavy boot landing on his already injured chest. Chase saw the mother scoop up the toddler and run off into the shadows of a forest.

Chase didn't know who the people were or what was going on, but he wanted this to stop. He laid helplessly on the ground as the screaming continued, and images flashed through his brain.

He felt the booted man's anger, the injured man's pain. He felt the woman's fear, and the cloaked man's worry. He felt the toddler's confusion, and the world's violent push on his body.

He saw a flash of a woman's eyes, filled with terror. Eyes that looked a bit familiar, but he didn't know where from. He saw the tip of a sword slice at flesh, a shimmering jewel, three drops of blood landing on crystal snow. The screaming got shriller, and he heard the woman cry out, "NO!"

There was a blinding flash. And then it was over.

Chase lay on the ground, breathing in short gasps. He sat up without a problem, the overwhelming pain and fear and anger he'd felt earlier gone entirely. Hands shaking, he reached for his sword…but stopped. There, next to his blade on the ground, were three drops of crimson red on white snow.

CHAPTER 3

"Tara, dear, be a doll and refill my glass, will you?"

Tara barely glanced up at Aunt Beatrice when she heard her speak. Her fingers worked nimbly with her needle, lacing white thread in and out of the silky material of Aunt Bea's favorite gown. Her aunt had torn the skirt on a thorn in her rose garden (which was tended to daily by yours truly), and Tara was stitching it back up for her. Aunt Bea sat across the dining room table, supervising her work.

"Tara, sweetie? I asked you to refill my glass. When you get the chance, would you mind?"

Tara still paid little attention, lost in her own little world. And her own little world was lovely. Funny, her daydreams were always exactly the same, every time. She always pictured walking down a path lined with buttercups and daisies. Butterflies and bumblebees flew round her head. It was springtime, and the sun warmed her skin. Pleasant music played in the back of her mind as she strolled along the dirt trail, passing a stream where turtles sunbathed and frogs played in the shallows. She imagined dipping her feet in the cool, refreshing water. She would always fantasize about spending the whole day at that creek, far away from her terrible aunt. She didn't have to listen to any yelling, anyone telling her what to do, anyone continuously screaming her name… everything was peaceful, beautiful, and happy. "TARA!!!"

Tara jumped a foot, pricking her finger with the needle as she did so. A tiny dot of blood appeared on her index finger. "Ow,"

Tara whispered. She looked up at Aunt Beatrice with distaste. "What?" she asked irritably.

"QUIT DAYDREAMING! I TOLD YOU TO REFILL MY GLASS!!!"

"Actually, I believe your exact words were, *'When you get the chance.'* I haven't gotten the chance yet, I apologize." Tara continued to sew.

Aunt Bea shoved her empty glass in Tara's face. "REFILL MY GLASS, YOU UNAPPRECIATIVE BRAT!!! *NOW!!!*"

Tara lifted her gaze angrily to meet her aunt's but bit her lip hard. *Be kind,* she reminded herself. *Be kind.*

"Okay," Tara muttered with difficulty. "What do you want to drink?"

Aunt Bea sat back in her chair. "Wine."

"All right."

She rose and walked gracefully into the kitchen, but once she was there, she scowled. "Unappreciative brat, huh?" she muttered softly. "Well, what exactly do I have to be appreciative for?"

She popped open a bottle and poured the bitter, dark red liquid into Aunt Bea's glass. She scrunched her nose at the sickly-sweet fumes. Tara hated the smell of wine. She walked back to the dining room, plunked the glass down on the table, and picked the gown up again.

"What? No napkin?!"

Tara forced a smile. "Oh. I'm sorry. How silly of me." She grabbed a cloth napkin from the cabinet behind her and tossed it down next to Aunt Bea's glass.

"No, no, no." Aunt Beatrice snapped her fingers. "Fold it for me."

"Why? You're going to unfold it anyway in like two"—"FOLD IT FOR ME!!!" Tara quickly folded the napkin into an elegant swan shape.

"Much better," Aunt Bea announced. Tara continued her sewing, trying to ignore the loud slurping noises her aunt made as she drank. She also had to block out the boring lecture her Aunt Beatrice was making about the state of her bathroom's east window pane.

Ugh, I hate this, Tara thought miserably as Aunt Bea continued to talk. *Not that hating it really does anything, of course. Honestly, how many times a day do I think that? And what's changed? I'm still stuck here, listening to this woman tell me what to do. This is hopeless. I'm going to be stuck here until my parents return.*

With the final stitch, Tara stood. "Your gown is finished."

Aunt Bea smiled, her teeth stained a pale red from the wine. "Good. Now you can go wash it for me! Oh, and while you're at it, get around to doing the laundry, as well. What's it been, three weeks since the last load?"

"One day," Tara said tightly as she stalked out of the room. "Not like you're any help, either, you lazy rat," she spat once she was alone in the laundry room upstairs.

Tara looked around the dull, dusty room, anger building up inside her. She had looked at the enclosing walls, day after day, for what seemed like centuries. And she was facing another eternity of the same trapped view.

No, she stopped herself. No, she wasn't spending any more time here. Not with Aunt Beatrice. Not like this. She'd had enough. In her fury, she threw the gown to the floor, sending up a cloud of dust. Tara kicked at the dress, stomped on it, picked it up and threw it back down, until it was covered with dirt and muck.

When she was done, Tara gave the dress one look, and immediately felt guilty. She felt guilty for ruining such a gorgeous gown, for being unkind by messing it up, despite her promise to her mother, for having only made more work for herself.

She just couldn't help it. She was so mad at Aunt Beatrice, she couldn't bear to do another thing for her. She was sick of the house, sick of the lifestyle, sick of her aunt. She had to get out of there. She would take care of herself until her parents returned. She would run away and never come back.

2

Crreeeeeaaaak. The kitchen door groaned in protest as Tara slowly pushed it open and tiptoed through the doorway. She held a candle in front of her to light the way through the darkness. It was near midnight, and Aunt Bea's steady snores trailed from her room upstairs, assuring Tara that she was asleep.

It had been several days since Tara had first decided to run away. She had made plans and packed in secrecy, and now her heart was pounding with the peril of the moment.

She entered the kitchen, opened a cabinet, and removed some sausages, a loaf of bread, and some dried fruits. She filled a small wineskin with water and slung it over her shoulder, then wrapped the food with cloth in a basket. She wasn't sure where Aunt Beatrice kept her coins, so she figured she'd have to make do with the few coins she had managed to stash away for herself. Unprepared though she was, she had plans to go straight to the market and find some sort of work. She could lay low there as a humble craftswoman or vendor to make money.

As she was leaving the kitchen, she spotted her sewing tools lying out on the countertop. She grabbed those, too, in case her gown ripped or she needed to make new clothes.

She had a knapsack on her back that contained a change of clothes and a blanket, and she held her walking boots in her hand. Her change of clothes consisted of the *one gown she'd managed to smuggle into Aunt Bea's house on her first day, and a brown cloak that she never wore, for fear of Aunt Bea seeing it and confiscating it.* She'd brought some nicer shoes, as well. The unfashionable walking boots were only for traveling.

She pulled her tattered winter coat over her shoulders, slipped her boots on, and scurried to the back door. Fingering her crescent moon necklace—a gift from her mother that she never removed—Tara took a deep breath and opened the door. She hesitated for a moment, looking out into the night, breathing in the anticipation of freedom. Finally, she stepped outside, letting the door close behind her with a dull thud. She'd have to be fast.

Tara ran around the side of the house, ducking to avoid her aunt's window. Racing down the hill, the only thing powering her forward was the possibility of Aunt Beatrice discovering her absence all too soon. She forced herself to keep going, although she was already very tired. She didn't run very often.

She sprinted up another hill, which she discovered to be uninhabited. She reached the bluff, then finally stopped to catch her breath. Sweat trickled down the back of her neck, plastering her hair down. *Ew,* she thought, pulling her curls up into a bun. She collapsed in the brittle, frozen grass, her brain overflowing with thoughts and emotions that she couldn't name. The cold from the ground seeped into her clothes, cooling her off quickly.

After a moment, Tara stood, examining her surroundings. What she saw was stunning, gorgeous beyond words. The view was one of untouchable beauty that she definitely hadn't expected from such a terrifying escapade.

It was a clear night, probably the last there'd be until spring. A full moon shone silver rays that illuminated a diamond sky. The castle loomed in front of her, and all of Jisara's capital was laid out before her. If she turned one way, she could see the forest on the edge of the city. If she turned the other way, she saw the smaller, neighboring hill, on the top of which was a house. A house that seemed so familiar, yet so far. Tara stared at that house for a long time. A bubbly feeling rose in her chest, for she knew she'd never have to return there again.

Her heart soared. She could do whatever she wanted. She'd never have to listen to Aunt Beatrice again.

Tara was so overwhelmed with happiness, she felt incapable of doing anything. She felt that she had to do *something*, however. This was a celebration! So, she did the only thing she could think to do. She sang.

She sang a soft tune that her father had always sung her to sleep with as a child. Quietly at first, then louder and louder… until she was ecstatic with joy and laughing and singing on the top of the hill. A breeze swirled past, and she pulled her hair down, letting the wind blow through her blonde curls. She closed her eyes, laughing as she spun in circles, her arms spread wide.

"I'm free," she whispered, rather unable to believe it herself. She spent the rest of the night singing with the wind, dancing until dawn lit the sky.

CHAPTER 4

That same night, while Tara celebrated with the stars and the sky on the outskirts of the city, Chase was trying as best he could not to fall asleep. He laid under a willow tree in a public place near the castle, catching glimpses of a full moon through the long, vine-like branches that hung down around him like a curtain of solitude. He had been greatly shaken by his vision…or whatever it was. He knew that the blood on the snow had not been his. He had checked himself thoroughly and found no cuts.

He leaned back against the willow's thick trunk, running his hands through his hair. He was baffled by what he'd seen. He'd later asked around, only to find that no one had heard screaming of any sort. So now he had it in his mind that he might be going crazy. How fun.

The way he felt, sitting there that night, made that idea run deep. Because, for the first time in his entire life, Chase wished he wasn't alone. He wished he had someone to sit and talk with; a loving parent, or a trusted friend. For the first time, he felt sad upon realizing that he had neither of those. And that made him believe that he'd truly gone mad. Never once in his life had he ever mourned his lack of companionship. Everyone knew that friends could only lead to restrictions. To pain.

Chase sat up for hours, talking to himself, testing his own memory, trying to assure himself that he wasn't insane. He asked himself questions, answering them aloud and focusing on keeping the replies as accurate as possible. He got overtired, though, and began dozing against the tree.

"No," he whispered suddenly, jolting himself awake. "It can't happen again." He was deathly afraid that if he fell asleep, the screaming would haunt him again.

However, he soon couldn't fight it any longer. He laid down flat, and let his eyelids slip closed. The second they did he knew he'd regret letting it happen. For the blanket of slumber brought with it a wave of horrors—visions much, much worse than the first. Chase would soon learn the hard way: his experience in the forest had only been the beginning.

There was no screaming this time. Instead, there were voices. A man's voice, fragile and raspy, "Hurry, Maria. Quickly! Bring the child with you. We must be hasty. He is not far behind." Chase saw the same woman from before, dark-haired and dark-skinned, holding the same baby. The tall cloaked man was speaking.

"No!" cried the woman named Maria. "I can't leave Charles. I must go after him!" The woman turned and rushed back into the house from which she'd come, leaving the child with him. "Maria!" the cloaked man called after her. There was a blinding flash, and the image changed.

This time, Chase saw a man standing bound to a wall by ropes so tight his hands were purple with numbness, hanging his head in defeat. Maria rushed in, empty-handed. "Charles!" she cried out, running to him.

"Maria, Maria! Darling Maria, quickly, he will be back soon."

Maria pulled a knife from her belt and cut through Charles' bonds. "Run! Go!" he shouted, and they sprinted out of the room together. "Wait!" Charles stopped suddenly, rubbing his pained hands as blood returned to them. Maria came to a halt.

"Where's Loviti? Where is he?"

Chase, even in his sleep, felt his heart lurch at the name. *Loviti.* It sounded so familiar.

"Raka has him. He is waiting outside for us."

Suddenly, a harsh, deep voice bellowed from the room they'd just left. "CHARLES ONAJ!!!"

Onaj. That sounded familiar, too.

"Go. *Go!!!*" Charles screamed, pushing Maria ahead of him, as they began to run again.

"YOU'LL NEVER ESCAPE!!!! NEVER!!!" the voice thundered.

With another blinding flash, the image changed again. Maria and Charles were running through a forest, the cloaked man keeping up with them and holding the baby, who'd begun to cry. "Raka!" Maria cried, turning to the cloaked man. "You must leave. Go, now!" She looked sadly at the baby. "Take him with you. Keep him safe."

"No," Raka replied fiercely. "I will not leave you, Maria. We will fight him together." The image faded.

Chase was suffering greatly. He did not feel the emotions of the people in his dreams this time. Instead he felt his own emotions…but they were ones he didn't understand. He felt angry at the man chasing the people. He felt like he needed to help the people being chased. He felt as if, for some reason, he had to keep them alive. He felt like his own life depended on their survival.

The next vision was the worst one of all. Chase saw heavy boots trampling through the forest. He heard the evil man's voice, saying words he couldn't quite make out. He saw the man's strong fist hit Charles across the face, sending blood spattering from his lips as he went reeling to the ground. Charles dropped his sword in pain, and the man picked it up in triumph. "Yes," he said, as he slammed one boot down on Charles' chest. Hatred shone in Charles' eyes. "I have won. I have won half the game, and it was easier than digging a three-inch hole in fresh farming soil. You are finished, Charles Onaj. Give up."

Chase was almost certain that Charles would get up and punch the guy in the face, shouting, "I'll never give up!" But no. Charles laid back his head and let his body go limp. He stopped struggling. The man raised Charles' sword.

No, Chase thought in his sleep. *What are you doing?*

Charles held perfectly still as the man sliced the barest tip of the sword across his chest. Three drops of blood landed on the crisp white snow beside him, making Charles gasp shallowly. He suddenly began to look very old and frail. His breathing became ragged, his hair turned white. His skin was papery thin and milky.

The evil man hoisted Charles up and began binding his hands. Chase saw that same flash of the woman's terrified eyes, which still looked so familiar. He heard her, once again, scream, "NO!" Raka pulled her back into the darkness of a forest.

Chase then saw the evil man pulling a bound and gagged Charles through the woods, in the opposite direction. "Don't you worry, Charles. You'll be reunited with your family very soon." The man chuckled cruelly, sending a chill down Chase's spine. There was a blinding light, and Chase saw the three drops of blood on white snow. Why such a small amount of bloodshed disturbed him so much, he didn't want to know.

Chase woke up with a start, only to find himself... in the forest. He was surrounded by woodland sounds and the musky scent of underbrush, dappled moonlight faintly illuminating the ground. Gazing around in confusion, he realized that he stood under the same tree he'd fallen from earlier that day. And somehow, with a chillingly mysterious understanding, he knew that this was the same tree beneath which Charles fell and was defeated in his dream. Concern for Chase's sanity numbed his thoughts.

Sleepwalking, he told himself shakily. *Just sleepwalking.* But why, and how, had he returned to this tree in the middle of the night—the same tree where Charles fell and was cut by that sword?

The same tree… under which three drops of blood still stained the snow. Chase's whole body shook in fear as he stared at the ominous crimson droplets. What was happening? He slapped himself, hard, in case he was dreaming, but the only result was a painful sting on his cheek.

As though that wasn't frightening enough, nothing could shake the ghostly feeling that he knew every single one of the people in his dream. The feeling that he knew those eyes. Knew Charles and Maria, knew Raka and the evil mystery man. He especially recognized that name…*Loviti.* It all seemed so familiar, like the whole thing was a huge flash of déjà vu. As though time had wound back, taking him into the past…or maybe even into the future. All Chase knew for certain was that the visions, and the sleepwalking, and that blood on the snow…they had now truly terrified him.

Chase sat up the rest of the night, fighting desperately to stay awake. It was now almost morning, and the moon was beginning to sink in the sky as the horizon began to turn a lighter shade of indigo in the east. Chase's eyelids began to droop uncontrollably. When the sun finally emerged over the hills, Chase felt like the weight of the sky had been lifted off his shoulders.

The horrible night was over, but the sunshine didn't rid him of sleepiness. Chase figured that since the worst dream had come at night, then it must be safe to sleep during the daytime. So, he laid down in broad sunlight to rest. He slept a dreamless sleep for hours, calming his angry, frightened, confused thoughts. And he almost got away with it, too.

The visions were very, very short this time. He saw clips from his former visions. He first saw Maria releasing Charles from his bonds. He heard the evil man bellow. He heard Charles say the name but leave out the rest of his sentence. *"Loviti?"* He saw Raka running off with Maria. He saw Charles fall, watched as his blood fell to the snow as he seemed to age a thousand years.

He heard Maria's scream, saw her eyes. The image didn't change after that, though. It stuck on her eyes, which flashed with fear and anger. Chase was so close. So close to the truth. He could feel it, even in his sleep. He knew those eyes. He'd seen them somewhere before, not too long ago. They were so familiar, yet so mysterious, it hurt his brain to think about it. And suddenly, he lurched awake.

He'd been sleepwalking again, apparently, for he now stood in the heart of the marketplace. He looked at the cobblestone ground beneath him, half expecting to see the blood droplets there, but there was nothing unusual about the ground.

Chase had decided, at this point, that nothing was really coincidental for him anymore, so he was wary of his surroundings. Finding nothing abnormal upon looking down, he looked up, instead.

He stood in front of a glass shop in the marketplace, selling everything from mirrors to windows. It was probably around midday, and watery sunlight shone through thick layers of fog. Chase was standing right in front of a mirror that was on display in front of the store, positioned so that when he looked up, the first thing he saw was his reflection. At first, he saw nothing unusual. His hair was mussed up, and his clothes were dirtier than usual. Yet upon studying his face in the mirror more closely, he yelped aloud, drawing odd looks from a few commoners.

Chase knew where he'd seen Maria's eyes. He recognized that devil-may-care look, that dark, chocolate brown with flecks of amber and gold. Maria's eyes were in his own. There wasn't a single difference.

Chase swallowed hard. If that was supposed to make him feel better, it most certainly didn't. Not one bit.

He wasn't only afraid, but also baffled. What did it mean? What were his dreams trying to tell him? Or maybe they didn't mean anything, and he was really just dreaming. But then, how did that explain his vision in the forest?

Okay, Chase thought, straightening his clothes. *How about trying to forget about this for a bit? You still need to eat, after all.*

So, Chase strolled through the marketplace, looking for someone to steal from. He passed several people he could have easily robbed, but he was too shaken up to even consider pulling off a theft. He felt like he would make a mistake and be seen, and then he'd have to fight. He was still too drowsy for that.

Instead, he started looking for some clueless, innocent person to distract. The type was easy to find; they walked around oblivious to their surroundings and always seemed a little too happy. He saw several of the girls he'd fooled the day before, and he nodded in their direction, making them squeal and shriek when they thought he was out of earshot. He shook his head and laughed to himself, relaxing more into his familiar sauntering gait as he continued on his way.

Jisara's capital had grown on Chase, despite the fact that he had stolen from just about everyone in the place. He had lived his whole life on these streets, and although they may not have known about it, everyone around him had played some sort of role in raising him. Sometimes, when he got lonely, he thought about that, and it made him see the Jisarians as one massive family, all of them providing for him unknowingly—and probably unwillingly, but no matter. It felt comforting to weave his way through the bustling market, being jostled lightly by the crowds and hearing the talk of all the people around him. Slowly, his nerves calmed.

Midway through the marketplace, Chase noticed a girl he'd never seen before. She wore a considerably expensive dress that had no place in the middle of winter. A thick brown cloak covered her shoulders, and Chase's thieving eye caught hungrily on a silver crescent dangling at the base of her throat. She carried a basket of food in her hands, and Chase smiled to himself. Too easy.

Slowly, he moseyed his way toward her, then pretended to turn around to look at something just as he got close. He bumped into her on purpose, knocking her basket from her hands. She yelped softly in surprise. Two dried apricots rolled out, but the rest of the food stayed put in the basket.

"Whoa! I'm so sorry, I didn't see you there," Chase lied. Up close, the girl was beautiful. She was quite a bit shorter than him, but her smile was warm. Her voice was silvery when she said, "No, it was my fault."

Chase quickly shook his head, clearing his thoughts. "Here, let me help you." He knelt and picked up the apricots, but held them in his palms for a second. He almost didn't want to steal from her. He had expected her to be another wealthy brat, overpampered and completely spoiled. Yet she seemed kind enough, and she was so pretty…

Whoa, he thought. *Chase, snap out of it! Who cares what she looks like, you've got to eat!* Chase opened the basket and tucked the fruit inside, snatching up some sausage and a few apricots in the process.

He began to stash the food in his pocket when the girl kicked him with her toe. "Hey!" she cried. "Give that back!"

"Give what back?" He stood and handed her the basket, making sure his questioning gaze was convincing. She was harder to pretend around than most people.

"My food," she said, backing away from him. "You took some and put it in your pocket."

"Oh, come, now." Chase smiled suavely and reached out to touch her cheek. "You really think I would steal from *you?* A beautiful, wealthy young lady? And royalty, too, no doubt. Do you live in the castle?"

The girl pulled away from his touch, fear inching in behind her eyes. "You stole from me."

"Why would I ever do that?" He took her cold fingers in his, watched her tense.

She yanked her hand quickly away. "I… I don't know. But you just did. Give me back my food, please." Chase was actually rather surprised that she wasn't head over heels like everyone else was. She was smart. But, nonetheless, he needed food. He smiled. "Goodness, milady, look at the time! Sorry, I'd best be on my way."

"Hey, wait a second!"

"Great meeting you!"

"No, stop!" she yelled, hurrying after him. Chase graced her with a bow, then turned and ran. Her cries of "Thief! Stop, thief!"

faded behind him as he lost himself in the thick coverage of the crowds.

He hurried through an alley as a few other Jisarians, hearing the girl's cry, began to come after him. He slowed, letting the men catch up, and then halted abruptly and turned, his body slamming into the closest man and sending him bowling into the rest of his pursuers. Not lingering to see if they would follow him, Chase rounded a corner and entered an even smaller back street, littered with unwanted objects and playing home to several scraggly cats.

There, he picked up an empty jug and threw it through a window that probably led into someone's kitchen. It crashed through the glass noisily, making someone inside scream in alarm. Quickly, Chase ducked into a shadow as the group of Jisarians stormed past. "In there!" someone cried, and they all clambered through the broken window. Chase waited until they were all inside so they wouldn't see him, then slipped silently away. He snuck around for a little while, staying in the shadows, but when it became clear that he was safe, he simply stepped out into the open and strolled along on his way like nothing had happened.

There was a quiet square near the edge of the marketplace, with a small fountain in the center and some grass peeking through the cobblestones' cracks. It was almost always vacant, and when he arrived, there wasn't a soul in sight. He sat down on the ledge of the fountain and pulled out the stolen food, just about to bite into the fruit when a voice stopped him.

"Don't. You. Dare." Chase whirled around to find the girl he'd robbed, standing with her hands on her hips, sweaty and trying to conceal the fact that she was out of breath. A loose curl hung over her eyes.

Chase wasn't startled so much by her catching up to him, but by the fact that she hadn't been charmed at all. She'd seen him take the food, and she'd come after him. That only happened when he wanted it to happen. And he hadn't wanted it to happen. Chase eyed her up and down. There was another thing about her, too.

It had been a long time since he'd seen someone that made him reconsider stealing from them. He'd seen plenty of pretty girls before, some even prettier than her. But none of them had affected him so strangely. Something about her was striking in a way he didn't understand, and he wanted to get away from it.

He sighed, tucked the food away again, and got to his feet. He'd been hoping to avoid this. The girl lunged at him, and he easily sidestepped. She tried to jump on him, but he dodged again and tripped her. She landed on her back, looking dazed and scared. He turned to run, but stopped. He felt…almost *bad*. Chase never felt bad about anything. This was turning out to be a *really* weird day. He approached her cautiously. Leaning forward on his knees, he looked down at her. "You okay?"

She stood, her clothes dirty and messed up. "No, I'm *not* okay! GIVE ME BACK MY FOOD!" *Ah. And that would be where the 'spoiled brat' facet comes into play,* he thought, beginning to like her a lot less. But it would still be fun to play with her a little. He'd always enjoyed giving rich folks a bit of exercise to get them off their plush satin chair cushions once in a while.

A mischievous smile slid onto his face. "You want your food? Come and get it!" he coaxed, turning and starting to run.

The girl's eyes blazed. "Fine! I will!" She took off her heels and threw down her basket, wineskin, and knapsack. She yanked a pair of walking boots onto her feet, reclaimed her things, and then came ripping after him. She was surprisingly fast, and Chase had to work a bit harder to stay ahead of her. But she soon wore out, and had to stop to catch her breath. Chase paused to yawn and crack his knuckles, then kept running.

The girl came after him again, but this time, he had an idea. He ran into a swampy mud puddle—which proved difficult, since it was beginning to freeze over—then stopped and just stood there in the middle of it. The girl came barreling towards him, but skidded to a halt, recoiling at the sight of the mud. Chase felt like his feet were freezing off, but he managed to keep a smug expression on his face. Her eyes burned with hatred, but she would not follow him into the mud.

"Give me my food. Now!" Chase smiled. "I told you. All you've got to do is come and get it." He held out the food, inches from her reach. The girl's eyes seemed to be turning to fire. She took a ragged breath, trying to calm down.

"Listen. I've got a long journey to make, I've got no money, and you just took almost all of my food. Why can't you get food from your family, or just steal from someone else? I'm on my own, and I need that. What I *don't* need is some slimy thug trying to take my stuff. So, can you please just GIVE IT BACK?!" Chase stared at her, completely forgetting the food for a moment.

"You're on your own too?"

CHAPTER 5

Tara stared at the boy in front of her, breathing heavily. Her face was hot, her hair was a mess, and her beautiful gown was covered in filth. Just to clarify, in case anyone hadn't guessed already, she hated that boy. She hated every single thing about him, with his infuriatingly hypnotizing charm at the top of the list. He was arrogant, he was sneaky, and he was devious. All great reasons why she was not letting him get into her head—or away with her food.

But his last sentence had calmed her rage a bit. *You're on your own, too?* It made her curious. "What do you mean?" she asked, making sure to keep her voice snippy.

He shrugged slowly. "I guess I just never thought that there might be someone out there like me."

Tara frowned in disgust, immediately forgetting her curiosity and replacing it, once more, with indignance. "Like you? You're a thief. A good-for-nothing, cruel, arrogant thief whose only concern is yourself. You're *nothing* like me." She had hoped her comment would hurt him, but his only response was a faint smile.

"No," he said softly. "I'm certainly not." He eyed her for a moment, then shrugged. "But who knows? Maybe we had similar pasts."

Tara scoffed, shaking her head bitterly. "Right. I'm sure that you, too, had to live as a slave to your aunt while your parents fought monsters all day long." As soon as the words were out, she bit her lip as if to take them back. She hadn't meant to say that much.

He looked surprised. "What?" Tara snapped defensively.

He shrugged. "I didn't really expect that from someone like you." His fingers swept through his hair in a casually dashing sort of way. His voice changed slightly, taking on a suave tone. "As I said before, you look… enchantingly royal."

Tara frowned reproachfully at him, unwilling to take his bait despite the hammering in her chest. He was unusually and unignorably handsome. He looked slightly amused as he continued, his voice dropping back to normal. "I had it rough, too, though. I still do. I guess we both"— "Stop," Tara snapped. "You cannot possibly relate to my past. Don't try to tell me what we have in common."

The boy cocked a brow, still looking more entertained than offended by her rudeness. Tara did not regret being harsh with him, but she honestly wasn't angry with only him. She was angry about everything that had happened to her, angry that someone would ever try to compare his sufferings to hers. He was probably just some spoiled rich boy having some "fun".

"Well," he said lightly, "I suppose you're right. You have it much harder than I do. I mean, you were walking around out here in expensive clothes, with food to eat and nothing to worry about. You poor, pitiful little charity case." Tara stared at him. He was *mocking* her. Toying with something that he didn't know anything about. Anger boiled through her veins, a furious scowl deepening on her face.

"This is not a joke, thief!" she raged. "You think it's funny because you cannot possibly relate to it, because you're free to do whatever you want and go wherever you please! You just *take* what others work hard for, so you cannot even begin to relate to the kind of hardships"—Suddenly, the words froze in her throat as the boy stepped forward…and held her food out to her. Easily within her reach. She stared at the fruit and sausage he was offering her, uncalculating. Her heart was racing from the adrenaline of her outburst, but in that sudden moment of silence, she was struck speechless.

"Take it," the boy said softly. Tara looked at him, then realized that her mouth was still hanging half open. She snapped it shut quickly. "Um…. What?"

"Take it," he repeated. "You need it more than I do." Tara stared at him for a few moments, dumbfounded, then finally reached out to cautiously reclaim her fruit and sausage. He let her take it.

Suddenly, Tara felt awkward. She didn't know what to do or say as they stood staring at each other. "Thank you," she managed, putting the food away in her basket.

The boy shrugged. "We're in the same boat, whether you like it or not. I get it. Besides, as you said, I can get my own food just fine. You can't."

Tara stared at him, unable to believe the act of kindness the thief had just displayed. She was amazed that he even cared about anything other than himself.

She stopped her thoughts, though, reminding herself to be wary. Just because he'd had some sort of pity on her didn't mean she could call him a friend. Not even close.

She turned to go but hesitated for some reason. That curiosity she had felt before was now nearly overpowering. What was it with this particular thief that made him behave in a nearly compassionate way? Thieves were not compassionate. Yet the one before her… was.

She hesitated a bit longer, and after several moments passed with neither of them moving, the boy smiled.

Slowly, he stepped out of the slushy mud puddle, stamping his feet to clean his black boots as he went. Scuffing his shoes on the ground, he said, "So you're a lady who's living like a slave. Not a particularly cheerful life, is it?"

Tara gripped her basket tightly, unsure of what to do. Somehow noticing that miniscule movement, the thief nodded to it. "You shouldn't carry food in an open basket like that. Thieves can see exactly what you've got, and they can swipe things more easily than if you keep them in your knapsack."

Tara blinked, looking down at the food she'd replaced in the basket. He was helping her. Why? "Why should I trust you?" she asked.

The boy stopped trying to clean his hopelessly filthy shoes to peer at her from beneath his hair. "From the looks of it, you don't have too many friends right now. Sad as it is, I'm all you've got, so that can be reason number one. Number two would be that I make a living off of clueless people like you, so I know these things pretty well."

Tara frowned slightly. "You make a living off of stealing?"

"No, of course not," he scoffed, seemingly offended. "I live off of my uncanny talent for embroidering tea cozies, and I steal from everyone as a side hobby." Tara stared at him for a moment in silence before she recognized his sarcasm. Somehow, his casualness made him seem slightly more humane. Not quite as frightening.

"So... you're not rich?" Tara asked tentatively. The boy snorted like it was a ridiculous question. "Of course, I'm rich. I'm just rich off other people's riches." Tara's lip curled slightly at that statement. "That's horrible, you know. There are people who really work hard for their families, who need the things they earn."

The boy eyed her, a slight smirk forming on his lips. "It seems like you question my morals a lot. If you don't like how my conscience works, I can take that food right back."

Tara glared at him silently, waiting to see if he would carry out his threat. He didn't. Instead, he walked over to a tree that stood near them and sat down at the base of its trunk. He went down with a lazy crash, leaned back, and eyed Tara with a half-lidded gaze.

"I'll make a deal with you," he said. "I'll help you with survival—food, shelter, whatnot—if you agree to help me with my own little problem."

Tara's lips parted in shock. Of all the things she'd expected him to say, it had not been that. "If I help *you*? With *your* problem? Your whole lifestyle is a problem." Her head was racing. What on earth was she getting herself into? "Why in the world would I trust you?"

The boy squinted at her. "Haven't we been over this already? We both need help, so let's help each other." "I don't need help," Tara snapped.

"You'll get eaten alive out here if you spend one night by yourself." He nodded in the vague direction of the sky. "Storm's due, too. So, yeah, you need help. Just tell me what's going on and I'll help you."

Tara scowled. "Absolutely not. I don't even know what I would be assisting you with. You might need help satisfying your bloodlust or something and just kill me as payment." Despite Tara's serious tone, her last comment drew a crooked grin from the boy. "That easy to figure me out, huh?"

Tara stared at him nervously, unable to decipher whether or not he was being serious. He leaned back, still smiling as though he found Tara wonderfully amusing. His expression was infuriating. "So, how about this, then? No payment. I'll help you out for free." "Why?" "Because I'm a nice guy." Tara frowned at him dryly as he continued airily, "So, tell me what's going on." "Why should I?" "Because you made me mess up my boots." Tara wrung her hands, choosing to ignore his last statement. He was a thief. A random stranger. She couldn't possibly trust him, let alone depend on him for survival.

And yet… he would be the last person Aunt Beatrice would expect her to be with. Her aunt would never even consider that Tara had made ties with a thief. The boy was also obviously good at what he did. He could undoubtedly sneak Tara around without them being seen. If her aunt came looking for her, he could help Tara hide. *I'm at literal rock bottom,* Tara thought, *if I'm actually considering this.* Yet if that was the case, things could only get better, right?

Tara bit her lip, hard, told herself she was an idiot, and then told the boy about her life. She explained everything, from her parents' job, to going to live with her aunt and her life there, to escaping and ending up with him. "So, I need a place to hide from her until my parents return from their journey," she concluded.

She paused for a moment, bracing herself, and then added, "You're a thief, so you must know about every hiding place in the capital. Could you possibly… show me one?"

The boy nodded slightly. "I could. But it sounds like you're pretty unaccustomed to roughing it." At the incredulous look she gave him, he smiled to soothe her temper. "I mean, roughing it on your own without food or shelter. If I were to escort you to a hideout and just take my leave, you'd be stuck with the dilemma of getting your own food. Not to mention the matter of fighting off other thieves and street thugs. Don't think for an instant that they won't take advantage of your inability to defend yourself."

Tara frowned in surprise. "There are others?" The boy's laugh was sharp and quick. "More than anyone would like to believe." Tara was quiet for a moment, wondering how far she should take small talk before anything went wrong. The last thing she wanted was to say something that would provoke him.

Tentatively, she said, "But none of them have parents, or families? Do they leave their homes to steal?"

The boy's reply was slow to come, as if they were approaching a subject he would rather avoid discussing. "No," he said tightly. "Nobody with half a brain would leave the luxury of a good house for a life of thievery." He was speaking carefully, as if he was anticipating the question to come. His voice had changed slightly, too, taking on a more hostile tone. Tara wondered if it would be wise to press but finally decided that if she was placing her trust in his hands, she at least needed to know where he was from.

"How about you?" she asked cautiously, bracing herself. "Do you have family around here?" His indifferent expression didn't change, but the muscles of his jaw clenched ever so slightly with his answer. "No. I'm an orphan."

Tara's lips parted in surprise and pity. She had expected as much, she supposed, but hearing it was striking nonetheless. "Oh," she said softly. "I... I didn't know. I'm so"— "I'm fine," he interrupted roughly, cutting off her condolence. "I don't need pity from some rich brat. I'm not a charity case."

She stepped back a bit at his harsh tone and insult. He glanced up at her, then exhaled. His brows slowly relaxed. When he spoke again, his tone was more controlled. "I'm over it," he said, but he did not apologize. His features were still sharper than before, and the rough edge on his voice belied his calm expression. Tara gazed at him for a moment longer in silence, then cleared her throat.

"Let's change the subject," she suggested hastily. "Why don't we introduce ourselves? I'm certainly not going to allow you to help me unless I know your name."

Rather than answering, the boy unsheathed the sword at his side and twirled it slowly between his hands, almost in an absent-minded sort of way. The tension about him slowly drained with that action, and after a few moments, all his former stoniness seemed to have dissipated. He didn't look at her or show any sign of menace whatsoever, but the sight of the weapon made Tara's pulse begin pounding nevertheless. What had she said to offend him? What would he do to her?

The thief looked up at her terrified expression and lifted a brow. Glancing at the sword, and then back at her, a small smirk grew on his lips. "You're one of those, hm? Scared of sharp things?" She didn't answer. He eyed her a moment longer, then sighed with a roll of his eyes. "I'm not going to kill you." He held the weapon vertically over the ground and stabbed it into the dirt beside his leg. "Not until you give me a reason to, at least," he added. "I'm Chase."

Tara dragged her nervous stare away from the sword protruding from the earth to look at him. "Chase?" she asked nervously, still wary of his blade. "That's it?"

Chase laughed as if she were being ridiculous. "Goodness, no. I meant to say, I'm Chase Cornelius Barnaby Frederic Archibald Henry Fitzgerald III." He yanked the sword back out of the ground and spat on it, using the hem of his shirt to clean the blade. "I'm an orphan, remember? I don't know my last name."

His first comment was light, but the second took on a harder edge. Tara shifted awkwardly, unsure of how to respond. That was definitely a subject to avoid. He was touchy there.

She had never imagined that thieves—much less this thief— would have insecurities. For that matter, she had never really imagined that they would have any emotions, either. She had always thought of thieves as hardened, cold, inhumane people. *Maybe,* she thought, *things aren't always as they seem. Maybe, beneath his anger and flippancy, Chase is hiding pain.* But Tara wasn't about to say that aloud. He would probably leap on her throat if she said that.

"Well, I'm Tara Florreson," she put out at last, attempting to sound as friendly as possible. Chase nodded slightly to acknowledge that he'd heard her, but remained occupied with wiping dirt off his weapon.

Tara stood uncomfortably in front of him, tightening her cloak against winds that were growing colder by the instant. It seemed like she was always either irritated or awkward in Chase's presence, and she was beginning to hate the latter state much more than the former.

Biting her lip, and praying he wouldn't take her outright words to offense, she stood straighter. "Are you going to help me, or not?" Chase inspected his blade closely, and, finding some miniscule blemish, spat on it again and continued wiping it down. "Hello?" Tara prompted, her voice lifting slightly. The thief didn't even shift from his lazy position on the ground, let alone spare her a glance. Tara waited for a few moments more, then felt herself deflate as Chase continued to ignore her.

Tara sighed as disappointment swelled over her like a wave. How could she have been ignorant enough to believe she would actually get help from a thief? Chase was as untrustworthy as they come, and he certainly didn't care enough about her to dedicate himself to her safety. He had probably just amused himself by toying with her for a while, and now he would simply ignore her until she left him alone.

Tara was now back where she had started nearly an hour ago, with nowhere to go and nothing to do except stand there and shiver as the air grew thinner and colder. It was going to snow.

She turned and began to walk away, gripping her basket with one hand and flipping up the hood of her cloak with the other. "Plan," she murmured to herself. "I need to make a plan."

"I wouldn't walk away if I were you," Chase called casually, stopping her. Tara halted and stared straight ahead. Small snowflakes had begun to sprinkle down around her, turning her cheeks and hands pink with the cold. Was it worth it to turn around, or was it just another waste of time? She took a deep breath, the cold air making her throat hurt.

"And why not?" she called back, still facing away from him. There was slight pause.

"Because without me, you'll either kill yourself or get killed," came his voice, softly, from directly behind her. Tara jumped in alarm, whirling to find Chase standing a mere pace away from her. His sword was now sheathed, and his black hair was freckled with white snow. She hadn't heard him approach at all, and he had moved faster and more quietly than she knew to be possible. Tara stuttered over her words in disbelief. "How... h-how did you... I didn't even hear..."

"Magic, darling," he winked.

Forgetting her shock, Tara recoiled instantly. *"Darling?"* she repeated in disgust.

Chase soothed her with a sappy, sarcastic look of apology. "Oh, I'm sorry, would you prefer 'sweetheart'? Or perhaps compliments just aren't good enough for someone as regal as yourself. Would 'princess' be satisfactory?"

"Tara," she growled, frowning in disapproval. "Tara will do just fine." "Whatever you need, your highness," he said airily, a hint of a smile tugging at his lips. "Come along." He walked past her and headed off in the direction of the market.

"Along?" Tara called. "Where?"

A heavy, freezing wind picked up suddenly, drowning out her voice. Glancing up from beneath her hood, Tara saw that the sky had grown darker. Snow was falling in heavier flurries now, the wind whipping it into freezing, miniature whirlpools as it descended. Her teeth had begun to chatter.

"Chase, where are we…" she trailed off as she looked back in front of her. He was gone. "Chase?" she called, slightly louder now. There was no response.

The wind whipped her cloak about, tossing her hood back and releasing her hair into the storm. Struggling to pull it back up, she squinted through the white, snowy void in front of her. The tall, black-clad thief was nowhere to be seen.

"Of course," Tara whispered bitterly. Snow was falling thickly now, turning into what was beginning to look like a blizzard. "No," Tara moaned. "Oh, please, no." Fighting to see through the white that surrounded her on all sides, she began to move in the direction that Chase had gone. She wasn't hoping so much to catch up to him as she was to simply find shelter in the marketplace. The last thing she needed was to be caught outside during a blizzard.

Stumbling forward, Tara didn't see anything in front of her for several minutes—until she found herself running straight into Chase. She yelped and stumbled, steadying herself and backing up. Glaring at him through the snow, she shouted over the wind, "Would you stop sneaking up on me?" Yet her furious expression belied her inner relief at finding him again. Even if he was a thief, it was comforting to know that there was someone with her.

Instead of answering her, Chase held out his hand. Tara stared at it, blinking snow from her eyelashes.

"Hurry up and take it!" he yelled, raising his voice in order to be heard. Tara looked up at him in alarm. "Take your hand?"

"Yes!"

She scowled. "No!" Chase scowled right back, making Tara step away from him. Any aggression from him was not good. It might be better not to provoke him.

"If you aren't holding onto me, you'll get lost again!"

Tara clutched her hood. "Lost? Where are you even taking me?" Her throat and eyes were stinging, every exposed bit of skin turning numb. All she wanted was to be indoors somewhere, but that didn't make her any less wary. "To my home!" Chase yelled back.

Tara still didn't move towards him, her brain moving sluggishly. She was trying to think around the cold that numbed her senses. Follow a thief to his home? She would have to be crazy to actually agree to that. What if he trapped her there and killed her? Beat her up and took her things?

Looking fearfully up at Chase, she was torn with indecision. If she didn't go with him, she would be left with no hope of finding a place to stay in time. Yet if she did, the risk of him doing something to her… suddenly, Tara realized something. Chase had stolen food from her, and then given it back. He had held a sword in his hands while sitting right in front of her, yet made no move to harm her. If he had wanted to kill her, he could have easily done so already.

Maybe following him would be the stupidest thing she'd ever done, but her thoughts were muggy, overcome with a single need: warmth. A real blizzard was forming, and frozen as she already felt, she knew that the storm hadn't nearly reached its peak. It had barely begun.

Pressing her cold lips together, Tara squinted up at Chase. "I'll follow. But I won't take your hand. You're not going to force me anywhere I don't want to go." She could have sworn he rolled his eyes, but with all the snow around them, it was difficult to tell for sure. "Don't fall behind!" he shouted over the storm, and then turned and ran off.

Tara moved to follow him, but quickly discovered that her numb legs were not functioning very quickly. She stumbled thrice, struggling to keep Chase in sight. Snow was blown under her cloak despite her desperate efforts to tighten it around her body, and the wind pounded her relentlessly with freezing air. Soon, in her struggle, Tara had fallen so far back that Chase was no more than a dark, splotchy shape moving ahead of her through the snow. Soon after that, he had vanished entirely. Again.

With a hopeless cry, she stopped moving, falling to her knees. *Why?* she thought miserably. *Why did I ever leave home? Why won't my legs work faster? Why can't I ever be in control of anything that happens to me?*

Her whole body began to shake, and whether it was from the cold, her misery, or her fear, Tara couldn't tell. She could die, she realized abruptly. She could freeze to death and die, right where she knelt. She should have stayed with Aunt Beatrice. Her life could have been longer, could have maybe even amounted to something more than this. Trying to ward off the wind and snow that buffeted her and battled her cloak for access to her skin, Tara huddled over her own body. "I'm going to die," she whispered through chattering teeth, tears threatening her lashes. "I'm actually going to die."

Suddenly, a hand grasped her shoulder roughly, breaking her out of her pathetic despair. Tara jumped up and twisted, breathing so hard that snow was ripped into her lungs. With a shudder, she coughed hard, then looked up into Chase's mildly frustrated face. "I told you to take my hand," he shouted irritably. "Just because I'm a thief doesn't mean I'm always wrong, you stinking rich girl."

Tara just stared at him, the insult slipping right past her. *Chase,* she thought slowly. *Chase might not be the worst person in the world.*

Maybe those were crazy thoughts, thoughts from a frozen mind, but she took his hand nonetheless. His fingertips were just as cold as Tara's, but his grip overpowered her weak, feeble one. With a sharp tug that sent a quick jolt up her arm, Chase began pulling Tara along behind him through the storm, moving deliberately along at a slow jog.

She stumbled along for several steps, trying to get her feet underneath her without stopping, but Chase sped up rather than slowing down. Tara tripped clumsily for quite some time before her nerves awoke and she began actually running, rather than being dragged. As soon as Chase felt the weight behind him lift, he broke into a full sprint, forcing Tara to keep up or reduce herself to a tow sack's position again.

Somehow, Chase managed to see through the blinding sheets of snow that fell around them, leading them away from open spaces and into the marketplace. There, Tara could vaguely make out the vacant shops and wagons around them, abandoned by people who didn't care to be caught in a blizzard. Chase's pace remained steady, but Tara was finding it increasingly difficult to continue pumping her legs fast enough to keep up. The air was thin and freckled with tiny flakes of snow, making it almost inevitable for her to choke on every breath. Yet Chase showed no signs of slowing, so she really had no choice but to continue.

After passing through the market, Chase led Tara toward the eastern side of the city. In all the trips Tara had ever made to the capital, she had never ventured into the eastern side. As Chase tugged her onward, his pace having slowed slightly to allow Tara to breathe, she was grateful that she had never seen this part of the city.

It was a town full of the most unfortunate folk possible, packed to the brim with ramshackle houses and overflowing with homeless people lining the streets. The few characters that Tara could see clearly through the snow were sheltered with even less clothing than her, huddled with young children around them. The poverty was excruciating to look at, and a sharp pain hit her chest as she realized that this might be where Chase lived. He still hadn't slowed down, and Tara tried to look around his shoulder to see where he was heading.

She yelped softly to see that Chase was sprinting head-on toward a sheer brick wall. It appeared to be the side of a house, one that was oddly out of place in the slums' village. They must have reached another residential area by now. Chase kept running forward without showing any signs of stopping, and a spark of alarm ignited in Tara. She squeezed his hand, trying to warn him that there happened to be a big slab of brick in his way. As if responding to Tara's warning, he stopped abruptly, a mere pace away from the wall. Tara collided with him from behind.

"What are you doing?" she shouted, feeling as though the sweat beads on her temples were freezing in place. Instead of answering, Chase did something very unexpected. He crouched down and yelled a command: "Get on my back!" Tara blinked. *Now is not the time for playing games,* she thought angrily.

"Why on earth would I do that?" she yelled back.

"Just do it!"

Tara glanced around. The homeless people hunched around them were beginning to stir slightly, staring curiously at the new-comers. She didn't want to be caught in this area—especially not in a storm. Yet still… grabbing onto his back? And whatever for? "Why?" she asked again.

Chase whirled quickly to face her; his brows knit closely. "I am freezing my tail off out here because I'm trying to help you!" he shouted over the wind. Taken aback by his anger, Tara shied a bit. "Trust me or don't, whatever you decide, but I'm not going to wait for you to talk to the angel on your shoulder. If you don't grab on, I'm leaving." Tara straightened, trying to contact some logical thoughts. Despite her struggle to find reason, her mind still snagged on one thing alone, and that was the possibility of shelter. Warmth. Fire. And her decision was made. "Okay."

Looking rather surprised at the simplicity of her answer, Chase turned around once more and crouched down. Tara tentatively hoisted herself up onto his back, locking her legs around his middle and lacing her fingers carefully in front of his throat. Confined as she was to her aunt's home, Tara had never even touched another boy her age. She leaned forward. "Why am I doing this, again?" she croaked around the icy air being sucked into her lungs. Her heart pounded with the awkwardness of her position.

Chase grinned and turned to talk in her ear. The closeness of his face to hers was unsettling. His teeth were chattering, too. "You'll see. But if you plan to survive it, you'll want to hold on a lot tighter than that." Tara began to demand a panicked explanation, but didn't get time to form a full sentence before the words were lost in her throat. Chase backed up a few steps, getting his body used to Tara's extra weight, and then sprinted at the wall in front of him and began climbing it.

Tara swallowed a scream and locked her arms around him with an iron grip, clinging to his jacket in terror. As it turned out, there wasn't much to fear. Chase found small crevices between bricks on which to plant his feet and hands and scaled the wall masterfully. The snow, making the bricks slick and wet, didn't seem to bother him in the least. He didn't slip once. What seemed like it should take years only took Chase a few moments—even with Tara strapped to his back like a large knapsack.

With a grunt of effort, he pulled them both over the wall and onto a rooftop, then knelt to let Tara unhinge herself from around him. She stepped away rather numbly, staring at Chase with wonder. He rose from his crouch to look at her, a smirk growing despite the blizzard around them. "Impressive?"

Tara could barely even respond. The boy in front of her had climbed a sheer brick wall, in the middle of a blizzard, with an extra person on his back—all within just a few heartbeats. That had possibly been the most incredible feat she had ever witnessed.

A sudden gust of snow sbowled into Tara with so much force that she stumbled. Up on the roof, the wind was stronger and faster, the air colder. Peering over the edge, all Tara could see was an epidemy of white. Nothing beyond four paces ahead was visible. Quickly forgetting her awe, she gripped her cloak.

"What now?" she yelled, noticing that her voice had grown weaker. Chase held out his hand again. "You follow me." Tara took his hand without hesitation this time, and Chase set off at a much slower pace than before. The houses beyond the poor village were large and strong, and Chase led Tara over the sturdy rooftops with careful ease. There was limited space between each building, so the crossing between two roofs was usually a simple hop.

Still, due to the strong winds, Tara followed Chase step for step. She didn't want to risk making the wrong move and falling. Finally, on the edge of a roof beyond which Tara could see no other homes, Chase stopped. Tara edged forward to crouch next to him, squinting through the snow. All she could see was a large, dark shape looming in front of them, much taller than the roof on which they knelt together.

"Is that a tree?" Tara called. Ignoring her question, he turned around. "On my back again!" he ordered. Tara frowned, but did as she was told with miminal reluctance. She had lost her will to argue. Once she had a firm grip on Chase, he stood, bent his knees like a coiled spring, and jumped off the roof.

Tara released a terrified cry as they flew through the air and that large, dark shadow that she had noticed before became visible through the snow. *It* is *a tree,* Tara thought—mere instants before she and Chase plummeted right into its naked, snowy branches. Tara yelped as twigs whipped at her hair and face, but she didn't let go of Chase as he slid down a thick branch and came to a halt on his feet. Clinging to his back, Tara's body was jolted slightly as Chase's weight shifted into a standing position again.

Tara frowned and gazed over Chase's shoulder. Peering downward, she saw a mysteriously dark circle beneath them, a stark gap in the endless world of white around them. With some surprise, Tara realized that Chase stood on the outer rim of a massive, gaping hole, wide enough to fit a small wagon into.

Branches and snow surrounded them; they were still in the tree. So, how could there be a hole so large, just beneath Chase's feet? With a start, Tara realized that Chase was perched where the colossal tree's branches met its trunk. Its hollow trunk. That massive, gaping hole was a hollow tree trunk.

Overwhelmed with amazement, Tara only faintly heard Chase's shout: "Get ready." Despite her detached state, she swore he sounded gleeful. Then he crouched and slid into the gap, plunging them both into darkness. Tara screamed as they rushed through the enormous trunk, losing her grip on Chase in the process. Her cloak whipped behind her as she fell, snagging more than once on a piece of bark.

Finally, the falling stopped, and she tumbled out the bottom of the hole onto hard ground. Tara fell with an ungraceful, painful *whump*, landing hard on her back with a weak groan. Chase fell in a feline crouch and rolled gracefully to his feet, smugly offering his hand to help her up. Tara wanted to smack him.

Brushing his hand away, she got to her feet, stumbling from the numbing cold in her legs. Regaining her bearings, Tara found that she was standing in a hard-packed dirt tunnel, dimly lit with torches stationed at intervals. She blinked several times, trying to accustom her eyes to the change in lighting. For the first time in what felt like years, she had a clear view of everything around her.

Light spatters of snow from the blizzard sprinkled down on her through the hollow trunk overhead, and she quickly scrambled out from under the gap. Once under the safe, dry roof of the tunnel, Tara let out an immense, if a bit shaky, sigh of relief. Despite being nearly as cold underground as it was above, there was no biting wind or snow down here to batter her body.

With a sudden gasp, Tara's eye caught again on a torch in the tunnel, seeing it with new eyes. "Fire," she breathed. Tripping over her cloak—now marred with several small, mysterious tears—in her haste, she ran to the nearest torch stationed in a stone sconce on the wall. Extending her shaking fingers over the flame, Tara sighed in pure bliss as the heat reached her skin. The warmth, if weak, felt so soothing that she had to restrain the urge to plunge her hands into the fire to warm them up faster.

Pulling her hands away from the torch, Tara leaned forward to bathe her face in the heat. Slowly, the snow clinging to her nose and eyelashes melted, and she felt a bit of the numbness slide out of her cheeks. Sighing again, Tara closed her eyes. The tunnel may have been freezing, old, and stale, but it was sheltered and sturdy, and it had fire. Fire was all Tara cared about.

She cried out in weak protest as Chase took her arm and pulled her away from the torch. "Why can't I warm myself up?" Tara asked, sounding painfully whiney to her own ears. Chase, she realized, had made no move to warm his hands or face, despite being obviously cold.

"Because it's freezing down here, and I don't want to stick around and watch you poke your nose into a candle," Chase answered, turning away from her and beginning to jog lightly down the tunnel. The torchlight on the path he was following illuminated several adjourning passages that Tara hadn't noticed before.

"Where… where are we going now?" Tara asked. As soon as she had stepped away from the small fire, she had begun shivering again. She was chilled much too deeply for a torch flame to cure her, she realized.

Chase's pace slowed to a walk, but he still didn't turn back. "You don't listen well, do you? We're going to my home." Tara frowned. "I thought you slept down here, though," she mumbled in confusion. Chase laughed, but said nothing. Gazing longingly back at the torch, Tara dragged herself forward to follow Chase. As soon as she started after him, he picked up into a jog again.

Tara sighed in exhaustion. She was freezing, hungry, and frankly, quite sick of running. Chase moved along through the tunnel with well-paced grace, apparently unfazed by the icy temperatures and unshakable numbness that plagued their limbs. Tara, on the other hand, was growing increasingly tired. No matter how fatigued she became, however, she would collapse before admitting as much to Chase. Trying to ignore the inviting light of the torches they passed, she followed him through what turned out to be an immense underground maze.

After what must have been a half hour at the least, Tara was struggling to take a deep breath. She had never run so much before, and if Chase went much farther, she would simply break down. Her heart was pounding heavily as she followed Chase around another corner and collided with him for the second time today. He had stopped abruptly, and appeared to have been reached up towards the roof of the tunnel before Tara bowled into him and nearly knocked them both over. He frowned and caught his balance. "Watch yourself, won't you?" Panting like an animal and too out of breath to respond, Tara simply stared at him. He shook his head and reached upwards again, muttering about stupid, clumsy gold-huggers. Tara refused to take offense.

Here, the tunnel sloped steeply upwards, the roof growing lower to the floor. Chase, shaking hard from the cold but only slightly winded, seemed to be attempting to make the roof cave in.

"What are you doing?" Tara hissed as he rammed his fist into the low ceiling again and again. "Killing us," he answered perkily, and then gave the ceiling one final blow.

With a groan, a hatch overhead swung upwards and the sharp wailing of a strong wind broke through the opening. Tara gasped as a hole appeared overhead, shedding icy, white light over everything and releasing a freezing gust of wind. The two nearest torches were snuffed out by an onslaught of snow that screamed through the open hatch, cruelly reuniting Tara with the blizzard overhead. She tightened her cloak around herself in misery. She had been hoping that Chase's home would be a nice, cozy place underground with a large fireplace and some hot food.

Following Chase's lead, she reached up, hooked her fingers over the lip of the open hatch, and pulled herself up. Grunting with effort, Tara hauled her body out of the tunnel and reentered the cold, white world of a Jisarian winter. She squinted to see Chase close the door through which they'd exited and realized that the top of the hatch was covered with halved river rocks. When the hatch was closed, it blended in with the other snow-covered stones around it perfectly. As cold and miserable as she was, Tara couldn't help being impressed. Both the tunnel entrances were incredibly well-disguised.

Nearly subconsciously, Tara reached for Chase in the snow. "What now?" she called, gripping his jacket sleeve tightly. He smiled. "You mount your steed," he said. Tara groaned, fastening her arms around his shoulders and trying to shield her face from the battering of the storm. The awkwardness of that position hadn't gotten any easier to bear. Once she was satisfactorily perched on his back, Chase took a flying leap off the ground, landing vertically on the side of a stone wall. Tara was unconcerned about him falling, considering the display he'd put on in the city, but the lurch still made her stomach jump a bit. She tightened her grip on him and prayed her shivering wouldn't cause her to accidentally let go.

Chase found hand and foot-holds in various cracks and grooves that, as they appeared conveniently again and again, seemed to have an almost regular pattern designed for easy climbing. As he continued onward and the ground got farther and farther away, Tara began to realize that, based on her surroundings, this was not a wall at all. It was a bridge, and a somewhat familiarly tall one at that. "Are we at Frog's Leap Stream?" Tara yelled. Before responding, Chase gave one final push and conquered the bridge, landing on his feet at the top of it. "Yes, we are," he called over his shoulder.

Tara had once been to Frog's Leap Stream with her mother, when she was very young. There was a massive stone bridge over the tiny creek, once a landmark for merchants arriving in Jisara's grand capital. Located far to the east of the capital's walls, Frog's Leap Stream ran through old, dried-up farmland that once provided the kingdom with food. Now, the fertile land was to the south, and the only things in the east were abandoned barns and weed-choked fields. The tunnels had taken Tara and Chase right underneath the walls of the capital.

Amazed with the distance she had travelled, Tara began sliding off Chase's back in a bit of a daze. At the very same moment, he began striding through the snow towards the other side of the bridge, causing her to yelp and scrabble for a grip on him. Tara didn't even have the faintest clue what to expect anymore; she only knew that she did not want to fall. Sure enough, she had held on tight for good reason. As soon as Chase reached the other side of the bridge, he occupied himself with jumping off of it. Tara began to scream but was strangled by the rawness that ripped at her cold throat as they tunneled through the air, her cloak streaming out behind her. With a grunt, Chase landed on a surface that was still far too high up to be the ground—a roof, presumably—and halted their descent.

The air was the tiniest fraction less frigid here than on the bridge, but Tara was nearly positive that frost was forming over her fingers. Shaking uncontrollably in the wind, Tara nearly protested when Chase lowered himself to let her off his back. She wanted to stay near his body heat.

Once he was relieved of her weight, Chase began kicking snow out of his path as he moved about on the roof of what Tara assumed was a barn. He shuffled around and cursed for a bit, as if looking for something, then finally stopped and brushed snow aside to reveal a handle. Gripping the iron ring in both hands, Chase pulled upwards with a grunt, opening a large gap in the roof. Warm, yellow light burst upward like an ignited hearth from the trap door, repelling the storm around it.

Tara gaped in awe. "Do you ever go anyplace by normal means? Like maybe a front door?" Chase grinned. "Never." And he shoved her through the gap.

Tara expected to feel the stabbing pains of betrayal and shock that she read about in books when something like this happened, but the fall was so short that she didn't even have time to think much of anything. She landed on a soft, plush sofa that half swallowed her on impact. Panting, shocked, and freezing, Tara hardly even noticed when Chase dropped down through the trap door, pulling it shut after him and landing beside her. For several moments, both of them just sat there silently. The only sounds were Tara's teeth clacking together and Chase's shaking, cold exhales. A few beats passed, and then Chase stood, shaking his hair out and brushing snow off his clothes.

"I'll start a fire," he said. "You can… well, I guess you can make yourself comfortable," he said slowly, as if the words were foreign to him. He must not have people over to his home often. With a bit of a start, Tara snapped her gaze out of its trance. She was in Chase's home. Alone with him… and his sword. She hunted for some sort of unease, but somehow found none, and quickly stopped thinking about it before she discovered fear.

As her thoughts became a bit more coherent, Tara realized that Chase lived in a spacious, high-ceilinged barn. The floors were covered in thickly woven rugs and the space was lit with numerous lamps. Against one side of the barn was a strange pile of assorted… things. Countless expensive-looking objects were stacked almost to the ceiling, tons of vases and purses and other oddities clambering over one another in a disorganized mound. Clearly, Chase had stolen those items, but why keep them here so carelessly? Why not use them? Deciding not to question the logic of a thief, Tara refocused.

Nestled against another wall was a stone fireplace where Chase stood now, tossing logs into the hearth and preparing a fire. Tara sat in wonder. The barn was large, but it was unbelievably homey. It reminded her painstakingly of her old life with her parents, when their house was always lit and joyful. Aunt Bea's was always cold and dim, smelling of dust no matter how much she cleaned. How this thief had come to own such a lovely place was beyond her, but her real concern at the moment was getting warm.

Chase had started a hearty fire and was busying himself with removing his wet jacket. Tara approached him slowly, hesitating for a bit too long and causing him to glance at her. There was a moment of awkward silence before the corner of his mouth tilted upwards in an imitation of amusement. "You can sit, you know." Feeling somewhat embarrassed, Tara took a seat on the floor near the fire in silence. She let her knapsack fall from her shoulders and undid the clasps of her cloak. Closing her eyes, she sighed contentedly as the warmth of the flames began seeping into her. Finally.

A soft shuffling beside her drew her eyes open. Chase was sitting next to her on the rug taking off his boots and removing a black leather strap that he wore across his body. When he took it off, Tara saw dozens of pockets hidden beneath the strap that she'd never noticed before. He emptied the pouches onto the floor, letting countless coins and jewels tumble out. Tara's mouth nearly fell open. He was rich. Insanely rich, as rich as any nobleman could ever hope to be. She felt a slight spark of anger towards him. Earlier, he had been complaining about how difficult his life was, but he was sitting with a pile of wealth in his lap. Completely oblivious to Tara's staring, Chase carried the riches to that massive pile on the opposite wall and threw them all into the stack like someone might throw garbage into the street. The money crashed noisily against other metal and glass items, finally settling into the growing pile. Again, she wondered what benefit anyone could possibly derive from an unused stash of money, but she decided not to ask.

Chase returned to the fireplace leisurely and began unbuttoning his shirt. Tara quickly cleared her throat, reminding him sharply of her presence as he made his way towards his abdomen. He glanced at her with a tinge of annoyance and refastened the buttons, leaving the top two open still. Letting her sudden irritation slip away from her, Tara inhaled deeply and looked around again, appreciating the comfort of a sturdy roof and warm fire. What did it matter if he was a hoarder? He had fire. That was all she cared about. She turned to Chase, who was sitting quietly and staring into the fireplace. The silence was overbearing, and Tara scrambled for a way to break it.

"How did you come upon those tunnels? They're very well hidden."

Chase glanced at her absently and pulled his gaze away from the flames, toying subconsciously with a coin he had kept.

"Found them by accident a long time ago. I slipped on the stones under the bridge and got my foot lodged under the hatch. Lifted it up and found the tunnels. They're ancient passages, an escape route for the royal family in case the kingdom's ever under siege. One tunnel comes up right under the palace kitchen." Tara's eyes widened in fascination as he laughed softly. "Learned that the hard way. I never knew how much it hurt to be hit with a bag of flour." Tara smiled before she could stop herself, barely even pausing to remember who she was talking to. "No one seems to know about it, and it's a great way to sneak in and out past the guards," he added, with just a bit too much enthusiasm. Her smile faded almost instantly. The reasons behind this madness were not wholesome. She could not forget that.

The fire crackled and popped, sending shadows dancing across the barn, and Chase laid down on his back in front of the fire. Silence settled in, and this time, it was not heavy. They both wandered off into thought, and soon the warmth of the fire and the steady hum of the storm outside weighed Tara's eyelids. As she fell off into a slumber that would not be denied, she thought of light snowfall and jingling bells, and the slightest hint of belonging in the air. Before long, her worries succumbed to dreams.

CHAPTER 6

That night, while snow fell heavily outside and wind stifled young trees' breath with frostbite, Chase sat up, tending the fire and watching Tara sleep. It felt strange to have another person in his barn. He wasn't used to that. At the same time, though, it felt good to know that he had a friend. He wasn't used to that, either. When he finally became exhausted, he got up and walked to his bed. He settled into its soft cushiness, pulled the blankets over his head, and let slumber envelop him. It had been a long, hectic day.

Chase's dreams showed him Charles Onaj chained in a prison cell. The man was skinny and sickly, and his shirt was torn to shreds. His black hair had turned gray and his eyes were sunken and sad. He looked up, and with a hoarse, parched rasp, he whispered. "Come, my boy. Come, Loviti, and save me. Quickly. I am fading. Come save me." Chase saw Maria and Raka with the child, who now looked a bit older. The trio was running along the northern borders of Jisara. He heard the roar of the evil man, saw Maria's—his—eyes flash with terror. She yelled out. "You will never get Chase. Loviti will never be yours. Never!" Chase did not see the man, but he heard his voice; deep and cruel, with a tone that rang of steely confidence. That was a voice he knew from his past and hated with all his heart. "It is not your son that I want."

Maria stood tall, shielding her child with her body, trying to look brave as the man continued. "I already took your husband, Maria. I already retrieved Ukrasen. I hold it now, right here in my sheath. As long as it is in my possession, you will always lose." Maria scowled. "Exactly. You have what you wanted. Why can't you let Charlie go and leave us alone?" The man laughed. "Plain and simple, my dear. You know too much." They elapsed into a moment of silence. "And memory charms," the man mused softly, removing a vial of purple liquid from his cloak and examining it, "are only so reliable." He replaced the vial decisively.

Chase heard the scrape of a sword being removed from its sheath, saw the blade being brought down. He tried to shout, but his voice didn't work. Everything went in slow motion. He saw Raka scream, "NO!" and jump in front of Maria. He saw the blade puncture his chest, saw him fall and lay lifeless on the ground, his body still twitching convulsively. He'd died for Maria. He'd died because of that man.

He saw Maria's eyes fill with shock, then with pure rage. "You killed him." Her voice shook with raw anger. "You killed my *best friend.*"

"No," the man's voice was steely. "He killed himself. He chose to jump in front of you. He knew what would happen." Maria's eyes shot daggers at the man in the shadows. His voice deepened and became more menacing. "Come with me now, Maria Onaj. Unless you want your son to be next." The color drained from Maria's face. She shook her head helplessly as the man tied her hands and legs.

"Loviti. What will happen to him? Please, don't hurt him. Please! My son has yet to live his life. You mustn't end it so early. Please! *Please!*"

"Shut up!" the man spat. With a cracking blow to her face, he sent Maria to the ground. "I have no reason to hurt him. But little ears hear quite a lot. And little minds remember even more. I will erase his memory of everything. The potion will work fine on such a youthful brain."

"But"— "Maria, you'd be wise to agree. I am being extremely merciful."

Maria gulped. "All right. But you must swear that you won't harm him."

A smile became audible in his tone, a sound more frightening than any amount of shouting could ever be. "Agreed." He dragged Maria away, leaving the boy standing alone. He screamed after his mother with heart-wrenching hoarseness, but Chase knew the child's cries were useless. The image changed to show the cruel man dropping Loviti down on the borders of Jisara…a place that seemed sickeningly familiar to Chase. The man dribbled the purple substance into the boy's mouth, and he fell asleep immediately after consuming it. As soon as the child was snoring, the man rose and walked away, leaving the boy sleeping on the borders of Jisara with nothing—not even his memory. The pieces were coming together. This was starting to make horrible, terrifying sense.

The image changed again. Charles and Maria Onaj were in awful shape, chained in the cell together, weak and starving. They both looked up with weary and withered eyes that looked centuries old. Their hair was white, their figures bony and frail. They spoke in raspy unison: "Come, Loviti. Come save us. Find the protection. Find Ukrasen, and bring it back. Come, our son. Come bring us home." And the dream faded out of existence.

Chase woke with a start, gasping for air. A cold sweat ran down his forehead, and his chest was rising and falling at an alarming rate.

He sat back on his elbows, trying to get a grip on some rational thoughts. All logic seemed to have left him entirely.

How had this happened to him? Just a few days ago, everything had been normal. Now he was having crazy visions that were giving him all sorts of ridiculous ideas. How could he actually believe that his parents were alive? That was complete insanity. The dreams were… "Only dreams," he murmured, as if he could drill that into his head enough times to make it true.

With a jolt, he sat up suddenly and leaned forward in his bed to look at Tara. He sighed with relief when he saw that she was still asleep. The last thing he needed was for her to find out about all this. Dragging himself out of bed, Chase dug around in a cabinet and found some bread to eat. He wasn't sure how long he had slept, but he was hungry. As he tore into his food, he found his attention drawn back to Tara. He stared at her with a confused sort of interest.

For some unexplainable reason, Chase had felt drawn to her. He had never previously invited anyone into his home, nor had he really extended very much kindness to anyone before. Wariness had always been a blockade. Yet he had felt a very strange urge to help Tara when he met her. When the blizzard had begun, he had gone back for her twice. It wasn't like love; Chase had been attracted to many girls before, but this was an entirely different feeling. It had nothing to do with her beauty, or even her personality. There was something there that he just couldn't identify, some sort of distant connection. She was another addition to the recent explosion of insanity in his life. He simply could not figure her out.

"I've gone mad," he mumbled with a shake of his head, finishing off his bread and venturing to his window. The glass was iced over, but the howling wind outside told him that the storm hadn't lightened any. It was likely that the blizzard would last several days, and he had no intention of venturing out into it again. Chase let himself get lost in thought as he traced a finger over the cold glass, drawing abstract shapes as his mind wandered.

"Where do you keep the food around here?" came a voice, startling Chase so much that he practically flew away from the window. His sword automatically sprang from its sheath, and a shriek followed his quick movement. Heart pounding, he scanned the room quickly and noted two things: first, that Tara was no longer in front of the fireplace; second, she was standing about four paces away from him and holding a blanket over her head like a shield. They stood in silence for several beats, and Tara slowly peeked out from behind the blanket. If Chase hadn't been so stupefied, he would have laughed at her meekness, but all he could think of was how Tara had moved without him noticing. And how few people had ever been able to do anything in his presence without his taking note of it.

Tara lowered the blanket a tiny bit more, then put a haughty expression on her face. "Well, that's quite a way to greet a guest after a long night's sleep. Good morning to you, too." Chase's mouth was half open, but nothing came out of it. Tara rolled her eyes. "Very hospitable, aren't you?" He fumbled for words, but somehow couldn't find any. He *always* had words. A new sensation was grappling with him: fear. Was Tara secretly a pickpocket, too? A spy? He was very doubtful that an average person could move that quietly.

"Would you put that thing away?" she snapped, her voice jolting Chase out of his thoughts. Slowly, he sank his sword back into its sheath. Tara promptly dropped the blanket that had been protecting her. That sign of relief—and weakness—restored Chase's superiority. "How long have you been up?"

Tara shrugged. "A few minutes. Is there anything to eat?" "No," Chase said, the lie flowing from him automatically. Tara frowned. "No food? How do you expect us to live through this storm?" Chase was silent for a moment. As a thief, he had never shared food in his life. Money and riches, surely, because some homeless couldn't steal or work for themselves, but never food. You ate what you could find and hoarded whatever was left for later.

"I saw how much money you have," Tara continued, gesturing at his mountain of wealth with an air of disgust that made his neck tighten. She had no idea what that was for. "You can afford to fill your belly. I am not naïve, so I know that you have food somewhere in here. Where?" Chase clenched his jaw at her bossy tone. If there was one thing he hated, it was being controlled.

"You don't own me all of a sudden just because you're from an upper-class family," he said tightly, trying to control his temper. "You're under my roof, and you answer to me." Tara crossed her arms and eyed him critically. "Well, I don't mean to be demeaning, but any gentleman knows that a host should always feed his guest." Her tone suggested that she very much meant to be demeaning. Chase hated it. Kind of hated her.

"Well, I'm not a gentleman, remember? I'm a filthy little thief off the street without a purpose. I take up air, right?" He must have sounded harsh, because Tara stepped away from him slightly. Her attitude diminished considerably.

"Chase, I didn't..." "No?" he interrupted. "Then don't expect anything from me. You can leave whenever you'd like, but in the meantime, you have to deal with my rules." Tara pressed her lips together, then turned and walked back to the fireplace. She settled down there and began rummaging through her newly dried knapsack, organizing whatever sparse and useless items she had left. She had somehow lost her food basket on the way here. *Figures,*

Chase thought. *Leave it to her to be careless with something as precious as food.* He took a deep breath and scrubbed a hand over his hair. He was never inviting anyone over again.

The rest of the morning was spent in silence. Chase busied himself with random household chores that he had never done before in his life while Tara folded and refolded her cloak, sewing up little tears with a needle and thread that had apparently appeared out of nowhere. Both of them seemed to be trying to find things to do, with Tara rarely sending a glance his way and Chase doing his best to ignore her, too. However, he was on sharp alert as he roamed around the barn. She would not surprise him twice.

Quite some time later, Chase was getting hungry again. He didn't want to eat in front of Tara, though. He couldn't give her the satisfaction of… *stop it,* his mind told him. He knew how irrational that was. Eating in front of Tara and denying her anything was absolute cruelty, and waiting until she was asleep tonight was unnecessary torture for both of them. Besides, he couldn't starve her to death.

Trying to focus on his newly invented pointless task instead, Chase frowned at the shirt he was attempting to fold. He had never folded anything before today, and he could not understand how to keep the sleeves from poking out and turning everything into a wrinkled mess.

This time, he heard it when Tara shifted. She was standing up. "That's not how to do it," she said. Her voice lacked the snappiness it had possessed earlier, but she sounded far from friendly. "This is how I do it," Chase replied shortly. Tara watched him silently for a moment as he struggled with the shirt, then spoke again. "It's not working very well, is it?" Chase thought he heard a hint of a smile in her tone, but when he turned to face her, he was met with an unfriendly expression. She stepped toward him once. Hesitantly. The tension in the room was stifling.

"Perhaps you'd like some help." Chase rolled his eyes and held the shirt out in her direction. "Do whatever you'd like with it. I love watching you demonstrate your well-to-do housekeeping skills in *my* house." Tara paused and lowered her gaze for a moment. She inhaled and said softly, "I wasn't that rich. And no matter what I had before, I think you forget that I have nothing now. You're better off than I am." Her voice was so quiet that Chase had good reason to suspect that those words were hard for her to say. He lowered the shirt and let it hang by his side. He could imagine plenty of sarcastic comments to hurl back at her, but something kept him from doing so.

He shrugged slowly. "Well, yesterday you threw a tantrum when I said we were in the same boat. I figured you would prefer it if I kept our differences in wider perspective. If I treated you the way a thief should treat a lady."

Tara glanced at him skeptically. "The way a thief should treat a lady? That would be stealing from her." A hint of a smile tugged at Chase's mouth. "I tried my best."

Tara tilted her head at that. Quietly, she mumbled, "No, you didn't." Chase lifted his brows. "Beg pardon?" "You didn't try your best," Tara repeated, slightly louder. "At stealing from me, I mean. You returned everything." Suddenly uncomfortable, Chase swiveled away and continued his vain attempts to fold the shirt. "Did I?" he asked casually, making a thoughtful sound in the back of his throat as if trying to remember it. He flapped the sleeves around some, then cleared his throat to break the silence in the room. "I don't recall that."

"You were kind to me," Tara said, more insistently. "Why?"

Chase felt like laughing. How was he supposed to know? Nothing made sense anymore.

Standing perfectly still, he searched for words. Something. Anything to break the silence. "Must've been drunk," he managed haltingly. Tara inhaled disapprovingly, giving him refuge. He turned swiftly to face her again, plastering on a winning smile and sliding an arm around her tiny waist. "Now, if you're finished with all your useless sentimental talk, I believe you offered to help me clean up. It would be such a help if you could only dust that"—

"You don't need to pretend to be tough all the time," she interrupted, stepping away from his touch. "Or amusing, or careless, or whatever you like to emulate." Chase clamped his mouth shut and stared at Tara incredulously. He wished, more than anything, that she would stop talking about things like that.

She continued, "I think that there might be something good, something buried underneath all your charm and stealth and trickery. Something in there." She jabbed a finger into his chest.

Chase stumbled back a bit, but it had nothing to do with Tara's force. She studied his face intently, then said quietly, "You don't have to run from that."

He just stared at her, feeling so unsettled that he began to sweat. Who did she think she was? To tromp around saying things like that when they had just met was unacceptable, and the fact that it bothered him so much was just as worrisome. Composing himself, Chase resumed his attempts with the shirt. "You don't even know me." His voice was colder than he had expected it to sound, and he knew instantaneously that he had just shut out whatever closeness Tara had been feeling to him at the moment. He should have felt overjoyed at that, but he didn't.

She sniffed briskly, then stepped away from him. "You're right. I don't. And I thought that perhaps it would be worthwhile to know you, but I guess I was wrong." Chase dropped the shirt to the floor and eyed her flatly. "Don't try to guilt me." With a long, dramatic sigh, Tara turned and walked slowly back to the hearth. "I guess I'll just sit over here by myself." She turned with an exaggeratedly wistful face to glance at him. "Hungrily." Chase frowned in her direction, but she simply sat in front of the fire and solemnly ignored him.

With a groan, he swiped the shirt off the floor and threw it at her. "I don't like you," he muttered, stalking to a cupboard on the far side of the barn and taking out a large clay bowl. He filled it with ripened fruit, nuts, salted fish, bread, and a few other basic foods, plunked a utensil into it, and grumbled his way back to her. Stepping in front of the fire, Chase thrust the bowl towards her with a gruff "here". Surprised, he stopped when he saw that Tara was holding something out to him, too.

In her hands and extended toward him like a gift was the shirt, pristinely folded and wrinkle-free. Each of them stared at the offerings being presented to them, then looked at each other. Hesitantly, Tara smiled. "You're not going to starve me, then?" Chase inhaled deeply as though considering it, then sat down and set her bowl next to her.

"No. Unfortunately, the screams of the starving are dreadfully annoying." Her smile wavered, but didn't slip, and she set the shirt aside to take the bowl into her lap. Chase rose to fix himself a plain meal like Tara's, and when faced with the choice between eating with her and sitting at his table alone, he surprised himself by reclaiming his seat on the floor beside her.

They ate mostly in silence, listening to the wind howl and the fire crackle, but Chase was really starting to think that maybe Tara wasn't so bad, after all.

Over the next several days, while the blizzard raged, Chase and Tara ate all their meals together. Fights melted into disagreements, and those dissolved into playful banter. Tara tried to teach Chase how to keep house, but Chase became so bored that he finally just told her that he never actually did chores; it had just been an act. Tara, in turn, confessed that her prissy attitude had been an act, too, and apologized for her poor decorum. Chase laughed at her for using the word 'decorum'.

And so it went, the bickering and teasing and strange space between friendship and wariness. There was also talking—real talking, the kind of talking that Tara had been trying to do when Chase stifled her sensitivity. Slowly, he became less afraid of it, and suddenly he found himself talking to Tara about many things. A certain degree of trust solidified between the two over the course of those days spent together, and both of them began to see the potential for a very unlikely friendship. Chase had never had anyone to truly talk to before, and it felt incredible to have a person to share his thoughts with. However, there were still some things that he wasn't ready to tell quite yet.

He had been having the same dream as the last—the one in which Charles and Maria Onaj were beckoning him—every time he fell asleep. The more times he saw it, the more he realized what it meant—and the stronger his urge to answer their call became. Chase was uncertain about sharing his visions with Tara, though. She probably wouldn't believe him to begin with, but if she did, what would come of that? Would she accompany him if he did decide to venture off and find the Onajes? Chase could barely imagine it. He didn't mean to be rude, but Tara would be dead weight on a mission like that. He had witnessed her endurance, fighting skills, and overall grace when he had attempted to rob her. It was unimpressive, to say the least, and he wasn't so sure he wanted her along.

Then again, he couldn't really dump her out on the street as soon as the snow lightened and leave her for her aunt to find. She would have to find out about the visions at some point.

Several evenings later, when the weather's rage was finally being pacified, Chase and Tara ate their supper before the fire, prepared a pot of tea over the flames, and went to bed. Chase fluffed his pillow and settled in, preparing for another long night of poor sleep and haunting visions. He had watched a knife pierce Raka's body enough times to make anyone go insane, but he had given up on trying to fight sleep. He got the feeling that the visions would only stop when he listened to them. *Tomorrow,* he told himself in a state of dreaminess. *I'll find them tomorrow.* He drifted into a restless sleep.

Sure enough, the same vision reoccurred again, and was, again, more vivid than it had been the previous night. Chase's mind suffered agonizingly through the entire thing. Every word spoken shook Chase to his very core. Maria's eyes were a reflection of his own, boring into him even when she focused on something else. Raka's body fell lifelessly for what felt like the thousandth time. And Loviti. Loviti meant Chase. Loviti was his name. All of this felt so close to him, so familiar that his heart ached for it to be real. But Chase could not touch it.

Finally, after enduring the entire dream painstakingly, he reached the close of his nightly torture.

"Come, our son," the voices echoed through his slumber. *"Come bring us home."* Those final words resounded through his skull as the image of a manacled couple destroyed by age blurred and vanished. He knew what had to be done. This was the last night. This would be the last vision he ever had.

After the dream faded, something unusual occurred that had never happened before. Instead of jumping awake immediately, there was blackness. Sleep. For just a few moments, white panic arose in Chase as he wondered if he would wake up. If he would ever wake again. And with a start, Chase lurched off the pillow into a sitting position in his bed, listening to his heavy breath. He was awake. His eyes were open, and there were no visions to stalk him here.

Sweating and practically trying not to cry from relief, Chase ran his hands through his hair, rubbed his face, and looked up to stare a very-much-awake Tara Florreson right in the eye. She sat before the fire, watching him.

"You screamed," she murmured. "In your sleep. You said… you said, 'I'll save you.'" She paused, looking at him worriedly. "Is everything okay?" Chase's mouth hung open, torn between releasing words and screaming again. Finally, he shook his head, feeling somewhat numb. He had to tell her. "Chase?"

He snapped his jaw shut, then found his voice at last. "This… this will sound crazy, but I've been having these visions…" Chase proceeded to explain everything that had happened thus far, trying not to watch her reaction too closely. He left out nothing, finishing with his most recent dream and being met with absolute silence. Tara was completely at a loss for words, and her speechlessness unnerved Chase.

"Won't you say something?" he nearly shrieked, terrified that she would flee in fear of his insanity. She shrugged, openmouthed. "I… I don't know what to say. What does it mean?"

Chase licked his lips, which suddenly felt brittle and dry. "Well…" *Just say it, you fool,* his head screamed. *Say it!* "My last name is Onaj. And I'm not an orphan."

"Hang on, wait a second. Let me get this straight. Your parents are alive? They're locked up in a cell somewhere and they need you to come rescue them?" Tara shook her head as if she could scarcely believe it. "How did you only remember this just now?"

Chase shrugged. "I already told you. That mystery villain gave me a potion when I was young to erase my memory." "And you… believe that?" Her tone was skeptical. "You think that's actually what happened?" Chase frowned at the ridicule in her voice.

"Well, how else would I have forgotten that my parents are out there somewhere, barely alive, with a monster of a man holding them captive? I know you don't think I have much experience with human compassion, but that's not the kind of thing that would slip my mind." He sounded harsher than he'd meant to, and Tara's face darkened a little. He cursed himself silently for being so rash. Things had been pretty peaceful between them for several days, and he had just taken them back to square one.

Tara's entire posture shuttered. "It's a little ironic how you suddenly remember everything and know exactly what's going on, don't you think?" she asked, her stiff mannerisms hinting at an oncoming outburst of her own. Chase frowned. "What's that supposed to mean?"

"It means, if this potion really erased your memory, then why do you suddenly have it back? Why do you suddenly know that Raka was your godfather and Loviti is another word for Chase? Why do you suddenly remember all of it?"

Chase shook his head incredulously. How was he supposed to know? Things were confusing enough without Tara making it all worse. "I don't know, okay? The man in the dream said that the potions weren't reliable. Maybe it wore off."

Tara shook her head. "I cannot bring myself to believe that. I thought you were somewhat more… well, logical." "Me, too, until I started having these visions that"— "Maybe you're going mad," she suggested, then suddenly realized what she'd said and backed away from him warily. Wonderful. Now she thought he was crazy.

"Maybe," he retorted, "it was magic. Those sorts of things never make sense to the simple-minded at first." Tara sneered, contorting her pretty face into an ugly, twisted thing. "Magic, Chase *Onaj,* does not exist."

Chase's brows fell over his eyes. Anger began clouding his vision. He had always had a quick temper, and Tara was igniting it again and again. "What's wrong with you? Why are you acting like this?" He was narrowly avoiding shouting. Tara frowned judgmentally at him, as if scorning his loss of control. "Acting like what?"

"Like I'm stupid and crazy. Like I would forget my parents!"

Tara eyed him coolly. No. Coldly. "You did forget your parents. You forgot them for years, and tell me what kind of family that makes." She glared at him expectantly, but he gave her no response. "A broken one, Chase. That is not a family, and no matter what ideas you have, you cannot rebuild one based on a silly little nightmare."

Chase clenched his jaw, gripping his own hands behind his back to restrain himself. Everything she said made him go just a bit blacker with fury, but behind the resentment blocking his mind, he held on to one logical piece: he could not hit her. In his past, Chase never would have let a fight get this personal or hurtful. He would have been taking swings long before things escalated this much—and had done so many times—but he had to control himself here. He couldn't attack Tara. He knew that if he allowed himself to, he would kill her.

Her eyes burned into his. "Another thing. If this potion made you forget everything, but now it's worn off, why don't you know where your parents are? Why don't you know what they knew, what the man was after? The only reason he erased your memory, Chase, was because you knew something that he didn't want you to know. How come you don't remember any of the actually *important* things?"

Chase bit the inside of his lip, hard. "My parents," he all but growled, "are very important to me. So shut your mouth and think for once."

Tara stepped away from him instinctively but composed herself and rose to her full height again. "Well, I'm not the amnesiac raving lunatic in the room, so I suggest you redirect that command. Maybe try the mirror."

Chase shut his eyes for a moment. *Don't. Don't do it. Control.* "And I suggest," he said through his teeth, "that you get out of my house before I make you sorry you entered it." Tara's eyes widened as his hand moved to his sword handle, and it took her a few seconds more to collect her wits than it had the last time. "I just think the whole thing is ridiculous."

"Then why are you still here?" Chase exploded, shouting in her face. She inhaled sharply at his aggression, but he didn't care. "I would die before I'd enjoy your company! I don't want you, and I never will! Nobody wants you, nobody likes you, so why don't you leave and take another burden off my shoulders?"

Tara quickly recovered with anger that blazed to match his own. "As if you have burdens. You steal from others! That's how you live. You do whatever you want, whenever you want to. You have the easiest life in the whole world!"

"Easy?" he sputtered. "You think it's easy, spending your whole life alone, thinking you're an orphan, wondering what happened to your family? And now, knowing your parents are in huge trouble and that you need to save their lives all on your own? You think that's *easy?*"

Tara glared at him, so close to him and so ferociously mad that he vaguely wondered if *she* would hit *him*. Chase had never fought like this before, where punches were taken verbally. He was worse at this kind of fighting than Tara was, and he wished he could take swings with his sword instead.

"I think your life is a gigantic joke," Tara hissed in response to his question. "And how about me? You think it's easy to have to live as a maid to your own aunt, with your parents in a foreign land that's packed full with deadly monsters? Having to constantly worry that they got eaten by some beast?"

Chase tried to speak, but Tara bellowed right over him. "What about escaping a life of literal slavery, living with the constant concern that your aunt is going to find you at any moment and reclaim you?" Her voice rose. "Beat you? Chain you? Who knows what?" Chase blinked, some of his anger succumbing to surprise at the rapidity of Tara's furious words. She was moving closer to him with every sentence, emphasizing words with aggressive gestures of her hands.

"How would you feel, Chase, if you ran away from a place like that, thinking you were finally free of cruelty, and your first experience out on the street was a robbery? How would you feel if you were raised to know that thieves were bad people, but you put your trust in one anyways?" He was silent and found himself actually backing away from Tara. She was pushing him towards the wall with her ranting.

"Would you be scared? Terrified? Worried for your own life? Because I certainly was, Chase, and I understand you don't know the meaning of the word 'empathy', but could you try, for one second, to stand in my shoes? Because I really thought that I had made a friend here. For once in my life, I had actual hope that there were good people in the world besides my parents—who, by the way, left me, too. Didn't want me, didn't like me, right? Just like everyone else, Chase, and just like *you!*" Chase's back crashed into the wall as Tara pushed on his shoulders with her hands. He stared at her openmouthed, trying to get words out but being run over by her again.

"I thought you were different! I put my trust in you, and you're throwing it back in my face!"

"How?" he finally managed to demand. Once Tara had taken a breather, she seemed to lose her sharp tongue entirely. Chase barreled onwards, looking down at her flushed, furious face. "How am I throwing your trust back at you? I sheltered you, fed you… all these things I didn't have to do but did. I don't understand what you got so worked up about in the first place! I told you about my visions, probably the most secretive part of my life, and you completely blew up! Why?"

"Because you're leaving me!" Tara burst out, her voice shaking. Chase began to retort, but stopped completely when he realized what she'd said. "You're leaving me here while you go off on your adventure." She shook her head slowly and said, much more softly, "I'm going to be alone again."

Chase opened his mouth, but decidedly closed it when he noticed her expression. Her former fury had been replaced with embarrassment and sadness, a heart-wrenching sadness that looked so horrible in her eyes. Her eyes… Chase took one slow, deep breath. Her eyes were welling up with tears.

He deflated silently, the last of his rage breaking into rubble. *Look what you've done,* his mind chastised him. He and Tara looked at each other for a moment, all the heat between them cooling slowly, and a single tear dropped from Tara's lashes. Chase watched it descend the curve of her cheek until she swiped it away, lowering her gaze and taking a step away from him. Then another. Even with distance between them, Chase didn't move from his position against the wall.

He had no idea what to do. He had never seen anyone cry at his hand before. People had screamed and cursed and bled, but never cried. For some reason, seeing Tara's tears made Chase's chest ache.

Still utterly unsure of what to do and not wanting to make things worse, Chase stayed where he was and said nothing until Tara's eyes dried. She swiped at her nose and took another step away from him. Her ears were pink with embarrassment.

Hesitating for a few more moments, Chase finally stepped away from the wall and walked silently across the barn, giving her space. He leaned against his bedpost and took a deep breath. "You're upset because you think I'm going to go running after my parents to rescue them and leave you by yourself." Tara avoided looking at him. "I don't *think* you are. I *know* you're going to leave. Everyone else did, and you have good reason to."

He frowned. "What do you mean, *'Everyone else did?'*" "I mean, everyone I've ever known and loved—which isn't very many—has left me. My parents left, my nanny left, my grandmother left… and my aunt wasn't always the way she is now. Everyone I've known has left me in one way or another, whether it be death or distance. I've been alone most of my life, so I suppose I should've known it was foolish to try and make a friend. Especially with someone untrustworthy like you."

"Well, first of all, quit with the insults, because that won't get you anywhere," Chase admonished. Lightening his tone, he continued, "Second, I'm not leaving you, so relax. You don't need to be so dramatic." She met his gaze, but she didn't look grateful. She looked as though she didn't believe him one bit. "Really? You're not going to go running off to find your parents now?"

Chase blinked hesitantly, chewing his lip. "Well, of course I'm going to"— "That's what I thought." Tara pressed her lips together. "I'm not accusing you of anything, Chase. You should go. I'd honestly think you were mad if you didn't. I don't want to hold you back." She paused, and Chase became at a loss for words. He felt sort of trapped here. She was upset with him for leaving but thought he'd be crazy if he didn't go. What was he supposed to do?

At last, she walked to the fire and pulled her cloak over herself, closing the clasp and shouldering her knapsack. Chase was momentarily confused about her intentions, but suddenly realized how soft the snow had become outside. It would be difficult, but travel was fully possible now. She meant to leave.

Tara flipped up the hood of her cloak. "I guess I'll just…get out of your way. You know, take another burden off your shoulders. Since nobody wants me." Chase winced, wishing he hadn't said any of that. She headed for the door. "Goodbye, Chase. I hope you find what you're looking for." She paused and gave him a small smile. "Thanks for everything. Really. You helped a lot."

Chase sprang forward frantically. "Tara, wait!" Tara's hand was on the doorknob, and she frowned incredulously at him. "Chase, I'm leaving," she said, as if he might not have noticed. "This is what you wanted all along. You should be happy." "What do you mean, that's what I wanted? That's the opposite of what I wanted!"

Tara just shook her head and twisted the knob, pulling. But the door wouldn't budge. She yanked and struggled, but to no avail. She turned to Chase with a scowl, waiting for an explanation. He smiled.

"Ah. Forgot to tell you. That trap door?" He pointed to the ceiling. "Only way out. The door is sealed." Tara's eyes followed a ladder all the way up to the ceiling where they'd come in earlier that night. She rolled her eyes. "That is truly ridiculous."

She spun on her heel and stalked off toward the ladder, but Chase rushed to stand in her path. She sidestepped and tried to continue on, but he blocked her way again, pushing her backwards with his arm. She groaned in frustration, trying to shove his arm away. "What's wrong with you?"

Chase smiled, giving her a hard push that sent her stumbling several steps backwards.

"Well, for one thing, my parents are missing. For another…I don't think I can find them by myself."

CHAPTER 7

Tara couldn't believe it. "You—you want me to come with you?" Chase folded his arms and leaned back against his bedpost. "Of course. You didn't think I was actually going to just pack my things and leave, did you?" She began to say something, but he arched an eyebrow ridiculously and she swallowed the sound, studying him carefully. She knew she was supposed to be mad at Chase right now, but he was hard to stay mad at. She was learning that quickly. "But…why?" she whispered. "I'm horrible at these things. I have no experience, I'm clumsy, I get scared by the tiniest things"—Chase smirked and touched his sword, simply proving her point— "and I couldn't win a fight if my life depended on it. Why would you want me tagging along?" He grinned crookedly. "You don't do yourself any solids, do you? I told you I'd help you survive. You'll die if you go running off alone, so you're going to go running off with me."

Tara frowned slightly at his choice of words, and Chase smiled captivatingly. "Let's elope, my love, shall we?" Ignoring him, Tara fretted with her hair. "Won't it be dangerous?" she asked nervously. Chase shrugged. "Not really. The last two times I did it, it was quite uneventful. Although there was that one woman from an island"— "Not the elopement, the journey!" Tara cried in exasperation.

"Oh. Well, that's a far less interesting topic. What about it?" Tara glared at him flatly and was met with a devious smile. "Just wait until the wedding's over," he whispered. Tara flushed instantly, choosing to ignore this. "Couldn't we die?" she asked. Chase nodded. "Yes, but only if we're stupid. Don't do anything stupid, and you'll be fine."

Tara's shoulders shrank a little. This was happening so fast. Maybe a little too fast. She had never been away from Jisara before. Who knew how far this journey would take them, or where they were even going? There was no way to tell what they might encounter.

"Chase, doesn't any of this still seem sort of crazy to you? You're heading out on a mission to find your parents, right? Well, you haven't the slightest clue where they might be. You don't know what their kidnapper looks like, either. And atop all of that, you really don't have a guarantee that any of what the visions showed you was true. You seriously can't tell, Chase. It's mental to set out with that kind of plan. Which is none."

Chase scoffed at her. "I have answers to all your childish concerns, Princess. Firstly, I have a fair idea of where to start looking for my parents. I know of a man in Iravvai, a small kingdom many days' travel from here. His name is Alejandro Vidovu, and legend has it that he is the Map Keeper." "Legend?" Tara intervened dubiously.

"Legends are always true," Chase countered swiftly. "In his chambers are all the maps of every place in existence, from hidden worlds to those right before our eyes. He knows them all like his own reflection, and he has led countless great people down their right path. If he can show us the way to my parents' prison—or even to someone else who could—it wouldn't matter whether or not we know what their captor's face looks like." He unsheathed his sword and examined it. "As for the reliability of the visions, you would know if you had had them," he continued, running the back of a finger over the flat of his blade. "It's all real. I just feel it."

Tara sighed. She wasn't sure how eager she was to go marching off on some unplanned quest based on Chase's feelings. Yet still…she didn't want to stay in Jisara by herself, and she wanted to help Chase. There was one little catch, though. Death was almost guaranteed on this mission—at least for her, it was. Chase could probably make it through just fine, but her? She didn't stand a chance.

"Chase, I don't think I'm going to come." Chase lifted his brows, looking very unconcerned. "After all that fuss?" Tara twisted her cloak in her hands. "Just because I didn't want you to leave me didn't mean I wanted to go with you"— "Well, I'm not staying here, so that is exactly what it meant," he interrupted, sheathing his sword and making a grab for her knapsack. "Give me that. You're not going anyplace."

Tara stepped away from him jerkily, swatting at his outstretched arm. "Chase, I'll die," she explained, twisting away from him. He wrestled her for access to the straps of her knapsack while Tara struggled to deter him. "I wouldn't last a day doing something dangerous like that," she insisted, but Chase continued his efforts unheedingly. "Stop it!"

Finally, he held still, giving Tara a chance to regain her dignity. She straightened her cloak and reached back to readjust her knapsack… which wasn't there anymore. Tara's head snapped up. The look on Chase's face made her want to kill him as he breezed, "It might be hard for you to survive alone, but harder yet without this." He tilted his head admiringly at the knapsack dangling from his index finger. "And even more so without me."

Tara made a grab for her property, but Chase stepped away with lightning speed and held the knapsack out of reach. "Now, here's my proposition," he said, using his other arm to restrain her. "No!" she interrupted before he could say anything else.

"There is no proposition, none whatsoever! I am not putting my life on the line for your insane mission!"

"When I leave," he continued, ignoring her completely, "I will take this with me. If you follow, you can have it back. If you stay, you'll have to live without it, and without help." Tara lunged for it again, but was met with the grip of Chase's free hand on her forearm, pinning her arm to her body and holding her back. "And, if you try to take it from me before I'm ready to depart, you'll wish you'd never run after me that day when I stole your basket." She frowned at him, and he smiled darkly. "I will make you scream for mercy. I will make you wish you were dead, wish that you had never even been. Believe me."

Tara shoved his hand away from her roughly and took several steps back, but she wasn't angry. She was mostly afraid. She was afraid of dying, afraid of leaving, afraid of staying here alone—and maybe even just a little bit afraid of Chase. Something about the speed and stealth of those hands was nerve-wracking, and his threats didn't help.

She glared at him and was met with the most stunning of smiles. A repelling, disgusting, nasty little smile that was so unfairly gorgeous, Tara could scream. No passing stranger would ever guess how fake it was. She took a deep breath. "Chase. Listen to me. I can't." Chase's brows tilted together in mock concern. "No?" "No." He regarded her slyly, then shrugged. "Fine, then. I give up." Tara folded her arms, not buying that for a second.

He slung her knapsack over his shoulders and drew his sword. Turning it over in his hands, he grinned with a wicked, boyish charm. "When you get your knapsack back, you can leave."

Tara scowled deeply at him. There was no way she was even going to try to best him, so she waited to see if he would cave. When several moments passed with neither of them moving, Tara deflated powerlessly. What was she supposed to do? Try to retrieve her bag from an armed swordsman? Try to get past him and leave without it? She didn't stand a chance with either option, nor with living on her own at all. Then again, she wouldn't stand a chance if she accompanied him, either. Why was everything so, so unfair? "Chase, please," she implored. "Don't make my life harder than it already is. I… I can do without you. I can't do without my life."

He stepped closer to her once, sending Tara crashing backwards to make sure she stayed away from his sword. With amusement dancing in his eyes, Chase said, "Those two are walking hand-in-hand right now, Princess. You take all or nothing." Then he swung his sword at her for emphasis, sending the blade sailing through the air with a speed that whistled. Tara wrung her hands and retreated from him again, then closed her eyes.

She never asked for this. Not to be forced to choose between losing her life one way and losing it another. The very person standing in front of her was a threat. She had begun to forget it, but Chase was still a criminal. His mind was wired differently from hers, and there was no telling when the hardened side of him would show itself. *And despite all that, you're still going with him,* she thought in disbelief. And she was.

When she opened her eyes, Chase's sword was at his side and her knapsack was being held out to her. Tara took her belongings back, and he let her have them. With a smile—a real, small smile instead of an artificially charming one—he inclined his head toward the trap door. "You heading out?"

Tara looked down at her knapsack and pursed her lips. Lifting her gaze and meeting Chase's deep brown eyes with her own, she shook her head. "No."

Chase shoved his hands into his pockets, looking entertained. "What? What are you talking about? You just got your knapsack back! You defeated me!" He nudged her leg with his foot, like he was kicking her out. "You're free. Go on, little independent lady. Run off into the world." Tara bit her cheek quietly, drawing a soft laugh from Chase. "Or are you finally deciding to trust me?"

She watched him slide his sword into its scabbard with a metallic *shink,* then fixed her gaze on the floorboards. "Will you let me down?" she whispered. Tara felt, rather than saw, his change in mood. Something about him went from playful to solemn in a matter of instants. He stepped towards her, then seemed to reconsider that decision and stepped back again. "Let you down?"

"Let me die," she corrected, but her first choice of words had been intentional, too. If he failed to protect her, it would be the greatest letdown of her life. It would, in fact, most likely be the end of her life. And what a short, sad thing it had been. Tara felt a burst of frustration within herself. She didn't want to have to be protected all the time; she wanted to break away from this helpless person she had become and learn to take care of herself.

"Tara." She lifted her eyes and was surprised by the kindness that she saw on Chase's face. Whether it was an act or not, she couldn't tell, but it was there and staring right back at her. With a small shake of his head, he spoke. "I won't let you down. I can promise you right now that you will live through whatever happens to us." He spoke softly, using his breath instead of his throat to form words. His gentleness struck Tara like a cold wind. While he wasn't particularly aggressive unless they were arguing, he wasn't normally quite so benevolent.

"And if you die?" she asked quietly. Chase frowned at that, and his softness dissipated so quickly that Tara might have imagined its existence. "Way to be optimistic, Princess." Feeling somewhat jolted out of her compassion, Tara straightened and blinked. The caring atmosphere between them had disappeared.

"I'm serious! What's to become of me if you pull some ridiculous heist in a foreign kingdom and get yourself killed?" Chase smiled lightly.

"You spend a lot of time worrying about yourself, don't you?" Tara began to respond but discovered that she had nothing to say to that. It was true. She was being disgustingly selfish. "I'm sorry," she mumbled. "You're right."

Instead of accepting her apology in a heartfelt, gentlemanly manner, Chase grinned. "Ah, I love those words. They're just so marvelously true, don't you agree?" Observing her disapproval, his smile shrunk down to a thin smirk. "Something wrong?"

"Yes," Tara shot. "You're childish and unforgiving." "Who said anything about unforgiving?" Chase said defensively. "I was never mad at you to begin with." Tara blinked in surprise. "Then why did you say I spent so much time"—

"Because you do. And another thing. If you hate me all that much, don't come with me. I'll only be allowing you to speak on the journey if you're telling me how wonderful I am. Insults and any other conversations that aren't about me are not permitted."

Tara rolled her eyes. "Who's the conceited one now?" "Me, obviously," Chase said matter-of-factly. "I've always been the conceited one. Only difference between us is that I don't care." She threw up her hands in exasperation, drawing a grin from Chase. He was living to irritate her.

"If we're not leaving now, I'd like to go back to sleep," Tara muttered after a moment. Chase cocked his head at her, smiling youthfully. "So, you really are coming with me?" She looked at the floor and shifted her feet. "I guess," she mumbled, almost inaudibly. As she moved towards the fireplace, Chase followed. "Beg pardon, Princess?"

She sat down in front of the hearth and sighed. "Yes," she surrendered, loud and clear. "I'm going with you." He smirked down at her from his standing position, his thumbs hooked over his belt. Even the way he stood was infuriating. "And I'm protecting you," he said softly, the sincerity of his voice belying his arrogant posture. Tara glanced up in surprise, then smiled. She didn't understand this boy one bit.

Chase ignored her grateful expression and said briskly, "We'll leave at dawn, heading east out of Jisara. We still have a couple hours left to rest." Glancing at her dirty dress and patched cloak, he sniffed in dissatisfaction. "That won't work. We'll get you some clothes on the way to Iravvai." Tara frowned. "What's wrong with my gown?" "It irritates me," Chase responded bluntly. "In fact, I would prefer it if you took it off right now. You'd look so much better without it." Tara's face reddened, drawing an amused look from Chase. "We'll also find you a weapon or two."

Tara started. "A weapon!" Chase nodded, moving away from the fire towards his bed. He kicked off his boots and unhooked his scabbard from his belt. "I'm going to watch out for you as much as I can, but you made a valid point earlier. If I die, or even get injured, you might have to take care of yourself. I'll teach you to fight."

Tara pressed her lips together. "But I'm a girl!"

Chase peered at her with amusement. "I noticed." He smacked a pillow into place. "Your point?" "I thought women weren't allowed to fight. It's certainly not ladylike."

He snorted. "Who even raised you?" He set his sword on the ground next to his bed and laid back onto his pillow with a sigh, pulling the blankets up over his body. Shifting and yawning, he mumbled, "It's not war, Tara, it's self-defense. That has no rules. Besides, women make the best warriors."

Tara stared at the fire, watching sparks pop away from the flames and burn out. The room was quiet, and even the snowfall outside had become too mild to be heard. "Only in the legends," she murmured absently. Tara thought Chase had fallen asleep, so it startled her when he spoke.

"Then become a legend," he mumbled, his voice husky with drowsiness. "You could be more than just a survivor, Tara."

Tara's lips parted at those words. *More than a survivor.* As she laid down and adjusted her skirts to be more comfortable, she thought about what that might be like. To live and thrive and enjoy life as it came without having to answer to anyone. To rule her life instead of trying to accommodate it. *One day,* she thought. Maybe one day this would all be worth the risk. Her eyes slipped shut.

Only a quarter hour after she had fallen asleep again, Tara was awakened by a cold draft. Shivering, she sat upright and chewed on her upper lip. She was freezing and had been every night since she'd come here. She'd never had the courage to ask Chase for a blanket, but now that he was asleep, she wondered if she could simply borrow one. As she sat there, wondering if he would wake up if she snuck over and grabbed a blanket, she heard Chase stir in his bed and groan drowsily.

"What do you want, Tara?" he muttered, sounding irritated. She looked over at his bed nervously, wondering how he had known she was awake and prepared to say that she was fine. Yet she wasn't, and she was tired of being so afraid of him. He hadn't done a thing to her yet; what would prompt him to hurt her now? "I was wondering if… um, if I could borrow a blanket. Please," she added quickly.

Chase covered his face with his arm, then got up and started dragging the top comforter off his bed, grumbling under his breath. Tara lifted her eyebrows in surprise. She hadn't expected it to be that easy. Bunching up the cover in his arms, Chase stumbled ungracefully over to her, tripping over the blanket and blinking half-lidded eyes. She had never seen him move so clumsily before.

Twisting her clothes anxiously and trying not to feel too guilty about interrupting his sleep, Tara held out her arms to receive the comforter from him. Chase squinted at her through tired eyes, then smiled blearily before dropping the blanket directly over her head. Tara yelped as she was plunged into darkness, groping about with the thick blanket to free her head. She glared at Chase and blew her hair out of her face, and he grinned his way back to bed.

Deciding she was too tired to pursue the matter, Tara laid down and arranged the warm comforter over her body, snuggling into its heat appreciatively. "Thank you," she said softly, forgetting his offense immediately. "Don't bother me anymore" was his gruff response.

She shook her head slightly. "I won't." "Good." There was a pause. "Good night, Tara." Tara closed her eyes and shook her head. Chase was completely bizarre and totally antagonizing, but he was good. Very, very good.

"Good night, Chase," she mumbled, and then found herself plunging into an ocean of euphoria, a place where the stars lay at her feet and her fears were too distant for her eye to see. A place that was starting to leak out of her dreams and into her life, like a trickle of water into a bland desert. Like a good dream into a sleepless night.

"Okay, now let me look at you… great. Now, just slide this ever so gently into your sheath"— "No. The leather's okay, but I'm not even touching the sword, let alone *wearing* it."

"It'll be in its sheath the whole time, Princess."

"Yeah, but what happens if it falls out?"

"It won't fall out."

"How do you know?"

Chase sighed. They'd left his barn at daybreak, and they'd now left Jisara entirely, the last kingdom for the rest of their journey. Everything from there on was just open, unclaimed, no-man's-land, so they'd made sure they stocked up on necessary provisions before they set out. Chase had also stocked up on pearl rings, silver chains, and sapphire pendants; none of which he'd paid for, and most of which disappeared mysteriously within the hour.

Tara looked down at her newly pilfered clothes: a white ruffled shirt, some black pants and black boots, a brown leather cross-body strap with hidden pouches like Chase's belt had, and an empty sheath hooked onto the back. It was all topped off with a deep brown leather jacket lined with soft animal skins. She felt ridiculous. She had never even worn pants before. Revealing, compared to the flared skirts that normally hid hips and legs entirely from view, but they were so… comfortable. *Why can't women wear pants all the time?* she wondered. She wanted to see a man try wearing a corset.

Chase stood behind her, trying to stick the sword he'd pilfered into the sheath. It was a nice sword, no doubt. It had a pure bronze hilt with a wrapped black handle. The hilt was lined with gold filigree, and the sleek blade was engraved with ancient inscriptions. Nice or not, none of that made Tara any more eager to own it, and Chase was growing impatient.

"I'm not putting that on! What happens if I lean forward and it pokes me? What if it punctures my back and kills me? What then?" He tried again, but Tara jerked away. "You said you'd protect me, not strap a sharpened weapon on my back!"

Chase looked exasperated. He'd been trying to convince her to take the sword for too long. "Come *on!* Nothing is going to happen to you!" Tara shook her head stubbornly. "Not doing it."

Chase squinted at her. "All right, you know what…" He stepped toward her with the sword and plunged it toward her shoulder. Tara screamed, thinking he meant to stab her, but he just sank the sword smoothly into its sheath.

Tara exhaled with relief, then let a whole new fear take over. She twisted around. "Get it off! Get it off!" she shrieked. Chase laughed. "You act like it's a tarantula." Tara stopped dancing in circles and glared at him.

"What's the matter, Princess?" He leaned forward and smirked in her face. "Scared?"

She scowled indignantly. "No. I am not scared. I just don't like the heavy…um, weight of it. It's too heavy for my back. It will ruin my posture." *Even though it's light as a feather,* she thought to herself.

Chase grinned. "Would you prefer to hold it in your hands instead?"

Tara was going to get frown lines from being around Chase this much. "I'm literally putting my life in the hands of a child," she muttered. Delighted with the opportunity to prove her point, Chase began whistling a slow, merry tune, traipsing around her in long, crooked steps and acting like a drunk. Every time his rotation led him behind her, his whistle rose an octave in a note that Tara was pretty sure wasn't part of the song.

She endured this merriment for three circles before she shoved him away from her. Chase spiraled backwards violently, making it seem as though Tara had hit him with a carriage.

She sighed. "Are you finished?" Chase straightened and dusted off his clothes. "Yep."

"Then let's go," Tara said exasperatedly. It seemed that they took turns being irritated with each other. "In a moment. I want to double check the map." Chase slid his hand into one of his hidden pouches and removed a rolled-up piece of parchment.

As he examined it, Tara surveyed her surroundings. It was wonderful to be able to breathe fresh, cold air again. She had missed sunlight, and although it was blotted with watery clouds and provided no warmth, it was shining brilliantly nonetheless.

Rolling up the map and replacing it wherever he was keeping it in his various layers of clothing, Chase took a breath. "This is it, then. You ready?"

"No." The corner of his mouth tilted up. "Don't worry, okay? We're going to keep each other safe. We'll be just fine."

Tara nodded, trying to make herself believe it. "It's just that… well, I've lived in Jisara all my life. To be leaving it, and under such risky circumstances…" She gripped her hair in her fist, then sighed. "I'm scared." She braced herself for mockery, but none came. Chase only nodded.

"I know. But remember what I told you last night?" Tara frowned. "Not to bother you anymore?" Chase flicked a finger against her forehead.

"You need to be more than a survivor. Life isn't worth anything if it isn't lived, and believe me when I tell you that fear is the only thing that will keep you from living. Look ahead of you, Tara. The whole world is out there, just waiting for us."

Following his gaze, she looked out over the horizon. They stood on the frontier of civilization. Ahead of them laid wild, uncontrolled lands with mysteries and secrets gurgling through streams and whispering on the wind. The roar of the previous night's storm had reduced itself to the soft descent of thin flakes, settling down to envelop the world in crystal white jewels of ice.

A thick layer of snow from the blizzard covered the earth, and light reflected off everything, creating a blue glow that wrapped around the trees and glided over the hills. It was beautiful. And as she and Chase stood there overlooking all this, Tara felt as though she'd reached the top of the world. She risked a glance at the boy standing next to her. He caught her looking and smiled. "And so, the journey begins."

Tara hit the snow-covered ground hard, falling from a tree, with Chase leaping after her. He brought his sword down on her, and she rolled out of the way, jumping to her feet. He slashed at her face, catching her hard across her jaw, and kicked her knee while her arms were lifted to protect herself. She cried out in pain and lost her balance, landing on her back with her sword a few feet away. She rushed to get up, but Chase was faster. He put one knee down on her chest and pressed his sword to her throat. She clenched her teeth in frustration, glad that the swords were harmless, wood-carved practice ones—and that Chase was a friend.

Chase stood and brushed himself off without asking if she was okay, not even sweating. They'd been traveling for a long, long time now, and the majority of winter had passed during their journey. Several days had been spent just huddling together and trying to keep warm during the worst of the storms. Earlier that day, Chase had predicted that they would reach Iravvai by morning tomorrow, so they stopped for a break and some training.

It had taken Chase forever to get Tara used to holding her real sword. Then he'd carved her a practice sword with his knife and taught her different moves. He explained how to parry and how to strike, how to fight offense and defense, how to anticipate the opponent's every move before it's made. They'd already fought each other countless times, and she'd gotten steadily better. She'd never win, though. Every time, Chase beat her so easily that it was embarrassing.

Chase got off her and helped her to her feet, nodding to her sword. "Pick it up." She obeyed, but held it blade down, indicating that she was done for now. She gripped the hilt tightly with aggravation and tried to ignore the pulsing in her jaw. "Why are you looking at me like that? I lost. Again."

Chase tilted his head. "You were just introduced to this, Princess. There's no shame in losing."

He took up his stance and motioned for her to do the same. They engaged briefly, but Chase advanced, got in close, and locked Tara's sword hilt in his, disarming her almost immediately with a quick twist. From there, she tried using her leg to sweep his out from beneath him, but he jumped over her motion with ease and grabbed her arm, twisting her body roughly against his and hitting her in the stomach with his dull weapon. "Plus," he said in her ear, "I'm spectacularly better than you." She sighed and pulled away to retrieve her weapon as he continued speaking.

"You're not putting your strength behind the moves. If you had a real blade and I was holding a wooden one, I could still do more damage to you than you could do to me."

Tara blinked in surprise, feeling a little hurt. "I'm trying." "I know you are. But you need to try harder. Your life could depend on this."

They engaged again as Chase coached her through the steps. "It's not all about defense. Damage control can only keep you alive for so long. If you don't have room to attack, you'll tire and lose." He pressed her a little harder. "Watch your footwork," he cautioned when she stumbled over herself. "Keep your feet apart." They disengaged, and Tara glanced at him for feedback.

"Don't try to hit my sword. Hit me." Tara frowned, then swung her sword low to the left and got a swat on his thigh. He nodded. "Better. Aim for the fatal lines. Legs are good, but if you're risking a strike at a lowline, try for the ankles. Your opponent can't fight without feet."

Tara sighed and reversed her wooden sword, her head swimming. "Am I actually good at this? Do I even have a chance in a real fight?"

Chase paused and drew in a breath before answering. "You're improving, certainly, and you clearly have potential. You just need more practice. Once this is all over, ask me again. I think my answer may have changed." Tara lowered her eyes and nodded.

"Don't be ashamed," Chase said quickly, taking the practice sword from her hand. "This takes time."

She still frowned, though. If she couldn't learn fast enough to defend herself in a real fight, she could die. And she knew Chase had sworn to protect her, but what if there came a time when he couldn't? She hated that feeling of defenselessness. Her whole life, she'd been wary of the world, always suspicious and afraid. She hated having to depend on someone else so much.

Sensing her change of mood, Chase smiled gently. "Take it easy on yourself, okay? You're doing fine."

Tara eyed him sideways. "Can 'fine' win a fight?" Chase considered the question. "Probably not. But at this stage, winning's my job." Tara sighed. "Will it ever be mine?" His smile deepened slightly. "Just you wait."

CHAPTER 8

Chase glanced behind him for what seemed like the millionth time. He and Tara had reached Iravvai that morning, and they were now walking through the villages and trying to find Alejandro Vidovu. So far, they'd had no luck.

This village in particular made Chase nervous. The people were odd, with sunken faces and wolfish smiles. No one seemed very friendly, and so far, they'd seen only two children, each looking scary and possessed. Their eyes were wide and they didn't blink, staring people down as they passed with their mouths hanging slack. Old women gave them wide, gap-toothed grins, but not in a welcoming way. More in an *ooh-what-a-nice-tasty-snack* kind of way. Others just gave them looks of pity, like they had strolled into a doomsday parade. Chase knew he was probably being ridiculous, but the place seemed strange. They had odd money, too. He fished his hand discreetly into a man's pocket and withdrew a diamond-shaped brown coin. He later dropped the coin into the purse of a woman, as recompense for the silver ring he'd snatched from her finger earlier. He hid the ring away in his pockets as he and Tara continued on their way through the streets.

The houses were like shacks, covered with cobwebs, crawling with bugs, slick with sludge and grime. They looked as though no one had entered them for decades, but people were going in and out of them regularly. It may have been his imagination, but Chase thought he saw a door open and close by itself.

This isn't right, he thought. *Something about this place feels different.* The cold seemed a little colder here, and it seemed…sort of empty. That didn't make sense, though. The village was packed full of people. Every movement caught Chase's eye immediately. His senses were sharp as knives.

He also felt like he was being followed, like a pair of eyes he couldn't see was watching his every move. Tara must've felt it, too, because she clung to him like a burr.

She stayed so close that their shoulders were pressed together. An old, hobbled man bumped into her, and she practically jumped onto Chase's head. She was so jittery. Every time somebody even looked at her, she squeezed his arm so hard that he swore he felt bruises forming. Finally, she pulled him off the main streets and down a narrow alley.

"I don't like this," she whispered nervously. "Everyone looks so creepy and haunted. I mean, did you see those children? It's like everyone's crazy, or drunk, or something. Look."

Chase gazed out at all the people on the main road. It was true. At random times, people would start doing odd things. One woman was looking at fish for sale one moment, then flapping her arms like a bird the next. An old man tackled a teenager, and they began rolling through the crowds together, fighting. The few children there were stopped every so often to grab the leg of a passing stranger, tripping them. It seemed like the people weren't in control of their actions and thoughts. Every move was jerky, as if they were being pulled by invisible strings.

But there was something else, too. Chase sensed that he was missing something really, really important. He just couldn't quite put his finger on it…

Suddenly he straightened. Tara leapt back at his sudden movement in alarm. "What? What's wrong?"

He clenched his hand over her mouth and pulled her closer to him with his free arm. "Shhh!" he hissed. "Listen. What do you hear?"

She relaxed a little in his grasp. She was used to that question. Chase had been teaching her how to foresee an attack before it happened. Along the road on their way to Iravvai, he'd stopped her at random times and asked her what she saw and what she heard, testing her senses. He'd taught her to always stay alert, to be constantly aware of her surroundings. Now, she studied the ground, her brow knit, holding her breath so as not to make a single sound that could interfere. She stayed that way for about a minute. Chase waited patiently. Finally, she tensed. Her eyes widened as she exhaled. She understood.

Her hands were shaking a little. "Nothing. I hear absolutely nothing." Chase nodded. "Exactly."

No wonder it'd felt so empty. The village was filled with people, all of them going about their regular business: shopping, walking, cooking, and cleaning. Their lips moved like they were talking. Feet hit the cobblestone, copper pots knocked together, birds flew by and wind blew. But the village was completely silent. Everything that should've made noise made none at all. None of the people seemed to notice, but it was a ghost town. Everything was noiseless.

Tara was pale. "Chase." Her voice was barely a whisper. She was clinging to his jacket, her knuckles turning white. "This isn't normal. Something's happened to these people; something really, really bad. We need to leave. Now."

Chase shook his head. "We can't, Tara. We didn't come all this way to get scared off." Tara's eyes darted back and forth anxiously. "You're not *afraid?*"

Chase ran his hand through his hair. "Of course I'm afraid, but we have to find the Map Keeper. We'll find him, get our information, and get out of here."

A deep voice came from the shadows, directly behind Tara. "Oh, no. It won't be that easy."

Tara screamed like a lunatic. Chase drew his sword, his heart thumping. "Show yourself!" he commanded, deepening his voice as much as possible. He tried to sound intimidating, hoping to scare the only other voiced thing in the village so badly that it would run to the next kingdom before stopping to look over its shoulder.

Yet when he'd said 'show yourself', he hadn't expected the man to *actually* show himself. When he stepped out of the shadow, Tara, who'd been frozen in fear, screamed again, even louder, and scrambled behind Chase, peeking over his shoulder.

No, he wanted to yell at her. *Don't show that you're afraid! That'll just make you look vulnerable!* He tried to send the message by kicking her, but that just made her say "Ouch!" and kick him back harder. Chase decided to just let that one slide. He focused his attention on the man that stood before him.

He was a big, burly man with a large frame that spoke of strength. He wore a bandana over his close-cut hair, and his eyes were so dark, they looked black. He wore a tight-fitted gray shirt beneath his winter coat, with dark green pants and black lace-up boots. From his belt hung two empty sheaths, and in each of his hands was a short cutlass with a wicked-sharp blade. His weapon of choice was easy to manage, but quick to cut.

Chase squared his shoulders. "Who are you?" he asked. His voice bounced off the walls and echoed back to him. The man grinned. His smile was different from everyone else's. It seemed a tiny bit friendlier. That didn't mean it was friendly, though. That just meant he looked like he wanted to kill them, not eat them alive. "I am Tetoviran, champion swordfighter and server of King Vidovu. And you are?"

Chase contorted his face into a sneer. "You announce your title with pride, but you let someone else own you. You're a servant. You're weak."

His smile widened. "I like you, kid. You've got spunk. Hate to take it from you so soon." Tara's heart was beating so hard, Chase could feel it through his clothes.

"You're not taking anything from me, except maybe my dignity. Now I'll have to tell everyone that I took on some king's miserable dog in battle. How much does a housemaid like you get paid these days?"

Tetoviran's smile faded. He stabbed both swords into the ground and closed in on them, drawing a small knife. Chase backed up against the wall behind him, trying to conceal Tara. She had gotten better with a sword, but there was no way she could fight this guy. This might prove a problem for him, too. He had never had to protect another person in a fight.

"You looking for a fight, or what?" he hissed. "I'm about three times your size and strength. I'd shut up if I were you." Tetoviran's breath was hot on Chase's face, and he heard Tara whimper in fear behind him. Hand tightening on his sword handle, Chase lifted his head to look the man evenly in the eye.

"You won't kill me." "That so?" He nodded, the smallest of smiles tainting his face. There was a moment of silence as the two stared at each other, but Chase had very little doubt that his attacker would allow curiosity to trample over bloodlust. He was right. Tetoviran sneered. "Why?"

Chase's smile grew so slightly, it was barely visible. "Because I can pay you." The knife didn't waver. "With what? Money? Weapons? I've got plenty. Know what I don't have? Heads. Heads mounted on my wall." Chase stepped aside deftly and, grabbing Tara by her hair, pushed her forward. Tara yelped in pain and alarm, and Tetoviran stepped away from her in surprise as she stumbled into him.

"Her," Chase said flatly. "You can take her."

Tara's mouth fell open in shock that seemed to paralyze her, and the swordsman took another step back in surprise. His knife was at his side. "The girl? What would I want with her?" Chase shrugged carelessly. "A wife. A servant. A slave. Whatever you want."

"You would exchange her," the man said skeptically, eyeing Tara, "for your life?" "Chase," Tara breathed, clearly on the verge of panic.

Ignoring her, he nodded. "Yes. You want her?" There was a short pause, during which Chase felt tension nearly pounding in his head. Tetoviran shifted, somewhat uncomfortably. "I'm not sure."

Chase grinned, practically laughing. "Oh, that was a terrible answer."

Wasting not a second more, he launched himself at Tetoviran with the speed of a panther, shoving Tara to the side and swinging his sword before the shocked man had time to react. Chase easily found the hilt of Tetoviran's knife with the tip of his blade, knocking the short weapon from the man's hand instantly. Just as Tetoviran's reflexes began taking action, Chase swung his leg around to the back of the man's knees and forced them to buckle, bringing him to the ground. In instants, he was disarmed and kneeling with Chase's blade positioned against the front of his shoulder—a deadly place, if punctured. Chase's free arm encircled Tetoviran's neck in a hold just barely loose enough to allow for the passage of air. It had happened so fast that neither of them was breathing quickly or loudly, so Tara's heavy panting became starkly audible in the silent city.

"It's always good to be certain of what you want," Chase advised casually. A beat passed, during which Tetoviran's initial shock hardened into controlled anger. "What do *you* want, then?" he asked.

"We're trying to find someone. The Map Keeper. He goes by the name of Alejandro Vidovu. Do you know him?"

"Why should I tell you?" the man scoffed, but the ridiculing sound was cut short as Chase pressed his knife closer to his throat.

"Should I ask again?" Chase inquired, met only with silence. "Do you know of Alejandro Vidovu?" he demanded.

Tetoviran pursed his lips. "Sort of," he mumbled ambiguously. "Sort of?" Chase repeated, increasing the pressure of his blade slightly. "You're unsure of things quite often, aren't you?" "He's my brother," Tetoviran spat quickly.

Both Tara and Chase stared at him. "What?" Chase asked incredulously, pulling back a bit. Tetoviran inhaled slowly. "Alejandro Vidovu is my brother. King of Iravvai, keeper of maps, blah, blah. And you're fast, kid. Pretty good fighter, brave enough, it seems. But you're nothing against him. Whatever you want from him, forget it. You can't beat him."

Unfazed, Chase began to pry. "You talk about your… brother… somewhat fearfully," he noted. Tetoviran shrugged, making little attempt to seem threatening now. "For good reason. You really think I'm working for him because I want to? I'd love to get away, be on my own. Roam around and kill evil, slightly terrorize nice kids like you… but I can't. King Vidovu is the most powerful man I've ever met. He just hasn't killed me yet because I'm his brother. I don't want to know what'd happen if I tried to run away."

Chase raised his eyebrows. "That bad?" Tetoviran began to nod, but found it somewhat difficult with Chase holding him in a headlock. "Could we persuade him to help us? Could you?" Chase interrogated. At that, the large man actually laughed. The sound resonated chillingly off the walls around them. "There's no reasoning with him."

Chase slowly loosened his grip on Tetoviran's neck. "Fighting, then? You must be able to help us beat him." Tetoviran snorted. "Kid, you're going to die."

Chase merely smiled. "You hate him, don't you?" "I never said that"— "So you must want to get away from him, right?" "Yes…" "Then why are you hesitant? Cowardly, or just indecisive again?"

Tetoviran inhaled sharply. "I don't know you, little devil boy, and you aren't dragging me into any of your adventures." "You speak with a lot of authority for someone with a sword across their chest."

There was a long moment of silence, then finally: "I just don't want him to die. He's cruel, but he's still my blood."

"If you help us, that's not a problem."

"Well, what'll I get from all this?" Tetoviran demanded.

"Freedom. You can get away from him," Chase reasoned. "And like I said, you get the damsel over there. Complimentary part of the package." "Chase!" Tara exclaimed indignantly, being ignored once more. Tetoviran took about half a heartbeat to consider the offer. "I don't want the girl, but I'm in."

Chase grinned and stepped away from him, allowing the man to get to his feet and dust himself off. He was feeling truly hopeful now. Who better to have on their side than the king's brother?

Besides, Chase doubted that King Vidovu was truly as horrifying as Tetoviran made him sound. The swordsman was far from intimidating when he stepped out of his brutish character, and Chase suspected he might have been exaggerating about the king's fighting abilities.

"So, then," he said satisfactorily and sheathing his sword. "Shall we begin mapping out a plan?"

With a single, wordless motion, Tetoviran turned and punched Chase right in the gut, folding his body in half. Chase grunted and stumbled back, holding his stomach in pain. He reached for his sword almost immediately, expecting that Tetoviran had tricked them and turned traitor, but there was nothing to fight against. The man had hit him once and then turned around to retrieve his swords from the ground, casually sheathing them and securing his knife at his belt.

"What did you do that for?" Chase demanded, trying not to wheeze. The man was agonizingly strong. "I'm not gonna get beat up by a kid," Tetoviran said simply, and that was the end of it.

As Chase recovered and began to painstakingly straighten, he found himself facing a new foe: Tara. Her arms were folded expectantly over her chest, her small body mounted into an angry stance. Chase began to say something, but Tara interrupted him by yanking a piece of his hair hard enough to make his eyes water.

Chase slapped her hand away from him instantly, shocked by how much it hurt to have his hair pulled. Everyone was beating him up today. "Jerk," Tara hissed. "Oh, relax," he soothed, massaging his scalp and holding his stomach. "I would never let anything happen to my dear little pawn."

Tara looked about ready to kick him, but he stopped her with a mischievous smile. "Ready?" She frowned, puzzled. "For what?" Chase eyed Tetoviran, who now looked almost giddy with anticipation. Returning his gaze to Tara, he proclaimed, "For bringing the Map Keeper to his knees."

⌇

When Chase saw Alejandro Vidovu for the first time, he laughed. Tara cracked up, too, and Tetoviran kicked both of them and told them to shut up. Tetoviran's true colors had shown through very quickly, and he was somewhat childlike beneath his aggression. He had eagerly agreed to their plan, and escorted them to the King's home, the largest and cleanest of the shacks in Iravvai (which wasn't very large or very clean). The "throne room" reeked of rotting food and was decorated with nothing but an abnormally large, plain wooden throne in the center of the room.

Tetoviran had tied Tara's and Chase's hands loosely behind their backs with ropes so thin, they could've passed for straw. He walked behind them, occasionally prodding them in the back with the butt of his sword. "Come on, move it!"

He bowed before the King. "King Vidovu…my brother. I found these intruders in Iravvai. I bring them to you as a sacrifice, my lord."

Chase suppressed a smile, and Tara's shoulders shook with silent laughter. The man in front of them was so ridiculous, Tetoviran had to kick them nearly five times before they gained control of themselves.

So, let's get the facts straight. Alejandro Vidovu; king of Iravvai, keeper of knowledge and history and maps, giver of nightmares to full-grown wrestlers…you'd think he'd be about sixteen tons of sheer muscle. The great and glorious king stood exactly five feet tall, and every single inch was made up of skinny.

Yes, it was true. King Vidovu was the size of a child. His red velvet cloak rolled around his feet, maybe forty sizes too big for the man. His crown was too large for his tiny head, falling down over his eyes, and his shoes fit so poorly, he couldn't take one step without tripping.

Yet as Chase gazed at the laughable figure before him, something rang in the back of his head: an old, old voice whose face he'd long forgotten. The voice of a woman, who'd warned him when he was young: *Never underestimate your opponent.* He studied Alejandro Vidovu carefully. Maybe he was more powerful than he let on.

The king rushed forward, stumbling and tripping the whole way. "Well done, Teto." Chase looked at Tetoviran, but his 'capturer' wasn't paying attention. He was focused on his brother, whose eyes slid slowly over Tara and Chase, a narrow smile forming on his lips.

"Now, what have we here? Nice, happy… living…humans. Wonderful. I suppose you've come to my city for information? They all do, you know. Shame my brother captured you, but I suppose I can still speak with you. What do you want?"

Chase explained the situation carefully, making sure he didn't leave out any details about his visions. The whole time, the petite man seemed to be only half listening, looking around the room and tapping his oversized shoes impatiently. Chase finally finished speaking, but King Vidovu didn't even look at him.

After a few minutes, Tetoviran spoke up. "I found them at the borders, my lord. I followed them…" As Tetoviran recounted his side of the story, Chase leaned over to Tara. "Well, now we know why it felt like we were being followed on our way through"— "Shhh!" Tara hushed him.

Only then did he realize how silent she'd fallen, how she was holding her breath. She was so still, he thought maybe she was paralyzed, but she was listening. "You hear that?" she whispered.

She was hearing what he was: the sound of creaking floorboards. It was so faint, it could've been in another house. But it was coming directly from the small door behind the king. There was apparently an additional room, and whoever was back there was tiptoeing, trying to stay unheard.

Chase smiled. "I heard that the moment we entered. Amateur." Tara shot him a dirty look as he squinted at the doorway, trying to snatch a glimpse of the person, but King Vidovu's voice snapped him out of his focus.

"Well, let's see, now. You want me to tell you where to find your parents. Am I wrong?"

Chase nodded. "Yes, sir. I mean, no sir. I mean"— "You're correct, Your Majesty," Tara saved him. The king nodded. "Yes, yes, of course I am. Well, let's see. I know precisely what you must do to find them. I will give you all instruction, all direction, all advice and guidance and words of wisdom that you"—"Actually, just a map would be perfect."

Chase knew instantly, by the amused look in the man's eyes, that it wouldn't be as simple as a map, or a location. Of course not. Chase cursed himself silently. How could he have thought it would be that easy? The villain who'd kidnapped Charles and Maria Onaj wouldn't be dense enough to drop them off a few kingdoms away and hope no one would find them. They were probably very, very well hidden, somewhere so far away that it would take years to reach them. Yet if there was hope…

Chase looked expectantly at King Vidovu, waiting for him to elaborate, but the tiny man was bouncing on the balls of his feet, humming to himself and admiring the moss growing on his walls like he hadn't a care in the world.

Chase cleared his throat. "King Vidovu."

"Hmm?" The king looked over at him, as if just noticing him there. "What do you need?"

Tara smiled, forced and patient. "We'd like you to tell us who the man is that captured Chase's parents, and where he's keeping them."

The Map Keeper smiled cheerfully. "Ah! Yes, yes, of course. Well, I'll tell you everything you need to know, but I think I should warn you before I do: nothing, my friends, is free. Nothing. For everything, every word, every wish, there is a price to be paid."

His ebullient grin was unwavering as he continued seamlessly, "I'm not sure if you're aware of the fact that I built this kingdom with my own two hands. I named it Iravvai—Frightened City— because frightened is exactly what it is. It is filled with the poor souls who had their minds, their memories, their voices—their lives altogether—taken from them. They all paid their prices."

Chase narrowed his eyes. He had lived amongst liars and tricksters all his life, and he knew the tone of King Vidovu's voice like his own reflection. The man was deceiving them; the only trick was finding out how.

The Map Keeper tilted his head at them. "Yet perhaps I can make an exception for youths like yourselves. It wouldn't hurt me to do a good deed every now and then. Perhaps I'll help you and send you on your way free of charge. We'll just shake hands on the way out, as country people do."

His friendly smile fooled neither Chase nor Tara, judging by the expression on her face. Unfortunately, she was terrible at hid- ing her suspicion.

Chase, on the other hand, kept everything in his head. He watched King Vidovu, reflecting back on every word he'd said and trying to decode or crack open any secrets he was hiding. He came out with nothing. The king had clearly given them some sort of clue, but Chase simply couldn't figure it out.

"Yes, every citizen of Iravvai is my very own kin; my children quite like their lives here. I make sure of it." There was something about the kingdom. The city. There was a key hidden there that would unlock the king's mysteries, and Chase intended to dig it up. Leaning closer, he sold the king an interested look. "Tell me more."

King Vidovu smiled. "Yes, I suppose I should tell you about my kingdom. This city especially. You'll want to get used to it. It'll be quite some time…" Chase's patience was waning. There were more and more clues being presented to him, and he only needed a bit more. He was so close.

The Map Keeper continued with extravagant gestures of his hands. "I have given every person in Iravvai a new life to enjoy—a new world to live in. They have each had horrible, tragic pasts like the two of you"—both Chase and Tara's muscles tensed—"so I have given them refuge from their nightmares."

"What do you mean by refuge? Do you erase their pasts?" Tara inquired in poorly disguised alarm.

The king considered the question with much more thought than the average person would have. "Something like that."

Chase's mind was practically screaming at him. Enough of this. "Tell us where Maria and Charles are," he said abruptly. "I want to find them."

King Vidovu nodded sadly, pity adorning his features. "Yes. I wish you could."

Tara took a huge breath, as if mustering every ounce of courage in her body, then expelled it all in a rapid series of sentences: "We can. It doesn't matter how far away they are or what we have to go through. We're going to find them."

The king smiled at Tara like he found her tragically childish. "Of course. Now, the problem with this is that your parents' location, Chase Onaj, is protected by magical barriers. No one can find it, no matter how hard they try. The place is invisible, and you can't even detect which part of the world it's in."

Chase's mouth tasted like metal. Magical barriers. How clever.

Unsympathetic, the king continued, "The only way to get them back, as I see it, would be to retrieve Ukrasen. Of course, I have absolutely no clue if Tarnik is still with it, but I suppose we'll have to find out when we see it, eh? Now, where was I? Ah, yes! Now, you will find your answers in the land of"—

"Hang on." Tara interrupted, looking baffled. "What's Tarnik? And…Ukrasen? Isn't that the…sword? It's a sword, right?"

King Vidovu's smile vanished. "I don't believe it." He looked at them bewilderingly. "You don't know what happened?"

Tara frowned, shaking her head. She looked just as confused as Chase felt.

"Well, then," the king said, leaning forward eagerly as if about to tell them a great secret. "I'll have you know, young lady, that a few years ago, your kingdom, Jisara, was pillaged by villains and thieves. During that time, the most cunning of the thieves got ahold of the kingdom's most precious, valuable artifact. It was very ancient, and very powerful. Soon after that attack, griffins invaded. Did you ever wonder why the monsters came?"

Tara nodded slowly. "Yes. But I never found out. No one would ever tell me why."

The king nodded, practically crackling with excitement. "Well, *I'll* tell you why. It's because, those short few years ago, one thief was extra clever. That invasion, and then the monsters directly after? That was no coincidence. The Sixteen Kingdoms were—and remain to be—at risk. Because not long ago, Jisara was robbed."

CHAPTER 9

Tara's brain was completely overloaded as she knelt in King Vidovu's throne room. Attempting to follow the Map Keeper's story, pay attention to the noises coming from the back room, and stifle her fear over what they were going to attempt in mere moments—all simultaneously—was proving very difficult. The King had been talking for several minutes while her thoughts roamed elsewhere, and she finally realized how much she had missed.

Quickly, she interrupted King Vidovu mid-sentence. "So, Your Majesty…you're saying that Ukrasen is a magical sword? It has a special key, correct? A jewel called Tarnik that fits into the hilt and produces its power?"

The king nodded in confirmation. "Yes. And, as I said before, Ukrasen was given to Jisara for safekeeping. As you know, it was a protection for the Sixteen Kingdoms. It created an unbreakable barrier against monsters and demons of the Beast."

"The Beast?" Chase asked. "You say that like it's a name."

The Map Keeper ignored this comment, raising the hairs on the back of Tara's neck. "But one villain," he went on, "the cruelest of them all, had an old grudge. He was an immortal monster, one with a hatred so strong that he killed members of his own family for revenge on the creatures he feared—and hated—the most."

"What angered him?" Tara inquired.

King Vidovu laced his fingers together. "Well, the villain's history begins with a young boy that lived in Kaarnan—an ancient city quite far from here. The boy belonged to a very wealthy family, yet a very harsh one. They were cruel to him and did not love him at all. One day, he tried to sneak away from his home to see his friends. They were going to walk to the market together and play pranks on the shoppers." Chase smiled.

"The boy got lost on his way, took a wrong turn at a fork in the path. He traveled all through the night, retracing his steps, exploring new places, trying to find his way back home. Dawn arrived, and he still was lost. He became afraid, and stumbled across a very, very ancient part of Kaarnan.

"There, he found black stone ruins that may once have been a castle or temple. The rocks were crumbling, and the curious—perhaps foolish—lad that he was, he entered the remnants of the place. He found gems and gold coins and ruby encrusted goblets; more than even the richest of men could imagine. He continued through the structure's skeleton, finding that the deeper into the heart of the ruins he ventured, the more the place seemed to age, as though it had been built up piece by piece, with centuries between each construction.

"The boy finally reached the oldest room, where the walls crumbled and disintegrated with the touch of a finger. The floor cracked with every step he took, the cracks turning into wide fissures. And then, he saw it. Lying in the middle of the room, with sunlight creating rainbows that rippled over its muscular pelt. Its mouth foamed, its eyes were ablaze. It had fangs sharp as knives and razor-blade claws.

"The creature came into focus. The boy realized it was a lion—the king of all lions, and the first of their kind. Huge, powerful, and fierce, the animal circled him. Slowly, slowly, slowly…" King Vidovu's voice was so soft and soothing, Tara relaxed her tensed muscles. She felt as though she was listening to one of the stories

Gramma Kate used to tell her. She was a little girl now, hiding under her covers while her grandmother told the scary parts, making her tremble with fear. But then came the happy ending, where Tara would crawl out from under the blankets with a big smile. But King Vidovu was no Gramma Kate.

"BANG!" Tara jumped violently, her heart pounding. Chase hadn't even flinched, and he sent an amused glance her way.

"The lion pounced. The boy slammed into the wall, which began to shift and groan, threatening to collapse. The boy was exhausted and weaponless, certainly in no shape to fight. He tried to wrestle the lion, but it was no use. He was soon pinned, and the lion raised its paw to finish him off."

Tara waited for the heroic warrior to barge into the story, or the boy to suddenly find inhumane strength. However, there was no such luck.

"*Slice!* One swift chop, and the boy was dead." What kind of story was this?

"His spirit left his body. He came to Tea and Jeff, who thought highly of his boldness. Wrestling the lion king took a lot of audacity, and they pitied his sad childhood, so they switched the boy's place with the lion king. They turned him into the king of the creatures, made him immortal. They then transformed the original king back into a helpless little human. This former king was so angry at Tea and Jeff that he marched straight to their palace and put knives to their throats, threatening to kill them if they didn't reverse what they'd done.

"However, they refused to turn him back into a lion, for he was monstrous. He killed without reason, attacked anyone within six leagues of his territory. That body gave his murderous mind too much power. But he declared that he would not tolerate being a regular mortal. So, Tea and Jeff, tricky maidens that they are, made him an *immortal* human. They then claimed that they'd given what he'd wanted; he was no longer a regular mortal. In fury, the king left."

Tara frowned, stopping his story. "Wait… Tea and Jeff? What kind of names are those? Who are they? Why do you go to them when you die?" The king smiled dryly. "Quite talkative, aren't you? I think your little friend over here can explain it."

She looked at Chase questioningly. He caught her gaze and shrugged. She searched his eyes for any signs of falseness, but he seemed genuinely confused.

"So…" Chase spoke, prompting him to continue. "What happened to the king?"

Alejandro smiled. "So glad you asked. Well, he was angry, in case you hadn't guessed. He was mad at Tea and Jeff, mad at his new body…but especially mad at the new king of lions. He was mad at *all* lions. He wanted revenge. So, he took time. Years and years and years. He visited sorcerers, mixed potions, brewed spells, crossed breeds. He worked on his project for centuries. And then one day, it was finally complete. He created the one true enemy of lion. The only creatures that were descended from the sleek, beautiful beasts, and turned into rabid monsters." Vidovu's eyes gleamed. "*Griffins.* Griffins were of his own creation. They were bred to attack and kill anything in their path. He had trained each one to share his bloodthirstiness, and to especially seek revenge on lions. They are one of the few things every lion fears. The king was vengeful, looking for any way to release his rage into the wild.

"However, these beasts weren't free to roam the wild and kill as they pleased. The griffins were considered monsters and were therefore confined to lands outside of the Sixteen Kingdoms— the majority imprisoned in Paroaff, if you know of that forsaken place." Tara tightened her jaw but said nothing.

"This made the king even angrier than before," Vidovu elaborated. "The sword—Ukrasen—was keeping his creations from attacking, and he refused to let his hard work go to waste because of a barrier. So, let's all take a guess what he did, shall we?"

Tara felt like someone had forced a boulder down her throat. King Vidovu nodded. "Oh, yes. He tried. He snuck into the palace of Jisara at night and got into the throne room where Ukrasen rested in its case, keeping Paroaff's monsters at bay. He almost got away with it, but he was caught by night guards and locked away in prison."

Tara's brain was overflowing. This was all starting to make sense to her.

"But he escaped somehow, didn't he? He got out. He stole Ukrasen from Jisara and hid it away so that no one could find it and restore it to power."

King Vidovu nodded. "Yes. He initially hid it in one of the Sixteen Kingdoms, which is why his griffins remained unable to attack. Tarnik—the source of the sword's power—was still intact, and the sword was still within the kingdoms. It was still keeping them safe." The Map Keeper gazed down at Chase, who knelt before him with an impassive expression, and granted him the smallest of smiles.

"A search party was organized. Maria and Charles Onaj led it, and they were the ones who found Ukrasen and tried to bring it back to Jisara. However, they could not best the lion king. He locked them away and forced them to surrender to his power. They were no longer threats to his plans."

Tara practically gasped in realization as everything began to make sense. "So afterwards, he hid the sword properly, far away, and hid the Onajes behind this magical barrier you're talking about. The sword must enforce that barrier, too, which is why they can't be found until Ukrasen is retrieved and brought back to Jisara. *That's* why griffins invaded Jisara and why there have been so many more attacks than usual. The barriers have finally broken." She looked up to find the dumbstruck faces of Tetoviran and King Vidovu staring down at her. Even Chase looked surprised.

The petite king before her cleared his throat. "Well, um, yes. Precisely. So, the sword must be replaced in Jisara's throne room. Then all the work of the king shall be undone. The griffins shall disappear back into the heart of Paroaff, Charles and Maria shall appear, healthy and young again…"

Chase's expression did not change other than a slight, confused dip of his brow. "What made them age so fast in the first place?" he asked, stepping lightly over the king's attempt to lure him. "Why did my mother and father seem so weak, and my father give up when he could have continued fighting?"

King Vidovu sighed softly and paced, then stood still after tripping on his robes three times. "Do you remember the place in the woods, Chase Onaj? The place under the tree where Charles was stricken, where blood stains the earth?"

Chase looked like someone had slapped him. "How did you"—"I know things, as you were so keen to notice when you chose to find me here. Ukrasen has bad powers along with good ones. As I said, everything comes with a price. When Tarnik is in its proper space in the hilt, the blade has the power to weaken whoever it cuts. It doesn't need to be a deep wound. Stabbing someone with a sword kills them, magic or not." The Map Keeper's eyes flitted over Chase as he shook his head. "But murder is hardly cruel when compared to torture. Imagine being preserved for an eternity, Chase. Locked in a cell with nothing to eat or drink, living endlessly with the pains of fatigue and old age. That is the blade's power. The smallest amount of blood drawn from a man who survives the cut will become his downfall." Chase's jaw was painfully tight.

"Wherever the blood falls, it stains the ground there forever. If snow falls over it, it reappears atop the snow. If a rockslide tumbles down, the blood appears on the stones. It's a permanent mark, indicating that someone's strength was taken on that soil. In a way, Ukrasen is a horrible, horrible weapon. Can't you imagine it, Chase Onaj? Unable to move, to walk, even to breathe properly, with vivid memories of the strong physical shape you were once in. That never-ending false sensation of old, old age." King Vidovu was nearly whispering.

The veins of Chase's hands were visible in his clenched fists. Cold, controlled anger was hardening features that Tara had grown fond of, and her heart hammered in her throat at the molten mercilessness cooling in his gaze. The chilling expression on his face brought thoughts to Tara's head that she thought she had finished conjuring, reminding her that he was dangerous. A thief. Criminal. Most likely a murderer. A childhood like his could leave rough edges that might never smooth out.

"What's this king's name?" Chase asked, his voice level but horribly soft. "Araknan," King Vidovu responded, gazing at Chase calculatingly. He was waiting, Tara realized, to see what Chase would do. He was waiting for his aggression to snap. Ever so subtly, Tara tucked her ankle over Chase's in a half-comforting, half-warning gesture. There was a tightness to his posture that loosened just the slightest bit at her touch.

Making eye contact with the king, she drew his attention to her. "I think we've heard enough legends for now. How do we find Ukrasen?" The Map Keeper hesitated for a moment, then slowly withdrew a map from his robes. How he had just happened to have the right one in his sleeve before they even arrived, Tara couldn't imagine. Stroking the rolled-up parchment in an almost absently loving way, he said, "This will lead you exactly where you need to go. Follow the map, and you'll find the sword. Other than that, I've told you everything you'll need to know."

Tara's fingers curled around her loosely tied bonds in anticipation, but she didn't dare make a move before receiving a proper signal from Tetoviran.

Tara glanced warily at the king. "You said you'd let us go after we got our information."

He nodded, a gleam in his eyes. "Yes, and I am a man of my word, I assure you. Teto, be a good fellow and lead them to the door, will you? As I said, I'll give you the map, and I'll bid you farewell with a handshake."

Chase's ankle tensed under Tara's all of a sudden. Going still, Tara waited until King Vidovu turned and began his precarious shuffle towards his front door to turn to him. "What—" He leaned forward and cut her off as Tetoviran broke their bonds. "Get out of here. As fast as you can, Tara. Don't wait for me. I'll grab the map and follow," he whispered, his voice closer to frantic than she'd ever heard it.

"What's going on?" she fretted.

"Just do it. Don't stop for anything. Get out of this shack. Get out of this city. No matter what you hear, no matter what you see, don't stop."

King Vidovu snapped his fingers behind them. "Come on, now! Hurry up!" Chase gripped her shoulders and stared her in the eyes. "Promise me, Tara."

Fear closed up in her throat. "Chase, what's happening?" "There's no time!" "But how will I find"— "Once you're out, just stay put. Don't go anywhere. I'll get the map, get Tetoviran out, and find you. Just promise me you won't stop for anything. And don't let the king touch you, either. He'll hurt you, Tara. Worse than death."

Tara's mind swam with confusion and fear. What was he talking about? "Chase"— "Promise me!" His eyes were so full of worry. She swallowed her fear as best she could. "I promise." Chase nodded, satisfied. He stared at her for one second more, then turned and walked to the door.

Tara walked after him, trying to imitate his quick, confident strides. What was happening? Chase had made some sort of realization just a moment ago—a realization terrible enough to terrify him. Reaching the door, King Vidovu held out his hand to Chase.

"I wish you the best on your journey, young man. It was a real pleasure," Alejandro intoned with a slight curve to his lips.

Chase nodded once. "Mutual. The map, please."

Alejandro shuffled casually to position himself between Chase and the door. "No, not yet," he said hastily. "We still have to do the traditional Iravvian handshake. It is a wish of luck on everyone who passes through. The handshake grants you abundance, safety, health"— "Mindlessness?" Chase intervened quietly.

The king's face dropped so drastically at that one word that Tara—confused as she was—could tell that whatever meaning was behind it, it had caught Vidovu somehow. There was a moment of silence that made the Map Keeper seem to shrink lower than his already tiny height and Chase to tower further above him. He had undoubtedly hit a target. Mindlessness? From a handshake? What on earth was going on?

Regaining his wits, the king's features twisted into a sneer so unlike his former behavior that it was alarming. All his former friendliness had vanished completely. "If you think you can outsmart me, boy..." Chase smirked. "You seem to forget that I already have. And that I will do so again, in roughly five minutes, so do not say I haven't warned you. Give me the map now. Make this easy on yourself."

Vidovu spat at Chase's feet. "You are nothing against me. Try to come and get your precious map if you desire it. I will make you bow to me until every bone in your back is broken."

Tara's brows jumped at the threat. Chase was making a big mistake. Whoever this king really was behind his friendly façade, he was dangerous.

Chase, however, didn't flinch. In fact, he smiled—yet without even the slightest hint of humor. "Ah, but even in death, my ribs will prod your heels most painfully as you crush them underfoot, old man." The Map Keeper smiled right back with equal malice. "Who said anything about death?" he asked softly.

Tara's heart was pounding in her throat. That sounded awfully close to Chase's warning just moments before. *Worse than death,* it had been. She was so focused on the exchange that she didn't even hear the boy come up behind her—until he was on top of her. He tackled her waist and covered her mouth, muffling her words for no reason. She was so frozen in terror that she couldn't have screamed if she wanted to.

Tara kicked his shin hard, but he leaned down and whispered in her ear. "Shh. Quiet. I'm here to help."

Silently, he pulled her away from the others and down behind the king's massive throne. The large build of the chair provided great coverage. Considering she was back there with a stranger, good coverage didn't really work in her favor. Tara could hear Chase and Alejandro continuing their verbal competition a short distance away. They apparently hadn't even noticed anything.

Tara turned and found herself staring at a young man a few years older than her, far closer to an adult than a child. He had blond hair, emerald eyes, and solid muscles shielding every bone of his exposed arms. He had a bow slung over his shoulder and a quiver filled with arrows.

"Who are you?" she mustered up the courage to whisper. "I'm King Vidovu's son."

Tara immediately began to stand, practically tripping over herself in fear. He yanked her back down, and Tara took terrifying note of his brutish strength.

"Just listen to me. I've been stuck here my whole life. My father watches me like a hawk. If I tried to escape, he'd…you know." He gave her a knowing look like the two of them shared some sort of inside secret. "But you guys know about him. You're the first ones ever to come here and know the truth. You'd be a perfect distraction. I could escape with you and your friend."

Tara frowned at him. "You're mad," she hissed. A beat passed, and when his earnest expression didn't change, she sighed. "You're not, then. So, you want to come with us?" He nodded. "Please. I can't stay here. I'm living in fear of my own father. I can help you get out."

Tara wanted to scream in frustration. This was so overwhelming. "I can't decide whether you come or not. I…I don't even know what's going on, or who King Vidovu truly is, and now"— "Wait. You don't *know*?"

She shook her head. "Apparently only Chase can figure those things out." "I take it he's your companion?" Tara nodded.

"Oh. Okay. Well then, I can help you. I've got a plan."

Tara scooted a little further away from him, not caring that she was risking being spotted. "Thanks, but no thanks. We've got our own plan. I don't even know you."

He shook his head. "It'll never work. You've got to trust me." "Trust you?!" "Shhh!"

Tara lowered her voice. "I just met you!"

He opened his mouth as if to protest angrily, then backed off slightly and merely shrugged. "Fine. Have fun getting killed on your way out." Tara scowled at him. For a stranger, he was certainly easy to dislike.

She wished she could just curl up and go to sleep. She'd had enough adventure for one day. For a lifetime, really. But then again… she knew how it felt to be trapped in a place you couldn't stand.

"All right," she decided reluctantly, hoping she wasn't making a bad decision. If she had misjudged this boy, Chase would never forgive her. "But if this is a trick"— "It's not. I promise." She bit her lip. "Okay. That's…that's fine. Not like it's going to get any better from here."

He nodded. "I've got your back." Tara stepped out from behind the throne and scurried back behind Chase. She tried to be subtle, but the king's eyes landed on her almost immediately.

"Where did you go off to?" he asked. "Who"—His face went slack as the boy casually stepped out from behind the throne. With a tilt of his head, he smiled. "Hello, father."

CHAPTER 10

When the strange boy that had been making all the noise in the back room snuck up behind Tara and yanked her behind King Vidovu's throne, Chase had kept his worry at bay. He knew that his hesitation would point out her absence to the king and put her at risk. But staying put and continuing to exchange threats with the pint-sized little goat, knowing that Tara had just gotten snatched by a strange boy in the middle of Alejandro's possessed city, was probably the hardest thing he'd ever done. He kept the king's attention as best he could, throwing out insults and poking humorless fun at his threats, but only a blind man could have missed Tara's reentrance. Silently cursing his luck as Vidovu spotted her, he turned with the king to look at Tara, who froze instantly.

Now, Chase had been expecting the stranger to come out from behind the throne at some point. He hadn't expected him to come out and tell lies, though.

When the tall, blond, rugged young man appeared and called King Vidovu his father, Chase almost laughed. The king was five feet tall with oily black hair, whiter-than-white wrinkled skin, and a horribly misshapen face that looked like it'd been kicked by an angry horse several hundred times. This boy stood over a foot taller than his father, had tanned, muscular arms and shocking green eyes, and handsome features that made him look like a prince (which he would've been, if the king was *actually* his dad—but he clearly wasn't).

Trying to take advantage of the distraction, Chase edged closer to the Map Keeper. He was just getting ready to grab the map from King Vidovu's tiny hands when the king spoke.

"What are you doing here, son?" Chase's subtly outstretched hand lurched back immediately. These two…related? It seemed impossible. Yet if it was true, that meant that the boy was probably tricking them. There was very little chance that he would go against his own father in this situation.

He gripped his sword hilt anxiously, trying to come to a conclusion about what to do. In that time, the king's son had taken several slow steps toward his father, shrugging nonchalantly. "Came to see the show. It always is inspiring to watch you expand your city." Passing an unreadable look over Chase and Tara, he continued, "These two will make a great addition."

Tara's gaze flicked back and forth between the boy and Chase. She looked pitifully scared. She didn't have a clue what was going on.

Chase drew his sword and stepped forward, his blade slicing the air sharply as he maneuvered it. "He's right, you know. It's simply such a shame that we have to leave." The king gnashed his teeth. "You won't be going anywhere. At least, not without my permission, you won't. You want your map? Take it!" He tossed the parchment to Chase, who quickly switched his sword hand and caught it. "As if it will be of any use to you now."

Tucking the map into one of his hidden pouches beneath his clothes, Chase eyed the king triumphantly. "You made the wrong move, pixie," he said, somehow managing to sound taunting and threatening at the same time. "Now that map is mine. Tell me, do you ever get headaches from holding so much inside such a tiny head?"

Fire blazing in Vidovu's eyes, he tore off his crown and threw it to the ground. "Enough of this! I'm sick of you, boy!" He snapped his fingers impatiently. "Teto, hold the rat. You, son, get the girl. Let's teach them a bit more about the customs of Iravvai, shall we?"

Chase sheathed his sword quickly as Tetoviran stepped forward and grabbed his arms. As he was pushed to his knees, Chase's mind spun. Tetoviran would not turn on them, but he didn't even know the other boy's name. What if Tara had misjudged him? He craned his neck to watch as the king's son took Tara by the wrists and used his shoe to buckle her knees and make her kneel. Chase could easily see that the prince was being gentle, which was a promising sign. Yet there was no real way to tell whether he could be trusted or not.

Forgetting the matter for the time being, he refocused on King Vidovu, who laughed and shook his head pitifully at him. "I will soon forget that tongue of yours, boy. As will the rest of the world."

He had only taken three steps toward Chase, his hand outstretched, when Tetoviran released Chase's arms and jumped over his already-ducking head with a sword drawn. Caught completely by surprise, the Map Keeper stumbled to back away, but Tetoviran was too fast. Putting all his strength behind a swing, Teto slammed the pommel of his weapon into his brother's gut, making the small man fold over in pain. Tetoviran liked hitting people in that spot, it seemed. With a grin, Chase unsheathed his own blade and joined in. As they both beat him with the butts of their swords, the King flailed in his robes and screamed in rage.

"Traitor! How could you do this? How could you do this to your own brother, Teto?"

During this opening, Chase became vaguely aware of the new boy pushing Tara out the door. Pausing before following her, he turned back towards them, slung his bow off, and drew an arrow.

Chase got the message and ducked at the same moment as Tetoviran. The young man let the arrow fly, then nocked another, and another, until his father was pinned down, unhurt, by his oversized, flowing robes. Chase nearly collapsed with relief that the boy had not turned traitor to him or Tara. A shot like that would not make a good enemy.

The boy then turned, shoving Tara outside, and slammed the door behind them both. King Vidovu was still screaming, trying to reach the arrows and pry them out, with no luck. Finally growing impatient in his outrage, he stopped struggling and lifted his voice. "My children! My citizens! My army of souls! Hear my command and obey me, your king! Do not let them leave this city alive!"

Chase looked at Tetoviran, who opened the side door. "That would be our cue to leave." Chase grinned. "After you." Together, the two of them ran out into a silent city full of mindless souls.

Chase slashed his sword in a wide arc, clearing a path through the inhuman people. Tetoviran sprinted behind him, yelling at the crowds to get out of the way and receiving no response. They'd received orders from their ruler, and they were following them. It appeared that these souls had some sort of ghost-like powers, for they were no longer silent. They hissed and rustled, their hollow voices reaching Chase and somehow forcing painstaking images to enter his mind. Their magic was strong, and he was struggling to ignore their words and images.

He saw his parents, suffering and weak. They were dying, chained in an invisible prison. Voices hissed from the mouths of the souls all around him. *"It is too late to save them. You will never make it. Give up now, and you will die quickly and peacefully."* Tetoviran smacked the back of his head.

"Snap out of it, kid! More running, less contemplating. Are you getting lazy? Kid, you'd better not be getting lazy!" The muscular man puffed the words out through his rapidly pounding footfalls.

Chase shook his head, hoping to clear it. "I'm fine." "Then what are you waiting for? Get moving!"

He surged onward, swinging his blade at anyone who tried to touch him. The citizens didn't have as much power as the king, but Chase preferred keeping them as far away from him as possible. He and Teto moved through the crowds as fast as they could, but the ghouls were undeterrable.

An image of Tara, sleeping before his fire the first day they met, popped into his head. The souls surrounding him chanted eerily, *"You have brought her into grave danger. She will suffer and die a slow death with you. Stay here, and she will return home safely. You have the map. She will not be able to continue without you. Just lay down here and make this easy on yourself. Save her. She will stand by your side and endure whatever you must. You will eventually endure death. Do you really want her to die because of you?"*

Chase's swings slowed. Maybe it *was* best to just let them kill him now. After all, he had to die at some point, and—*Stop. Stop it, Chase, you idiot, they're working their magic! Focus. You're almost there.*

He could see the city's gate in the distance. With every breathless, frantic step, the visions became more vivid, the voices more insistent. They showed him things that he didn't remember.

Two old ladies, sitting in rocking chairs and talking to a little kid with shaggy black hair and chocolate eyes, knitted large quilts before a hearth. *"You will face them soon. Do you really want to go through all that again?"*

He saw his deceased godfather, Raka, reading a book to a baby. *"He loved you so very much. He sacrificed himself for your mother, who will soon die along with your father. Your family will be gone. Come, join your godfather. Wait for your parents to arrive. Greet them at the gates. You could be with them forever."*

Chase swallowed. He was getting closer to the city walls, and the souls were getting desperate.

They began wailing and shrieking at him. Tetoviran still moved behind him, shooing the ghouls away. Chase looked up, his breath heaving. A few more steps, and they'd be free. His feet felt like cement, and voices raged into a blur of chatter around him as his sprint slowed to a trudge. Tetoviran couldn't contain himself at the last moment and ran right past him to safety. Chase was one step away from doing the same, but the spirits were determined not to let him go.

They began showing him things that never happened. He saw Tara in combat with a huge monstrous creature, fighting for all she was worth. Her sword was knocked from her hands, and the monster's mouth opened, just over her head, to reveal six rows of gleaming white fangs dripping with poison. The gaping mouth came down on Tara's head just as the image was wiped out.

"You see what you lead her to? You can prevent all this. If you die now, she will return to Jisara. Simply let us kill you. Protect her from this venomous monster and all the others with far worse weapons than poison to come. All you have to do is lay yourself down right here. We'll finish the job." Chase fell to one knee, breathing hard. If that thing really was a challenge they'd have to face, if the souls could tell the future… *No. No, come on, Chase, you're inches away!*

He shook the panic out of his head. That wasn't real. These things couldn't tell the future at all. He began to crawl forward, but one hand reached out and grabbed his right leg. Another seized his left. And as he struggled to break free, more souls jumped upon him. Soon, all but his head and his left hand, which he'd stuck over the border and clawed into the ground with, was being pulled back on by the locked grip of a cursed spirit.

Tetoviran grabbed Chase's free hand and pulled as hard as he could. The big man was, by far, stronger than any of the ghouls, but there were a whole lot more of them than of him. For a moment, a game of tug-of-war transpired between the two sides, but the harder Tetoviran yanked, the more of Chase's body was pulled outside the city. The souls were trapped in Iravvai, so they were forced to let go. Just as Chase's body felt as though it would rip in two, Tetoviran gave one final pull, and Chase went flying out of the city and onto snow-covered hills. There, he tumbled over himself, somersaulting three times before finally coming to a stop, lying on his back, staring up at a gray sky. Snow was falling softly outside the city, and Chase was soon coated with it. He laid still and tried to catch his breath as his chest heaved.

He was exhausted. He just wanted to stay there and rest. Judging from the dark shade of the sky, nighttime was almost upon them. His eyelids were turning to lead.

Tetoviran stood over him, clucking his tongue like he was disappointed. "All these young kids. They don't know real exhaustion. Why, I once went four days without sleeping! One puny little possessed city and soul-sucking king, and you're completely beat! Pathetic. Just pathetic." he muttered disapprovingly.

Chase groaned, suddenly angry at the man. "Well, it would've helped a lot if you'd told us who King Vidovu was! The Map Keeper? The reason he's so knowledgeable is because he takes on the knowledge of every person he possesses. I heard stories about him growing up. He's the man with poison touch. He sucks out your soul if he touches you, and he gains control of your body and mind." He shuddered, then propped himself up on his elbows. "You know that if he hadn't given us so many hints, I never would've figured it out? Do you know what would've happened if I *hadn't* figured it out?"

"You would have been fine," Tetoviran scoffed. "I knew."

"Then why didn't you tell us?" Chase spluttered. "I just forgot to! I'm so used to it, I didn't really consider his powers." Tetoviran paused. "And I also wasn't so sure how much I liked you guys yet, so I may or may not have kept it to myself."

Chase scowled. "You're the biggest idiot I've ever met."

Tetoviran sneered at him. "I would say it's mutual, but my blonde nephew is your better-looking equivalent. It's the girl I'm worried about. I like her. Uses her brain. Much better than you two self-absorbed blabbermouths. All you boys ever do is talk and talk and talk and"— "Wait." Chase sat bolt upright and shook his head. "Oh, what's wrong with me?" Tetoviran leaned in a little closer to examine him.

"Lot of things. First of all, your hair looks like a rat made a home and got halfway through a family tree in it. Second, you talk too much. Third"—

"I don't mean like *that!* I mean, how could I have forgotten? Come on! Tara and the boy… what's his name?" "Fin." "Tara and Fin went out the front door, so they would be this way," he decided, pointing to his left, "if they left the city in one direction. We have to find them." He stood and brushed off his clothes.

"Wait, hang on a second, kid. I'm just getting started. I've got a whole list of things that are wrong with you. Seventy-nine of 'em, and I just met you today. Now, where were we, number three? Ah, yes…"

Chase sighed and began to jog around the city's walls, heading for the southern side of the city and praying Tara was still alive.

It was still hard for him to grasp how much he had come to care for her over the course of their journey. He had never really cared about anyone before, and he wasn't sure how much he liked it. Worrying about her wasn't that fun.

He and Tetoviran hurried along the borders until they finally came to a spot where Chase could see King Vidovu's shack in the far-off distance of the kingdom. There were a bunch of souls lined up along the border, screaming soundlessly in agony and still trying to carry out their king's wishes. Chase searched the path from the border to the trees and back again. "Uh, Tetoviran?"

The guy was still talking. "Seventh, your jacket looks like a bunch of walruses had dinner on it."

"Tetoviran?" "Eighth, you get tired too easily."

"Tetoviran!" "Ninth, your knees are too knobby. Tenth"—

"*Tetoviran!*" He looked up, annoyed. "What?"

Chase sighed, wondering how long it would be before he strangled him. "Do you see them?"

Tetoviran turned and scanned the area. "No. Tenth, you interrupt people too much." Chase nodded, panic rising in his chest again. "Okay, that's great, but we *need* to find them. Do you think we should go back into—Gahh!"

He shrieked as he was tackled down from behind, struggling for his sword as he turned over to look up at… "Tara!" he cried, his thumping heart slowing. "You're okay! And you're an idiot, because I almost killed you!"

She nodded giddily, completely ignoring the last part. "Yeah. Did I scare you?" Chase laughed and sat up, pitching her onto her back in the snow. She was always one to get straight to the point. "There's a fine line between *scared* and *startled.* I'd say startled fits better."

Tara grinned. "But you didn't hear me?" Chase even surprised himself as he said, "No."

Probably too busy insulting Chase, Tetoviran, who had been wandering around in the snow nearby, hadn't noticed Tara until just then. He hastened to her side with a smile and helped her to her feet as Chase stood. "Tara! You're here! Oh, thank goodness you're alright!" Tara laughed. "I'm fine. It's good to see you, too, Teto."

Chase smirked. "Yeah, *Teto.*"

Within about two seconds, Tetoviran packed roughly ten pounds of snow together and hurled it at him. It happened so fast, Chase didn't have time to think, and he flew backwards covered in snow. He slammed into the ground, spitting out little crystals. Tara looked at him with wide eyes as he groaned and rolled over onto his stomach, cursing. "What was that for?"

Tetoviran shrugged and leaned casually on a tree like nothing had happened. "No one calls me that but Tara and my brother. Who is gone, so now only Tara."

Chase rolled his eyes and got up. The blonde guy—Fin—was sitting on a rock a few feet away, watching the scene with amusement flickering in his eyes. To Chase, he looked okay. He wasn't wearing some sort of *I'm-planning-something-that's-going-to-kill-you-all-mwah-ha-ha-ha* look. He noticed Chase staring and lifted the corner of his mouth in a hesitant half-smile.

"Chase, right? I'm Fin." Chase nodded. "So I've heard." "I, um… I know this is sudden, but I was really hoping to join you all on your journey to find your parents."

Chase lifted a brow. "And I suppose Tara told you about all that?" Fin nodded, then realized that Chase might not be very happy about that and started to shake his head instead. Chase shot Tara a glare, but she just smiled at him sheepishly.

"I can shoot," Fin piped up randomly, splitting the awkward moment. "If… that could help you at all. And I could see your confusion about my father's story about Tea and Jeff. I know all about them, truly. I can gather food, or build fires, if you'd like. I could even"—

"Fin," Chase interrupted with an air of amusement, "you helped us defeat your own father and saved Tara's life. We owe you, and if you want to come with us, you can." Fin's face lit up with relief. "Thank you."

Tara shivered and glanced at the sky, which was swirling black now. Her curls whipped around her face. "I'm exhausted. Can we try to find shelter?"

Fin nodded immediately. "I know a place. It's not far from here; just outside the city." Chase nodded. "Good. Let's get going." Tetoviran nodded in agreement, pulling Tara closer to him. "Hurry up. Poor girl's going to freeze to death." Tara rolled her eyes at him as they began their trudge forward. "I'll be just fine, thank you very much. I'm not a puppy."

Chase and Fin glanced at each other hesitantly, neither of them fully comfortable with the other quite yet. They walked on in silence for a while until Chase reached into one of his hidden pockets and removed a gold chain.

"Here," he said, offering it to Fin. The blonde boy's mouth hung open in shock. His hand flew to his bare neck where the chain had rested less than an hour ago.

"How did you"— "I have my ways." Eyes wide, Fin took the chain and refastened it around his neck. "Remind me to watch out for you."

Chase smiled. "I'll do nothing of the sort." Several cold steps later, they reached the summit of a hill and found a small stone cottage nestled between a few stark trees. Its windows were dark, but Fin walked right up to it and opened the thick door with one powerful kick. "Home sweet home," he said satisfactorily.

CHAPTER 11

A fire crackled comfortingly in the stone fireplace, warming the small building and lighting the remnants of a meal. Hard wooden floors creaked under the weight of four people huddling together over one piece of paper. Tara, Chase, Fin, and Tetoviran had all eaten and warmed up before finally coming to this crucial moment. Together, they leaned closer to Chase as he pulled the map out of his pocket. The paper was old and yellowed, and unrolling it displayed the Sixteen Kingdoms and everything for hundreds of leagues around it. A thin red line drawn in ink ran between two of the locations: Iravvai and a forest called The Sumadine Woods.

"North," Chase murmured. "It's a straight line north." Marked in the center of the woods were the letters D and F, side by side in swirling penmanship.

Tara was puzzled by this.

"The Sumadine Woods? I've never heard of it," Fin murmured. Tetoviran shook his head. "Me neither."

Chase stared at the map for a while longer. "That's quite a bit of ground to cover," he commented slowly. "And without horses… if we're planning on getting there anytime soon, we'll have to leave first thing tomorrow."

Tara and Fin groaned simultaneously. Chase elbowed both of them in the ribs, then rolled up the map and turned to Fin. "Who are Tea and Jeff?"

Fin smiled slightly. "First of all, it's not Tea and Jeff. It's *D and F.* Single letters." Chase and Tara blinked. "Ohhh," they muttered simultaneously.

"But it has to mean something, right?" Chase asked. "What do the letters stand for?"

Fin shrugged. "No idea. I just know that they're the initials of two powerful beings. Something like gods, from what I've heard of them. Supposedly, when you die, your spirit goes to them. They judge you, based on the life you led when you were alive, and… well, let's just say they decide whether you go up or down in the afterlife. Sometimes, if they sense that someone is going to have a really important life, like if they have a destiny to save the world, they come to that person and speak to them about their future in confusing ways. They say things sort of like… you know, fortune-teller prophecies. My mom told me about them.

"They always kind of scared me, how they could see the future, decide what happened to you, make people immortal, give them a different body…all kinds of good stuff like that. But I'm guessing that since their initials are there, they live in the Sumadine Woods. So apparently, we're going to find *them.* They'll tell us where Ukrasen is, but it won't actually be in the forest. This is just our first stop." He muttered a few unsavory words about his father and his tricks.

"But why did King Vidovu think Chase could explain them?" Tara asked.

Tetoviran spoke from a few feet away. "Maybe because he just passed out?"

Tara turned quickly in alarm. Sure enough, Chase was lying sprawled out on the floor, his eyes closed. His breath was shallow, and Teto was nudging him.

"He's not asleep," Tetoviran said. "I dumped a cup full of water on his face. He didn't move." "Teto!" Tara scolded. "What? He deserved it."

Tara's hands shook as she brushed Chase's hair away from his face. He was sweaty and pale, and looked about as good as one of King Vidovu's souls. She looked at Tetoviran. "What happened?"

He shrugged. "How am I supposed to know? As soon as Blondie over here started explaining the tea-time god-zappers, he just muttered something like *'Pour a cup of water on my face, please'* and passed out."

Fin arched an eyebrow. "I never said anything about any 'god-zappers'. And Chase didn't say that." "How do you know? Were you there?" "I was right here." "Not the same. You weren't listening."

Fin rolled his eyes. "Chase isn't stupid. He would never say something like that."

"Bah. Kid's plenty stupid. And besides, the situation itself was calling to me with its own voice. It was so perfect. The kid lying there, unconscious, big cup of ice-cold water right next to me... it was just too tempting. Irresistible, actually. Once in a lifetime chance."

"Visions," Tara muttered. Fin had his mouth open, ready to retort, but he stopped. "What?"

"The visions. This is exactly what would happen whenever he got a vision. Even if he was sleeping. He would get really pale and short of breath... and then he'd start saying things and screaming"—Perfectly on cue, Chase broke out in a bloodcurdling shriek. Fin jumped nearly a foot in the air. Tetoviran leapt up, ran across the room, grabbed a pillow, and came running back to smack Chase in the face with it, who promptly stopped screaming.

Tara glared at Tetoviran. He saw her face and dropped the pillow. "Well, at least it got the kid to shut up." She glared even harder.

"What? I panicked. When I panic, I hit stuff. I also hit stuff when I'm sad, or angry, or happy, or anxious, or calm… actually, I hit stuff a lot. Big passion of mine. One of my favorite things to do, really. Especially when I'm hitting something as annoying and self-absorbed as this far-too-talkative kid here. And honestly, would you look at his hair? It's a disgrace to the world! I mean, if the kid wants to do shaggy, the least he can do is brush it once in a while! And the jacket! Oh man, the jacket makes me sick to my stomach. Just take a look at it! Walrus feast going on there! If somebody gave me a jacket like that, I'd take it and go hit whoever handed it to me with it, and then kick him a few times, just for good measure. Ooh, no, never mind. I'll whip out the buttons on him! That steel can hurt! Trust me, once I gave an ugly jacket like that to my brother, and let me tell you, that did *not* end well!"

"*Teto.*" The big man lowered his head sheepishly. "Sorry," he mumbled. Tara refocused on Chase, unable to believe how quickly Tetoviran had grown comfortable with them. He was just a big kid.

Chase turned from side to side, thrashing and flailing. He muttered inaudible things, his pitch rising and falling from time to time. His mutterings became fiercer and harsher, and at one point, he recoiled like someone had punched him in the stomach. Then Chase began screaming nonstop, a piercing, guttural sound that screeched through the room, releasing the pain and agony of every death, every loss, every injury ever endured. Even Tetoviran looked shaken up when he finally stopped. He went silent and laid peacefully for a few moments.

Fin's voice cracked. "Should we wake him up?"

Tara shook her head adamantly. "No. He needs to see the whole thing. It could give him answers. What I don't get is why he's getting more of these now. He told me they were done. But passing out..."

Tetoviran frowned. "You know, I never went to school—and yes, I know it's hard to believe, I was just naturally born this intelligent—but my mom told me that people aren't supposed to scream unless they're having a gruesome, violence-filled, action-packed, completely terrifying nightmare where the whole world dies. Don't think gruesome, violence-filled, action-packed, completely terrifying *visions* where the whole world dies count. I mean, if you're unconscious, shouldn't you be... you know, kind of half dead?"

Tara stopped breathing for a second when she heard that. *Half dead.* That was not how she wanted to picture Chase after he'd just escaped from a city full of half dead people—and almost become one of them.

Tetoviran continued on. "I thought you weren't able to move or speak when you're unconscious. Or maybe my mom was wrong. Wait, no... Mom was never wrong. She was so very wise; a wonderful philosopher, too. One day she told me that hitting people is like eating a midday snack of roast turkey and vegetables—you've just got to do it. Isn't that just the most extraordinary thing you've ever heard?"

Fin was trying not to smile. "Grandmother sounds very interesting, Tetoviran. She seems... exactly like you."

Tetoviran grinned, puffing out his chest. "Mom was a brave one. Huge compliment. Thanks, Blondie. Speaking of Mom, is there any roast turkey and vegetables in this place? Can't forget the midnight snack, either. I mean, midday is pretty special, but midnight! Now *there's* an essential."

Fin shook his head in amazement. "He's just so… so incredibly idiotic. I've never seen anything like it."

"Guys, look." Tara nudged Fin with her elbow. "I think he's going to wake up."

They all studied Chase as he began to stir. He sat up, but his eyes stayed closed as he got to his feet. "Sleepwalking?" Fin muttered in confusion. But that was far from the end of it.

Chase's eyes snapped open, but they were glazed over like one of King Vidovu's possessed souls. He trudged across the room with his eyes open, staring straight ahead and never so much as blinking. He opened his mouth, and in a horrid, choked voice that sounded nothing like Chase, he wheezed, "Fate. My fate…"

Fin looked like *he* was going to pass out next. Tetoviran looked ecstatic. "This is incredible!"

Chase plodded to the couch and suddenly turned sharply, a look of pure fear overtaking his face. His eyes seemed normal, just for a split second, but then they went glassy again. "Fate…" He seemed to be having trouble breathing.

He collapsed on the sofa, and his eyes slid shut. Fin peeked over Tetoviran's shoulder, his hands shaking so hard that the veins in his forearms were visible. "Do you think it's over?"

Suddenly Chase screamed so horribly, Tetoviran turned and grabbed a steel pitcher that had been resting on the countertop nearby. He raised it above his head just as Fin hit Chase in the face with the pillow.

Chase continued to scream, though, so Tetoviran stepped forward with his pitcher at the ready.

Tara leapt forward and grabbed his arms. "Teto, no! You'll hurt him!" Tetoviran looked around desperately as Chase continued to howl. He snatched the pillow from Fin's hands and began beating relentlessly at Chase's head. "Why—won't—he—stop?!" Tetoviran yelled frantically.

Tara tried to grab the pillow away, but stopped suddenly in unison with Fin and Teto. They all heard the difference, and they all froze at the sound. Chase was still screaming, but it was a few octaves lower now and sounded much more like him.

Finally stopping their chaos to look at Chase, the three of them saw that he was sitting up on the couch, his arms up to shield himself from Tetoviran's pillow. When his screaming finally died, he lowered his arms and glared up at Tetoviran.

"Seriously? You know I could feel that the whole time, right?" Fin was crouching down, holding his hands up like a shield. "Are you all right?" he stammered. "I mean… are you sane?"

Chase shrugged. He didn't seem very shaken by the whole thing at all, which was possibly more startling than the episode itself. "I don't think I ever was. Whatever just happened… well, I remembered something about my past. Or, it was shown to me, I guess. I don't really know. This whole vision thing is getting tiresome." Tara noticed that Chase himself sounded quite tired.

"When I was leaving Iravvai with Tetoviran, the…citizens… showed me these two old ladies, sitting in rocking chairs and talking to this child. I think… I think it was me. They told me I'd have to face them again soon. At the time, I didn't understand why two elderly women would be so frightening"—

"Well, they must be plenty frightening!" Tetoviran yelped. "You practically scared the hair off Blondie's head, screaming like a lunatic. Not that I would've minded the kid being bald for a few days. I could take him into town and have his portrait painted. Hang it on my wall and laugh at him for the rest of my life." "Gee, how thoughtful of you," Fin grumbled.

For once, Chase didn't have a sarcastic comment to offer. Instead, he closed the doors of lightheartedness with a single glance at the pair and continued. "The vision I just had took me back to when I was really, really young. I remembered these two family members… Aunt Destiny and Grandma Fate. Both of them were very old, and they always sat in these two rocking chairs and knitted. They were identical to the women the ghouls showed me.

"I guess they kind of scared me when I was a kid, because I could feel my emotions in the vision. It's sort of hard to explain, but… they always just sat there and watched me. They never even seemed to move. They never ate anything, never drank anything, never said anything. Just sat there and knitted.

"One day, I asked them what they were making. They didn't respond. They just kept knitting and staring at me. So, I tried again two days later. And then the day after that, and the day after that. Pretty soon, I was asking them daily what they were making, and walking away daily after they just stared at me. This went on for a long time.

"Soon, though, I began to realize that Mom and Dad didn't even acknowledge them. If they were my aunt and grandma, they must've been related. So, one day, I asked my parents why they never talked to Aunt Destiny or Gramma Fate. From that day on, they thought I was making imaginary friends and family. They didn't even know the women existed.

Once, I walked them right up to the two rocking chairs. The ladies just observed and knitted, as usual. I wasn't really expecting anything else. But my mom just smiled like she thought I was being cute. She walked around in the area I was pointing, but she didn't even see them. My father actually walked straight through one of the chairs, like it was made of smoke. I wasn't imagining it. I know I wasn't. They were real."

"Are you sure?" Fin asked hesitantly. Chase eyed him somewhat chillingly. "If you think I'm crazy, explain your father's city. Tell me how that's more realistic."

Fin frowned, taken somewhat aback. Tara held her breath for a moment as the boys stared at each other. Finally, Fin dipped his head. "You're right. I'm sorry." Chase didn't give him a response, but Tara saw a look of slight appreciation come over him. She knew how hard he found it to admit he was wrong, so she figured he had respect for Fin's ability to do so.

Tetoviran was staring at Chase. "So that's it? Two ghost ladies were just hanging out in your living room and knitting? That's what you screamed about? And I thought Blondie got scared easily!"

Chase rolled his eyes. "No, that's not it! I remembered something else, too. I remembered a day—the day before Raka was killed, Mother was captured, I lost my memory—I asked the women what they were making again. I wasn't expecting an answer. It had just become a habit. So, when they started talking to me…I screamed. And cried. I was so scared, I thought I was going to die. I remember thinking that that day would be the last one of my life. But something told me that whatever these ladies had to say, it was important, and that I should listen.

"They had these really raspy, hollow voices, and their lips didn't move as they spoke. They talked in a different language. I don't even know what it was, but for some reason, I could understand it. It's the strangest thing. I never even knew I had had this experience about five minutes ago, but now the whole thing is clear as day to me. They said…"

Chase pulled his eyebrows together thoughtfully, then spoke. *"Mend what's been torn since the day you were born. Decide where you'll turn. When the choices get hard, remember what you've learned. You will find help in the most unlikely of places, far from where you belong. The tiniest things make all the difference, and what will save you is the memory you've been forgetting all along. Stitches woven tight, like destiny's plan, can still be removed if one believes they can. Fate may be fickle, the future too sad. But rewrite what's been written, and reunite the two halves. Both pieces need each other, both patches side by side. Find out what happens when two worlds collide.'*

Everyone in the room exhaled when the incantation was over. Those words carried weight that felt inexplicably familiar to Tara. Though she had never heard them before, she felt as though the power behind them had overtaken her before. Glancing at his companions, Chase continued slowly.

"Then they held up this big quilt—what they'd been sitting there, knitting all that time. It depicted this boy…me, when I was older, although I didn't know at the time. About the age I am now. I was standing with my parents and seven other people. I was holding Ukrasen, and we were looking over Jisara at sunset. We were all so happy. And then, they each grabbed a side of the quilt and ripped it straight in half. *'Behold, little one. Your horrors begin tomorrow.'* The two of them exploded into purple dust, rocking chairs and all. And just like that." He snapped his fingers. "Gone."

Fin was frowning so deeply that his eyebrows were practically touching. "Did you recognize anyone in the picture?"

"Not then. Now, as I'm remembering it, I recognized Tara, Tetoviran, and you, Fin. My parents, too. There were also two people… this doesn't make sense, but one of them looked just like an old friend of mine. And the other… well, it's impossible that she could be involved in this, so no matter. But there were two other people I've never seen before."

A thoughtful silence filled the air. The only sound was Tetoviran munching loudly on a carrot. Everyone turned and stared. He looked up. "What? Stress eating." Fin snorted. "You don't hit stuff when you're stressed?"

Tetoviran scowled. "'Course I do! Here, I'll prove it." He took the carrot he'd been eating and whacked Fin on the head with it.

Chase grabbed the carrot from Tetoviran's hands and tossed it over his shoulder. "Focus! Do you guys not get it?" Blank stares.

He sighed. "Fin. You said that sometimes these special beings—D and F—come to important people and speak to them about their future, right?" Fin nodded, rubbing his head where Tetoviran had hit him.

"Is there any possible way for them to come in a disguise?"

Fin nodded again. "According to the stories, yes. They never appear in their true forms." Everyone but Chase seemed to take this as light, casual news. He looked at them expectantly, then snatched the pitcher from Fin's hands and banged on the floor with it when he got nothing. Tara started at the aggressive noise.

"Come *on!* Think, you three. D and F. Aunt Destiny and Gramma Fate. Women of smoke knitting a quilt that showed me with my friends in the future. Ripping it apart. Strange words that make absolutely no sense. Disappearing the day before everything with Araknan and Ukrasen began, predicting that my horrors would start the next day. Put the pieces together!"

Tara was the first one to get it. The shock was so heavy, she stumbled and fell back onto the couch next to Chase, trembling. "Chase," she said, her voice barely a whisper. "That quilt. They were sitting there, weaving your fate. Your happy life. And… and they ripped it in half." Her voice broke. By that time, both Fin and Tetoviran had understood.

Fin's mouth had fallen open. "D and F. Destiny and Fate. Two... two *women* are destiny and fate? Or... beings, I guess? But I thought those were just myths, or words, or something that you got to make for yourself. These *people* decide what happens to you?"

He fumbled his hands as he spoke. "And if they came to you... uh, Chase? Hey, I don't want to bring you down or anything, but when D and F—I mean, Destiny and Fate—visit someone, that person is usually a really important guy who's destined to make a little, ah, sacrifice in his future that saves the world. Meaning, the person usually"—

"They can't!" Tara's face burned. She stared at the black leather of Chase's jacket, unable to look at him. "They can't do that! Just deciding to take someone's life away isn't fair!"

Tetoviran twisted his shirt. "Tara?" She looked up. "Listen. My mom told me about Destiny and Fate once, too. She told me that sometimes, when they see that something really bad is going to happen, they choose someone special to fight for what's right and conquer the enemy—you know, your average save-the-world-become-an-adored-hero-live-on-to-be-the-richest-most-famous-person-in-the-entire-universe story. But... Blondie's right. Usually, that person doesn't live long enough to *become* rich and famous. Usually, they just carry on a legacy of a brave, heroic death that saved everyone. And once they choose someone... well, the choice is made. Permanently."

CHAPTER 12

Chase stared out the window into the dark, swirling snow. It had to be at least midnight, and the others were already asleep. A moon strong enough to shed light through the clouds illuminated his view.

A wolf's howl seeped through the cracks in the window pane from outside. Tara turned over in her sleep. Several more voices answered the call, coming together harmoniously, sharing their songs of sorrow and solitude. An owl cut across the clearing, swifter than a lion running through flatlands. *Lions.*

The idea made Chase's fists clench so tight, they trembled with anger. If it wasn't for that stupid, disgusting, wretched fiend Araknan, none of this would've happened. Why couldn't he just accept that he was a human and get over it? At least he got to keep his immortality. That would've made Chase overjoyed. He wouldn't have to worry about old prophecy ladies, or ripped quilts, or a destiny to die… he wouldn't ever have to die.

This was all so unfair. It wasn't his fault. He never asked to be involved in this. He never asked for his parents to be captured. He never asked for Ukrasen to be stolen. Why didn't Destiny and Fate give this problem to someone else? Why him? He was a stray boy who thieved his way through life. How could anyone expect him to take on something this huge?

"Hey, kid."

Chase jumped so hard that his head banged into the window. Tetoviran stood behind him, looking bleary-eyed and sleepy.

"Geez, Tetoviran, don't scare me like that. You gave me a heart attack." Teto grinned. "That's what I was going for."

Chase sighed. "Did you just wake up to scare the life out of me, or do you actually need something?" "No, no, I don't need anything. But you, my good fellow, *do* need something."

"I do?" A beat passed. *"Good fellow?"*

Ignoring the second question, Tetoviran nodded. With one hand, he picked up a thick, heavy chair and set it down next to him. "Sit."

"I'm not going to sit." "Why not?" "You're being nice." "So what?"

Chase narrowed his eyes. "So, why are you being nice? Don't you hate me?"

Tetoviran plopped himself down in the chair. "No, kid. I highly dislike and despise you. But I don't hate you. You've done a good job taking care of Tara. I'll give you credit for that. And… well, you're not bad, Onaj. You've got a real messy past. For everything you've been through, you're okay." Chase stood in uncomfortable silence under the compliment while Tetoviran stared out the window. After a moment, he sighed and met Chase's gaze.

"You know how many people would get angry thinking that none of it was their choice? That they shouldn't have to deal with it? They'd take their anger out on anyone even remotely connected in any way. The fact that you stayed whole on the inside, kid, is the real feat. It shows that you're strong."

Chase raked his hand through his hair and leaned against the window pane. "Yeah, that'd be great, but I *am* angry. I'm not okay with any of this. Like you said, it's not fair. I didn't ask for any of it."

Tetoviran shrugged. "But you've kept it leveled. Some people let their emotions rule them. The trick is to rule your emotions.

Trap them up in a feeling-proof box before they overflow. That way, you don't accidentally push away the people you love."

Chase arched an eyebrow at him. "You don't. You act like a baby." Teto shrugged. "Difference is, I'm not scared of pushing anybody away. I don't like anyone."

Chase laughed shortly, making Teto frown defensively. "What?" "Nothing. Those words are just so familiar." They sat in silence for a beat, until Chase pulled a knife from his boot and starting cleaning the blade with his shirt. Tetoviran glanced at it nonchalantly, then looked again with wide eyes.

"Hey! That's mine!" He checked the sheath strapped on his ankle, even though the knife clearly wasn't there anymore. Teto glared at Chase and snatched the knife back, replacing it and making sure the sheath was secure. Chase made no effort to stop him, and Tetoviran scowled.

"Why do you steal things from us if you're just going to give them back?"

Chase tilted his head, giving Teto a look so arrogant that a schoolmaster would've beaten him to death for it. "Can't get out of practice, now can I?"

Tetoviran sneered at him before heading back to his spot on the couch. "Go to sleep, kid."

Chase nodded. "I will. And, Tetoviran?" "Hm?" "Thanks." There was no response, but Chase caught the man smile before he rolled over in his blanket.

He watched the snow falling outside until he heard Tetoviran begin to snore again. He looked over to the couch on which Tara and Teto laid head to head, deep in slumber. Fin was sprawled out at the foot of the sofa, mumbling in his sleep.

Well, Chase, he thought to himself as he grabbed a blanket and laid down next to Fin, *you've done pretty well. A while ago, you were Chase what's-his-name, the confused, lonely orphan boy, Jisara's expert at stealing and trickery. You were friendless and on your own. Now look where you're at. Chase Onaj. You've got a last name. You've got a family. Not to mention three new friends, your parents to save, the world at risk, an evil immortal robber to beat, and a ripped up happy ending that settled you down with a destiny to die. Doesn't get much better than this.*

And he slipped away into his dreams.

Chase yanked out the map and studied it. The afternoon sun was muffled by a wool mitten of fog, making the air warm and humid. Icicles were dripping, and mounds of snow were slowly melting away to fresh, clear streams that ran down the mountaintops and into glittering blue lakes.

A bird chirped in the distance, and Tara smiled beside him. "Spring's almost here." Chase took a deep breath. The air smelled like cobblestone right after a rainstorm and fresh blossoms blooming. Honeysuckle tinted the breeze.

It brought back bittersweet memories of his first springtime alone in Jisara. He was young and innocent, still unaware of the pains of the world. He heard birds chirping as he ran splashing through gurgling brooks and skipped stones. He danced through meadows full of dandelions that sent golden dust up in the air to tickle the breeze, wrapping ripe cotton clouds and sun-dappled butterflies in its sweet perfume.

He missed that carefree life. But having an untouched heart with no friends and no worries was far worse than having six million things to worry about and your three closest friends by your side. Even if they were your three only friends.

Thinking about his childhood made his thoughts wander to more recent times. A few years ago, he'd been pilfering leather and swords, sitting back in the shadows and trying to look tough. The truth was, back then he'd been terrified. At first, he was fine with being on his own, but he got older and realized just how vulnerable he was. He became guarded and afraid.

When he grew older still, his confidence lifted and he found that he had finally become what he'd faked for so long. He could stride through crowds and not carry the fear of meeting someone bigger and tougher. He carried himself in a way that made people clear the way for him, avoid eye contact, try to pretend that they were otherwise occupied.

Unless, of course, he brought out his smile. That changed everything. Girls giggling like idiots, mothers swooning and calling him a gentleman, young children toddling after him and puffing out their tiny chests trying to impress him. Little did those children realize that the boy they so longed to be like had been stealing from their father just moments ago.

His expression must've been reflecting some of his thoughts, because Tara smiled and bumped his arm. "Feeling a little better?"

"I was before I had to look at *that,*" he teased, gesturing to her face. Tara shook her head at him, and they walked in silence for a short time before she turned to him and halted his strides.

"I'm… glad you're okay, Chase." Her voice was coated with a sudden seriousness he'd never heard from her before. He'd heard exasperation and irritation and fear and pure rage… but he'd never heard her tone as serious as it was now. It kind of scared him.

He laughed nervously, trying to lighten the mood. "What do you mean? Of course I'm okay."

"They could break your body into a hundred pieces and you'd still be okay." He smiled. "Nine lives, Princess." Her forehead crinkled. "Yes, and pretty soon you'll only have eight." "Eight more chances to do something completely stupid that kills me."

That made her angry, and she shoved him with her hands. "Chase, this isn't a joke, and you need to stop acting like it is! What do you not understand? Death is not something you can cheat your way out of."

Chase frowned a little at that. "Who ever said anything about cheating?" "That's how you treat everything! You think you can just smile that stupid smile and talk your way out of everything. You act like all your problems can be solved just like that, like everything's fine. But nothing's fine! You haven't done a single thing to deserve this."

"Are you accusing me of being lazy? Because Tetoviran was just getting started with me on that the other day when"—"Chase, I'm serious!" *Yeah, no kidding.*

"Are you so naïve that you're not going to worry about this, or are you arrogant enough to think you can control it?"

Chase turned his face away from her. "When did you get so snappy?" Tara took a breath. When she spoke again, her tone was softer. "I'm worried about you. Aren't you upset, Chase? Aren't you afraid?"

He pressed his lips together and squinted thoughtfully at her. "Yeah. I am. I'm upset and afraid. Also, I've got this burning desire to pull an oak tree out of the ground and bash Fate and Destiny over the head with it a few times." Just the thought was enough to make him smile.

"You aren't just going to sit around and let them decide what happens to you, right? Aren't you going to do something?"

He hesitated. Part of him, the smallest part in the back of his head was screaming, *Yes, I'm going to do something! I'm going to kill those stupid grandmas and kill Araknan and punish every single person, monster, lion, whoever, that got me into this mess, including you!* But the rest of his brain slammed a door on that voice's face.

"I'm going to change this. I don't know how, but I'm changing it. I'm not losing my life, or my parents, or anything else. Maybe I can reason with them. They're Destiny and Fate. Reason is probably their great-nephew or something. They'll listen."

The plan sounded ridiculous, even to his ears, and Tara's face told him that if he thought the plan was bad, he didn't want to know what she thought of it.

"Hey." He slung his arm loosely around her shoulders. "It's all going to be okay. I pro"— "No promises, Chase," she interrupted, pushing him gently away. "I don't want you to make one you won't be able to..." her voice trailed off. The unspoken word hung in the air between them like smoke. *Keep.* She believed that he was really going to die. But the real question was, what exactly did *he* believe?

Again, he tried to lighten the mood—this time with some success. "They can't kill me," he said. "I'm too handsome. My death would take away the meaning of every girl's life. Yourself included, however immune to my charm you may pretend to be." He dipped his head to hiss in her ear, "I know you whisper my name in secret, falling over your own heart in adoration."

Tara rolled her eyes, but a smile was creeping its way stealthily onto her face. "Grinning because of my irresistible beauty?" The smile quickly vanished, replaced by a sassy pout. "Now you're just dreaming," she muttered.

He punched her arm without force. "Don't give me that. I don't have good experience with dreams." "Clearly. They're making you crazy. *Irresistible beauty.* That's the best joke I've heard all year."

He gave her a dirty look, and she suppressed another smile. There was a moment of silence, and she pulled her hair away from her face. "But… you're okay?" He nodded. "Always."

She opened her mouth like she wanted to say something more, but clamped it shut again. Sounds of Tetoviran and Fin arguing traveled back to them, followed by a sickening crunch and Tetoviran cursing like there was no tomorrow.

Chase tugged a piece of her hair. "Come on. Let's catch up. Those two are going to slap each other senseless one day, I swear." She laughed. "Race you?" He smirked. "I'm still faster." "We'll just see about that." And they took off, side by side, racing into the promise of spring.

⌇

"All right, guys. Sleep well tonight. I'm sure everybody's tired." Chase tossed a handful of branches into their campfire. The heat flew higher, sending up sparks that danced like fireflies in the sky before disintegrating to ghosts of flame.

"What are we supposed to do once we reach the Sumadine Woods? According to the map, it's a huge forest. How are we supposed to find Fate and Destiny in all that space? That is, if they're even there," Tara said.

The fire cast weird shadows over her face, illuminating her eyes and making their usual vivid blue look icy gray. "Easy," Chase said. "We just make fun of them. Say things that'll make them angry. They'll come out to confront us. Works every time." She frowned. "What if they're really angry and blast us to pieces?" Chase blinked. "Uh… then we bring out Plan B."

Fin arched an eyebrow. "And that would be…?" Chase paused. "We'll talk about it later." Fin folded his arms. "You have no idea, do you?" "Of course I do!" "Okay, then. What's the plan?" "I'll tell you later!"

Fin rolled his eyes. "Let me just do it for you." He put on a devious smirk and ran his hand through his hair. Using his best Chase Onaj impression, he said smoothly, "Plan B. We get blasted to pieces. What shall we do? We shall die. But hey, I'll look great doing it, so it all works out for the better."

Chase kicked him. Tara smiled, and Teto's grin stretched across his entire face. "Hey, that was pretty good, Blondie! You ever consider looking into the acting business?" "Uh, no."

"All right, fine," Chase admitted. "I don't have a Plan B. Also, my Plan A sounds like the dumbest of dumb people thought it up." Tetoviran smirked. "It doesn't just *sound* that way." Chase kicked him, too. "Look, let's just figure it out tomorrow. I'm tired, and we all need rest."

Fin nodded, resting his head on the ground and pulling a blanket over himself. "Good night, everybody."

Teto plopped down on his back and fell asleep without any covers at all. Tara bedded down slowly and carefully, smoothing one blanket beneath her and pulling another over her, using her knapsack for a pillow. Chase, however, had been lying about being tired. He was wide awake, full of energy.

He surveyed the area and climbed the tallest tree he could find, hoisting himself up onto the highest stable branch. They were on a hill that overlooked a huge valley, and he soaked in the scene from his treetop view as everything bedded down for the night.

A twig snapped behind him. He didn't turn, didn't move, only smirked. "Hi, Tara."

She stomped her foot. "Aargh! I was so close this time!" He leaned back against the tree's thick trunk, swiveling himself to smile down at her. "I'm up in the tree. What were you going to do from down there?"

She shrugged. "Say boo?" He laughed. "Come up."

She eyed the tree up and down. It was enormously tall, and Chase was perched at the very top. "Uh…" "Come on, it's a nice view."

She took a deep breath. He heard her mumbling under her breath, and he couldn't help smiling.

She grabbed the lowest branch and swung one leg over it, then the other. She tried to stand up on the branch but wobbled and fell, hanging by her knees upside-down.

He examined his nails with a bored expression and she glared at him, hopelessly trying to swing herself upright. Finally, she dropped down and rolled until she was lying on her back on the ground. He feigned a yawn. She got back up and tried again. This time, she got up four branches before toppling over.

She huffed in irritation. He sat down on his perch and rested his chin on his fist. "Any day now, Tara." She gave it one more shot, and got about halfway up the tree before she lost her grip and slid down the trunk, landing hard on a low branch.

She groaned and stared up at him. Even from this distance, he could spot small cuts on her hands from her failed attempts. "You going to help me or what?"

He grinned. "And the high princess finally admits she needs my help. Okay, first, pull yourself upright. Now, grab that branch to your left… that's your right!" "That's my left."

He shrugged. "Okay, grab that branch to your right, then."

She sighed but did as she was told. Slowly, she made her way up the tree. He called down instructions until she was a few feet away from him. He offered his hand, but she waved it away.

"I can do it myself," she insisted. Sure enough, she pulled herself up to sit next to him, completely out of breath. She stared into the tree.

"All that for a bunch of leaves?" He laughed. "Turn around, Princess."

Tara carefully maneuvered herself on the branch to face the horizon, then stared into the valley. The stars had come out, making the sky look like a glass bottle of black ink had shattered, spilling heavy darkness over glittering shards of fragile beauty. The moon was in its second day of roundness, and the sounds of crickets and nightingales played a soft melody in the symphony of night. Warm breezes drifted by, ruffling Chase's hair and causing Tara's curls to lick her cheeks like a puppy.

Tara's eyes sparkled. "Wow," she breathed. He nodded. "It's nice, huh?" "Nice is a *huge* understatement."

She rubbed her arms and shivered a little, then smiled. "You know something? I'm really glad I came with you. You can be the most obnoxious, obstinate boy I've ever known sometimes, but being out on an adventure, here with Fin and Teto and you… it's more than I ever could've imagined. This is like my own little fairy tale."

Chase took a deep breath of the crisp night air as she laid her head down on his shoulder. "And you're the princess."

CHAPTER 13

Falling off a cliff with a boy she just met was not something Tara had expected to experience in her lifetime. Yet here she was, screaming like a banshee and plummeting towards the earth.

As she fell, clinging to the stranger's neck, she tried to imagine that she would live. That everything would be fine. And in that moment, she realized why Chase liked to act like nothing was wrong. It distracted from everything that was, in fact, very wrong. Such as the lack of safety nets below her.

The ground rushed up to meet her, and she squeezed her eyes shut, bracing herself. That morning, while she, Chase, Fin, and Teto were traveling, they came across a lone boy walking through the woods. He introduced himself as Devon Arani, a guy around their age with close-cropped dark brown hair and pale skin. His eyes were blacker than charcoal. He'd explained that he'd run away from home because his parents were cruel to him, and discussion turned into quick friendship. As they walked, their path had taken them to the edge of a canyon.

Chase and the others had just begun warming up to Devon when the rocks under Tara's feet began to crumble. Fin tried to run after her, but a boulder fell between them, and he was forced backwards. Teto and Chase ran out to help him get away from the edge of the cliff, but Tara was hanging onto a ledge with three fingers as the rocks fell and hit her repeatedly in the face and arms. She heard Devon call her name as she began to slip and felt him grasp her wrist just as she couldn't hold on any longer. But the cliff was crumbling quickly, and Devon soon lost his footing, too. He fell along with Tara, off the edge of the cliff, down a sheer drop into a ravine. A river rushed at the bottom, and jagged rocks lined the banks. Other sharper boulders from the rockslide were falling with them.

Devon yelled something, but over the wind whistling in her ears, she couldn't hear him. The water hit her face like a brick wrapped in sandpaper. Her gut stung, her face burned, and her lungs screamed. Her legs went numb almost immediately, and she felt herself begin to lose consciousness as the current swept her downstream.

Her wrist was caught once again, but it was a subconscious awareness. Someone was pulling her body out of the water. She gasped for air just as the current washed a mouthful of water into her lungs, and she came up coughing and spluttering. Devon was holding onto a rock that broke through the surface with one hand and gripping her arm in the other. She forced her legs to move and propelled herself against the water's flow until she reached the rock. Dragging her body from the river, she took deep, gulping breaths of air.

She collapsed against the rock, coughing and retching, heart pounding in her chest. The freezing water washed over her in waves, and she shivered uncontrollably. Her fingers and arms were scraped and bloody, but she couldn't feel them. The air had been completely knocked from her lungs on impact, and every breath was a struggle.

Her head dipped under the water, and Devon dragged her back onto the rock by her jacket collar. "Whoa, there," he mumbled. "Careful."

She swallowed. They were in the middle of the river. "Okay," she said. Her voice was grainy and rasped. She cleared her throat, which felt like someone had broken a jar full of fire in her esophagus. Trying to collect her thoughts, she mumbled, "So… what now?"

Devon grimaced. "We swim."

She groaned. Devon glanced nervously from her to the riverbank, then began swimming across. He plowed through the water like a knife slicing softened butter and dragged himself up onto the shore. He fell onto his back with his legs still submerged, then called tiredly to her. "Come on. The current's not too strong."

She took a breath. *It'll be fine,* she tried to remind herself. She pushed off the rock and began to swim. Devon had been very, very wrong about the current. It was stronger than a hundred horses. The water slapped against her, pulling her down the second she left the rock. It took every ounce of her strength just to stay afloat, and the current was taking her away.

Devon thrust out his hand, but she was too far away now to reach him. She heard Fin shout out to her and caught a glimpse of him next to Chase and Tetoviran, a few feet away from where Devon stood. The son of King Vidovu was limping mildly. Tetoviran ran down the shoreline next to her. She tried to call out but got a mouthful of water again and began to choke. Panic took over as her lungs filled with water, and a sudden burning pain shot through her head as her skull clunked against a sharp rock in the current. She began to sink beneath the surface. Her head spun, and the last thing she saw was Teto jumping into the river to rescue her before the world went black.

Tara's eyes fluttered open. Yellow spots danced across her vision. Everything was blurry, and she couldn't remember her name.

"Hey, guys! She's awake!" The fuzzy silhouettes of four people crowded around her. She blinked a few times, and everything came into focus.

Chase shook her shoulder gently. "Tara, can you hear me?" She was about to nod, but a sudden jolt of pain shot through her leg, causing her body to spasm in a quick burst. The shock was wearing off, and soon her whole body hurt.

White-hot pain flared through her gut. Her legs ached, her neck was twisted, her head was on fire, and she could feel bandages running up her arms. Tetoviran handed her some sort of herb, and she chewed it quickly. "That should help," he murmured. He was right; after a few minutes, her pains began to subside to aches.

She sat up shakily, feeling the weakness in her neck. "How…" she swallowed. Her voice sounded foreign to her. "How long was I out?" Nobody answered, so she looked at Chase, who pressed his lips together. "Couple hours." His face was kindly, but she could tell by the way he gripped his sword hilt that the expression was pasted on. She closed her eyes for a second. She was such a screw-up. Time was of the essence, and she was wasting it because she was too weak to cross a river. "I'm so sorry."

Chase shrugged. "It's nothing. Besides, you couldn't help it." Tara squinted curiously at him. His words were telling her some-thing completely opposite of his face, and even that was shifting between expressions. She couldn't even begin to imagine what he was thinking.

"Can you stand?" he asked abruptly. She glanced at her bat-tered legs. "Uh… I can try."

With Tetoviran holding one arm and the other draped around Fin, she attempted to get on her feet. She wobbled as pain exploded in her knees, and she would've landed flat on her face if her friends hadn't been supporting her. Slowly though, as a bit more of the pain faded, she began to walk step by step until Tetoviran and Fin let go of her and she kept going by herself, carefully stretching her muscles a little bit at a time. At one point, she stumbled accidentally into Devon, who caught her instinctively. Her face burned with embarrassment and she pushed away from him.

In doing so, however, she lost her balance again and stumbled in the other direction. She hated being injured. Hated being helpless.

Chase jumped in and caught her arm just as she was about to hit the ground. That, she didn't mind. But Devon… well, she barely knew him, but the way he looked at her made her uncomfortable. He seemed a bit mysterious and a little sad, as if he was carrying a heavy burden he wanted to drop but wasn't allowed to let go of. When their eyes met, she felt strange. Butterflies danced in her stomach. That'd never happened to her before. She couldn't place the feeling, but she knew that she had bigger things to worry about.

A short while later, she was walking on her own, decently stabilized and only slightly dizzy now. A knot had formed in the back of her head that throbbed persistently, but otherwise her pain had mostly drained away.

That surprised Tara, because although she wasn't experienced in this sort of thing, she hadn't thought pain of such intensity faded that quickly. She wouldn't question it, though, because no matter how or why, she felt better. That was all she cared about.

The group climbed back up the valley until they were where they'd started out before the rockslide. A huge chunk of the cliff was missing from the edge. As they continued on their way, Chase narrated a summary of their situation to Devon, who had suffered little more than some scrapes. While they talked, Tetoviran fell back to walk with Tara.

"You okay?" he asked. She wanted to say yes, but the word just wouldn't form in her mouth. It wasn't true. She wasn't okay. She was a complete and total mess.

After a beat, he smiled knowingly. "It certainly shouldn't take that long to answer."

She shrugged helplessly. "I just can't believe what my life has become. Everything is all about surviving another day." Teto shrugged. "Surviving is always good." "Yes, I know. But not too long ago, I was living in a house like a civilized person—if not with very civilized company. Too much has happened far too quickly, and the devils seem to be cursing us with the rottenest possible luck. I bet you that something terrible is going to happen before we even get to the Sumadine Woods."

"No, it won't. It's a straight line forward, and we have the map, don't we? There's no way anything could go"—

Suddenly, a loud cracking sound came from behind them. Before anyone could even process what was happening, a huge tree fell on its side, and landed dangerously close to Tara's feet. She screamed and scrambled out of the way.

"—wrong," Tetoviran finished with wide eyes. "Did I jinx that?"

Tara's heart was jumping around in her throat.

Devon, Fin, and Chase had come to join them now. Looking around, Devon frowned. "Where did that come from?"

Fin shot him a puzzled look. "What do you mean? A tree fell."

"Yes, but look at where it fell from. There's no stump. There was never a tree standing there." Tara scoffed, her racing pulse slowing. "Don't be ridiculous. Trees don't just appear out of thin air and crash to the ground in front of you."

Immediately after the words left her lips, however, another fully-grown tree, this one larger than the last, dropped just in front of Tara with a ground-shaking smash. Again, there was no stump to show where the trunk had cracked off.

Yet another massive plant followed suit within the moment.

Chase's sword was drawn in an instant, as was Devon's, and Fin had an arrow nocked in his bow before Tara could blink. There was nothing for him to shoot at, though. The three trees just laid on the ground like…well, like trees.

Tetoviran reached for one of his two blades uneasily. "Men—and woman—I think it's begun to rain." Fin shook his head, baffled. "Where are they coming from?"

Tara could scarcely breathe, but her confusion was currently overriding her alarm. It was impossible for trees to fall from the sky, so what was going on? "There must be a logical explanation," she tried to reason.

A dark brow was raised in her direction. "Really? What about this journey you're on is logical?"

Devon's question was lost to the sound of a bush falling through the air and landing right on Fin's head. He yelped and pushed the foliage out of his face. "What in the name of—gah!"

Another bush fell and landed on Chase, then another on Devon. When a fourth came for Tetoviran, he was ready. He swung both his blades through the air, slicing the bush to pieces before it could hit him. Instantly, a sound like a faint wail echoed through Tara's ears.

The others froze, telling her that they'd heard it too. On a hunch, Tara stepped towards one of the prostrate trees. She snapped a branch off and a little hiss escaped from the break. Smoke curled up from the end of the bough she held in her hand. "It's almost like they're… alive."

She turned to find an unusually pale Fin. His eyes were wide with recognition. "That's because they are." His hands shook a little. "I've heard of these. They're *cuvari*. Guardians of the Suma-dine Woods. Earth spirits. They're just one of several things protecting the woods. Their job is to keep other people out."

Tara stepped out of the way of a falling shrub. "Why would they want to keep us out?" "Destiny and Fate only have conferences with the living if they've seen that they're worthy of their time. Meaning, we have to go through all these tests and trials—fight these… things—and get to the woods alive."

Chase slashed a bush out of the air, eliciting a shrill shriek. "What do they do, possess the plants? I really hated the possessed souls. Now we've got possessed plants. Just get yourself some men, for Death's sake!"

Devon shook his head. "No. I've heard of these things, too. They don't possess the plants. They *are* the plants. All these trees and bushes have a spirit within them, just like we do, and they're awakened when strangers step foot in their territory."

Tetoviran cracked his neck. "That is the weirdest defense mechanism I have ever heard of, and my brother had a city of brainless slaves. How do we kill all of them quickly so we can move on?"

Before anyone could form an answer, a vine as thick as Tara's waist slithered out of nowhere and moved over the ground at lightning speed toward Fin. With a cry, Fin fired an arrow at it, but the green snake of the earth didn't hesitate at the juices or smoke flowing from its new wound. It wrapped around his body and covered him from knees to throat, muffling his shout of alarm and forcing his bow from his hands. The vines coiled tighter and tighter until they were squeezing the air of out him.

Tara blanched, barely aware of Chase diving to rescue Fin's bow and slinging it over his own shoulder. The barest moment of empty, motionless horror passed, and then came a sudden onslaught of aggression from Tara's companions.

Devon lashed out with his sword to cut through the vines, joined by a more skillful but equally energetic Chase. The air was filled with the howls and screams of the plants as they were cut apart, and Tara felt an odd aching in her chest begin to burn somewhat insistently—undoubtedly from horror. Tetoviran's weapons were blurs of strength, but even with the combined efforts, it soon became clear that blades were not the answer. Each time one vine was cut away, another shot out of the grass to replace it.

Instead of trying to join the useless chopping, Tara scanned her surroundings frantically for a better solution. However, the second her attention strayed, a new bunch of vines slithered forward and seized her legs, lifting her up into the air.

She screamed as her limbs were locked into a grip tighter than anything she had ever known, cutting off circulation and pressing her knees together painfully. Hanging upside down, she was dangled in midair for a short time… and then she was plummeting back towards earth. The vines slammed her body against the dirt, then lifted her back up and brought her down again. Again. Again. She was finding it increasingly hard to inhale.

"Tara!" Chase cried. He sheathed his sword and ran toward her, leaving Tetoviran and Devon to continue their violent attempts at helping Fin.

Tara's already weak body hit the ground yet again, and Chase managed to grab her arms as she was about to be lifted for the third time. The vines simply lifted him into the air with her, though. Chase screamed a whole volley of curses as his feet left the ground, teaching Tara more than a few new terms as he began hitting the ground and coming back up again with her.

Slowly, the repetitions grew faster and more forceful. The ground rushed up and away quicker and quicker, and the earth itself seemed to be getting harder. It began jarring Tara's bones so violently she was sure something must have broken. Her body was already weak from the fall. She couldn't handle much more of this.

At one point, Tara felt Chase—who had been clinging painfully to her arms this entire time—find a new grip on her belt. Then he found another on one of the vines encircling her legs. Carefully, in between blows, Chase began to climb over her. Five up-and-downs later, he was standing precariously on the thick vines around her ankles while she dangled upside down.

Tara heard a metallic scrape and an earsplitting wail, and felt the vine suddenly stutter. She heard chopping sounds, and felt herself falling again. This time, she hit the ground and didn't come back up.

She knew she couldn't waste time lying around, but Tara wanted nothing more than to curl up and go to sleep just then. Lifting her head woozily and feeling like she'd never be whole again, she saw that her legs were no longer wrapped in vines. Chase laid a few feet away, his sword in one hand and the halved, smoking plant in the other.

"You cut it?" Her voice was shaking a little.

He nodded breathlessly as the agonizing shriek of the murdered plant faded. He had leaves and twigs entangled in his thick, dark hair. She could only imagine what her own curls must look like.

Before she could even begin to get up, another huge vine just like the last snaked down from the sky, wrapped around Chase's torso, and began beating him against the ground again. This time, his arms were pinned to his sides, his sword lying forgotten on the ground. Another came down and grabbed Teto from Fin's side. The blonde boy had gone limp.

A vine slithered down towards Tara, and she rolled to the side as it clamped the ground right where she'd been. More came after her, and she quickly got to her feet, ignoring all pain, and ran. She dodged a flying bush and jumped over a slithering green vine, grabbing Chase's fallen weapon as she did so. Pausing to catch her breath and trying to figure out how anyone managed to hold that sword with one hand, she saw that her friends weren't having nearly as much luck as her.

Devon was soon carried off, and the already unconscious Fin began getting pounded relentlessly against the ground as well. More vines surged toward her again, and everything seemed to move in slow motion.

Plants, she thought. *We are getting killed by a bunch of* plants. At seeing everyone so helpless and being slammed into the earth over and over again, rage began to build up inside her. She wasn't going to fail because of some stupid vines. Fin wasn't going to die. Everyone would live. They were going to make it.

She concentrated hard on those thoughts, but the vines began squeezing life out of her friends. First Devon lost consciousness. Then Tetoviran's head lolled back, his face purple, and only Chase was left. He wore an expression that Tara had never seen on him and hoped never to see again: panic.

Blood pounded in Tara's ears. She felt a burning sensation on her chest and looked down to find her mother's necklace—the one with the crescent moon shape on it—glowing the color of white-hot flame, scalding her skin. The heat was radiating through her whole body, and her hands had begun to shake with intensity. She didn't know what was happening, or why she was somehow unafraid of it, but then Chase lost consciousness. And Tara's anger broke loose.

CHAPTER 14

Terrifying. What Chase had seen before he blacked out, before the sky turned upside-down and his breath left his body, could only be called one thing: terrifying.

Devon, Tetoviran, and Fin had all been unconscious, lying limp in their vine cocoons. Tara stood, watching the scene and barely noticing the plants snaking towards her for the attack. That part alone was scary because he'd never seen her so angry, nor so perfectly calm in the face of danger.

Yet then her necklace—that moon-shaped one she always wore—began to glow. Golden, white light so bright it made yellow spots dance in Chase's vision and forced him to squint. A wind rose up, strong and fierce, and soon a sort of hurricane was encircling Tara. The swirling air stung Chase's face, and he struggled to stay conscious as the vines squeezed him tighter.

Peering past the twigs and leaves circulating in the miniature storm, he caught a glimpse of something else that was glowing— her eyes. Tara's normally blue eyes were shining with a fluorescent orange light. Already, Chase was nearly certain that he was hallucinating, but Tara wasn't finished.

Luminous figures and creatures painted in deep browns and golds began to dance across her irises, perfectly visible to Chase despite the distance. They looked like animals, almost. A huge, proud stag with thick antlers ran across her eyes, then a wild horse. An eagle soared over her blazing pupils, then a plump salmon pursued by a large grizzly. He saw fresh soil and crisp green grass dappled with dew. He saw roses and morning glories, cherry blossoms and tiger lilies.

Finally, he saw a gray wolf, howling up at a full orange harvest moon that was represented by her pupils. All the world seemed to have been encompassed in those short moments, the entire wilderness of this earth displayed in her eyes. A large sword, seeming utterly familiar to him but unplaceable, slipped from her hands and clattered to the ground. Chase passed out just as the earth groaned and folded beneath him, under the complete control and command of Tara Florreson.

"Chase, wake up. Wake up." "Kid, don't be lazy. Get up."

Chase opened his eyes somewhat reluctantly to three people leaning over him. He sat up wearily, rubbing sleep out of his eyes and trying to get his hair under control. "What—what happened?"

Fin shrugged, looking abnormally anxious. Considering the recent events, Chase supposed that was acceptable. "We have absolutely no idea. The three of us just woke up on the ground. Oh, and here," he added, holding Chase's sword out to him. "This was lying over there," he gestured in a vague direction as Chase took his familiar weapon by the handle and sheathed it.

There was a moment of silence during which he tried to sort out reality from illusion in what he'd seen. Slowly letting his senses recover, he began recounting what had happened before he passed out. Tetoviran chewed on the end of a grass blade somewhat vengefully until he finished talking.

"Do you think you could've imagined it?" Devon asked, sounding nearly hopeful. Chase wished he could give an answer, but he honestly didn't know. How could he possibly discern what was real and what wasn't in the state he'd been in?

Fin cleared his throat nervously. "Well, ah… here's the thing, Chase. We haven't exactly been able to *find* Tara."

Chase had been trying to stand, but fell over again at this news. "What do you mean, you haven't found her?"

"Exactly that," Devon shrugged helplessly. "I was the first to come to, and she was nowhere to be found. We've searched all over."

Chase tried again to get to his feet and succeeded this time. Feeling a strange sort of stiffness in his posture, he reached for his back and felt his fingers brush something unfamiliar to him. It took him a moment to recall having slung Fin's bow over his shoulder, and now he removed the weapon with something close to shock. It was still in pristine condition. By some miracle, it hadn't been crushed.

He looked up to find Fin grinning in an almost hesitant manner, as though it might be too good to be true. "She's okay," he whispered, sounding as though he were talking about his sister or mother rather than his bow as he reclaimed it. He held it with so much reverence that one would think he worshiped it.

Chase, however, was not so easily distracted. Where was Tara? What had happened to her? Trying to clear his thoughts, Chase leaned back against a tree for support, resting his hands on his knees.

Suddenly, he jumped and whirled around. Tree. He was leaning back against a *tree.* "Why aren't there any plants attacking us?"

A beat. "Maybe we killed them all." He rolled his eyes at Tetoviran. "Then why is there a tree right here?"

He looked around curiously, then reached up to snap a branch off of the tree above his head. It broke cleanly, but no steam or wailing ensued. Everyone seemed to hold their breaths for several heartbeats afterwards. When nothing happened, Chase frowned in puzzlement. "There are still plants, and there are still *cuvari* in every single one of them. They just stopped…guarding."

Tetoviran frowned. "Okay. We passed the first test, I guess. We'll just be readier for the next one. More importantly than all this, where's Tara?"

"The first test?" Chase interrupted.

Devon nodded. "Don't you remember what Fin and I told you? There are a bunch of tests—like monsters, spirits, temptations—all these trials that we have to go through in order to get to the Sumadine Woods. Destiny and Fate want us to prove that we're worthy of their time."

Chase looked around cautiously, but took note of nothing suspicious. "Okay. Where are we now, then?"

"We're in between the last test and the next one, I think. Otherwise, something would be trying to eat us right now," Fin muttered. "In a little while, if we keep travelling, we should come across the next trial."

"Okay, let's slow down for a second," Chase said, feeling overwhelmed. This was all going way too fast. "Before anything else happens, we need to find Tara." The others all nodded in agreement.

"Well, we came from this direction," Devon said, heading back the way they'd come. "Maybe she's still back—ow!" He tripped over a stump and fell flat on his face, biting a few words far less unsoiled than 'ow' on his way down. He sat up, spitting out dirt, then stared at the stump in perplexity. "I could've sworn nothing was there before."

Fin groaned. "Here we go again."

Cautiously, Devon got to his feet and inched toward the motionless tree stump. He nudged it ever so slightly with the butt of his sword, then jumped when the stump began to move. It twitched slightly, but made no attempt to attack. Fin nocked an arrow, and Tetoviran advanced with his blades.

It may have been a comical sight—four armed, muscular males panicking at the sight of a tree trunk—to any common bystander, but those four were not eager to have the air crushed out of their lungs again.

"Wait," Chase stopped them all of a sudden. He inched forward until he was standing directly above the stump. He squatted down and squinted at it. Was it just his imagination, or did it look like a…?

Suddenly, the tree trunk grew. Visibly. Or rather, it popped a little further out of the ground like a gopher popping its head out of a hole. Chase now saw that it wasn't a stump at all. He'd been right. Sticking out of the ground was the sole of a leather boot.

Fin frowned in disbelief. "Wait a second. Is that… a shoe?"

Teto nodded excitedly. "Yes. And don't you see? It's not just any shoe. It's Tara's shoe!"

Devon looked somewhat exasperated. Chase could hardly blame him. The day had been mindboggling from start to finish, and it was still mid-afternoon. "There's no way. How would Tara's shoe get buried under the earth and suddenly start coming back up all by itself?"

"Maybe," Chase said, warily eyeing the boot that looked plenty like Tara's, "if it's *not* coming up all by itself." Fin gave him a look, and Teto rolled his eyes.

"Come on," Devon ridiculed. "You don't honestly think she controls the earth spirits, do you?" Ignoring him, Chase bent down and softly poked the leather of the shoe. It was now thrashing a bit more fiercely in the ground, and as it emerged a bit more, he saw the silver buckle on the ankle, determining that it was indeed Tara's boot. He squeezed the toe a bit, and jumped back, crashing into Devon.

"What? What's wrong?" he asked frantically, scrambling for a grip on Chase's clothes.

Chase's hands shook ever so slightly. "The shoe," he said. "There's… there's a foot in it. And if that's Tara's boot…" He didn't need to finish.

Fin and Tetoviran rushed forward simultaneously and began tugging at the shoe, trying to yank it from the earth. Once he regained his balance, Chase joined in, quickly followed by Devon. Everyone tugged with all their strength, but to no avail.

"This is insane," Tetoviran grunted. "We're trying to pull a girl's foot out of the ground, and we can't do it. We're basically failing at an exhumation."

Chase gave him a sharp glare that made the man go silent, but neither of them could get much further before they were interrupted by yet another phenomenon—and most likely one that would try to kill them again.

There was a sudden low rumbling, and ground began to tremble under their feet. Cracks snaked out from Tara's shoe, splitting the hard dirt violently.

"Uh… I don't think this is good!" Fin shouted, sounding close to panic.

"The boulder!" Tetoviran pointed. The four of them quickly stumbled away to take cover behind the large rock a few horse-lengths away—and not a second too soon. The moment they were all safely concealed from the earthquake, the thin fractures in the land exploded.

Bits of soil, blades of grass, and flowers of every assortment flew from an eruption of earth. It was as though they'd been simmering in a volcano, deactivated and waiting for the slimmest chance to burst free.

Chase's teeth clacked together, and he bounced up and down on the heaving earth as though he weighed nothing. He didn't dare try to speak any of the curses he was thinking, for fear that he would bite his own tongue off. The shaking was so violent, he worried the rock they were hiding behind would crack up and dissolve.

He heard a few sickening crunches and saw Tetoviran accidentally sit on Fin three times, making the blonde boy curse in a manner that would've made Tara wash his mouth out with soap. Even Chase learned a few new words. Devon hit his head on the boulder repeatedly, and Chase felt flying pebbles scratch his face. Something sharp hit him in the eye, making him shout wordlessly. The ground groaned again, seeming to grow tired from all the action, and the shaking suddenly stopped. Chase's senses spun at the sudden halt in motion. Just as quickly as it'd started, it was over.

Everything was silent, and a few seconds later, birds started chirping again in the treetops. Rubbing his watering eye, Chase slowly peeked around the side of the rock.

Tara Florreson was standing in front of a huge, smoking crater in the ground. Her hair was a disaster of dirt and leaves, her face smudged with soil. Chase had never seen a creature so wild.

Devon, Fin, and Tetoviran cautiously looked out from behind the boulder in time to see the glow on her necklace beginning to fade away. Her eyes had been alight, as well, exactly as Chase had remembered them. His head spun. He truly hadn't imagined it. He wondered if he wished he had.

Each of the lights slowly subsided until they both diminished completely. Together, Devon, Fin, Chase, and Teto slowly emerged from behind their shelter. The four of them walked towards Tara carefully, each with a hand on their weapons. Chase hated it, but he found himself loosening his sword in his sheath. He didn't know what would happen or what had occurred in Tara's head.

"Okay," Devon whispered, his voice hoarse. "Maybe she *does* control the earth spirits."

Tara spotted them approaching and stood waiting as they walked to her. Once close enough, she took two large steps forward and embraced Chase, startling him.

"You're okay," she whispered, seeming to collapse against his body in relief. Chase was horrified by his hesitance to return the hug. Whatever had happened, she was powerful. Really, really powerful and, from the looks of it, fairly unpredictable, too. That was a dangerous combination. Tara pulled back just enough to look Chase in the eye. He carefully avoided her gaze, putting his arms around her to avoid any questions. His conscience shouted at him for being afraid of Tara—which he knew was wrong and unfair—but he was, and his ego shouted at him for fearing a girl who cried all the time and couldn't hold a weapon without quaking. Chase hated listening to his ego. "How did you do it?" he whispered softly. A stiffness formed between his two arms, and Tara was pulling away from him before he could say anything more.

Pretending not to have heard him, she embraced Fin and Tetoviran, making an extra effort to avoid eye contact with Chase. The others murmured gauche greetings, but nobody seemed at ease. As she turned to Devon, she seemed to hesitate, then awkwardly put out her hand for a shake. He took her by surprise, though, and wrapped her up in an embrace. Her expression went from shocked, to shy, to happy as she returned the hug. Her cheeks got a little rosy, too, although she seemed unaware of it.

Chase took careful note of the exchange but said nothing.

"So, Tara," Fin began. His voice cracked, and he cleared his throat. "I…um, didn't know you could do that. How—how long has that been happening? I mean, I'm very interested in the properties of this necklace you wear and how it can cause earthquakes and dig massive pits in the earth. It's just an incredible talent you've got there, I mean… that's a really lovely skill to have. Is it a certain technique you use with your eyes to make them look like flaming sockets of lava, or is it just a trick of light?" His tone was high-pitched, his words clearly a product of nerves.

Tara laughed with equal discomfort. "I—well, it's a very complicated subject, actually. The specific details can just drag on forever, if you know what I mean. There're just so many careful explanations and equations that need to be explained in order to succeed in fully comprehending the potential essence of the"—

"We'll talk about it later tonight," Chase interrupted, eyeing Tara carefully. What was so bad that she would refuse to discuss it?

"We'll talk about it tonight?" came Devon's disbelieving tone. "We all almost died, Tara saved our lives by controlling the spirits of the earth with a magical necklace that buried her underground for who knows how long, she comes out unscathed… and you say we'll talk about it *tonight?*"

Fin nodded, seeming to gain confidence from Devon's confrontation. "Yeah, that's not just something you can dismiss with a flick of your hand. That needs an explanation. Now."

Tara inhaled slowly, looking at the ground and seeming to shrink more with every heartbeat. "I'm… um, I'm tired. From the exertion of it all. I just want to rest right now." Fin's brow pinched, but he said nothing. Reluctantly, Devon backed off, too, and turned away from Tara. Chase barely caught her quiet mutter, "It wouldn't kill you to understand that I'm scared, too." He tugged gently on a piece of her hair from behind, saying nothing but letting her know that he had heard.

Tetoviran, who had been quiet up till now, glanced skyward. "Speaking of later tonight, kid… uh, we've only got a little while before later tonight's here." It was true. The sun was slipping away below the horizon.

Devon sighed. "Great. We need to find shelter in a place that's guarded by a bunch of monsters."

Tara started at that. "Shelter? But…we have to keep going. We already wasted a ton of time."

Fin shook his head. "Tonight, we all need rest." He hesitated before muttering, "You especially, Tara. It can't be easy making the earth bend to your commands." Tara's face shuttered visibly, and Chase might have yelled at Fin if he didn't secretly feel the same way.

"If we bed down right here, we should be safe. The next challenge lies ahead of us. It shouldn't bother anyone here," Fin continued.

In about twenty minutes, they had a small fire started up and thin blankets laid on the ground. Everyone passed out almost immediately from sheer exhaustion. Everyone, that is, except for Chase. He was tired and worn out, but sleep wouldn't come. He laid awake, staring up at the stars.

This had better not be a joke, he thought to himself in the silence. *We're all going through so much for this, and if I find out that it wasn't worth it—if I never find my parents, if I die in the end, if all this is just pointless…* he shook the thought away. He smiled up at the moon, despite everything, and, so quietly that it was barely audible to his own ears, whispered, "I'm coming for you, Mother and Father. I'm going to find you. I promise."

His secret oath was whisked away on the wind, and he looked up at the constellations that lit the heavens like jeweled droplets of magic patterning across the sky, decorating the darkness with silver sparks of hope. There *was* hope. It was always there, burning like a flame that never died. Energy sparked through Chase's body, and suddenly he felt strangely content. Just for that one moment, he could pretend that everything was perfect. He wanted to take those few golden seconds and freeze them in time, replaying that feeling of happiness over and over again. But the moment would fade. It always did. It was the depressing truth that filled Chase's chest up with heartache.

As he pushed away his blanket and headed for Tara to wake her, though, he realized something. He realized that the tiny little flicker of hope was there for a reason. It was what assured him that no matter how many times a good feeling faded, another would always come, like the rising sun. At nighttime, when it's dark, it feels as though the light will never come again. But those tiny little stars keep telling you that brightness and joy are still out there, even though you can't see it. And, sure enough, the sun comes the next day, brilliant and gold and glorious. *It will always come,* he told himself. *Only to slip away again, but always to return. Always to come. And I will come. I promise that, Mother and Father. I will come.*

CHAPTER 15

"Talk. Now." Tara tried to pretend she was still half-asleep. Anything to keep away from this subject. Chase had woken her and walked her away from the others, and they were sitting on the ground with their backs up against a boulder. She drew her knees to her chest and yawned half-heartedly.

"I'm *so* tired, Chase," she complained overdramatically, drooping her eyelids for effect.

"Then you're only hurting yourself, because I'm not letting you go back to sleep until you tell me what's happening." "Can't we talk tomorrow?" "No."

Tara mumbled in protest, then let it trail off as she pretended to fall asleep. Chase gave her a whisper of a backhand. "You might be able to get away from the others, but I'm not leaving you alone."

Tara tried a new approach. "You know, I really don't believe I trust you anymore, though. After I fell into the canyon, you were acting suspicious. You never told me why. I don't think I should tell you any of my secrets if you refuse to tell me yours."

Chase blinked at her. Momentarily, he was at a loss for words as he groped for an excuse. "I…" he opened his mouth and then closed it again.

Tara looked wide awake now. "Yes?"

"I can't tell you that," he managed haltingly. Her eyebrows lifted. "Really."

He held her gaze firmly, but Tara had never seen such hesitance in his eyes. They sat at a standstill for a few moments, her waiting expectantly while he struggled for words.

"Yes, really," he said abruptly, recollecting himself and assuming dominance over the conversation once more, "and acting a bit strange is nothing compared to making the ground roll. Tell me." His change had been so quick that it was obvious he had forced it.

Tara folded her arms. "You tell me about you first." "No. Now."

She glanced away from him nervously, then took a deep breath and shrugged a shoulder slowly. Clearing her throat, she mumbled, "I don't exactly…know what happened." She inhaled sharply as if about to cry. "I'm so scared, Chase. This is just as confusing for me as it is for"—

"Oh, quit, Tara, you're a pathetic liar. Would you please just talk to me?" She made a big show of pretending to debate over this and came to a quick conclusion. "No."

"Tara." "I don't have to tell you anything if I don't want to." "Tara."

He fixed her with a hard, cold stare that forced her to look away. She tried to look interested in the grass, plucking a blade and twisting it around her finger. She snuck a glance his way, but he was still staring at her like he'd send her to her grave and then spit on the stone with a smile. Tara swallowed. He could be really intimidating sometimes.

"Chase, don't do that." "Then tell me what's going on. How bad can it be?"

She stared at the moon, in the sky. It was a crescent tonight. She held up her necklace, aligning the identical shapes. The silver light behind her necklace seemed to give the jewelry a halo.

Chase rolled his eyes. "Quit stalling. I'm tired of this game."

She didn't respond, but continued to stare at her necklace, outlined with the silver shimmery glow of the real moon sprinkling its luminescent dust over the earth. She thought about her mother and father and Gramma Kate…but especially her mother. Her heart felt heavy, and a lump formed in her throat. It couldn't be. Her mother would never burden her like this. Her mother loved her.

After a few minutes passed, Chase shifted to sit in front of her, and she jumped. She'd almost forgotten he was there for a moment.

He pressed his palms into her knees and gave her the meanest stare she'd ever seen. "Tara Florreson, if you don't tell me what's going on right now, I'll beat you until you cry, tie you to a tree, and leave you here to rot all alone while we go finish the journey."

She snorted over her jump of alarm, and his expression hardened even more. "You think I can't?" His voice was deadly calm, her knees being gripped with such intensity that they ached.

She shook her head quickly and looked down. "You wouldn't." He leaned forward, resting his elbows on her knees and bringing his face so close that she could see each one of his eyelashes. "Bet." She tried to focus on him. Anything but her mother. Anything but the fact that it was all her mother's fault.

"I…" Her voice failed her. She looked at the moon again, shining proud and bold amongst the stars. "It's complicated. It's really, really complicated." One tear slid down her cheek, even though Tara wasn't really sure why. Somehow, he could see that she wasn't faking it this time.

Chase's face softened into a long sigh. He pushed away and replaced himself next to her in a somewhat defeated manner and she began to cry. Horrible, wrenching sobs that seemed to tear Chase to pieces. "Crybaby," he murmured tenderly through a tight mouth. She buried her face in his shoulder and cried harder than she'd cried since Gramma Kate died. There was just so much happening at once—too much. And now this with her mother…

Chase pulled her into him slowly, holding her while her tears flowed, trying to release all of the worry and pain and fear that'd been trapped up inside her for months—no, years. She'd held it in when Gramma Kate died; when her parents left; all those years dealing with Aunt Beatrice; and now, here with Chase, knowing what dangled on that chain around her neck, knowing the power it possessed… just thinking about it made her cry harder.

Chase smelled like dirt and his clothes smeared dust across Tara's face, but she didn't care as her tears wetted his shoulder. He rested his chin on the top of her head. "If you don't want to talk about it, Princess, you don't have to." And that was probably the nicest thing he could've said.

She leaned against him and cried herself free of tears before she finally stopped and wiped her eyes. "Forgive me," she mumbled in embarrassment.

Chase shook his head slightly. "There's nothing to apologize for." Even after she quieted, he continued to hold her. She took a breath. This was going to get trapped up inside of her, too. She couldn't let that happen. She needed to tell someone, and if there was anyone she wanted to tell, it was Chase.

"I was very, very young when I found out."

Chase pulled away, and she felt his eyes on her. "Tara, you don't have to"—"No, I know I don't. But…I want to. Someone needs to know."

There was a moment of silence. "Okay. If you're sure." She nodded and mustered up her courage.

"It was my birthday. I opened all my presents and got things like toys and dresses from my friends and relatives, but I remember that my mom gave me a really small gift. It was a little jewelry box, wrapped in blue paper. I opened it and found this necklace." She fingered the pendant nervously. She was losing confidence fast. She tried to remember that this was Chase she was talking to. He was her friend. There was nothing to be nervous about.

"Well, I thought it was really pretty. My mom asked me if I wanted it, and I said yes. Absolutely." She began choking up but forced herself to continue. "My mom fastened it around my neck and told me that if we were ever separated, I should look up at the sky. Look at the stars, and know that she's watching the very same moon, thinking of me. Then she told me that I had to be careful with the necklace; that I was taking on a huge responsibility in accepting it. She warned me never to let anyone else touch the necklace and never to take it off. And I… I made a promise. It was binding, unbreakable… irreversible. If I were to ever break it, then—well, bad things would happen."

Chase arched an eyebrow. "How bad is bad?" "Very." He nodded like he'd been expecting that, then paused as if deciding his next words. "What exactly did you say?"

She swallowed. Here it was. What she'd been afraid of. But she had to tell somebody. "I said…words."

He snorted, and she rushed onward before he could ridicule her. "Ancient phrases and promises, and this one"—she held up her necklace—"has been in my family since the dawn of time."

He frowned, trying to keep up. "That necklace is a promise?"

She nodded slowly. "Of a sort. But my oath… well, my ancestors said these words for the first time to Life and Death, millennia ago. But I said them, too."

With that sentence, Tara opened herself to her memory. She felt a sensation like a dam being broken within her and water rushing forward. *Open,* she thought. *Stay open to the memory.*

She pulled the words, the promise she knew so well, from the darkest depths of her mind. Reciting it felt as though she was ripping a piece out of her soul. The words were so powerful that they tore at her chest, warning her not to misuse them. But she said them anyway.

> *"I solemnly swear on Life and Death,*
> *The forces of good and evil,*
> *The founders of Land and Sea,*
> *To all that live and reign on the Thrones of Creation*
> *Hear my call, hear my oath, and respond to me now.*
> *I hold this power to the responsibility and safekeeping of myself*
> *To protect and defend, dead or alive*
> *For all eternity unless taken by another of my own blood.*
> *To hold it, cherish it, treasure it;*
> *To summon the rising sun*
> *And cast off the strikes of darkness.*
> *To bring life to the nature of Heaven's works*
> *And use it by that of my own choice.*
> *Forever may this rest, at my hand, and under my wings.*
> *I henceforth shall permit this magic to thrive under my control*
> *And use it wholeheartedly with the best of my intentions,*
> *Whether it be assisting the forces of good or evil,*
> *The choice of which is mine.*
> *To this oath I dedicate myself*
> *My whole life long*
> *Until relieved of duty and crown.*
> *To keep all vows*

Unless it is desired to be banished, exiled, and executed entirely
From the world and cast down to the pits of Eternal Hell
Where Suffering never dies and Pain lives forever.
I entirely accept and embrace this power of Life
And promise to forever hold this oath to my heart
Through hardships and miseries
As my ancestors did before me
And as my descendants shall proceed to do after me.
Until the end of time and the dawn of a new age—
I promise this."

Tara concluded her recitation with a jolt, as though she was waking up. She found herself breathing heavily and shaking. The weakness of her liquified muscles forced her to collapse against the rock behind her. Her bones felt as though they were disintegrating and blowing away in the night wind. The pledge was so binding, so powerful, that it had sapped her very essence straight from her body.

Chase watched her warily, as if debating whether he should say something. After some deliberation, he finally opened his mouth to speak, but she beat him to it.

"Centuries. Centuries, Chase, and more. This necklace has been in my family since the beginning of time. The words are not mine. They were built into me from the moment I was born. And now… now I remember the story. I remember how it all began." And she launched into a tale that she'd never witnessed, never been told and never heard of in her entire life, but that she somehow knew like the back of her hand.

"In the beginning, there was only flat, barren rock. No sky, no air, no land, no water. Just two beings. One was called Life. The other was Death. They were the first of all the Creators. Just as Destiny and Fate are the creators of everyone's future—their own destinies and fates—Life and Death were the original creators of all life and all death. So, they created their children—the rest of the Creators. They had Sky and Earth, Destiny and Fate, Heaven and Hell. Those were their six original and only children. Each of their descendants had their own children, who had their own children, and so forth. Sky brought forth clean air and vast blue expanses. He gave birth to five children: Sun, Cloud, Bird, Storm, and Wind. Each of them had children, as well, and this resulted in the making of the moon, the stars, rain, thunder, lightning, and all the birds that fly in the sky.

"Earth brought forth grass and trees and plants of every size, shape, and color. She gave life to two children: Land and Sea. They had children, and this brought on all animals great and small, all beasts of the earth and all fish of the sea; all mountains and prairies and vast canyons. Heaven gave birth to Happiness and Repose. Hell brought forth Suffering and Pain. Heaven and Hell quarreled with one another often but were partners in business with Destiny and Fate, who were both strict maidens. They'd never had children and pledged to keep it that way. They sent animals and plants alike to their deaths, then decided whether they should go to Heaven's realm or Hell's. Since the dawn of time, the siblings have been in competition, trying to see who could uphold the larger population in their own land of the dead."

Chase frowned. "I've never heard this story before. I knew about the Creators, but I didn't think everything was here because of them. I guess I thought they were all just... up there."

Tara smiled drily, starting to feel a bit more collected. "Well, that's not how it goes. And for the first time, I know something you don't." Chase rolled his eyes, and for once, it was her turn to smile.

He jabbed his elbow into her ribs. "So, what happened?"

"The world was living in perfect harmony. Except for the constantly flowing arguments between Heaven and Hell, everyone got along well. A few years passed, and the Creators stopped having more children. Soon, it became a law on the Thrones of Creation that none of the original six Creators could ever have any more children. Everyone obeyed these laws. Everyone, that is, except for Earth. She saw what her realm looked like, and she felt as though it was missing something. So, she broke the rules. She had not one, but two children, and named them Man and Woman. They were Creators—not humans—but the creators *of* humans. Before Life and Death could find out, Earth ordered her children to make a species to live on her land and thrive off her animals. Man created the first human in his own image and named him after himself. Woman did the same, creating the first female human and naming her woman. They were taken from Earth's essence; created of her own land and her own water, sewn together with the blood of Life. Earth put the two in charge of her realm. They were to look after and care for her children; to rule the plants and animals with kindliness and fairness.

"Well, the man failed. He proceeded to kill more than he needed and ridicule the belief that all nature had a spirit and a life of its own. Earth became angry and disappointed. She was thankful to the woman for staying loyal to her, and expressed her gratitude by sharing some of her power with the woman. She gave the woman a special necklace, only to be worn by her own kin and passed down generation through generation. The wearer of the necklace was never to take it off, unless it was taken by her children and descendants of blood. Earth had so much faith in the woman, she gave her control of her realm. The woman accepted the necklace eagerly, happy to serve her original mother and excited at the idea of such power.

"A responsibility as great as that needed a formal authorization of Life and Death. Earth admitted to her forefathers that she had, indeed, broken the rules and had children—the descendant of which was this woman. But Life and Death gave her no punishment and wrote an oath for the woman to recite if she wished to take the necklace and its power. Without thinking of her family to come at all, the woman declared the lines clearly, and the power was hers. Earth named her Avaline Florreson, her last name meaning 'life of the flower.'

"The necklace reacted to Avaline's emotions. Only when they were strong enough would the power activate and come to life. The spirits of plants and animals alike bent to her commands, feeling the blessing of their mother, Earth, in her power. Avaline was thrilled with this privilege. Man and Woman created more of their kind, and soon, she had a child. Her daughter took the necklace at a young age, spouted her oath, and accepted the power. And so it went, passed on and down the long line of Florresons. Only a woman could wear the necklace, for man had broken the trust of Earth forever. If the wearer broke her oath, she would be sent into Eternal Hell—Hell's most torturous land, where the devils and Dark Angels live. Each Florreson child must keep her mother's last name, contrary to custom, and none will ever be unable to have children.

"Through the first dozen Florreson girls, the necklace was a wonderful opportunity. But soon, they began to realize that the necklace was dangerous. It was a risk to their lives, and the lives of everything else in Earth's domain. And it soon became more of a curse than a blessing, as it was passed on to my great-grandmother, my grandmother, my mother, and now to me."

CHAPTER 16

Chase plucked a blade of grass from the ground, staring at it with a new perspective now. Fin, Tetoviran, and Devon were listening carefully to Tara's story, the same one she'd told Chase last night. The image just wouldn't form in his mind. Tara Florreson. Sweet, timid Tara in charge of the entire realm of nature? That was just too much. That was insanity. A responsibility that huge, in her hands… She must be terrified.

"So now the necklace is mine," Tara was concluding. "And until I have a child—a daughter—I can't take it off or give it away, and if I die before passing it on, I'll suffer endlessly."

"Wow. Earth's a real sweetheart, huh?" Fin commented after a beat.

Tetoviran frowned. "What happens if you decide to be a maiden?" She shrugged. "Not an option, I guess."

A thick silence hung in the air. Devon's voice cut through it, thickly concerned. "If you've had this necklace since you were three, how come the earth never did what you wanted it to do before?"

Tara smiled a little in his direction. "Simple. I just wasn't aware of its power. I didn't remember the promise I made directly after I made it. No one ever does. It's kind of drilled into your mind when you're born a Florreson. Once I became aware of my powers, my emotions became strong enough and the memories came back… well, the magic sort of activated itself. But you have to understand, I can't just use it whenever I feel like it. I can listen to and understand nature, yes. Their language is mine. But the true power only comes when my emotions are too strong. And sometimes it happens when I don't want it to. Sometimes it's *against* my will."

"So, you can speak to plants and animals?" Fin asked curiously.

Tara scrunched her nose. "I don't know, actually. I've never tried. I can hear them, though. Right now. The grass is happy and young, but uncomfortable under this rock over here." She picked up a small stone and set it atop a larger boulder. The green blades which had formerly been compressed against the ground immediately regained a healthy, upright position, and bent slightly in Tara's direction as if bowing down in gratitude.

"And there's a squirrel in that tree up there, warning his son not to eat too many nuts, or he'll get a bellyache." Four people looked to the tree in disbelief, but Tara shrugged as though it was no big deal. "I've always loved nature. The outdoors called to me with its own voice, in a way. I guess I just assumed it was longing, but now I have to wonder if the earth was speaking to me all along. Maybe I just couldn't hear it quite as clearly."

Chase drummed his fingers on his knee. "Can you control water, too? It's part of Earth's realm, right? Her son, Sea?"

Tara smiled wryly. "If only. Land and Sea had a big feud some billion years ago, and it ended with a separation between the two. Those worlds are now divided, which is why fish can't live on land and land creatures can't live in water. Water is sort of like enemy ground for me."

Tetoviran took a cautious sip from his wineskin, as though afraid that since the water wasn't on Tara's side, it might bite. "What does it feel like being able to hear and understand everything around you? Doesn't it get confusing?" the burly man wondered aloud.

"Yes," Tara said immediately. "It sounds like I'm in a giant city full of people, all talking at the same time. They all blend together unless I'm focusing."

Devon stood, seeming suddenly bored with the conversation. "Maybe we should keep moving. Once we get past all the guardians, we still have to get through the Sumadine Woods, find Destiny and Fate's home, stay sane through the whole wind thing…" he trailed off as the entire group turned to stare at him. Chase frowned in confusion. "What wind thing?"

Devon looked at his companions as though it should be obvious. "The Sumadine Woods? Their whispering winds? Don't tell me none of you have heard of them."

"No, we haven't," Chase said. "What whispering and winds? They make you go crazy?"

Devon ran his hand through his hair. "Usually." Chase glared at him. "Usually?"

He huffed. "It's complicated. You see, there're these winds that"—he suddenly stopped short, his eyes locked on something behind Chase. "What's that?"

Chase rolled his eyes impatiently. "Please. I'm a master thief, and that's the oldest trick in the book. What about the winds, now?"

Devon shook his head. "No, seriously. What *is* that? Chase, look."

Chase still hadn't turned around. "So, there's really something over there, huh?" Devon nodded insistently, but Chase only cocked his head. "Could it possibly be a reason to avoid warning us about potential dangers we don't know about?" Confusion registered on Devon's face. "Why would I ever"—"Maybe that way, you can survive while we all die. You could even take Tara's necklace off her dead body and try to use its power like the wretched fool you are."

Chase heard Tara bite his name in shock at his accusation, and Devon gave him a sharp look. "I would never"—

"Really?" Devon stared at Chase with a mix of outrage and shock. "Of course not!" Chase shrugged. "Okay, then come with me and show me what's threatening our lives." Devon moved to lead him away, but Chase stopped him by the shirt. "If there's nothing there, I'll force those secrets from you. Mark that." He heard several alarmed inhalations behind him from their companions, but he didn't care. He had missed being aggressive every now and then. It didn't really matter whether or not he actually hated the person.

Devon scowled at him, shifting in his own clothes from Chase's grip on his collar. "You're wasting time!" He paused for a second, then tilted his head. "How come you're the only one who gets something out of this bargain? If there's really something there, what do I get?"

Chase laughed lightly and thought about it. "I'll steal you some gold or something." "Compared to torture, that's not much."

Chase eyed him levelly. "Fine. You can hit me ten times, as hard as you'd like, and I won't defend myself. Deal?"

Devon didn't miss a beat. He simply smiled and put an arm around Chase, guiding him away from Fin, Tara, and Tetoviran. "Deal."

"This ought to be good," Chase muttered. Although, as Devon steered him up towards the crest of a hill, he couldn't help thinking that nobody would be stupid enough to have that much confidence in their excuse if it was faulty. Which meant two very, very bad things: there really was some sort of terrifying thing over the top of this hill, and Devon would be allowed to beat him without retaliation.

As the two of them reached the top of the hill, their friends following close behind, Chase did, indeed, see something. At first, he wasn't even sure what he was looking at, and he became more confused than afraid. The sight before him was so weird and unthreatening that he wasn't fully sure how to react.

Some sort of shaggy creature, waddling low to the ground, approached over the top of the hill. The animal's fur was greenish-brown, caked with mud and tangled with twigs and leaves. It was short and stout, walking on four legs, with only its large nose poking out from under its shaggy mane. Two thick, dark brown horns protruded from its head, and its unruly tail was thick and long. Chase stared on in curiosity, wondering what the odd animal might be.

"Tara, do you know…" his voice trailed off as he turned to look at her. She was shaking. "Tara? What's the matter?"

"That… that thing…" she could barely form her words. Chase took a concerned step in her direction, but before he could say anything, a chilling sound unlike anything he'd ever heard pierced the air. It sounded like some sort of gnarled howl, and Tara released a despairing wail of her own afterwards.

"Well, that's it!" She began pacing quickly, gnawing on her fingernails. "They declared war. I'm dead, you're dead, everyone's dead! We're all going to die."

Chase stared at her. She was turning into a raving lunatic. "What? Who did? What was that noise?" "Them!" Tara cried, throwing a finger in the direction of that odd animal.

Chase was puzzled. How could that one little shaggy ball of filth hurt anybody? He turned to look down at the place where there was formerly one little creature—but where there now laid hundreds. Chase's jaw went slack. A huge sea of green and brown surged forward, each animal grunting and snorting and occasionally screeching out a cry like the first they'd heard, directly followed by growls and snarls of agreement.

Devon hit the back of Chase's head. "Told you."

Fin looked rather amused. "Cute little devils, hmm?"

Tara whirled on him and seized him by his shirt collar, yanking him into a crouch so he could look her in the eye. "This is not a joke, Fin Vidovu!" The blond boy's eyes widened in shock. That was the first time he'd ever heard Tara yell. "This is real. Those animals out there? They're monsters. Killers."

Tetoviran huffed and folded his arms across his burly chest. "Why does that not surprise me? If it's not one thing, it's another. I never should have agreed to any of this."

"Listen to me." Tara stared at him. "Those things are known for being indestructible. Their skin is harder than steel; they might as well be made of stone. They're immune to fire, swords, arrows—people have tried burying them under avalanches! They still come out alive! Nothing can kill them. Instead, you have to gain their trust. Otherwise, they see everything as a threat. *They will kill you.*"

The others began to shift uncomfortably, realizing for the first time that these funny-looking, almost cute creatures were, in fact, very dangerous.

"They're *teskos*—steel monsters. One *tesko,* years ago, leveled an entire kingdom all by itself. Another single-handedly defeated a whole army, a thousand strong, in less than an hour. These things have caused worldwide destruction while traveling solo. We're looking at hundreds of them! So right now, right here, we need a plan," she concluded anxiously, waiting for someone to announce their genius idea.

Instead, everyone stared blankly for several seconds before Tara shrieked in frustration. "Come on! We're running out of time! We need to get them on our side! What can we do?"

Chase racked his brain for an idea, but he couldn't concentrate. Tara sitting there screaming at them to hurry wasn't helping him focus, either. He was starting to panic. If one of these monsters could take down a whole army by itself, what could this many of them do? Easily take down five weary travelers. That would be nothing for them.

Suddenly, Chase snapped his fingers as an idea came skipping along and slapped him in the face on its way. "Tara, you can understand animals, right? Well, can you understand the *teskos,* too?"

Tara nodded slowly. "Yes… they're all chanting that they want to eat our bones and drink our blood." "Great," Chase said dismissively. "You also said you'd never tried talking back to them? Well, I need you to try that."

Tara stared, dumbfounded. "That's your plan?" Chase nodded, spun her around, and steered her towards the approaching army of *teskos.* "Yes, and I need you to go with it."

"Chase!" she screamed as the sea of shaggy monsters shuffled onward, getting closer to her with every second. She resisted desperately, scrambling against his strength, but he continued to shove her toward the army.

"Just relax and everything will be fine. Early morning wake-up calls transmit the same level of irritation that you're probably feeling towards me right now and I know it's difficult not to punch me in the face, but you just have to go with it because if you don't, we're going to be tomorrow's breakfast, and I'm pretty sure these guys don't like bacon."

"Are you *babbling?*"

"Just go talk to the nice little doggies."

"Chase, I can't just *do* that. I already told you, I don't know how." He shot her a charming smile. "Maybe it'll just come naturally."

She shook her head. "No! That's not how it works! And besides, my emotions aren't strong enough. If they were, then maybe it would begin to come naturally, because I'd have the full power. But right now, nothing's happening."

"Shouldn't fear be strong enough?" Chase spluttered. She shook her head frantically. "I would think so! I don't know! Apparently, there's just not enough of it right now."

Fin spoke up from behind Chase. "Well, get more scared, Tara! Make the emotion strong enough!"

"That won't work! It has to be genuine! I can't just force something out of me."

"No?" Tetoviran asked suddenly. "Then what if we did it for you?" Tara glared at him. *"What?"*

The *teskos* were getting very close now. They'd be upon them in instants. Tetoviran turned to Fin, Devon, and Chase. "All right, you worthless children. We've got almost zero time to make Tara's emotions strong enough to give her all that Earthly power. It's going to be great! Zap with the power here! Zap with the power over there!"

Chase nodded excitedly, silencing Teto as he realized where he was going. This might just work. "Anger won't work. She can't get mad at us too easily; she's way too nice for that. I say sadness. She's got plenty of sad things in her past. Talk about them. Insult her. I don't know. Just make her sad enough; it's the only thing that'll save us."

The others looked a bit uncomfortable with the plan, but nodded reluctantly. One by one, they took up shouting out to Tara, filling her head with as much emotion as possible. At first, she looked confused, but as she listened, sorrow and memory filled her eyes with hurt, and she seemed to be staring right at Chase as the *teskos* got closer.

He called out to her, "Think of your grandmother. She was vibrant and alive, but what did her life amount to? She was

Earth's tool, and then she died. Remember the day she left you? What had she given the world?" Her eyes grew glassy with tears, and Chase's gut twisted. He was being cruel. Part of him knew it, and a smaller, sickening part of him had missed acting this way. That alone made him nearly sick with guilt. But the more the others called out, the more Tara's sorrow seemed to rise—as did the growing glow of her necklace. He shook off his misgivings and continued reminding his best friend of her worst nightmares. *This is necessary,* he told himself repeatedly. *It's necessary for survival.*

The necklace began to glow blindingly. It was working… even though they were sort of using her. He knew they shouldn't take her for granted, but this was the only way. She'd said herself that the monsters were indestructible. Five young voyagers would be a tasty snack from their perspective. Besides, using her powers wasn't just saving his life; it was saving all of theirs, so it was completely for the better.

Chase reminded Tara of that one time when she'd felt so betrayed by him in his barn that first night. He even went so far as to tell her he hoped she had been hurt by it. Her eyes overflowed with tears, and then the explosion came.

A huge blast of white light dancing with ghost animals and phantom plants burst across the sky, radiating pure power. Chase stumbled back into Fin, shielding his eyes. The light subsided, and Tara stood with glowing gold eyes, phantom land-walkers lighting up her pupils and ghostly wheat stalks highlighting her irises. All the plants, animals—every blade of grass and fallen twig seemed to bend in her direction, waiting for her command. The *teskos,* which were now mere feet away from Tara, had stopped short and bowed their shaggy heads low. Tara slowly approached the leader of the pack, and placed her hand gently on his head.

A small growl escaped from the back of the creature's throat, but he let her stroke his ears and smooth his fur.

For several minutes, Tara simply stood, petting the *tesko*. As the monster began to relax a bit more, she brought her hand around in front of his nose, and held her palm out. Chase was pretty sure he heard Tetoviran yelp, and both Fin and Devon winced, half expecting the *tesko* to open his mouth and bite Tara's hand clean off. But the animal merely sniffed her fingers. After a moment, his small pink tongue peeped out from behind his razor-sharp teeth and licked Tara's hand, and it wasn't until the creature rubbed affectionately up against her leg that Chase exhaled a huge breath of anticipation and anxiety that he hadn't even realized he'd been holding in. The other *teskos* shuffled forward and began to lick and nuzzle Tara, as well. They liked her! The animals communicated with a series of grunts and snorts, and she spoke back to them in the exact same language.

Chase felt as though he was watching a miracle unfold. An entire army of monsters had been about to attack them, and not a single weapon had had to be lifted. He beamed with pride as Tara made a few hand motions, sending the *teskos,* one by one, back down the hill in the direction they'd come, no doubt using some sort of convincing bait—*there's a whole pack of worthless weaklings just like us down there!*—until only one remained.

He was tiny, the size of a fox, and clearly young. His fur was short and light brown, and his horns were just little brown stubs on the top of his head. He had big brown eyes that made him look rather much like a puppy or baby goat. He was actually very cute. Tara shooed him away as the last of the light faded from her eyes, but he only snuggled closer to her leg. So, Tara finally bent and picked him up, petting his head and grunting soothingly.

She walked over to Chase and the others, who were grinning with triumph. Teto congratulated her, quickly to be echoed by Fin and Devon. Chase reached out to embrace her. "You did so well!" he cried. But he stopped short when he saw her stony glare. "Tara?"

Her next words were extremely unexpected. "I hate you."

CHAPTER 17

Tara seethed, trying to use anger to cover the immense pain that clamped her heart like a fist. She'd never felt so used in her entire life. Chase and the others stared on in confusion at her harsh choice of words. The baby *tesko,* whom she'd decided to keep after he cried to her about how his mother had abandoned him and the other, older *teskos* were always picking on him, licked her hands comfortingly. She'd decided to name him Rebel, since he'd chosen to leave his herd.

Devon looked taken aback. "Tara, what's wrong? You did it! That was almost too easy."

She glared at him, her fingernails carving thin crescents into her palms. "Easy for *you.* You used me." She passed her gaze around to each of them, trying to cool the rage that each of their faces ignited within her.

"My power is not supposed to create an easy route. It's not meant to help you cheat your way out of something. It's supposed to be used when you've fought with your life, after you've given it everything you've got, and you just can't win. It's not supposed to be used for the advantage of four terrified boys that are too lazy to even try and put up a fight. You're just as bad as the original man, taking Earth's power for granted. Just because I'm here and I have power, what you did is not okay with me. You can't start depending on me to save you from everything you're afraid of."

Fin offered a small smile. "Tara, we don't. Trust me. We just kind of panicked this time. Besides, think about it. If we hadn't done that, we would've died, you would've died, all nature would've died… we did you a favor, in a way."

Chase nodded. "Yeah. If we hadn't made you upset, the power never would've worked."

Tara couldn't believe them. Here they stood, her best friends, telling her that by forcing her to cry and using her powers before even trying to put up any effort themselves, they'd done her a favor. "I wasn't crying because of what you were saying," she burst incredulously. "I was crying because I'd never felt so betrayed in my entire life. How could you? Telling me to think about my own grandmother's death. My own mother's mistakes. Who do you think you are?"

"Tara, think about this rationally," Devon cut in, using a tone of voice that was meant to soothe her but only infuriated her further. "Would you rather focus on the petty, meaningless emotions you're feeling now, or appreciate the fact that you're still alive?" Chase winced. As soon as the words were out, Devon seemed to realize what an enormous misstep that had been. Anything he could've said to make up for it was lost in his throat.

"Tara"—Teto started quickly. "Save it," she interrupted sharply. "I need some time alone."

With that, she stormed off over the other side of the hill, leaving the mumbling, guilty voices of her friends and her new pet behind her.

"Please, Tara. Please just listen to me." Chase stood in front of her, begging her to accept his apology. His hair hung over his face. "I know I was mean. I… I know what betrayal feels like. But you've got to realize—" he gestured back in the direction of Fin,

Devon, and Tetoviran—"We're your friends, Tara. More than that. We're like family, and we need to trust each other."

Tara's heart sped up, and anger rushed in her ears. All she'd wanted since as far back as she could remember was a person whom she could call a friend. She had thought, so strongly believed, that she *could* trust Chase. When she had first thought he was leaving her that night in his barn, the feeling of betrayal had been nothing compared to this. She felt her eyes begin to burn and tried to keep herself under control. "Do you think I don't know that? Don't you think I want to trust you?"

He inhaled slowly, his eyes revealing nothing interpretable. He seemed much, much smaller than usual. "I know it's been tough for you to get used to me, but this… this is just who I am, Tara. You seem to forget that I'm a thief. Your expectations for me are far too high."

Ignoring the sadness lacing his tone, she rolled her eyes. "Please. Don't feed me trash. You're perfectly capable of choosing right from wrong, and I've watched you be kind."

Mustering up a small amount of dignity, Chase bristled. "Yes, Tara, I can be, okay? But that's not me. I'm not…naturally like that. I've lived for myself alone for as long as I can remember, and being considerate for you takes a lot of effort on my part. I have to *concentrate* on being nice to you, because it's natural for me to start fights over nothing just for the sake of hitting someone. Don't you understand? I'm working hard to become more than a thief, and you have to let me make mistakes sometimes."

All this time, Tara's mouth had been working silently, her lips pressing together impatiently.

"Tara, please. You have to trust that I'm trying."

She waited a moment to see if he was done, and when he said nothing more, she exploded with an angry push to his chest. A frown closed over his face at the gesture and his fists tightened, but he didn't retaliate.

"You, Chase Onaj, have made it completely impossible for me to trust you. Or any of you, for that matter."

"Tara—" he interjected, only to be cut off by another aggressive shove.

"If you want me to trust you, then try harder," she hissed. "I'm trying as hard as I can, Tara!"

"Great, then. This is your hardest? Thanks for showing me who you really are. That you'll never be more than a thief. And that you, of all people, are no friend of mine." As she said those last words, a circle of grass around her immediately turned black and died. She blinked hard from the sting in her eyes. Power sent slight tremors through her body.

"What is this?" she whispered, more for her own ears than for Chase's. "What have you done?" She shivered under the pressure of anger that now burned brighter with her newfound alarm at the dying plants, feeling her eyes burn. "Look what you've done!" she all but screamed at him, lifting her hands as if to hit him but only lowering them again.

She took a step, and the death followed her. Another, another. All plants within twenty steps of her created a trail of ash as she went. This was not her. This was not Earth. Earth was queen of life, but Tara strode forward as a queen of death. Darkness shrouded her with every step—within and without.

She paused and stared back at Chase with luminescent eyes. The feeling within her was terrifying. He had hurt her, and she felt an aching desire to hurt him back. "So, this is what you call a family? Perhaps your parents are better off without you, then."

She heard him suck in a sharp breath behind her as she continued to stride forward and away. She'd hit a sore spot, for sure, and that was alarmingly pleasing to her. The smallest part of her wanted to run back and comfort him, tell him she hadn't meant it. But she couldn't. This was retaliation, nothing more.

Besides, she had a bigger problem to concern herself with. Plants were dying. *Animals* were dying. She could sense the fleeting panic of thousands of insects and several rodents as she passed them, their small hearts suddenly ceasing to beat and failing to restart. She ran a few steps, trying to escape this horrible thing, but it followed her.

Her head swam, her mind being overrun with the terror of those animals and plants as they died. There was life, and then death, and it was more than enough to make a person go mad.

Tara desperately tried to calm herself. She tried using her willpower to make the death stop. She commanded the plants and animals to stay alive, but the death continued to follow her everywhere she went. She heard footsteps behind her and froze as a sudden fear swallowed her. What if it this became unstoppable? What if nature now died wherever she went?

She swallowed that thought as Chase caught up to her and seized her by the shoulders. "Tara, please listen."

She cried out, trying to pull away. Her former anger, which had seemed so important just moments ago, was now nonexistent as she realized the danger that he was in. "Chase, no!" She struggled in his grasp. Her eyes were still alive. She felt them burning. "I can't control it! Chase, let go, I might hurt you!" He didn't loosen his grip. She gasped as she felt power surge through her body. Something was building, something more monumental than the destruction she was wreaking, and it was building up under his touch. "Chase, listen to me!" she cried frantically, beating her fists on his chest.

But he wouldn't. Tara felt the buildup grow, expand, and then… burst. A grunt of pain was drawn from the pit of Chase's stomach as her power struck him. He gasped out a strangled noise, and a wracking terror tore through Tara, ripping at her core. She felt his hands clench spasmodically on her shoulders as her vision began to blur from the strain of her power. She could feel herself filling with something. Something… something like energy. Chase's energy. She was leeching his very soul from his body, filling herself with his strength.

"Stop," she desperately implored this horrible magic. "STOP!" But it didn't. It continued to slowly eat away at Chase, torturing him from within. He was painfully hunched, his muscles twitching from time to time. His eyes were rolling back in his head, bloody foam bubbling in his mouth. She was killing him. Her breathing grew sharp with panic. *She was killing him.*

"Tara," he wheezed suddenly, his voice strained and forced. "Tara…" She stared at him with wild fear, shaking more violently than he was. His neck trembled with the effort it took for him to raise his head, but he did it. "Look at me," he panted.

She stared at him unblinkingly with fear. The flow of his energy into her body was growing steadily. A sharp, burning pain was biting at the back of her head. The strangest things were in sharp focus to her. His face was slick with sweat, the veins in his forehead pulsing visibly.

"Not my face," he grunted, his voice breaking off at the end as he gasped for breath. "Eyes!" he demanded forcefully. Barely able to see from the panic clouding her vision, Tara did as she was told.

Looking into those eyes, she found a deep comfort so sharply contrasting with everything going on around her that her head spun. Rich brown, with flecks of gold as though the sun had passed through, Chase stared back at her. While his whole body shook and strained against the power that was eating at his lifeline, his eyes were the same as ever: present and relaxed. Her power was destroying him, but he was there for her.

Without really even realizing it had happened, Tara's breath had slowed. Gradually, she felt her anger and fear seep away, sucking her gently back into reality. The power within her ceased to rage and she felt the life she had stolen from Chase rush out of her body. Her eyes stopped burning, leaving her to blink from the tears that ensued. The air around them grew heavy, and then the pressure lifted all at once.

Chase's muscles gave and he collapsed to the ground gasping. Tara's eyesight cleared, and she, too, fell to her knees as the pain she had felt in her head continued to throb. She felt drained, sapped of all the strength she had consumed from Chase. She wasn't sure if she was crying from pain or shock or horror. Her hands still twitched convulsively and she fought desperately to calm down. As she inhaled slowly, her gaze fell on something peculiar.

She saw that the wide trail of ash she had left in her wake was dotted with shoots of pale green. Tara's head thrummed with a new, cleansing sort of energy: rebirth. She could sense the plant spirits recovering, could feel new life reverberating through her bones as though it was her own energy.

Yet that feeling of relief was very quickly gone. The animals that had been killed by her rage were lost beyond revival. She was supposed to give life to nature, not kill it. And Chase… she looked down at him, her heartbeat jumping again as her mind replayed what she had done to him.

He was lying on his back breathing heavily, staring up at Tara with a look that appalled her: awe. Who would be fascinated by what she'd just done? Why was that look not one of horror? With a groan, Chase rolled onto his side and pounded his fist lamely into the ground, spitting blood out of his mouth. Tara gasped at the sight. "By the Devil, Tara," he breathed, a husky chuckle escaping his throat, "you must really hate me."

She inched closer to him, afraid to touch him. "What happened?" she whispered. "What did I do to you?"

He shook his head and blinked hard. "I don't know, but it sure hurt."

Tara looked at him for a moment longer, her stomach churning as she remembered the pained look on his face as her power clawed at his vitality. Even now, he was continuing to cough up blood. Her horror was apparently obvious, because Chase's fingers coiled around her wrist. There was a surprising amount of strength in them after what his body had just endured. She had just pulled half of his soul, strength, and life out of his body and then slammed it back into him all at once.

"Relax," he mumbled. "So, you've found something new in this little gift of yours. You'll learn to control it. Just calm down." Tara's mouth almost fell open. He made everything sound so simple. She could barely control the magic that worked in her favor, but this... whatever had just happened had been completely beyond her control, and that worked in nobody's favor. Her body was just a vessel for that abominable force.

"Man," she whispered suddenly, her mind making a horrible, horrible connection. "Man and Woman were Earth's children. That means that my power... my power can affect human beings."

Chase tasted a curse with his infuriating laugh. "You don't say."

Tara tried to pull away from his grip. "Don't touch me," she warned, her tone hitching. "Not until I know what's happening. Maybe not ever again."

Chase gazed up at her, holding one hand over his eyes and keeping the other around her arm. His thumb stroked a protruding vein on the inside of her wrist. "I'll tell you what's happening. Your powers are coming back to you bit by bit. This thing with humans apparently only applies in certain extreme situations." He paused to wipe blood from his lips. "Which means that I apparently messed up even worse than I thought. Whatever you did to me, the pain was strange. It wasn't like a wound or a burn, and it was slow. At least, until the end." He chewed his lower lip thoughtfully. "My guess would be that since you just used that power for the first time, it's still weak. That's most likely the only reason it didn't kill me."

"But that wasn't my willpower," she exclaimed as he sucked blood from his teeth. "I wasn't trying to hurt you or anyone else. I didn't *want* any of that to happen. I tried to stop it, but nothing happened." "You were freaking yourself out," he reasoned. "You had some sort of panic attack and lost control. Besides, things are as simple as this: Destiny and Fate will be able to explain everything to you. When we get there, we'll figure all this out, and you'll be fine."

Tara stared at him incredulously. "How in the world can you say that?" she practically shrieked. He grimaced at the volume of her voice. "How can you be so calm about this? I just *tortured* you! You are cleaning blood out of your mouth as we speak!"

He offered her a small smile. "Two reasons. Firstly, I'm not in pain anymore, so I don't care what you did to me; second, you forgot you were mad at me."

She bit her lip and folded her arms. "I most certainly did not. If you're as uninjured as you claim, get up." He did so somewhat hesitantly, but he didn't so much as sway. With a triumphant grin, he swiveled to look down at her. Rather than accepting the gloved hand he held out to her, though, Tara sat back on her heels. Her head had stopped hurting, and she wished this new discovery would fade just as easily.

"Chase, what'll I do?" she asked softly. "I'm a monster. What if I kill someone before we reach Destiny and Fate? Before I can control this?"

"Just make sure you aim at the enemy," he answered seamlessly, slipping his arms beneath hers and pulling her to her feet despite her protests. "Because if you ever do that to me again, I'll knock your teeth out of your head." Tara broke away, putting distance between them. "Chase, I'm serious. This is really scary." She could hear the tremor in her own voice. Her head was spinning with thoughts too numerous to separate.

He studied her for a beat, then offered the smallest of smiles. "Tara." He opened his arms to her, and she stared at them. Her heart hammered in her chest. How could she be certain that she wouldn't harm him?

"I don't want to hurt"—she began, but he grabbed her by the shoulders and pulled her against his chest. She yelped and almost began to protest, but his arms enveloped her and she suddenly realized how wonderful it felt to be held. Her complaints and worries fell away as she melted into his warmth. Where Chase's physical contact usually had something to do with alluring her or embarrassing her, its sole purpose now was to comfort her. His arms encircled her back and head, pressing her into his chest.

"You're not a murderer. I'm alive and well, okay? And look." He directed her attention to the shoots that were sprouting from the ash she had caused. Grass peeked out from beneath the destruction, slender and young and growing so fast that the process was visible. "There's always hope, Princess," he murmured. "Forget this for now."

She felt cold when he stepped away from her and released her from the comfort of his hug. "We should keep going," she said after a moment. "A lot of time has been lost already." He nodded slowly, and she put an impulsive hand on his arm. "Let's not tell the others about this yet," she said. "I don't... I don't know if they'll be as accepting of it as you are. The last thing I need is for them to fear me."

Chase eyed her carefully, appearing to run through that proposal and every possible outcome of it within a heartbeat. "Okay," he said at last. "And... I haven't forgotten why you were angry, Tara. Am I forgiven? Are they?"

Tara had to think for a moment to understand what he was talking about. That anger seemed so trivial now, so distant. "It doesn't matter," she said dismissively, trying to collect herself. *Put it aside,* she thought of her power. *Forget it for now. Nothing will come of worry.* And, to her utmost shock, her mind listened.

Chase turned towards the hill over which he had followed her. On the other side, hidden from view, waited their friends and Rebel. He paused, looking down and running a hand through his hair before looking back at her. "I *am* sorry, you know. I wasn't just saying that. I really feel bad about what happened. They do, too."

"I know that," she said. "You need to control your mouth sometimes, though, Chase. How could you pick a fight with Devon the way you did?"

He shrugged casually. "It didn't mean anything, Tara. He knows that. Neither of us will hold onto those words." "I'm sure he'll hold onto *your* words. It might be amusing to watch him beat you up." Chase smiled at her. "Really? More amusing than watching me fall to my knees in agony? You truly did enjoy it, didn't you?"

She glared at him, and an all-too-familiar antagonizing smirk appeared on his lips as they began the tiresome trek up to the top of the hill. Regaining his solemnity, a short bit later on the hike, Chase cleared his throat. "Honestly, though, Tara. None of us would ever try to hurt you. You need to understand that."

She tried to hide a smile. She'd already told him several times that she wasn't mad anymore, but he kept trying to apologize. It was almost endearing, although he'd kill her if she ever used that word to describe him aloud.

"We're your family now," he went on, "and families fight sometimes." She cocked her head, and for the first time since she'd met him, Chase's cheeks reddened. He cleared his throat uncomfortably. "Not that I would know. I barely remember my family. But… I've watched people."

He turned away quickly, trying to cover the first sign of embarrassment Tara had ever seen from him. She almost wanted to laugh aloud. He was always so cool and nonchalant, as though he knew he was better than everyone else and above silly things like embarrassment. Yet of all the things to be ashamed of!

"You know," she called after him, "Prince Charmings don't usually turn red in the face."

He stopped walking and turned to her, his face a normal color again and his smirk showing off the Chase she knew. "And princesses aren't usually murderers." She gasped, and he laughed as he turned and continued walking. "I am not a"— "Better hurry up, Tara." He picked up his pace to move on ahead of her. "We're out here all alone. I might just decide to get revenge."

She rolled her eyes, but a shiver went up her spine nonetheless as she moved to catch up.

As soon as she got back to the others, she was hit with a barrage of apologies, hugs, and pleas for forgiveness, which she granted almost immediately. "But it'd better not happen again." Her friends swore up and down that it wouldn't, and they quickly began moving again. Devon and Fin hiked up in front of everyone, with Tetoviran close behind. Tara walked behind him with Rebel, and Chase took up the rear.

They walked on for several hours during which Tara endured the aches in her feet and the pressing anxieties in her head silently. *Push it away,* she kept repeating to herself. *Away, away, away.* She couldn't bear to think about what she had done to Chase, nor what it meant. Not now, at least.

At some point, she noticed that the terrain had become rather rough on their path, frequented with sharp outcrops and rocky trails. The sky had become bleak, with clouds of pale gray shielding the earth from sunlight. As they went, it grew ominously darker until the clouds were almost black. The air smelled heavily of rain, and thunder sounded in the distance.

Devon and Fin began to walk slower, as did Tetoviran and Rebel, until the entire group was walking together in one cluster.

Rebel whined. "It's going to rain, Tara."

She nodded absentmindedly, watching the sky as the clouds grew darker yet. Tetoviran glanced down. "What'd the pig say?" Rebel looked curiously at Tara. "What'd the man say?"

When Tara translated, Rebel snorted in outrage. "Pig? I'm not a pig! I'm a *tesko.* A monster. You'd be quaking in your boots by now if you knew what was good for you, old man. You should be terrified!"

Tara barely lifted the corner of her mouth to smile.

Teto rolled his eyes. "I can't understand you, pipsqueak." Tara told Rebel once more what Teto had said, and the young monster began ranting angrily again, but Tara stopped listening.

"Chase," she whispered. "Is the sky supposed to get that dark?"

Chase shook his head. "No. I…I've never seen anything like this."

"We must be heading for a pretty serious storm," Fin commented worriedly.

Even Tetoviran and Rebel stopped bantering to glance skyward. "Whoa," Teto breathed when he saw the clouds. "What *is* that?"

"It's the sky."

Teto glared at Fin. "I see that, Blondie. But it's still late afternoon. The sky isn't supposed to be *black.*"

Rebel wrinkled his nose. "The air smells bad," he said.

Tara turned to look down at him. "What does it smell like, Rebel?" "Bad stuff." "Like what?" "Bad stuff."

Tara smiled through lightly clenched teeth, trying to remain patient. He was just a baby, after all. "What does the bad stuff smell like?" "Bad stuff. What else would it smell like?"

"Rebel, what kind of bad stuff do you smell?" "All kinds." "Like what?" "Bad stuff."

Tara shrieked in frustration, trying not to pull her hair out. The others looked on as though she was crazy, which probably seemed quite apparent at the moment.

"Like monsters."

Tara stopped fuming for a moment and looked down. "What?"

"It smells like monsters. But not the normal kind. It smells like… the bad kind." Tara stared at Rebel. Weren't all monsters bad? "Are *teskos* the bad kind?"

Rebel shook his head. "No. The bad kind are much worse." The little *tesko* burrowed his face into the crook of Tara's arm. "And I smell them. Lots of them."

Tara quickly translated to her friends. Fin frowned. "Monsters that an indestructible killing machine is afraid of? I don't think I want to meet them."

Tara shot him a look and picked up Rebel defensively. "Rebel's not a killing machine." "Yes, but he's a monster nonetheless, and if there's something out there that makes him turn tail and run, I don't want to meet it."

Thunder boomed again, and Tara held Rebel closer to her chest. Chase was still watching the sky. "Funny," he mumbled.

"What?" Tara, Fin, Devon, and Teto asked simultaneously. "The sky. It's black, and the clouds are thick. Thunder's rumbling, too. But there's no sign of rain. The air's thick with the scent of a storm, but nothing's happening."

The group was moving very slowly now, all five of them on end.

A hawk flew by overhead and screeched, and everyone jumped—even Chase. That was not a comforting sign for Tara, who had rarely seen something surprise Chase Onaj enough to make him flinch. Everyone was on high alert, but Tara couldn't really tell why.

She opened her mouth to say something, but Devon silenced her. "Shh. Can't you feel it?"

"Feel what?" she whispered.

"The tension."

Chase nodded, turning slowly to walk backwards, his hand on his sword hilt. "We're being watched. I can sense it."

Rebel pressed closer to Tara's chest. "The monsters are close, Tara. Really close." She hugged his little body tighter and tried to slow her breathing.

A twig snapped in a small grove of trees to the left of the path, and Devon, Teto, and Chase drew their swords simultaneously as Fin nocked an arrow in his bow. Tara jumped, more so from the quick brandishing of so many weapons than from the sound in the trees. The four of them stood, silent and waiting, each one watching the trees where the sound had come from. For a moment, everything was quiet. The silence was heavy and thick in the air, as though a heavy blanket of suspense had been dropped upon them.

Another twig snapped. And another, and another, as the underbrush in the trees began to rustle softly. Chase took a slow, careful step forward, turning his blade. The rustling grew slightly louder, but he didn't back away. He cast a warning glance back at Tara as Rebel began to cry loudly.

"They're so close, Tara! So close!" Despite his protests, Tara gently eased him into her knapsack and softly spoke to him. "Stay quiet, Rebel. We'll protect you."

The rustling grew louder and more intense, and soft sounds like muted hissing came with it, also growing more audible by the moment. The language was foreign, even to Tara's ears. Fin shot her a questioning glance, and she shook her head. She couldn't understand a word.

Chase took yet another step forward, hesitating slightly as the noises grew louder. He cast a look back at Tara and frowned at her empty hands. The look he gave her was so disapproving that it hurt. She still didn't have the guts to hold a sword in her hand after all this time, but his disappointment was enough motivation.

She took a slow breath and reached for her sword. Her real sword, not the wooden practice one. *This* was real. This was not practice. Her fingers closed around the handle, and she paused. She could do this. Finally exhaling, she pulled the blade from its sheath, and, as she did, she felt a strange sense of community with the people around her. They were protecting one another, it seemed, and she was a part of that in the same way as everyone else.

Together, with weapons in hand, the five of them advanced slowly on the source of the noise. The sounds grew louder and louder with every step they took, until they were standing mere feet away and no one could hear themself exhale.

And then the noise ceased. Silence filled the air for a millisec-ond, and Tara let her muscles go slack as she peered forward with curiosity. But Chase put his arm out. "It's not over." And the sky exploded.

CHAPTER 18

Lightning hit so fast, Chase didn't have time to think. The blast of electricity struck at the speed of sound, and the trees it hit caught fire twice as fast. From the flames sprouted the sources of all the rustling—ten ghost-like apparitions, each practically translucent but the color of dark blood. They surged and expanded in the flames. Each was dressed in the faint suggestions of cloaks that cascaded over wine-colored gowns. Chase had never seen anything like them before. Their hissing and indecipherable whispering was haunting, and Chase felt chilled from merely listening to this language. He couldn't understand the words, but they spoke of darkness. That much could be felt.

The phantoms had wild hair and yellow eyes with black irises that seemed to swirl with a constant motion of their own. They held no weapons, and their rotting, molded skeletons were clearly visible through their clothing.

Chase noticed something peculiar about them, though: they clawed at him and hissed with aggression, but they never moved out of the flames. More than once, a ghost grew impatient and reached out for him but screeched and recoiled at the touch of air. Straying outside of the fire seemed to burn or poison them, confining them to their hellish homes.

They shrieked and screamed as the fire began to spread, and more of the spirits protruded from the growing flames.

At one point, Chase made the horrible mistake of looking one in the eyes. They began to suck him in like black holes. His logical side told him to look away, but for some reason, he couldn't. Darkness seemed so inviting. Serving the cause of evil… after all, he was one of them. He was a thief, a person of crime and deceit, a person who had grown to loathe the "good" people, the "righteous" people. The opportunity to get his revenge was right in front of him. The power of darkness was all his. Why not claim it? Why keep fighting the evil when evil always wins? Why not join the victorious side?

An indecipherable voice whispered in Chase's ears, but the ghost's mouth didn't move. Just eye contact. Those swirling, black eyes, staring unblinkingly at no one, nothing but him. They cared for him. They welcomed him. So few ever welcomed him. The fire flared towards him, getting closer as the heat became unbearable. He began to sweat, yet he moved closer still. He had always wondered what it felt like to touch fire. Didn't everyone? He longed to know…

"No!" Tetoviran cried out, slapping him across the face and breaking his eye contact with the ghoul. Chase stumbled backwards dizzily, barely able to hear Tetoviran as he spoke. "They're Hell's servants, you idiot. Fire demons. They hypnotize you into stepping into flame with them; then they torture you before pulling you back to Hell's domain. You serve an eternity of slavery there."

Chase's breath hitched as his consciousness began returning. So close… that had been *so close*. And those eyes…

He shook his head, cheek stinging, and quickly surveyed the scene. Fin was in a trance, trudging drunkenly toward the flames with his bow cast carelessly aside. Tara and Devon stood back-to-back, their swords at the ready but completely useless against the fire.

Chase returned to Tetoviran. "You get Fin. I have an idea." Teto nodded and ran off toward Fin while Chase hurried in the opposite direction. He reached Tara and Devon and gently slapped each of their shoulders, turning them to face him. "I know how to beat these things. We have to"—

He was cut off by Fin running up to him in near hysterics after breaking away from his hypnosis. "The demons… the hellish things… Life, Chase, I nearly…"

"Calm down," Devon interrupted, laying a firm hand on his shoulder. "You're fine." Fin nodded shakily, still panting, when Chase heard an eerily cheerful tune in the midst of this hypnotic inferno. He turned to see Tetoviran standing behind him and whistling. Chase stared at him. Actually *whistling*. "Tetoviran, what are you doing?"

"What do you mean, what am I doing? I'm staying calm. That's what everyone always tells me to do in an emergency."

Chase put his head in his hands, then spotted something through his fingers. "Fin! Save your bow!" The flames were licking dangerously close to the boy's weapon. With a yelp, Fin scrambled to save it and got there just in time, quickly retreating from the flames. He kissed the bow and slung it over his shoulder.

Once they were all standing together again, Chase got down to business. "These things can only live in fire. The more the flames spread, the more phantoms come. We need to get to the stream we passed. If the fire's put out, we're safe."

"Can't we just run?" Fin asked.

"And let this thing burn? Hardly. We need water." The others nodded. "Oh, and something else. Don't look into their eyes. Ever."

With that, the group raced down to the bottom of a gentle slope in the land where a small stream tumbled along, peaceful as ever amidst the inferno raging at the top of the hill. The group formed a transportation line that kept movement minimal, with

Chase filling wineskins and passing them to Fin, who passed them to Devon, and so on until that water was tossed onto the flames. The empty ones were cycled back again.

After several trips up and down to meet Fin, however, Chase's legs were aching and threatening to collapse when he pushed them too fast. The others were slowing as well, and despite their efforts, the fire seemed no smaller than before. In fact, it seemed to be spreading more quickly now. Chase also noticed that the flames seemed to follow them wherever they went. They were spreading more slowly than they could run but gaining nonetheless.

Finally, he gathered everyone into a huddle again. "This isn't working," he gasped, out of breath. "We're never going to get anything done like that."

Tara leaned forward on her knees; her curly hair was matted with sweat. "What if we tried to kill them with weapons?" she gasped. Devon shook his head. "This is a fight we can't win with swords, or arrows, and your powers don't extend over fire." He was almost shouting to be heard over the earsplitting sounds of hissing phantoms. "Water isn't working, either. This takes brains, and nothing more. We just need to come up with a plan."

Tetoviran grunted. "Good luck, kiddos. The fire just surrounded us." Everyone looked up to find that the flames had indeed somehow formed a ring around them, licking the sky at heights impossible to jump.

"Don't look for that long!" Chase shouted at all of them, hitting the heads of Devon and Fin hard towards the ground. "You'll catch their eyes."

Tara was wringing her hands frantically. "Uh, Chase?" she asked, her voice on the verge of panic. "We're trapped, you know. Very much unable to go anywhere or get any help, very much about to *die!*"

Devon snapped his fingers suddenly. "I've got it! Tara, use your powers to turn up the earth. The dirt will smother the flames."

"And swallow us with it!" Fin hissed.

"Only if you can," Devon added, ignoring Fin. He and Tara seemed locked together for a moment. "Please, please try."

Tara nodded, taking a slow breath. "Okay." She closed her eyes and went silent, leaving the rustling language of the ghouls to fill the space.

Chase ground his teeth together anxiously. He could feel the heat rising around them, and the smoke was strong enough to make his eyes water. They didn't have time for Tara to stand there doing nothing. His fists clenched impatiently with the desire to do something. Anything to help them survive.

"I…" Tara's voice came, straining through a sharp breath. Everyone looked to her hopefully, but her eyes fell open in despair. "I can't." Fin released a laugh humorless enough that the devil might approve.

"I'm sorry," Tara whispered, barely loud enough to be heard, and Chase's heart thrummed through his chest. She thought they were going to die. But didn't he? They were out of tricks and completely helpless. All of them were forced to stare at their feet to avoid making eye contact with the innumerable phantoms swirling around them. Some were getting bolder, too, bearing the pain of reaching out of the flames for longer periods of time before wrenching back to safety.

A strange sound, different from the voices of the ghouls, suddenly reached Chase's ears. It sounded like some sort of animal snorting and grunting. Momentary panic flared in him until he realized that it was Rebel. Tara was communicating back with him as naturally as if it were her own language.

Rebel, Chase thought suddenly. His head clung to that as if it was important, but he couldn't figure out why. What could Rebel do for them? Suddenly, he gasped, feeling like an idiot. "Tara! Tara, your *tesko!*" he said rapidly, scrambling for words. "Take… take him, he'll eat it! He eats, right? Everything? The fire, have him eat the fire!"

Tara stared at him as though he was crazy for a moment, trying to pick apart the words that had flown right over one another. "Make him eat the fire," he pronounced frantically. A heat wave blasted him in the face, and he shielded himself behind his shoulder. "Hurry up!"

"No! He's too young!" she cried back.

"I don't care!" he all but screamed back.

"Do it, Tara!" Tetoviran agreed, breaking off halfway through with a cough. "He's indestructible! He can't get hurt!"

There was a pause, and Chase was nearly ready to strangle Tara for wasting so much time when she reached behind her and pulled Rebel from her knapsack. "He said he can do it," she said, her voice laced with anxiety as she set him on the ground.

The small animal looked around, then tossed his head and growled fearsomely. Chase couldn't see what was going on beyond his feet, but he heard the wails of the ghouls and felt the heat of the flames. Rebel left their feet and ran off towards the fire, leaving Chase's line of sight. He heard a snarl to his left and the shriek of a phantom, followed quickly by a sharp yelp from Rebel. Tara clutched his arm, and he laced his fingers roughly through hers. The heat grew more intense, and Chase began to sweat as he felt Tara's fingers slip with moisture on his knuckles. He swept his other hand across his forehead and gripped the hilt of his sword until he thought his muscles would cramp. *Come on, Rebel,* he thought. He hated every bit of this, every bit of being so helplessly dependent on someone else.

The flames cackled closer, and the agonized cries of the demons became more and more audible.

Devon, who was standing a few steps away, suddenly shouted a curse and leapt into Chase frantically. Chase stumbled backwards from the impact and was saved from falling into the fire only by Tara's firm grip on his hand as she scrambled to pull him towards her. "What in the name of"—

"I got burned," Devon panted. Chase's head was spinning from fear and heat. He got burned? The fire was *that* close? For what was probably the first time in his life, Chase sent up a silent prayer. To whom, he didn't know or care. He just hoped somebody was listening.

Just when Chase thought he might faint from overheating, the wailing suddenly became half as loud as before. There was a series of sharp hisses, but these had a different tone to them: something like panic. All the heat on the left side of Chase's body was extinguished entirely as he heard a growl from Rebel. He welcomed the cooling air with a gulp of relief. Maybe… just maybe…

Chase's eyes began to clear with hope. That little monster just might come through.

The wailing subsided more and more with the heat, but still no one dared look up. There was a ravaging snarl and the sound of high-pitched shrieks in response. An animalistic cry. A flare of the wind, as though fire had swelled rapidly. And then, just as quickly as it had begun, the noise stopped with one final wail.

Slowly, and cautiously at first, Chase raised his head. The ground all around them was burnt and blackened to a crisp, and smoke trailed from the skeletal trees into the sky. Heat waves bounced off of everything and blurred the air, but the fire was, indeed, put out entirely.

Chase nearly fell to his knees in disbelief. He had been sure they were doomed. Sitting in the middle of this all was a little *tesko,* belching puffs of smoke and licking a blackened patch of fur on his back haunch.

Tara rushed forward in such haste that she tripped over her own feet and stumbled woozily from the heat damage to her head. She fell upon the little creature and squeezed him in an embrace. "You did it! You did it, Rebel! Oh, thank Life, I'm so proud of you!"

Fin threw his head back and breathed the air, smoky as it still was, and Teto crouched down and ruffled Rebel's fur. "You know, you're not the bloodthirsty monster I pegged you for. You're one brave little *tesko.*"

Tara smiled as Rebel lifted his head proudly at the praising voices surrounding him.

Chase laughed aloud in relief, then cast a glance at Devon, who had remained on his knees since the fire had been put out. Unravelling his waterskin from his belt, he walked over to him. "Where were you burned?"

Devon fell from his knees to his rear, sitting on the ground with his left leg outstretched. A hole had been burnt through the lower leg of his pants there, the material around it blackened. The skin showing through the opening was raised and white in a blister that turned the surrounding flesh bright red. "Blasted thing," Devon hissed softly.

Chase winced at the sight and opened his wineskin, pouring water onto the bottom of his shirt until the fabric was soaked through. He pressed the material to the skin until his shirt grew hot, then wet another piece of the fabric and applied the fresh one. Devon's fingers, which had been curled into the ashy earth to withstand the pain, slowly loosened as the burn was soothed.

The others were still celebrating their survival, and by the time they noticed what had happened, the skin was warm, rather than scorching, and Devon claimed the pain was much better.

Chase stood in satisfaction and wrung out his shirt, then put away his waterskin as Devon stood up. He shook his legs and jumped a few times, then smiled. "See that, stupid fire? Good as new."

Chase nudged Tara's arm. "Hey. Look at the sky." They all looked up and saw that the clouds were no longer black, but a normal, rainy gray. A cold drop of water hit the bridge of Chase's nose, and Tara laughed. "Well, we should probably find shelter."

A light drizzle began to surround them, chasing off the smell of smoke. Devon shook his head suddenly. "No. We have to keep traveling."

Fin frowned. "Why? Pretty soon it's going to be storming out here. Besides, it's already dusk. We need our rest."

Devon squinted up at the sky. "Haven't you traveled before? We have a place to be, and it would be ideal to reach that place before a century has come and gone. We've already been delayed so many times, it's amazing we're all still young. Rain is nothing. It shouldn't slow us down."

"Good thing I grabbed these earlier, then," Tetoviran said abruptly, pulling three thick, dry sticks from his pack. Within a few moments, they were alight and serving Devon, Tetoviran, and Chase as torches to help them see through the darkness. As soon as Devon had his light, he began to walk, his feet crunching twigs and gravel in his path as the steady pitter-patter of rain grew louder. There wasn't so much as a limp to his gait, despite the burn he had suffered. Chase chewed his lip curiously. Devon didn't seem strong, but he was. He was amazingly tough.

Tetoviran shivered. "It may be better for us to keep moving," he agreed. "I'm getting cold from sweat, and we need to keep our body heat. Besides, Blondie over there is starting to look like a limp noodle with overcooked broccoli for arms." Tara looked at Fin's ripped biceps and lifted an eyebrow as Tetoviran continued. "He needs to build up muscle or he'll never amount to anything. Then again, kid probably wouldn't amount to much either way."

"Now listen here"— Fin began angrily, and the two walked off bickering, the rain bouncing off their backs as though it didn't exist in their quarrel.

Tara turned to Chase. "What do you think?" Chase frowned. "I… I'm not really sure. Continuing to travel is fine by me. Devon's right. We do need to move faster. It's just…"

"What?"

Chase shook his head. "Probably nothing." *Probably?* He offered a tired half smile. "It's nothing." Her eyes darted around nervously, and he tossed his arm lightly around her shoulder.

"Don't worry about it, Princess." She slid a glance behind them, and he hit her jaw gently with his shoulder, pushing her head forward again. "There's nothing back there but rain."

A gust of cold wind hit them in the face, slicing against their skin. Chase tucked his chin into his jacket, and Tara squeezed Rebel tighter in her arms and leaned against Chase's chest, using him as a windbreak. As the winds died down, Chase tugged her ahead. "Come on. We can't fall behind."

The rain was cold on his body, and his sweat from the fire was drying coolly on his skin beneath his clothing. He shivered. Tara cast a glance behind her once more, and Chase finally took his arm out from around her and used it to shove her away from him. Caught off guard, she stumbled backwards into a tree and barely saved herself from falling.

"How many times, Princess? You're scaring yourself over nothing. There's nothing there." She gave him a look after she recovered. "Chase, if there wasn't anything there, you never would've said something."

Yes, that was true. And he knew that there really *was* something there—or had been, just moments ago when he'd heard it—but Tara didn't need to know that. It didn't seem to be a threat, and there were few signs of it now.

"What, after three tiny attacks you're trying to say that you don't trust me anymore? This is *me* we're talking about. Chase, the gallant knight and fearless warrior who has saved you from blizzards, monsters, injuries, the wrath of wind"—

As if proving his point, another gust blew in, and Tara stumbled to his side as her hair whipped about her head. He smirked down at her. "And epic destruction. After everything we've been through? You can't back out on me now, I'm far too handsome."

"Of all the ridiculous"— "Be quiet, you fool, I'm trying to brag." She rolled her eyes and slid a now slumbering Rebel into her knapsack as Chase prattled on about himself. "Why, I even lent you my own strength once! My very soul!" To that, she gave him a solid punch in the stomach before continuing to ensure that Rebel was comfortable. Chase only continued as though nothing had happened.

Finally, he stopped and shook his head, a thin smile on his face. "Honestly, Princess. There's nothing to worry about. Trust me on this, okay?"

She looked at him hesitantly through the rain, the orange light of his torch playing across her wet skin, then nodded. "Sure." "All right, then, come on," he said, waving the torch towards her as if threatening to burn her with it. "We've got to catch up."

They jogged ahead together until they were walking behind the others again. The rain was coming in heavy sheets now, and everyone's hair was matted to their heads. Raindrops ran down Tara's face, and she wiped at her eyes often, leaving her eyelashes bejeweled with water droplets. Everyone fell gradually into silence, trudging quietly along and trying to scout out what was ahead of them.

While the others seemed to be falling asleep on their feet as they kept moving, Chase stayed alert. He knew he hadn't just been hearing things. There had been someone—or something—back there, and nothing else was sneaking up on them today.

They walked on for what must've been hours, until the rain was so heavy no one could see three paces ahead. Chase's feet ached and his back was sore. He could only imagine how Devon must feel with his blister. The others were groaning with fatigue and Tara's stomach rumbled loudly enough to be heard over the slapping of rain against earth.

At last, Devon halted. "We can stop here. Everyone's tired, and the weather's only getting worse. Divide and scout for shelter. A cave would be ideal. We'd all prefer to stay dry while we sleep tonight."

Chase bit his tongue softly at the commanding tone of his voice. Since when had he become the leader? He stopped his own train of thought in dismay. *Who even cares?* he thought in perplexity. It didn't matter who gave out orders; he agreed with them, anyway.

The group separated and went off in pairs. Chase went along with Fin. Together, they walked wearily through the sludgy soil, which clung to their boots in clumps of thick mud.

"'Keep traveling', he says," Fin muttered, mostly to himself. "Well, who bloody put him in charge? My socks are soaked though, and my boots are as good as ruined." He flicked wet hair out of his eyes and quickened his pace. "Come on. I want to get out of this rain as soon as possible."

Chase nodded. He did, too, but for an entirely different reason. Through the storm, he heard bushes rustling in ways that didn't match up with the way the wind blew. He heard quiet coughing and muffled yelps when it sounded as though their follower had tripped. Whatever had been behind them earlier, it had kept up. Chase eyed Fin, but he was too absorbed in finding shelter to take notice of anything other than his chilled feet.

Chase moved quicker, pausing every so often to loop around a tree or brush leaves over his footsteps in the sludge. However hard he tried to throw their tracker off his trail, though, the person managed to stay with him. It had to be a result of his torch, but he couldn't snuff the fire; they wouldn't be able to see.

Fin squinted through the hazy sheets of rain. "There!" he cried out, and Chase immediately cringed at the loudness of his voice. The footsteps behind him halted.

Chase stood directly in front of a thick tree shadowed deeply from the storm. He felt hot breath on the back of his neck and stepped purposely on a twig, causing the breathing to stop abruptly. Keeping one hand on his sheathed sword, he swept the torch behind him as if searching the woods for something. In reality, he was hoping to get the flames close enough to the person behind him to scare them off.

Fin ran forward, but Chase didn't move. "A cave! I see a cave, Chase! Oh, finally! Quickly, get inside and start a fire. I'll go back and tell the others."

Chase nodded and, with a sudden idea, stepped forward. "Thank Life on the Thrones! My feet are killing me."

Fin grinned through the rain. "Not for long! I'll be back in a few minutes."

"Great. I'll start collecting wood." Chase hurried through a small grove in front of the cave, then crouched down behind a tree. He swore aloud and concealed his torchlight in front of his body, away from the view of his pursuer. "Stupid thing," he said loudly. "Now I can't see." Once he was sure that the firelight wasn't visible to anyone behind him, he picked up a good-sized stone and hurled it as hard as he could in the other direction. It rolled, bounced, and rustled through the underbrush.

It was night, and the trees concealed the ground in shadows, so the noise the stone made sounded just like feet tramping through the bushes. The stone rolled further away, and the sound faded to a stop at such a perfect distance, it sounded like someone had simply gone too far to be heard any longer. Then Chase crouched, holding his breath, waiting. Rain still hit his face, but he barely noticed it. All he heard was the breathing, although a bit further away now, begin again where he'd formerly been standing. And then, sure enough, a figure emerged from the trees.

He moved silently to stand behind the tree, still hiding his torch as he observed what he could. From the looks of the silhouette—which was about all he could make out without revealing his position—it was a girl, perhaps a bit younger than him and uncommonly thin. She appeared to be barefoot, and loose material like an imitation of trousers clung to her legs. They were ripped off at the bottoms, and her hair seemed to be of medium length.

She moved slowly and cautiously, checking behind her frequently. As she approached his hiding spot, he thought quickly about what to do. She seemed to be a mere village girl who'd lost her way. She was no threat to him or anyone else. He should just let her be. But then that same small voice that he'd heard in Iravvai whispered in his ear, tickling the back of his mind. *Never underestimate your opponent.* She had followed them for a reason. He narrowed his eyes at the figure moving towards him, examining her more closely.

She was certainly aware of her surroundings, and she cringed every time she heard herself make a noise. She was now a very short distance from his hiding spot. Chase sucked in a silent breath, contemplating what to do. Finally, he decided that he could take no chances. When she finally was right in front of him, he tensed, waiting for just the right moment…

He leapt out at her from the shadows, jumping upon her and tackling her to the ground—somewhat impressively, in his opinion, considering he kept his torch above them both in one hand and held her with the other. She screamed and writhed as he forced her onto her stomach with his knees and pinned an arm behind her back. "Help! Help me!" she screamed, but there was, of course, no response.

"Who are you?" he yelled. She continued to scream. "Someone, please! Help!"

He gave her arm a sharp jerk, and she cried out in a yelp of pain. In the firelight of his torch, Chase saw that her skin was cinnamon-toned and frequented with scratches or messy cuts. Her cheekbones were very defined and her eyes deep-set and dark. He had never seen a person of her features anywhere near Jisara and vaguely wondered where she was from. "Stop! Please, stop! Help!"

"Who are you?" Chase demanded again, holding her firm. Her bare foot made contact with his knee, and he bit back a curse, wrenching her arm harder. "Tell me who you are, now!" The girl screamed again, and he inhaled in irritation.

He dug his torch into the wet soil beside him and let it burn there, then let his free hand go to his sword. He slowly drew it and the blade scraped against the sheath, and the girl stopped her hollering. He casually turned the blade, letting the rain drip down the steel. The flickering torchlight reflected off the silver. "If I were you," Chase said in a deadly casual tone, "I would talk. But the choice is all yours."

She kicked him again. "You can't make me!" He laughed and twirled his sword with lightning speed to rest the edge of it on the back of her neck. One motion of his wrist, and she would be dead. "You want to bet on that?"

The girl swallowed audibly, and he almost smiled. He often scared himself with the amount of pleasure he felt at having a person at his mercy. Whether most people would call that monstrous or not, he didn't really care. It was fun.

"Fine," she said at last. "M-my name is Grace Thoral. I've been out here for days, all alone, and when I saw you, I decided that maybe… well, I was hoping I could get some food."

Chase had to bite his lip to keep from grinning. Little thief, then, and a poor one, too. "By stealing?" She was quiet. He prodded further. "Who else is out there?"

"No one," she replied instantly. "I promise. I never meant you any harm. I was never going to hurt anyone."

Chase lifted his head at the sound of footsteps, pulling his sword away enough to allow Grace to do the same. Fin was back—and the others were with him. Chase hefted the girl to her feet, holding his sword across her stomach.

Fin held his arrow drawn tight in his bow, aimed at Grace's head and threatening to fly at any second. Three sharp blades glinted in the hands of the rest—even Tara's.

Devon smiled. "My, my, my. This is an unexpected surprise."

CHAPTER 19

"**H**ow did you get out here?" Grace shifted uncomfortably in Chase's grasp. Tara, Tetoviran, Devon, and Fin were crowded around a warm, hearty fire that crackled and sparked with warmth as the rain raged outside. Their cave was bright and dry, and they'd unrolled their blankets to sit around the flames. Rebel snored softly by the fire, mumbling in his sleep. After everything had been set up in their little shelter, everyone had seated themselves in a circle around the blaze and interrogated the newcomer. In the light, Tara could see that she was very beautiful. Her obsidian black eyes glinted sharply, and her high cheekbones highlighted dark skin.

Chase was sitting cross-legged, holding Grace's arms pinned behind her back with one hand and looking mildly bored. She was so skinny that he could encompass both of her wrists in his palm. She sat beside his knee and kept trying to edge away from him—probably more out of fear than anything. She kept glancing warily at the sword in his other hand, and Tara smiled, remembering those first couple of days when she'd believed he might hurt her with that blade.

Chase nudged the small of the girl's back with his knee. "He asked you a question."

"And I have no intention of answering it."

"Answering our questions is not optional." "Then I suppose there is no option for me to speak."

"You have a lot of mouth for someone in your position."

Grace thrust out her jaw and stared at him coldly.

Chase narrowed his eyes and laid his sword across her chest. Tara's smile faded as she watched. "Do you want a taste of this blade?" he asked quietly. "Not particularly, no. Metal tastes horrible."

Chase curled his lip. "You sound like you have experience." "Well, they wouldn't be so bad if you put a little salt on them."

Devon snorted, but Chase lifted his chin and glared at Grace darkly. "You're very, very lucky I'm in a good mood tonight."

"What do your bad days look like?"

"If this were one of them, you'd be out in the storm right now."

"I'd much rather be out there than in here with all you idiots. None of you even have families or a place to call home. Not to say that I can blame people for rejecting you. You are without doubt the most pathetic group I've ever seen."

Chase grabbed her by the collar of her shirt and yanked her close to him so she was forced to look him right in the eye. "You, Grace Thoral, are lucky for another thing, too. You're lucky you aren't dead. Because if I was any other person in this world, I would've killed you by now. But instead, you're here in our cave, by our fire, with our blankets wrapped around you. We're also feeding you with *our* food. You have no right to talk back to me or anyone else, and if you think for one second that I'm going to tolerate you acting like a brat, then think again. I'm sick of banter, and if there's one more word out of line from that blasted mouth of yours, you're getting thrown in the dirt with a few new scars." He spat the last word in her face, and pushed her roughly away from him, dumping her to the floor of the cave. She grunted and sat up slowly.

Fin asked again. "How did you get out here?"

She just stared at him. "Well?" Chase sighed, unfolded his legs, and stood up, holding his sword tip leveled at her face. "You know, I'm getting really fed up with you. Talk to us!"

She shook her head, scowling indignantly. "You told me not another word. I clearly can't say the right thing, so perhaps it would be better if I said nothing at all."

"Quite," Chase growled, "the contrary." Grace didn't respond beyond a cool gaze. Chase took a step forward and dug his sword tip under her chin. She backed up against the stone wall of the cave in panic, arching her neck to get a breath. "Talk."

"A-alright, fine, if you want to be mean about it. I wanted to get out of my village, so I snuck out of my home and followed my father and brothers on a hunting trip. I branched off after a while and got lost. When I saw you, I thought… well, I could eat. The food you gave me was the first meal I've had since I left home." She glanced at the blade, then back up at Chase. "Thank you," she mumbled.

He lifted an eyebrow, leaning a little closer. "What was that?" Grace leaned forward angrily, as if to get up. "I'm not repeating it! You don't deserve it, the way you've treated me!"

Chase dug the tip of the blade further under her chin, and she drew in a breath, fear finally edging into her eyes. "One more time, darling." She stared down the length of the blade, then finally rolled her eyes. "Thank you," she said, loud and clear, her voice choking as her throat convulsed immediately afterwards. Chase tilted his head in satisfaction and pulled his sword away. Grace's hand flew to her throat and massaged it until her breathing slowed again.

Chase straightened and twirled his sword in his hand, and Tara blew out a sigh of relief. Despite his murderous expression, Chase's habits showed through. He wasn't planning on harming this girl.

Tetoviran slurped his tea loudly while Chase paced back and forth slowly in front of Grace. She sat shivering against the wall on the floor, looking up at him timidly.

"Please don't hurt me," she stammered finally, changing tactics. Tara arched an eyebrow. She had certainly gotten a quick sense of humility. "I won't pretend to respect any of you, but I know I don't stand a chance if I run or fight. I won't cause you any trouble from now on. Just let me live." She hesitated before reaching out to touch Chase's leg. He had been ignoring her completely while she'd talked, and now he looked down at her sharply. "Please," she implored him.

He eyed her emotionlessly, then pulled away. He turned his pacing away from her, not breaking stride but smirking at Tara as he walked past her. She couldn't help but roll her eyes. He was really *proud* of how badly he'd scared Grace.

Finally, he stopped and turned to face the stranger, his expression deadly again. "We're not just going to take you in, Thoral. You need to know that before anything. We'll talk about it together and make a decision. For tonight, you can stay here." Grace let out a huge breath of relief. "Thank you! Oh, thank you so much!" She rushed to her feet.

"But," Chase continued, pushing her back down to the floor with only one arm, "You aren't free to say or do whatever you want. You aren't getting any more food or drink than you've had. You can sleep by the fire and use these blankets, but your opinion—or eavesdropping—will not be tolerated in any of tonight's conversations. Basically, if you speak or act out of turn, you're out of this cave, out of our lives; possibly out of yours. Do I make myself clear?"

Grace nodded vigorously. "Yes, of course. Thank you so much. Thank you, thank you, thank"—

"Quiet! That's enough. You're going to give me a headache."

He sheathed his sword, a frown on his face, then turned to her. "I'm Chase." He jerked his head toward the others, who in turn introduced themselves.

Grace nodded curtly to each of them and crawled with obvious fatigue to the fire. Laying down beside it, she curled her body up in an effort to leave as much room as possible for the others. She pulled the thinnest of the blankets over herself and watched the flames dance in front of her face. Tara studied her carefully. At least she knew *how* to be humble. Rebel opened an eye, saw Grace lying there, and dragged himself to his feet. The others watched as the little *tesko* shuffled up to Grace and dropped his small body with a huff in the crook of her arm. Grace smiled and stroked Rebel's head as he drifted back to sleep. She looked up and saw everyone watching her, and she offered a small smile. Tara returned it; Chase kicked her lightly for that. Grace's eyes, which had lit up slightly at Tara's sign of friendship, shuttered at Chase's hostile actions. She closed her eyes with a creased brow, and within minutes her breathing became steady with slumber. Her facial muscles relaxed as she fell out of this world.

Tara remained seated, watching Grace thoughtfully as the boys filled a small dish with water to shave. The soft splashing of water and low mumbling of their conversation were the only sounds besides the crackling fire and pouring rain. Fin laughed at something someone had said, and Devon splashed his face with clean water from a flask. Tetoviran emptied the water outside when they were finished and left it out to collect rainwater.

Chase sat down next to Tara and warmed his hands by the flames. "You didn't have to do that," Tara mumbled, still thinking of the disappointment on Grace's face before she'd fallen asleep.

"Nonsense, you're just too nice. She ought to know she's not welcome. Besides, it was funny." His grumpy façade had vanished, replaced now by the boyishness that tempted him to light sticks on fire and wave them around to make shadows dance on the cave walls.

Tara couldn't help smiling as he entertained himself, but he soon grew bored with this and began to eat instead. The wind howled at the mouth of the cave, but it was decently warmed inside. Tara turned her face away from the flames for a moment to cool her skin, then laid out flat on the floor and sighed tiredly. Fin, Devon, and Tetoviran mumbled amongst themselves, but Chase sat silently now, twisting a silver ring around his finger, then pulling it off and tossing it aside as though it was a worthless piece of junk.

He noticed Tara watching him and gave her a lopsided smile. "What?"

"You're a pretty good actor, you know that?"

"Well, of course I know that. Poor girl was scared to death." He chuckled softly and stretched his legs out. "Almost felt sorry for the little horror."

"She *was* being rude, though," Tara said, sitting up again.

Chase nodded. "Yes, but she reminded me of myself. All she needed was to be set in her place. I think she'll be fine."

Tara snorted. "You still need to be set in your place."

Chase grinned. "Top of the food chain, Princess. I'm standing in it." She rolled her eyes as he continued. "You're way down there." He pointed to the ground, then poked her belly. "Everything else eats you up."

"Uh-huh, until this little trinket"—she held up her necklace— "lights up, and I bury you alive under the earth."

Chase whistled lowly. "Dark humor, huh? Well, if we're going in that direction, why don't you just kill me from within while you're at it? Little bit of power abuse never hurt anybody, right, miss torture master?" He spread his arms. "Look at my weak little human body, just waiting for you to shred it to bloody pieces."

Tara gasped, her stomach rolling sickly at the description. "I said I was sorry a thousand times, Chase! I would never do that!"

"Oh, take a joke, Princess."

She frowned grumpily. "I would, if you made funny ones."

He smiled, pushing her jaw gently with his fist. "I'm impressed, by the way." He unsheathed his sword and twirled it, spinning it dangerously close to his nose. "You drew your sword twice today. Congratulations."

Tara bit her cheek. Both times, she'd been terrified, but Chase didn't need to know that. She lifted her chin and nodded. "Yes, I know. I'm quite proud, really."

He laughed and balanced the pommel dangerously on his palm. "Don't even try, Princess. I see fear in your eyes. Even right now." He spun the blade again just as it started to tip off his palm, stopping it inches from her face. She squeaked and then tried to swallow the sound, making a strange, choked noise.

"See? You're never going to get over this."

"What if you made a mistake, though? What if you hadn't stopped your blade just now?" "Then I'd be rid of your endless chattering complaints."

She stuck her tongue out at him. "Oh, that's real mature," he snorted. "Princess, I won't make a mistake."

"But say you did. What then?"

He thought for a moment, his face growing serious. "I really can't say. I mean, there would be so many difficult decisions to make. A giant party, or a smaller event? A colorful theme, or an all-white dress code? Celebrating the death of someone as pitiful and repulsive as you would be a very special occasion."

"Seriously?" "No." "Then what?"

"If I actually killed you?" He exhaled once. "I honestly have no idea, Tara. You're… you're the first person I've ever really cared about." He shot her a quick sideways glance. "If you ever bring this up, to me or anyone else, I'll"— "Kill me?" she asked in amusement.

"Precisely."

"And then spend the rest of your life wallowing in your own despair?"

She had been completely joking—and her tone had clearly implied that—but Chase took a slow breath.

"Perhaps I shouldn't try to talk about this. I'm deathly afraid I might start crying, and if there's one way to wound your pride, it's crying in front of a pretty girl."

There was a moment of silence as Tara registered that. When she did, a smile slid over her face. She lifted her brows at Chase, who was staring straight ahead, smile lines playing around his eyes but his mouth betraying nothing.

"Pretty?" "Hush."

Tara lowered her eyes, a blush creeping up on her. "Thank you," she mumbled. Chase tilted his chin up, considering this, then dropped his face again. He didn't further acknowledge her thanks, and Tara figured that was as far as he was willing to go in the sweet and sappy areas right now. She was wrong.

He drew a sigh. "Tara, I have absolutely no clue what I'd do if I killed you by accident. I can't even fathom the grief, so I only pray I never go through it. But I haven't made a mistake in a pretty good amount of time. I'd say you're safe."

"As would I," she agreed. The corner of his mouth turned up, an easier smirk. "You have faith in me at last, I see."

"I always did. I think I simply doubt you less than I believe in you now."

For a while they just stared at the fire, Chase twirling his sword and lost in thought. "What do *you* think about Grace?" he asked suddenly.

Tara glanced at the girl sleeping across from her. "I think she's... she's okay. She's trying to survive, like the rest of us. She's just really scared. Of course, you didn't help with that very much." Chase smirked as she continued. "But Rebel seems to like her, and she's capable of being modest, too. Perhaps she was only rude to you before because she was afraid of you. After all, you attacked her in the middle of a storm and could've killed her if you'd wanted to. She's probably terrified of you."

He grinned, rubbing his freshly-shaved jaw. "You really think so?"

Tara swatted his arm gently as Tetoviran turned to face them. "What do you two think?" he asked.

Tara looked up. "About what? Grace?"

Fin nodded. "Yeah. What are we going to do with her?"

Chase shrugged. "I'm not really sure. She seems okay. She's younger than most of us, so how much can she be capable of?"

Devon half smiled and fiddled with a piece of wood. "We thought the same thing about Tara."

"And you too, Chase," Fin added. "You said everyone in Jisara thought you were innocent, but while they were busy watching your smile, you were emptying their pockets." He tossed it out in a slightly accusatory tone—probably not on purpose—but Chase just smiled as though it was the best compliment anyone could've given him.

"Yeah, for once the kids are right. This girl could be dangerous." Everyone nodded in agreement with Teto, but Tara intervened.

"We can't just leave her out here. We have to at least escort her to a safer place. A town, maybe, or—better yet—her village. I'm sure her family is worried sick about her."

Devon nodded. "Yes, but we could also bring her with us. Like Fin said, she could be powerful. Think about it. If she has powers—or fighting skills, or anything useful at all—she could help us."

Teto snorted. "That's the dumbest thing I've ever heard! Why would she try to help us, you imbecile? We attacked her, kidnapped her, and forced her to talk like professionals. By the way, how amazing was that? We were sitting there, interrogating her, and when she refused to talk, the kid over there got in her face, yelled at her a bunch, shoved her into a wall… it was spectacular to watch him pretend he's tough."

Chase rolled his eyes, and Tara nodded. "Tetoviran's right. Even though we let her stay and gave her warmth and food and shelter… we were anything but friendly. Maybe we should've considered that," she said, glaring pointedly at Chase.

He shook his head. "She couldn't see us as anything less than strong. Otherwise, she'd try to take advantage of weak points. She had to be afraid, or she would've tried something tricky on us."

"Yes, but now she'll never want to help us," Tara argued.

Devon sighed in exasperation. "Don't any of you have a brain? She's *afraid* of Chase. Scared to death. If he threatens her, she'll do whatever he wants. We can bring her with us, and Chase can make her do whatever we want."

Fin nodded thoughtfully. "That would work." Chase and Tetoviran agreed instantly, but Tara spoke again.

"On one condition." All eyes turned to her. "We can't treat her like a slave. She may be driven out of fear, but we aren't going to take advantage of her. And besides, you never know. She may come to realize that Chase will never really harm her at all and try to get away. We can't make her feel stuck with us, as though she's trapped with no way out. Otherwise, her only goal will be escape. Even if we don't trust her, she has to be treated equally. We needn't necessarily tell her everything yet, but she should at least be accepted as our traveling companion."

The others nodded. "That's fair," Devon said. "Besides, we shouldn't be cruel."

Teto yawned. "Yes, but in the meantime, we all need some rest. Good night, idiots." He paused. "That doesn't include Tara." With that, he plopped his muscular bulk down and began snoring seconds later. Tara just shook her head. He was impossible.

She flattened her own body out on the ground and settled down. Shivers ran along her arms from the cold winds outside, but she was far too tired to get back up to fetch a cover. She decided that she could live without one, and she was just dozing off when she felt the cozy warmth of a blanket on her shoulders.

She looked up through tired eyes to find Chase looking down at her. He crouched to kiss her cheek with warm lips. The kiss was brotherly, but Tara sensed realness in it that was absent from the lavish, lip-locked kisses he handed out to random girls like free food. "We making this a tradition, or what? Are you ever going to get your own blankets?" Tara smiled. "Never." He kicked her in the side, making her yelp and roll away from him. "Yes," she corrected herself, even though the strike hadn't hurt. "I definitely will."

"Good," Chase said with false aggression. There was a pause, and his tone changed. "Good night, Princess."

He stood and walked to the other side of the cave, sitting with his back against the wall of the cave with Devon, who was carving something out of wood. Tara watched them together, talking in hushed tones and helping each other with the careful whittling of the wood. She looked at Tetoviran and Fin snoring by the fire, and then she looked at Grace, still holding a slumbering Rebel in her exhausted arms. She too, was asleep. Tara smiled contentedly and let her eyelids slip closed as she fell away into her dreams.

~

Tara awoke to sunlight filtering into the cave in brilliant rays. The small fire was a blackened pile of twigs, and droplets of water fell off the top of the cave outside from the previous night's rainstorm. Today, the sky was blue, and the air was crisp and fresh. Despite the frigid early-morning temperatures, birds sang their melodious songs. The plants were green and happy from the rain. Everyone else still slumbered, and everything was just as it should be. Yet there was one thing…

Tara gasped. Rebel lay snoring peacefully near the burned-out fire—with a flat blanket next to him. Where was Grace? Tara looked through the whole cave frantically, then roused all her friends. "Up! Up, get up!"

They rose reluctantly, yawning and groaning. "What?" "What's wrong?"

"Grace is missing!"

Immediately all sleepiness was extinguished. Fin rushed to the spot where she'd been sleeping that night. "What? How?"

Devon rushed into his boots, and Tetoviran did the same. "Who was on guard duty?" someone demanded, receiving no response. Nobody had been.

"How long has she been gone?" Chase asked Tara.

"I don't know. I woke up a couple minutes ago and she was just… gone."

He groaned, grumpy from his rude awakening. "Why did she leave?" "Probably because she was *scared.*" Chase blinked, then frowned slowly. "Are you saying this is my fault?"

Fin pushed between them to the mouth of the cave and screamed her name out into the woods. "Grace! Grace? Grace Thoral!"

"Well, I just think that maybe if you'd been friendlier, she might have stayed," Tara said matter-of-factly.

"I can't believe you're blaming me! It's not my fault." "Then whose is it?"

Devon was fumbling through the bags. "Did she take anything with her? I swear, if that little rat stole anything from us…"

"Well, you certainly didn't help the situation!" Tara continued her bickering with Chase. "No, you had to be all big and tough and scary. Sometimes that's not the answer!"

"Well, what should I have done, let her take our food? She said herself that's what she was planning on doing!"

Fin was still screaming outside. "Grace! Grace, we're not going to hurt you!"

"Where's our bread? We had an extra loaf of bread! It's gone! She took—oh, wait, never mind. It's right here." Devon rummaged aimlessly through the food.

"You know, if you would just listen once in a while and not be so concerned with your reputation all the time"—

"Well, if you would stop being such a little goody two-shoes"—

"At least I don't pretend to be someone I'm not just to boost my ego!"

"Grace, where are you? Are you out there?"

"Maybe she took the smoked meats! And do we still have all our blankets? Check the blankets!"

"I'm really just getting fed up with you, Chase! You're always being so ridiculous. You never think before you act, and furthermore, I"—

"BE QUIET!!!" Tetoviran screamed over all the chaos. His voice echoed through the cave and boomed in Tara's ears. Everyone fell silent, watching Teto. "Stop running around like a pack of wild apes. Thoral can't have gone far. All we need to do is find her. Now would you all please *shut up* and follow me?"

He harrumphed and started off towards the woods, muttering about the pure stupidity of young kids these days.

Chase put his weight on his left side, purposely hitting Tara aside with his hip. "You know, I just thought of something. Why do we need to go after Grace, anyway? We're better off without her. And besides, she didn't take anything."

Tara scowled at him and hit him back with her own hip, but it hit his leg and had no effect on him due to their height difference. She had almost never felt smaller, and it made her cheeks flame with fury and embarrassment.

Tetoviran smiled from the mouth of the cave. "True enough. She didn't steal anything. At least, nothing of any importance. Just your sword." He threw the last part out casually, then turned and walked away.

Chase's hand flew to his side. *"What?* No! I… I took it off last night before I went to bed and… aargh! She took my sword?" he roared.

Fin shook his head. "What a little…"

"Of all people. Look who's finally been robbed," Tara muttered.

Chase clenched a fist at his hip. His eyes looked darker than she'd ever seen them before as he glared at her coldly. For a split second, she thought he would hit her.

She swallowed and took a tentative step back. "Chase, are you…"

He didn't give her a chance to finish, just shrugged on his jacket and pushed past her abruptly. "Let's go."

The five of them walked through the trees, almost silent except for the occasional crunch when Chase kicked something in his fury. They followed crushed twigs, footprints, and Rebel's sense of smell for a long time before they finally saw her.

Grace was running with Chase's sword in her hand, tripping and stumbling often as she went. Tara winced each time she hit the ground. Chase clenched his jaw and raked a hand through his thick black hair. "That pint-sized wretch."

"Maybe you should take a more peaceful approach this time…" Tara suggested, but Chase didn't look at her.

"Oh, yeah. I'm sure if we ask nicely and say please, she'll give it back and we can all go sing around the campfire and frolic through meadows, too. Grow up, Florreson. Not everything's a fairy tale."

Tara was astounded at the tone of voice he used with her. He'd never spoken to her like that before.

Before she could say anything more, Chase jumped out at Grace, pouncing on her and knocking her to the ground. She screamed as he wrestled his sword out of her hand. "You know, we've got to stop meeting like this, Thoral."

Fin, Devon, Rebel, and Tetoviran closed a circle around them while Tara stood on the outskirts of the ring, watching. Grace's face was as white as a sheet. "Please. Let me explain."

"Explain what?" Chase growled. "Explain why you stole my sword and ran off with it while I was sleeping? Explain why you did that after I spared your life when I could've killed you? After I fed you when I could've let you starve? Please, explain. I'd love to hear your excuses."

"I'm sorry! I… I was afraid. I wanted to run, but I knew you would come after me. So, I thought that maybe if I took your sword, then if you caught me you wouldn't be able to hurt me."

Chase stared at her for a second, pinned underneath him, breathing hard and pale with fear. "That," Chase sighed, "is the stupidest thing I've ever heard in my entire life." He spoke calmly, and Grace relaxed a little. But in his next statement, he was yelling at her. "What were you thinking? Why didn't you just run? We wouldn't have come after you if you hadn't taken anything!"

"I don't know! I was nervous and I didn't know what you'd do. I thought maybe if I took your sword you wouldn't be able to harm me."

"Oh, you think I can't hurt you without my sword?" Chase tossed his scabbard aside and pressed a hand to her throat. Grace froze, and for a moment, she just lay there, shaking in fear. "Since you were so eager to take the risk," Chase said, "you can find out." He pressed harder.

"P-please, Chase," she choked. "Please don't hurt me. Just let me go. I'll run. I'll run far away and I'll never bother you again. Or I'll stay here, I'll do whatever you want. Just… please… don't hurt me."

Chase scowled down at her. His jaw was tight as he considered what he should do. After a few tense moments, he pushed to his feet, taking his sword with him and reattaching it immediately to his belt as he released the last of his anger in a hard kick to Grace's ribs. She curled into a ball and gagged while her throat recovered.

"You'll do anything I want?"

Grace nodded, practically tripping over herself in her haste to stand. "Anything. Anything, I swear."

Chase turned to the others, who gave nods. He spoke then to Grace. "Travel with us. For now, at least. We can use an extra pair of hands, and another set of fighting skills."

Grace's eyes lit up. "Really?"

Chase turned away from her growing smile and started off in the other direction. "But you're going to have to learn how to hold your tongue, Thoral. That's going to get you into trouble someday, and I'm bound to run out of mercy sooner or later." Yet Grace looked much too relieved to care.

CHAPTER 20

Chase walked quickly through the tall grasses of an open field. Weeds choked out the occasional wilted wildflower, and yellow stalks of wheat grew so tall that Chase had to push them aside to walk through. He heard the light footsteps of his companions behind him and saw Grace out of the corner of his eye, walking just a little behind him and to his left. He noticed how she took care to keep up her pace, so as not to slow Fin, who was walking behind her. She also watched Chase's scabbard hitting against his leg, keeping a wary distance from the sheath.

He was bearing little ill will towards her now for what she'd done. In fact, he felt somewhat connected to her sympathetically. He saw himself in her personality quite often, in her stubbornness and attitude.

He walked a little slower, attempting to put himself in stride with Grace, but she slowed with him, lessening her pace as he did. As he was walking, he pushed apart a crowd of wheat for her to pass through, holding it after him like he'd done millions of times before with doors in Jisara. But Grace just shifted a bit to the right and passed through the wheat herself.

Chase frowned as he continued to walk. She was either deathly afraid of him or completely disgusted by him, and he suspected the former more than the latter. She barely dared to get near him.

Obviously, he'd dealt with this before in girls, but he couldn't try to charm Grace. He wasn't going to steal from her, and it would probably seem strange if he suddenly started flirting out of the blue after almost killing her. Maybe Tara was right. He could've been a little nicer. Although, after the sword theft, who wouldn't be angry? He'd come to depend on the protection of his sword during his lifetime.

He cast a mildly resentful glance back at Grace and was surprised to find her staring at him. She quickly looked away when his gaze fell to her, but not nearly quickly enough. Chase frowned and turned back around. Perhaps he could simply try talking to her. Start up a conversation. He would still have to be gruff, obviously, but if he opened up more as they talked, maybe she would see that he was actually nice. She might come to trust him quicker that way. He turned slightly towards her, then motioned to her with a sharp look.

"Come," he said. "Walk up here."

She looked behind her, then back at Chase, as if asking, *who, me?* He nodded, and she quickly scurried to his side. "What's the matter?" she asked.

"Nothing. Just wanted to talk to you."

Grace frowned uncertainly. "What?" "I said I wanted to talk."

She began to fidget nervously. "Um… what about?" "Anything."

Grace stared at him. "Really?"

He rolled his eyes. "Oh, so what, you've never heard of a conversation before? This is how it works. I say something, and then you respond to it, and the subject we're talking about unfolds until we're rambling on about a bunch of nonsense without stopping for air. Ring a bell?"

"I've had a conversation before," Grace said indignantly. "I'm just a little surprised. I thought you might want to talk about my place of birth and exactly who I was friends with when I was four years old. Questions, questions, questions. That's all you ever ask!

Why can't you just relax and try to make some friends for once in your life, instead of being so grouchy?"

He shot her a warning glance, and she stared at the ground silently. "Why do you always do that?" he asked suddenly, trying to put a bit more gentleness in his voice.

Her surprised look came again. "Do what?"

"Get angry and confident and speak your mind—make a big statement—and then back off if I give you a dirty look. Why do you do that?"

She shrugged, as if the answer was so obvious, she'd never given any thought to it. "Well, I guess I… uh…"

Chase smirked. "Still running like a rabbit from a fox, tail tucked between your legs. Don't be such a coward, Thoral."

She folded her arms across her chest. "I'm not a coward. I'm actually very brave." Chase quickened his stride, not pausing to look at her. "Oh, really?" "Yes."

"And exactly what, pray tell, have you done that is so bold and fearless in your lifetime?"

Grace pumped her legs faster in an effort to keep up. "I helped my mother fight a wolf out of our village, and I snuck out of my home in the middle of the night to follow my father and brothers on a hunting trip, which is strictly forbidden where I'm from," she said smugly.

"Oh my, that took courage. I'm quivering at the mere thought of doing such things," Chase said flatly. "My bravery is no match whatsoever. I only survived an evil immortal's magical amnesia potion, took care of myself and raised myself up from a child, taught myself to fight, stole from other people in my kingdom to live, fought with countless men six times my size and thrice that of Tetoviran's, set out on a journey with only one other companion to complete an almost impossible mission, escaped from a village full of deadly, haunted souls, outwitted a king who could take over your mind with the touch of a finger, battled an army of living plants, withstood an attack of indestructible monsters and another of fire demons, and, last but not least, attacked, half strangled, and interrogated the most annoying little thief in the entire world."

He gave her a pointed look, tossing out a teasing scowl. Had she smiled? Maybe a little bit? "I'm ashamed, really," he continued. "Your feats are marvelous and courageous, but mine are miniscule and unimportant. Pale in comparison, really. It's actually embarrassing to be in the presence of such a fearless, bold, reckless leader with incredible audacity that reaches levels beyond compare. I'm really just enthralled, Miss Thoral. You are such an admirable person. In fact, you shouldn't even be a *person,* you're so amazing. You should be made a Creator, you're so brave. Can't you see it? Grace Thoral, up on the Thrones of Creation, daughter of Life herself. Why, wouldn't that be something? All those incredible deeds would finally be rewarded, and you would get"—

"Chase, shut up," Grace said.

He did as he was told. She was definitely smiling now.

"See? It's not that hard to talk to me. I'm not going to murder you for saying something. For stealing my sword, well, yes—consider yourself lucky that all your limbs are still intact—but if you simply talk to me, I'm not going to do anything to you. Besides annoying you to death, perhaps."

She narrowed her eyes. "The last time I tried talking to you, I got you yelling in my face, holding me by the shirt."

"Because you were being a brat."

Grace bit her lip. "Uh, about that… I'm sorry I was so rude. I was just really scared. You have a million reasons to hate me,

Chase, and if you got angry enough… do you have any idea how easy it would've been for you to kill me?"

"Yes, I do."

"And just imagine, I don't know any of you. You're all day-old strangers to me, and that's really scary. I don't know if you're going to turn on me, or if you're going to try leaving me behind… I don't know anything around here. Nor did I in my village. I've always been kind of clueless, and I was just hoping… well, I was hoping that maybe that would change if I went off on my own. I could be different from everyone else and maybe be admired for once, instead of looked down on."

"Hey," Fin called out from behind them and stopping whatever response Chase might have had. "There's a town up there!"

Everyone looked to find that they were staring into a shallow rift with a tiny village in the center of the valley.

"There's a town all the way out here?" Tara asked in surprise. Devon shrugged.

"I guess so." "Well, that's good," Tetoviran said. "We can restock and get Thoral some shoes."

Grace beamed. "Really?" Her smile quickly faded, though. "Wait, but… I don't have any money."

Devon grinned. "Neither do we." She looked at Chase, confused. "Then how…" she gasped. "You don't mean to steal, do you?"

He smirked. "Please, darling Grace, are you suggesting that I would steal? Me?" He shook his head. "Never stolen a thing in my life. I am a man of honor. How dare you imply such a thing?"

He turned and started into the valley. He could picture the scene behind him perfectly: Tara rolling her eyes, Fin, Teto, and Devon trying not to smile, and Grace staring after him in confusion.

"Come on, guys. You're lagging," he called over his shoulder. Quickly their footsteps sounded as they rushed to catch up with him, starting their descent into the valley.

Chase strolled through the streets of the charming little village, smiling politely at grown-ups and flashing charming smirks at young girls. Devon, Fin, Teto, and Grace had gone off "shopping" with the promise to meet up again in a bit. Surprisingly, it turned out that Tetoviran wasn't a bad pick-pocket himself.

Chase walked alongside Tara with awkward silence. She'd tucked Rebel safely into her knapsack, and now she stopped and said hello to everyone they walked past, pausing at stands and shops to admire jewelry. She seemed to be enjoying the friendly bustle of people after all the horrors they'd encountered in the past few days, and Chase couldn't deny his own contentment at being back in this kind of environment. Tara paid special attention to one pair of earrings, seeming very interested until the vendor informed her of the price.

After she walked on, Chase held back. He strolled casually up to the cart, pretending to examine the jewelry.

The vendor chuckled. "Lookin' for something to give your mum, boy? Or has a wee lass got under your skin?"

Chase looked up and put on a phony shy smile, making his voice sound higher. "The latter, sir. Could you recommend anything?" The man leaned forward over his belly, his belt straining against his enormous gut as he examined his jewelry.

As he was looking through his selection, Chase slid a hand into the leather purse on the vendor's hip and removed a small sum of money, deftly rolling coins over his knuckles and into his palm.

"This would be a fine pick for any young one," the man said obliviously, gesturing towards a plain necklace that cost very little. Chase considered it carefully, then pointed to the far side of the display. "What about that one over there?"

"Let me have a look, lad." The man leaned further away, and Chase closed his hand around the small box containing the earrings, slipping it discreetly into his pocket before the man turned back around with another box in hand. This one held a wrist cuff.

"Here y'are, lad. That's twenty."

"Perfect." Chase handed the vendor's own coins back to him with a smile and took the box from him. "Thanks, sir! Keep the change for your trouble."

The vendor took the money in delight. "Why, o'course, lad! Glad to help."

As soon as the vendor looked away, Chase put the box containing the wrist cuff back on his cart and walked off. He caught up with Tara in the bustling crowd and slipped the box of earrings subtly into her hand.

She jumped when she felt him touch her, but upon seeing it was him, she stopped and examined what he'd slid into her palm. Her eyebrows shot up. "Chase! These were really expensive! Why would you steal"—

Chase slapped his hand over her mouth as shoppers glanced over curiously. "Shut up," he whispered in her ear, giving out apologetic smiles and steering her away from the crowds while feeding them some excuse about her mental instability. He led her around a corner into a quieter side street, then pushed her gently back into a wall.

"You idiot," he whispered. "Number one rule about stealing. Don't ever tell anyone that you've stolen something. Ever. You'll get me killed."

Chase turned to face Tara as she hesitantly put on the earrings, looking a bit guilty. "I feel a little bad putting these on, but… thank you. They're really pretty."

He nodded, a quick jerk of his head. Sensing her tension, he sighed. "I'm sorry. For the things I said this morning."

She smiled, her whole body going slack with relief. "Me too."
"Better be."

He then told her to wait where she was as he sauntered back into the street. He spat in his hands and worked his hair away from his face with it, then approached a girl who stood alone.

Catching her eye immediately, he sauntered lazily towards her. "Excuse me, I'm new in town," he said, drawing close. "Could you possibly direct me to a good place to eat? I'm famished." Her eyes lit up with friendliness, and she reached out to touch his arm welcomingly. "Of course! There is wonderful food on the corner down there, and if you care for soup, there is a small inn that serves a wonderful stew just down the street."

Chase nodded, pretending to listen, and then glanced at her sleeve. "Thank you very much! I must say before I go, the pattern on this material is absolutely beautiful," he said, reaching out as if to examine the fabric. "Oh, thank you! I bought this just a week ago," the girl said excitedly. He drew his hand away and adjusted his own sleeves. "It is simply gorgeous. Thank you for your help!"

She nodded her response as he moved away and returned to find Tara. "You, darling, just witnessed a master at work," he proclaimed with a flourish when he reached her.

She shook her head. "Did you interrogate that poor girl just for fun, or did you do it for a reason?"

Chase smiled and pulled the girl's compass from his pouch, wiggling his brows childishly.

Tara sighed. "Of course." Chase studied the compass without expression for several moments, turning around a couple of times, then snapped it shut and slid it back into his pocket.

"Come here," he said more seriously, leading Tara further away from the crowds and down a back street. Once he was assured that no one was within earshot, he turned to her.

She frowned slightly. "Is something wrong?"

Chase ran his hands through his hair and messed it up again, pushing it all back into his face and ruining the work his saliva had done. He put an arm around Tara and tugged her forward as he took up a leisurely, slow pace. "Walk with me." She looked at him with concern. "I haven't told the others about this, Tara, but we have a problem. We're off course, and way behind schedule. I had suspicions that we had strayed, but the compass confirmed that. We should've reached the Sumadine Woods yesterday." Tara's eyes became wide. "We started off in the wrong direction after the *tesko* encounter, and then when we went after Grace, we took up traveling a long way off the road. We shouldn't have found this town, Tara. We should've found more trials, more monsters. Also, before the *teskos* attacked us, Devon mentioned something about whispering trees. I never managed to get back to him on it, but we need to find out more about that."

He shoved his open hand into his pants pocket. "We need to start traveling right away. I don't want to stay here long."

Tara nodded. "Yes. We can't wait any longer." Then she side-eyed him suspiciously.

"Is there another reason why you want to leave so soon? Is someone *else* following us that you're not telling me about?"

Chase smiled. "No, Tara. Nothing's wrong this time." She arched an eyebrow, and he sighed in exasperation.

"I swear, no one's following us."

Tara nodded. "Okay. Good."

"Except for a few bloodthirsty assassins. Only a few." He grinned and released her from his arm. "Come on. Let's go find the others."

Once they found Fin, Devon, Tetoviran, and Grace, they quickly explained the situation and hurried to continue traveling. Grace, Chase noticed, had indeed gone on quite the shopping trip and was now traveling in a long skirt and a purple cowl. Ankle-height soft leather walking boots adorned her feet, and her thick, glossy black hair had been brushed to frame her coffee cheeks beautifully.

Her dark eyes darted around nervously as she walked. She jumped at the slightest movements around them. Her mind seemed to be conjuring up strange things, turning trees into beasts and shadows into monsters as she became more and more paranoid of something that Chase couldn't see. Nobody else seemed to be on edge like that.

Tetoviran walked next to her, babbling on about the time he dueled a giant with one hand tied behind his back, wielding both blades in one hand, but Grace didn't seem to hear a single word. She kept glancing back at the path behind them, and Chase caught her trying to push dirt over her footprints more than once. Finally, he fell back to walk with her.

"What's wrong?" he asked.

She shook her head. "Nothing."

"Is your mind just making things up, or do you know something?" "Probably the former," she said, clutching at something on her belt underneath her new cloak.

"Uh-huh." Her jaw clenched at his skeptical tone.

"Can't you please trust me for once? I'm just being stupid. While I was out on my own, I saw these strange men on horseback who wore black and had glowing red eyes. They blended into the shadows so well that if they closed their eyes, you couldn't see them if you were a few feet away. They scared me, and they followed me for a whole day. Once, I was standing inches away from one, and I didn't even know it. Well, that is, until he opened his eyes. Two glowing red sockets, boiling as if they were full of fire. He spoke to me. After that experience, I'm really paranoid, so it's nothing. I was starving and scared at the time, so it was most likely just delusional stuff."

She looked with embarrassment at Chase as if expecting him to laugh, but he frowned. "Red eyes?"

She nodded. "Yes. Glowing red, almost the color of blood, but with the heat of a flame. It's ridiculous, though. Things like that don't exist." "You'd be surprised what exists," he muttered, but his mind was on what she'd told him. He had never heard of anything like that before. *Men on horseback...* he racked his brain. "Were there many of them?"

Grace shook her head. "No. Usually I would only see one pair of eyes, from a distance. Sometimes two. Once I saw three, but I never again saw more than one at the same time after that. The last one I saw—when he snuck up on me and spoke to me—I ran from him, and I stumbled upon you and Fin mere moments after. I was hoping that maybe I could take some food from you and find refuge from the creatures."

Chase glanced over his shoulder at the trail behind them. Quickly he turned back to Grace and lowered his voice. "What exactly did this man say to you?"

Grace shrugged. "I...I don't know. It was all strange. Some prophetic garbage, about my fate or something... and destiny's loom…" Chase's puzzled face made her cheeks heat up. "I don't really remember."

He frowned again. "I need you to think as hard as you possibly can. This could be important, Grace."

She glanced nervously at the ground. "He… he said… 'So, it's true, then. The legend is real.' He said that mostly to himself, after he saw me. But then he spoke directly to me. He said… he said I need to be careful. He said, 'Be careful, child, and never take your eyes off the road behind you. The intertwining of fate, woven on destiny's loom, has stitched a pattern for you.' Uh… and then… 'Things are beginning to change. Be careful whom you choose to trust. Be watchful of your back. The beast is awakening. He is coming for them. Coming for *you*. Fate is cruel to you, child; Destiny looks with scorn upon you. You must make a choice that will change your life forever. We serve the beast, yet we warn you of his coming. You see, child; you can trust no one. No one is your friend. Not even I.' And then his eyes turned into actual flames, like they were burning in his eye sockets. He looked like Hell himself, just sitting on his horse and… staring at me.

"Then he said, 'Especially not I. Watch. Watch as the beast awakens. Evil will spread like…' What was it?" Grace fought to remember. "Oh, wine! 'Evil will spread like wine spilt on cloth. You will find your closest friends turning and stabbing your back; your own family will become your greatest enemy. The future waits for you hungrily. The past haunts you with nightmares. The present kills you with fear. There is no escape.'" Grace paused for a shaky breath.

Chase watched her with closely knit brows. "Was there anything else?" he asked carefully.

She nodded. "Yes. 'Run. Run, and watch yourself, child. For I will return. And next time, I will be under his control. Even now, he consumes me. So, go. Let the legend live in the future—not the present. But it will catch up with you. Run as fast as you can, as far as your human legs will carry you. I *will* catch you. The beast *will* find you. For you can never outrun your fate.' And then I did exactly as he said. I ran. And… and, Chase, when I looked back, I saw two red eyes watching me go." She shuddered as she concluded the story, and she looked up in surprise to find that the entire group had been listening to her as they walked.

Tara's eyes were wide with worry, while Teto's were saucers of glee. Devon and Fin were both frowning deeply, as was Chase.

"You swear this is true?" Devon asked slowly.

Grace pressed her lips together. "I saw it, but I don't know if I was imagining things or not."

"Nobody imagines things that vividly," Fin muttered, scrubbing a hand through his blonde hair. "It must have been real."

"Hang on," Chase said. "If you saw that thing—man—whatever it was—close to where we were, then that means that even if we were off track, we were still within reach of the guardians. Because that cannot have been a man. Men don't have eyes of fire. It must have been one of the monsters guarding the woods. So, there was a town in the middle of a land full of monsters and phantoms?"

Devon shook his head. "It seems unlikely."

"It's pretty unusual," Fin agreed. "Nobody would be stupid enough to build a city in the middle of monster-infested land. It's not as though the guards would leave them alone just because they're residents."

"Unless," Tara interjected, "those riders with red eyes aren't guardians of the Sumadine Woods at all. Maybe they don't have anything to do with that. They spoke of a beast and a legend. That doesn't seem like something that has to do with the Sumadine Woods."

The others were silent as they took this into consideration. "Right, because the woods thing isn't enough. They have to send some beast, too, just to top things off," Tetoviran grumbled.

"Destiny's loom," Chase muttered. "I wonder what that's supposed to mean."

"It means," Devon said, "her weavings. Fate and Destiny weave patterns that depict the future. Their tapestries and quilts tell the tales of tomorrow. It's said that everything they've ever woven, since the beginning of time, is kept with them in the Sumadine Woods. That's what you saw, Chase. Your quilt was your future, and they ripped it. Somehow, you have to make your destiny right again. That's what all of it meant. Grace is somehow tied in with us, but it sounds like her picture isn't pretty.

"Those creatures sound like *deriniums*. They're monsters that serve a beast called Myderev. He's supposedly a monster that has slumbered for eight thousand years. But there's a legend that says that someday a girl—the daughter of a great king, a beautiful princess therefore—will wake him again. And his wrath will doom the world." Everyone stared blankly at Devon. "You don't happen to be the daughter of a king, do you?" he asked Grace, oblivious to the looks of the others. She shook her head, but Tetoviran was interested in something else.

"How do you know all this, kid?" he asked. "You seem to know quite a bit about everything the rest of us haven't a clue about. You trying to get tricky with me, kid? Because I'll knock your two front teeth out if you are."

Devon just rolled his eyes, but Chase crossed his arms and studied Devon. "Yeah. You do seem to know a whole lot about strange topics. And you still owe me an explanation. Before the *teskos* attacked, you said you knew something important about the Sumadine Woods. How come that's never come up in our conversations?"

Devon only smiled. "I also still owe you a beating. How come *that's* never come up in our conversations?"

The corner of Chase's mouth lifted in a half smile that could make a girl pass out. "All right, then. You get to hit me… what was it, ten times?… if you tell us what you know." He was hardly concerned that Devon would hit him hard, and he was anxious to know everything he possibly could about what they were up against.

Devon nodded. "Deal."

Chase yawned and stood slouching casually with a half-amused expression as Devon readied to hit him. This would be somewhat embarrassing, if nothing else. The first five hits were light—just barely enough to ache at the end. This was all he had expected, but it was still somewhat relieving that he didn't have to endure any real pain.

Yet after the fifth punch hit his arm, Devon glanced at Chase and smiled mischievously. Chase immediately began to step back. "Whoa, there, hold on"—

Devon hit him the sixth time, square in the stomach and forcing a grunt of pain from his mouth. Grace gasped as Devon hit him again with his entire strength, and again… and again… without letting him recover. When there was a pause, Chase tried to bend over to relieve the pain in his stomach, nearly gasping. He couldn't even breathe.

"To Hell's domain with you, Devon," he panted. "I swear on all the Creators that if I could hit you back right now, you'd be eating dirt." He wasn't truly angry—after all, he was the one who'd asked for this—but he sure was in pain.

Devon grinned. "But you can't, can you?' Chase winced and looked up at his friend through his hair. "And there is, I believe, one more to go."

Chase shook his head at the ground.

"Devon, maybe you shouldn't"—Tara began hesitantly, but Devon was already swinging his arm before Chase could even properly brace himself. With that final punch, he stumbled backwards and crouched to the ground, breathing heavily with his eyes closed. His stomach muscles were tense with pain, but at least it was over. He heard Devon step closer to him, and his eyes flew open as he lifted his hands warily.

"Hey, you already got your ten"—he started, but Devon leaned down and held out his hand to him. Chase looked at it, then looked at Devon. He was smiling and definitely trying not to laugh.

Chase shoved his hand away and stood on his own, still bent over and trying to catch his breath. "Filthy rat," he hissed through a chuckle.

"Sorry," Devon said, sounding nothing close to it.

Chase shrugged. "Don't be. If I had the chance to do that to you, you'd be unconscious and I wouldn't have any regrets." Devon grinned, and Chase was quite pleased that he could say things like that—and possibly mean them—without any hatred brewing between the two of them.

"I guess brothers beat each other up, huh?" Devon mused.

Chase blinked in surprise at that—*brothers*—then quickly checked himself with a thin smile. Straightening his posture with a groan, he shook his head. "Guess so. What's wrong with the woods?"

Devon stared at him for a moment at the quick change in subject, then began giving his answer as everyone started walking again. "Well... a number of things. First off, Destiny and Fate have a palace in its heart; the very center of the woods, with equal distance in all directions, and equal hardships every way. So, there are no shortcuts. Second, the Sumadine Woods are the only known habitat of the *Aljenez Zijer*—Shadow Monsters. And since they have nowhere else to live except Paroaff, there're a lot of them in the woods. They prey on happiness and hope, and they'll suck you into such despair and depression that you'll go mad. They feed off of good feelings, so you have to constantly try to stay in the sunlight."

Fin frowned as the group continued walking. "But that doesn't make any sense. What happens at night?"

"Well, I was just getting to that," Devon grimaced. "No one has ever survived a night in the Sumadine Woods." There was silence as everyone processed this.

Devon continued anxiously, "The *Aljenez Zijer* envelop the mind and drive people insane with hopelessness. People go crazy."

Chase frowned worriedly, still holding his side with one hand to appease his pain as he walked.

Devon went on, "The worst part is"—

"There's more?" Tetoviran interrupted. "You know, maybe it's not worth it to go talk to these old ladies. We can meet some ugly grandmas anytime. Trust me, they're everywhere. It's creepy how many old ladies with saggy eyeballs drink weird tea and eat pastries for a living. Maybe we can just find Ukrasen ourselves."

"That's ridiculous," Chase argued. "Ukrasen could be anywhere in this world and anywhere in billions of other worlds, too. It would be impossible."

Tara nodded. "There's no way we'd be able to find it in time to save Chase's parents."

"Well, yes," Chase said, "but even besides that, there's a lot riding on this. The Sixteen Kingdoms are in danger, too."

Grace put up a hand. "Slow down. What's Ukrasen? What's wrong with Chase's parents? Why are we going to see Destiny and Fate?"

Chase stopped walking and turned abruptly so she walked straight into him. He smiled down at her pleasantly as she stumbled. "Because they have the answers to all of *our* questions, you obnoxiously clueless child."

Grace opened her mouth again, clearly still confused and probably ready to throw an insult back at Chase, but he spoke over her. "So, what's the worst part?"

Devon grimaced. "It's the wind."

Fin snorted, staring at his friend incredulously. "The wind. Right. Devon, we have been attacked and threatened and injured by so many different monsters that each of us could fill a book. We can deal with a little bit of rough weather."

Devon shook his head. "No. It's not weather. The wind speaks."

Chapter 21

Tara's gaze kept wandering to the road behind her as they went, searching for a pair of red eyes staring back at her. A sharp wind buffeted her face, turning her cheeks pink with the cold. Winter's final breaths were always the fiercest of them all.

"They whisper to you," Devon was saying, "and each person hears something different. The winds speak of your past, of your deepest secrets, wildest dreams, most desperate desires. They know. They know all of it, and they tell only the truth. The winds know men better than men know themselves, and these truths told back to them is enough to drive them mad with fear and regret. It's said that"—

"What do the winds do to women?" Grace interrupted, and Tara smiled.

Devon blinked. "What do you mean?"

"Well, what makes men so important?" she asked. "Why do people always talk about men, but never women? Men are a bunch of ridiculous bungling trolls."

Devon held up his hands defensively. "I never even meant"—

"Even ask Tara!"

Tara gave a start at her name. "What?"

Grace nodded firmly. "Yes." She turned and stared accusatorily at Devon, who looked more baffled than anything as they continued walking.

"Tara gets tired of men, too. She told me about the time you all betrayed her, and she was *not* pleased with you."

Tara's eyes widened. She'd told Grace not to tell them she'd said that! Immediately Chase, Devon, Fin, and Teto all snapped to attention. Tara laughed nervously as Grace continued.

"She is getting sick and tired of you guys stepping all over her like dirt. She even told me all about her several fights with you, Chase, and let me tell you, she is not a huge fan of *you* right now." Tara closed her eyes. She was never telling Grace anything ever again. "And you know what else Tara's fed up with? She is fed up with"—

"Ah, Grace? Grace, sweetie… um, can we talk for a minute?" Tara grabbed her by the shoulders and pulled her aside as the others glared at her. "Grace, when I tell you not to tell people something, that's when something is called a secret. And I'm kind of expecting you to keep my secrets. All right?"

She glanced nervously at the guys standing a few feet away, then back at Grace. "Look. I got really upset with them for that incident, and I got really upset with Chase those times, but I'd prefer if you didn't tell them *everything* I told you. Especially those select few things I specifically told you *not* to tell them."

Grace shrugged. "I don't get the big deal. You clearly feel as though you can't speak up for yourself. They need to know how you feel. If you hate someone, you can't just pretend you like them."

Tara almost laughed. "Yes, but sometimes it's best that people don't know you hate them. That's how fights start. Besides, I don't hate any of them. I never have."

Grace frowned. "Huh."

"So why don't we just go on over there and not say anything about the things I've told you, okay? Great."

She stepped quickly away from Grace and started a light, bouncy pace down the road past the boys and Tetoviran. "Are you guys coming?" she asked, pinching her jacket hard between her fingers. This was bad, to say the least.

Slowly, one by reluctant one, the footsteps followed her. She could almost feel Chase's hard stare on her back, and she tried to ignore it. Grace hadn't meant to cause any harm. She'd just gotten a little carried away trying to make a point. *A point that didn't need to be made,* a tiny voice growled in the back of her head. But she just took a deep breath and walked a little faster.

After a while Devon awkwardly cleared his throat and continued what he'd been saying before. "It's said that these winds can tempt you. They sort of egg you on to do crazy things, and if you can't ignore it, then it'll get into your head and drive you mad. They'll plant weird seeds, so I've heard. They'll get you thinking about some pretty awful things. I heard a story; once two young boys wandered into the woods by accident. They were only about ten or eleven, and they came in weaponless and unknowing. The two had been best friends since birth, born side by side, and their mothers were friends as well. These two had never had a single disagreement in their entire lives, and the winds started talking. The two turned against each other, and the next day both bodies were found dead, one beaten to death and one stabbed in the chest. The one who'd been beaten laid holding a long, sharp rock and the stabbed one a thick branch. They'd murdered each other. All those years together; that whole life together! They couldn't fight the voices."

Tara slowed her pace a bit as fear clenched her stomach. "And… we're going in there?" Devon's face hardened when he looked at Tara. The shift was very slight, and it passed to be very quickly covered by fake cheeriness, but Tara saw it. Devon had been offended that she'd been talking about the boys to Grace in private. She could tell he didn't appreciate the gossip. "Yes. We'll just have to get out before nightfall." Tara played with a piece of her hair nervously. "But if the forces are really that strong, how can we fight it? Who's to say we won't just kill each other?" Devon set his jaw. "You can try optimism if you'd like." Tara pressed her lips together at the aggravation underlying his polite tone. "I don't mean it like that. I just"— "What else might you not have meant to sound the way it did?" he interrupted aggressively. Tara stopped in her tracks and stared at him with wide eyes. Biting his lip as if to keep himself from blurting anything else out, he took a step away from her and graced her with a slight dip of his head. "Sorry," he mumbled after a moment, then brushed past her and continued walking. Tara watched him go, her heart thrumming in her throat. This could not be happening. Her and her stupid big mouth! The first group of real friends she had ever had, and this was how she'd decided to treat them? She wished she could just turn back time and actually think before she spoke. Devon was obviously hurt and angry, and the others were simply closed off to her. She didn't even want to imagine how Chase must be feeling. But had she truly done anything wrong? Why should she apologize for sharing her feelings?

Tara had stopped walking altogether now, her conflicted thoughts carrying her further into despair. What could she do? Try to discuss the matter with everyone? She really didn't have any excuses; she had just screwed up. But they had, too, by treating her the way they did.

There was a sudden lurch at her arm as Chase shouldered past her. "Chase..." she started, but he didn't so much as slow down. His face was stone, and he walked right past her without a glance. Tara was growing able to read Chase now, and she knew that in truth, he was probably more wounded than angry. He tended to vent pain through anger.

Cursing herself for being so thoughtless, she made the resolution to take responsibility. She had to go apologize and try to talk things out. It was the right thing to do. However, when she moved to catch up with him, she found that she'd been standing there lost in thought for so long that the entire group was already a long way ahead of her. She stared after them sadly for a moment. Grace was completely oblivious to her absence, but the others hadn't even bothered to stop and wait or to call her back. Even Tetoviran hadn't said anything, although he kept casting sad glances back at her.

Rebel squirmed out of her knapsack and dropped to the ground beside her, then laughed at her, lolling his little pink tongue. "Race you to the group, Tara!" he cried, and took off full speed, tumbling and somersaulting over his waddling little legs as he went. Tara smiled. Rebel was apparently her only friend at the moment, but he was one of the best she could ask for. She paused momentarily to laugh at his cute little stumbles, then drew herself up to begin running again.

In doing so, she caught a glimpse of something strange behind her: two brightly colored spots hovering in midair over the grass. Tara stopped and turned completely for a better view. She'd never seen ladybugs that bright shade of red before. She squinted at the two crimson dots, aligned perfectly side by side, seeming to move closer at the exact same rate, almost bouncing up and down in perfect unison. No bugs could do that, Tara knew. Then what on earth was…

Suddenly, something flickered. For a split second, maybe even half of that, the two red spots were no longer floating randomly in midair. A form built around them—a human body, a horse—then disappeared as if it were smoke. After the illusion dissipated, however, the two red dots still sat in the air, their form gone again.

Tara stood with trembling hands, her mouth open with no words escaping, trying to scream but having seemingly lost her voice entirely. The rest of the group was fading into a small grove of trees. She panicked even further at the thought of losing them completely. She needed help.

Tara whirled back around and almost laughed in relief at the discovery that unlike her voice, her legs still worked just fine. So, she ran. Fear grasped her lungs and numbness tugged at her feet, but she kept going. She tripped once and stood up to find a bloody hand and a ripped pant leg. Her hair was matted to her face with panicky sweat, and she looked up to see those two red spots coming closer to her. There was no time to dwell on the scrapes. She scrambled desperately to her feet and kept running. Where were her stupid powers now, when she really, really needed them?

The wind chapped her lips and rushed in her ears, ripping violently at her eyes and making them water until the land in front of her was blurry, but at this point it really didn't matter where she was going. Her friends probably wouldn't help her anyway, and her only thought was to get away from the monster. Away from those two red spots, the spots that certainly weren't bugs. They were eyes, eyes with a camouflaged rider to go with them.

Tara finally found her voice and screamed. She screamed as loud as she could and heard her friends' voices shouting in the distance a moment after. She barely had time to think a single word before the sockets were right in front of her, and the red lightning of fear flashed across her eyes. *Deriniums.*

She heard shouting continue distantly, but it was fuzzy and faraway, like an unreal dream. Tara knew there was no possibility of her friends reaching her in time. The *derinium's* body flickered into existence briefly, then winked out again. Finally, the entire phantom was visible and solid, standing right in front of her.

The *derinium* never dismounted, simply stared at Tara for what seemed like an eternity. She wanted nothing more than to look away, to erase the image of those fiery eyes from her memory forever. Yet something held her there. Why she didn't run, she would never know. She just stared right back at the *derinium* in silence, neither of them speaking or moving. For a moment, Tara thought she had felt a connection. She thought that perhaps the monster would not harm her. But then it spoke.

In a voice like that of a desert-bound vagabond dying of thirst, it creaked, "Beware, Flower of Earth. Your mother may smile on you, but other Creators do not. Others hate you, wish you dead, as your ancestor was born from disobedience. Fools, Life and Death, to let their unruly daughter get away with such arrogance. But if the Creators will not punish you, so be it."

He slowly drew a twisted dagger from beneath his cloak, turning it in his ashen, papery white hand as he slid from his horse. "My master is becoming strong again. He will awaken, and you are the key to his return to power. The beast demands you dead, child."

A scream filled Tara's ears, and she would only later realize it was hers as the *derinium* loomed over her with a dagger in hand.

CHAPTER 22

Pounding feet. Pounding breath. Pounding heart. Dirt flew and people tripped. Thorns snagged and skin bled. Thoughts swirled through Chase's head faster than a shooting star, each tail-ending the other and none tarrying more than an instant in his endless panicked stream of thought. He ran with all his power, surging forward and ignoring pain. Nothing mattered. Not the wind. Not the blood. Not the sting when he fell repeatedly, tripping on those in front of him and scraping his knees over and over again. Not the whirling thoughts. Not even his anger. The only thing that mattered was Tara.

Fin scrambled in front of him with clumsy speed, and flanking him on either side were Devon and Tetoviran. Grace proved to be surprisingly fast, but apparently had low endurance. She finally slowed with exhaustion, but Chase couldn't stop. Not this time.

He kept going, hurtling toward the *derinium* like a fireball. He watched as the phantom drew a long, twisted knife and raised it above its head. Chase wouldn't make it in time. He put all his power into it, but he knew it would be impossible. Either Tara would somehow dodge the first strike, or… Chase shook the thought out of his head and pushed harder. There was no *or*. Tara would avoid the first strike. She had to.

As the *derinium* brought the dagger down, Chase's muscles began to slow against his will. His legs turned to jelly and he stopped, staring with cold dread at the scene. He needed to move. He needed to help. But his muscles wouldn't respond to his brain. This was the last second and very possibly the end. The only thought he had was that Tara might die, and the last thing she'd known was anger. His anger.

He watched as that twisted knife came down towards Tara, watched it pause just the slightest bit, mere inches above her chest. At that point he turned away and shut his eyes tight, trying not to let his heart beat through his shirt. He waited for a scream. His entire body went rigid, and he found himself clutching Fin's wrist as they put their heads together in wrenchingly painful anticipation. But the sound that met their ears wasn't a scream, or the sickening squelch of a stabbing. It was a ring of metal clashing with metal.

Chase looked up and almost cried with relief. Devon made it. Or maybe Tetoviran. They saved her! But what he saw when he lifted his head made his eyes actually well up with tears. Tara laid on her back, holding her sword gripped in two hands, pushing back on the *derinium's* blade. And in that short moment, Chase felt his insides warm up with pride like he'd never known before. Fin stared on with wide eyes, as did Devon and Tetoviran, who were standing nearby.

Tara cried out wordlessly with struggle, and Chase snapped into the present, keen and alert. He quickly drew his sword and sucked in air through his teeth. Never had he been so afraid of a fight. Never had he been so afraid of making a mistake. Things were different now. He could *not* make a mistake.

"Don't screw this up," he muttered under his breath. Then he tugged up his boots and charged.

He pounded into the *derinium* from the side, bowling him over. The horse reared and kicked wildly while the rider crawled effortlessly to his feet and laid a hand on the mare's neck, calming it with a soothing voice. Whickering and snorting, it gradually relaxed and trotted to a small patch of tall grasses. From there it stood still as a statue, and before Chase's eyes, it disappeared. Camouflage.

Tara laid breathing hard on the ground, dirt painting bold lines across her cheeks and neck. Her eyes were full of many things; fear, confusion, relief, and gratitude all rather rolled into one desperate plea for Chase to forget what she'd done. Forget what she'd said. If even just for a minute, to just forget it long enough to keep her from being killed.

Chase met her gaze and his jaw tightened. She hated him. She'd told Grace so and had since failed to even attempt denying it. He didn't blame her. He had hurt her, hurt her too many times. And yet for the first time in his life, Chase knew true pain. He'd been kicked and hit and cut and broken, but this was different. This wasn't a pain that went away with proper care and rest. It was living inside him. *This is why,* he told himself. *This is why it's best to do things alone. People cannot be trusted. Love just ends in pain.*

Right then, staring at Tara, Chase became so caught up in emotion that he didn't even realize the *derinium* coming up behind him until Tara screamed. *"Chase!"*

He whirled seconds before being struck and deflected the blow. "Wretch," the phantom hissed. "I remember you."

Chase slashed and felt his blade graze the *derinium's* stomach. The phantom cursed and touched the wound. It took Chase a moment to register how quickly he'd gotten a cut in. This monster was clearly unskilled. But despite its new wound, the *derinium* lunged forward and began pressing Chase, engaging him violently and taking up all his focus. "I'd recognize that arrogant glint in your eyes anywhere." The *derinium* was fast. Chase barely parried a slash to his left and let himself watch the phantom's blade in his peripheral vision.

"I've been told I have beautiful eyes, but really. You needn't flatter me."

The *derinium* growled like a hungry animal and stabbed with its dagger. The shorter weapon forced it to expose its arms on an attack, but Chase didn't have the room to strike. He retreated several hasty steps, pivoted, and continued to exchange with it. There was a weak spot on the right of its torso, Chase noted. The phantom was taking extra precautions to guard that area, but it was slow to get there. It would be expecting an attack there. "Remind me again where we met before?" Chase asked.

The *derinium* grinned a hollow smile. "Ah, yes. Of course. How could I forget about the potion?" It continued with exaggerated laziness as their blades clashed. "You and I met for the first time long ago, boy. You were still a tot, which is why you don't remember the occasion. In ways that I will never understand, you still managed to have an attitude, even back then."

"Appreciate that stage, when I didn't have a blade behind my words." He feinted to the *derinium's* weak right side, and it moved to block the strike with full force as expected. Chase instantly swept his blade under its arms to deliver a cut to the exposed left side with all his strength, but a jarring impact that was not the *derinium's* body lurched up his arm and put agonizing pain in his elbow. Chase's sword had been met with a parry that shouldn't have been possible. All the *derinium's* momentum had been going in the opposite direction. Chase quickly found the line of the riposte and caught a parry of his own, but he was beginning to worry a little bit.

Their fight moved a bit to the left, and one quick glance told Chase that Tara was no longer on the ground where she'd been before. He concentrated and heard rustling off to his right. Another glance revealed her shadow on yellow grass, but she herself was concealed in underbrush. Tara still had so much to learn. Like making sure her shadow couldn't be seen, as she might as well be standing out in the open otherwise.

The *derinium* took a hard swing at the air, and Chase ducked as the blade sliced over his head. While he was lower, he struck for the *derinium's* legs. It had been anticipating this, however, and it lowered its blade to protect its lowlines. Chase jumped back to his feet for a blow at the unguarded chest, but the *derinium* straightened and met Chase's blade again. The phantom's moves were quickening even more, and Chase was forced to put all his skill behind his sword. He was shocked that the thing wasn't dead yet—and that it moved so easily despite the blood seeping from the thin cut in its stomach. Chase knew firsthand that those shallow cuts often stung worse than deep ones, yet the *derinium* fought on without missing a beat.

"Yes," the monster continued, "my master was stirring in his sleep, at unrest because of his nightmares of two people with a young boy who were threatening to ruin his alliance with a very powerful man."

Chase's blade locked with the *derinium's.* "Araknan," he growled, ignoring the strain in his trembling arms.

The phantom smiled cruelly. "Indeed. My master was working with the lion king for several centuries in a mission to open the Land of Monsters to the world. But your foolish parents almost destroyed their plan."

Chase lurched away from their standoff before his muscles gave and lunged at the phantom, catching him off guard at last and pinning him on the ground. He had probably been expecting Chase to falter at the mention of his parents, but no such luck.

Finally getting to catch his breath, Chase hissed, "I'm going to find Ukrasen. I'm going to restore it, and my parents are going to be set free again."

The phantom just smirked beneath him. "Oh, but you're far too late." At Chase's confused expression he laughed throatily. "You see, in your absence, monsters have begun to discover the barrier is gone. Your precious kingdom of Jisara is being attacked by beasts as we speak."

Chase's eyes widened, but he refused to be distracted. He pressed his sword to the phantom's chest as it continued talking. "Oh, but you needn't worry about finding Ukrasen. You'll probably go mad with grief before even reach the Sumadine Woods."

Chase frowned. "Grief? What are you talking about?" But suddenly, he appeared to be hovering in midair. He felt the *derinium* beneath him still, but it was now invisible, save for two glowing red eyes staring at him.

"I'm talking about the girl," the phantom replied slyly. "No. Don't you *dare* touch her!" Chase yelled, but the *derinium* was gone, leaving him lying on the ground and desperately searching his surroundings for two eyes he simply couldn't find.

Panic filled Chase's chest. He had to warn Tara. That is, if the *derinium* hadn't already found her. He couldn't give away her location, so he did the next best thing.

"Tara!" he shouted frantically. "Tara, the *derinium* is coming after you! It's invisible, camouflaged! Watch out for"—His warning was cut off by a sharp pressure in his shoulder that sent him lurching forward so hard that his neck snapped back. He swore loudly, whipping around to find two retreating red eyes gleaming maliciously.

Not stopping to examine the wound, Chase tore off after the phantom. He spotted his other friends coming nearer, Grace lagging a bit behind and Tetoviran in the lead, but he didn't slow. He ran after the two eyes, focusing only on keeping the two glowing dots in sight. Just as he was catching up, the eyes disappeared.

Chase pulled up and looked around. Where had he gone? He turned a full circle, searching desperately. Had the *derinium* found Tara? Where in the world had he— *"Aaaaahh!"*

Chase cried out as his heart practically lurched out of his chest. A hand seized his ankle so quickly and unexpectedly that Chase's blood stopped flowing for a second. An icy, iron grip seemed to seep through his boots and spread frost over his skin. He shivered and looked down, but nothing was there. Nothing except… an arrow. Just rather hovering a small bit above the ground. Chase swallowed. The *derinium* had been shot.

He looked closer and saw, sure enough, two red eyes staring back at him. But something was different in his gaze. His eyes no longer carried the fire of menace and hatred. They seemed dull and thoughtless, as though they had gone hollow. Slowly, the phantom's body leaked back into existence, and Chase saw that the arrow he'd seen was protruding from the *derinium's* gut— piercing directly through the first cut Chase had given it. The phantom's breath came short and shallow.

It looked up at Chase and rasped, "Do not underestimate, Chosen One. My horse is still alive. He will call others. And you will not live to tell the tale of my death. The beast is awakening. The end is coming."

Chase opened his mouth to respond but jumped instead as another arrow suddenly flew into the *derinium's* chest with a sickening wet thunk—right where its heart would be. Blood spilled out from its chest, and the *derinium* fell dead immediately.

Chase looked up and saw Fin crouching behind a bush, another arrow nocked and at the ready. "Is it dead?" the boy called.

Chase nodded a bit numbly. The phantom's grip had not slipped with its death, so he reached down and gingerly began prying its fingers off his ankle. At his touch, the phantom's body disintegrated, leaving just two arrows lying on the ground, covered in dark blood. His fear finally drained away, his heart resuming a normal pace after several moments. The heat of the fight leaked out of him.

The others crowded around, staring at the spot where the *derinium* had lain. Devon glanced at Chase. "What did he say to you?"

Chase swallowed. "Well…" he paused. He didn't know if he could even process what he was about to say. "He said that Jisara has been invaded. The monsters are beginning to discover that the barrier is gone. They're attacking." He glanced anxiously around him. "And they're not the only ones. The horse is still out there. The *derinium* said it was going to bring more of its kind after us. We have to get to the Sumadine Woods soon. They know what's in those woods. They won't follow. Nobody's that stupid but us."

Suddenly he felt weak, and he crumpled to his knees. Grace gasped. "Chase! You're hurt!"

Chase was suddenly very aware of the warmth seeping through his jacket. That pressure he had felt earlier had apparently been a cut. He hadn't even realized what had happened at the time. He gritted his teeth, more in frustration than pain. "It's just a scratch."

But one look at his jacket told him otherwise. It was soaked a deep red all the way down his back and forearm, and the pain was spreading just as fast. The initial shock of the wound was fading. Fiery heat singed his shoulder, and upon pulling off his jacket he found that his shirt, too, was soaked almost completely through with blood. He began to feel a bit faint, and Fin rushed to steady him as he swayed hazily. Grace quickly poured water into his mouth.

Teto suddenly pushed his way to the front of the small crowd. "Look, I care about the kid just fine and all, but before that… where's Tara?" he asked worriedly.

Silence followed as everyone began to think what no one dared to say. Rebel started whining. "No," Tetoviran whispered. "You wimpy squirrels, I'm going to go find her and hit all your sorry behinds when I find her alive and unscathed. Go dig yourselves a hole and cry somewhere." And with that, he stomped off determinedly, calling her name.

Devon glanced worriedly at the others but said nothing. Fin helped lay Chase down gently after a moment, propping him up against a rock. "I'll be right back. I'm going to go help look for"—

"Tara!" Teto's voice boomed across the field. A feminine scream that definitely belonged to Tara trailed after it, followed by nervous laughter. Fin's eyes lit up as the pair came into view. Grace quickly followed, and together, they made their way back to where Chase lay.

Tara was trembling in shock and terror from her trauma, but when she saw Chase, she flew to him and wrapped him in a hug. He grunted and tried not to cry out with pain. She obviously hadn't seen his wound.

"Thank you!" she cried, seemingly on the verge of tears. "Thank you, Chase. I know you were mad, and you still helped anyway, and you saved my life, and Fin, thank you for shooting him, and…"

She stopped and looked at Chase, then shrank a bit. "Are you still angry? Oh, Chase, I'm so sorry. All of you. I'm so sorry to all of you."

Chase smiled through gritted teeth. "It's fine. I'm glad you're okay."

She frowned. "Then what's wrong with"—she gasped. "You're bleeding!" Her eyes widened as she looked at his shirt. "A lot."

"Yeah." He closed his eyes and tried to focus on steadying his breathing. "I'm bleeding a lot."

She hurriedly moved away from him, mumbling apologies frantically as Devon carefully unbuttoned Chase's shirt to examine the wound. He slid the sleeves down, and Chase whimpered in a way that he was embarrassed of when Devon pulled his arm a little too far back. His eyes pricked, but he refused to let himself cry.

The others crowded around, and Tara looked sick as she stared at the gash in the meat of his shoulder. "Too much," Fin mumbled. "That's way too much blood."

Despite his effort to stay positive, Chase knew he was right. If they didn't find a means of helping the wound besides bandaging, he could very easily die. He'd always sort of figured he was immortal. Stupid, but helpful when he became afraid. He was very afraid now.

"What can you do for it?" Chase asked, scared of the response. There was a horrible moment of silence. "Answer me!" he shouted, his voice cracking unintentionally.

"Kid, there's not…" Tetoviran trailed off.

Suddenly Tara's eyes widened. "I can help!" she cried. She dug around in her knapsack, finally pulling forth a needle and thread. "I brought them along in the beginning," she explained, then turned to Devon. "Clean it, will you? When you're done, I'll stitch"— She stopped talking abruptly, her eyes fixed on the plants in front of them. Everyone followed her gaze.

"What now?" Fin growled, reaching for his bow. But a smile was slowly spreading on Tara's face.

"What is it?" Grace asked, squinting to see what Tara was looking at. "What are you seeing?"

"Leaves." Tara grinned like a child receiving a gift. "Those leaves. They can help us!"

Devon groaned. "Oh, wonderful. Now she's gone mad."

She shook her head quickly. "No. They're herbs. Earth… she's helping us. She sent us this plant." She scurried to the shrubs and plucked a handful of leaves from the bush, then handed them to Chase. "These will help you heal. They'll remove infection."

He was nearly panting with pain, his head spinning from a loss of blood. "Are you sure?" She nodded. "Yes. Chew these, and when they're in a pulp, spit it into your hands. We'll put the paste on the wound."

He frowned skeptically but put two leaves in his mouth and chewed. He immediately spat them out on the ground. "Ugh," he cried. "They're disgusting! I'm not chewing these stupid leaves!"

"Would you rather have someone else's saliva in your wound?" Chase chewed the stupid leaves. While he did, Devon used a small knife to cut Chase's shirt into strips. Half of them, he set aside for bandaging. With the rest, he got to work cleaning the wound.

Tara took the hand of Chase's unharmed side into hers, giving his fingers a slight squeeze. Chase spat out the pulp of bitter leaves and waved her away carelessly, shaking her hand from his. "I'll be fine." She looked anything but reassured but didn't press him.

Devon took the paste from Chase and began smoothing it gently around the wound. As he reached the slash, his arm and chest muscles tensed visibly and he clenched his jaw, digging his fingers into the dirt for relief of the pain. He closed his eyes briefly and moaned into his teeth. *You have to be strong,* he countered himself. *The weak don't make it in this world.* He opened his eyes gingerly, flitting his lids away from the light as though he'd been in darkness for hours.

Fin was crouched in front of him. "How are you?" he asked worriedly.

Chase tossed him a flat look. "Peachy."

"You aren't really expecting to keep going, are you? You're in no shape for travel."

Chase laughed shortly. "I don't have a choice at this point. We're not far from the trail. Once we find it again, we'll have to travel all night long if we're going to get there in time to beat the *deriniums.*" Fin pressed his lips together but said nothing more. They both knew he was right.

Devon stepped around to face him. "The bleeding subsided a little, and the herbs are definitely helping. Are you ready for the stitching, Tara?"

She gulped and gripped her needle, her fingers sliding on it from her sweat. "I… yes."

Chase took a deep breath and braced himself. "Go easy on me," he managed to murmur through his clenched teeth. Tara was trembling as she stepped around him. "Sorry," she whispered in advance, then slid the needle into his skin.

Chase cried out and jerked away when the needle first punctured his shoulder, and Tara yelped as the thread pulled tight. Whatever pain he thought he'd had before, this was worse.

"Chase!" she scolded. "You can't move like that!"

"It hurts!"

"I'm trying to help you! Keep still, you'll only make the pain worse." She continued to sew his wound together, and he cursed at her as she pulled the thread taut. She paused and frowned at him. "Careful." Her tone had a warning edge he'd never heard before, like she was telling him not to push too far.

"Sorry," he mumbled, and he kept still until she was finished, withstanding the stinging silently.

Finally, Tara used Devon's knife to cut the end of the thread. "There. It's all done."

Chase never thanked anyone for causing him pain, but he did anyway because he knew that she'd probably just saved his life. She nodded curtly, then put her sewing supplies away in her knapsack as Devon started bandaging him.

Chase studied Tara for a moment, then tilted his head back at her. "What's the matter?"

She looked at him, startled. "Nothing."

"Uh-huh." He waited a moment longer. She sighed.

"What if it's not enough? What if you still don't make it? After everything I did to you, you would die because you tried to protect me."

Chase rolled his eyes, trying to make light of things. "Kill the drama, Princess. I've been through worse, and I think you worked a little Earthy magic on those leaves. Tasted horrible, but helped a lot more than they probably should have." It was true. The paste had made him feel much, much stronger. Already the pain was beginning to subside. It was being replaced by itchiness, which he figured would get really irritating really fast.

Tara frowned slightly, clearly not believing him, and sat down beside him. "I'm sorry I hurt you," she said quietly. Chase got the feeling she was referring to more than stitching his wound, and he pressed his lips together for a moment. He had forgiven her for gossiping—almost losing her had been more than enough to take care of that—but it still felt odd to him that she cared enough to apologize. Of course, being Tara, she would, but he was still getting used to being cared about after all this time.

"And I'm sorry I swore at you," he returned, the words feeling odd in his mouth. "You didn't deserve that, despite what a backstabbing little rat you are. So now I will tell you that you're beautiful, and magnificent, and a wonderful girl all the way around"—he leaned back to glance suggestively at her rear— "literally, you know—to make up for it."

Tara reddened, shifting uncomfortably under that gaze and frowning at him. "You can't even give me a straight compliment, pervert."

"Well, I've got to have some fun, don't I?" Tara gave him a flat glare, and he lifted his hands in surrender.

They were silent for a moment until Chase shoved her. "Well, go on and say something nice about me, will you?"

Tara cocked her head a little. "Does it have to be nice?"

"Yes."

A beat passed. "Huh. I can't think of anything."

Chase fixed her with a glare. "When this thing's healed, watch out. I've got a feeling your skills aren't as sharp as the *derinium's*. And, in case you didn't notice, it's dead. Just imagine how quickly you'd go down." He smirked at her and wrinkled his nose. "One swift chop," he whispered, miming cutting her throat with his index finger and drawing a white line in her skin with his nail.

Tara grinned, refusing to be scared by his empty threats. "But in the meantime, I can do whatever I want. And when you try to kill me, Fin won't help you finish the job."

"Only takes one hand to strangle a person, you know." He held up his good arm, reaching for her neck again.

She just smiled wider. "It also takes a brain to be able to make that hand work. You're definitely lacking."

Chase let his hand close gently over her throat, his smile thin. "Push me a little further. I dare you."

Her smile wavered for a moment, and he felt her warm pulse beneath his fingers. He felt her *life* beneath his fingers, which was a weird thought. He literally held her life in his hand. How easy it would be to—*WHAT?* his brain screamed at the intrusive notion. Almost as if reading the random, unwanted thought, she frowned, tilting her head. "Would you do it?"

He pulled away in shock at her question. She seemed deadly serious. "No! Never, Tara, not if you begged me to."

She looked at him hesitantly, then nodded. "I… I know. I feel silly for asking now. You can just be very… persuasive. You made me feel like if I were to do something, you really might…"

"Really? After everything I went through just now to save your life, I'm not about to kill you." He paused. "Maybe later, though."

She rolled her eyes.

Once they stopped talking, Chase realized how distracted the conversation had made him. He was suddenly very aware of the itchy pain in his shoulder that made him wish he could scratch the stitches away. Devon was just finishing up and tying the bandage, and Chase's head began to wander to different subjects—such as the *derinium* who'd given him that wound.

Chase always tried to be brave, sometimes to impress people, other times because he hated relinquishing his pride. He'd immersed himself in a character that did not fear anything. Yet he did fear. Everyone did. The hairs on the back of his neck stood on end when he thought of those glowing red eyes boring into him, reading his soul like a book. That blade that never failed, the senses that seemed to anticipate every move he made. He wondered if *deriniums* were always watching him, always awaiting his next move with the knowledge that he was playing right into their hands.

Chase shivered as Devon came forward. "I wrapped it tight and secured it. We have extra cloth packed away, and Grace got more of those leaves. So, if you're ready…"

Chase held out his hand, and Devon pulled him to his feet. Chase cracked his neck and winced. "I've never felt better." And he'd told bigger lies before. He turned and helped Tara up with his good hand. "Let's go."

CHAPTER 23

Tara stumbled blindly over a tree root in the darkness. Thin branches seemed to reach out for her face, and the wind hissed through the leaves, rustling her nerves right along with the trees. Deep, thick clouds covered a small moon, making it nearly impossible to see. The night was cold and heavy with ominousness. Owls cooed and shadows lurked. Tara's imagination was a greater enemy than anything that could've been hiding in the darkness.

She didn't know why she was so nervous. Fin was walking right in front of her. She was flanked by Rebel and Tetoviran, and Chase was behind her, but she was still afraid of the night.

She stepped carefully, avoiding underbrush as they followed the trail on their way to the Sumadine Woods. So far, there had been no sign of trials, monsters, or *deriniums,* but the night was still young. From the dark, a raccoon scurried across Tara's foot, and her heart leapt so fiercely that for a split second, she felt her eyes awaken. Her necklace glowed with the strength of fear, and the plants all around her bent to her for two heartbeats, before she took a breath and calmed herself down. Everyone turned to look at her, and she flushed with embarrassment.

"Sorry," she mumbled. How was that even possible? Her powers ignited from her fear in the woods, but not when a *derinium* was trying to kill her? Her necklace was some kind of ridiculous joke. *Or maybe there's something in these woods that should be feared more than a* derinium, her stupid imagination suggested.

They continued on in this sort of fashion for several hours, Tara's powers waking six more times, until she felt a hand on her shoulder. She jumped out of her skin and turned with her fist already flying. Chase caught her punch with his hand before she could hit him in the face, laughing softly.

She exhaled with relief and held her chest while her heart slowed, practically sagging with fatigue. She was exhausted, and her jitteriness didn't help.

"Relax, Tara. Can we talk?"

She nodded and fell back in stride with him. A cold wind passed through the trees, and Tara shivered in her jacket. She glanced at Chase and immediately pitied him. His shirt and jacket had been ruined with blood, and he was walking with only the bandages around his shoulder for warmth. His exposed skin prickled with goosebumps. She was still worried about his wound. Even though he said it wasn't bothering him and he wasn't betraying nearly as many signs of pain as before, she knew how good he could be at hiding things. He could still be in horrible pain, for all she knew. She'd seen him twitching strangely many times, as though he needed to scratch something, and he was consuming so much food and water to keep lightheadedness away that they would be out of provisions in a few days.

"What do you want to talk about?" she asked. He glanced at his lightly stepping boots in a slight hesitation before responding. "Am I really that bad, Tara? Do you really hate me the way you told Grace you do?"

Tara immediately recoiled, stepping away from him. She felt horrible about that. He smiled gently and pulled her back to him by her elbow. "I'm not mad, Princess. I just want to know. I'm still sort of... new... to the whole friendship thing."

She shook her head and watched their feet moving in sync, being careful not to look up. She was so ashamed for having said that. "No. No, you're not at all bad. At that point, I wasn't still upset with any of you. I just hadn't really had anyone to talk to about it when it happened, so I took the opportunity and just kind of vented. I told Grace about everything, but I didn't necessarily expect that she'd... um..." She trailed off, staring at Teto's back in front of her.

"Tell us?" A smile hid behind Chase's tone. "I just wanted to make sure you weren't actually mad at me. And that I'm not actually so horrid. I know I've been mean, but I really am trying. I really am sorry."

"How could I stay mad at you after all this time and all you've done?"

Chase smirked and put his good arm around her. "How could anyone stay mad at me for more than a few moments? I'm adorable."

Tara finally looked up, elbowing his stomach so gently it was more of a skimming. He folded his body over and stumbled like she'd hit him with a hammer. Recovering with an overexaggerated groan, he shivered suddenly. "Holy Death, it's freezing."

Tara smiled. "It's not that cold. You're just not wearing anything. Do you want my jacket?"

Chase smothered a snort. "Sure, sure, offer me clothes. Pretend you don't like seeing me shirtless. Besides, you really think I could fit into *your* clothes? With muscles like these?"

Tara squinted at his perfectly chiseled arms and chest as if searching for something. "Which muscles would we be talking about, now?"

In a single, impossibly quick motion, his good arm encircled her neck from behind, his biceps flexed hard enough to push against her throat. "These ones," he chirped as she gasped reflexively, grabbing at his arm and trying to push him away. The feeling of being choked from behind certainly wasn't easing her nervousness.

Finally managing to shove him off, Tara gagged to recover and shot him a disdainful look, which he returned with an impish grin. "If you're so great at being charming and sweet, so why don't you ever try being that way with me?" she grumbled. "I offered you a jacket."

"Because strangling you is more fun," he began, ticking off the first reason on a finger, "you aren't deserving of my charm," he counted, "I don't really care at all whether you like me or not," he continued, "and I don't want your jacket." Tara curled her lips at him in irritation, and he dove forward as though to lean in and kiss them. She pulled away quickly, giving him a rough shove for good measure.

"If you want to be rude, then suit yourself and freeze," she muttered, moving to walk on ahead of him.

"That's impossible, I'm too hot to freeze."

Tara frowned slightly, turning back over her shoulder. "But you just told me how cold you"— Chase smirked as realization hit her. "For the love of Earth," she muttered. "I have never met a more conceited person in my entire life."

"Well, that's just because no one else is handsome enough to be this conceited. Look at me."

"I am," she said flatly.

Chase waved his hand at her in exasperation. "I don't expect you to understand. You couldn't truly relate since you're so pitifully ugly, but if you looked like me, you'd be bragging constantly, too, believe me."

Tara gave him a disgusted look, which he returned perfectly. "Ugh," she muttered. "I'm going to walk with Teto." Chase smiled as she quickened her pace to catch up with Tetoviran.

Rebel rubbed against her foot as she walked. "How much farther, Tara?" the *tesko* mumbled sleepily. "I'm exhausted."

Tara smiled down at him as his eyes began to droop. His steps were dragging slower and slower. He fell back with Chase, who picked him up and handed him to Tara. "Little guy's falling asleep on his feet," he said.

Tara nodded. "You can rest, Rebel." She tucked him away into her knapsack, kissing his soft head before closing it. "Sleep tight, baby," she whispered in his silken ear. He purred softly before quiet snores overcame him. Tara tightened the drawstring and pulled the knapsack shut, readjusting it carefully on her back.

Chase stepped down on the back of her shoe. "You like him more than me. How come I've never gotten that treatment before I go to sleep?"

"Because Rebel doesn't try to kill me every three seconds." Naturally taking his cue, Chase grabbed Tara by the back of her neck and dragged her body backwards, making her stumble enough that she nearly fell. He gave the sides of her throat an unpleasant squeeze before releasing her, drawing a yelp as she felt her face fill with blood for a moment. Regaining some balance, she brushed herself off shakily and tried to control her urge to punch Chase in the face. It probably wouldn't end well for her, anyways, and she knew he was only playing.

"Rebel also isn't a conceited arrogant pest," she muttered sourly.

"Aw, you love me."

She debated pretending to be mad at him, then relented, "Not half as much as you love yourself."

Chase cracked a grin. "I can hardly deny that."

They walked quietly for a while longer until it was probably near midnight. Tara took a breath and let the sweet scents of clean, cool air and fresh trees envelop her. In the strangest, most backward way possible, Chase's threats had calmed her nerves a bit. Somehow, the night didn't seem quite as scary now. It seemed peaceful and quiet in a beautiful way. The world was resting, silent and serene. Everything was just as it should be.

Just as Tara was finally reaching this peace of mind, two people leapt out at her from the trees. She screamed in alarm as they ran toward her, one of them holding a small lantern the size of his palm. Small and easy to hide as it was, it emitted a strong light that allowed Tara to see the attackers. The one with the lantern was a boy with scraggly, unkempt red hair and a spattering of freckles across his nose. He carried a dagger in his other hand and had the biggest green eyes Tara had ever seen.

The other appeared to be a girl from the dark braid sweeping past her waist, but Tara couldn't tell for sure. She held a long curved scythe and wore a long black cloak over her hunting clothes. Her hood was pulled up over her face, completely shadowing her entire head all the way to her shoulders.

The two charged out from opposite sides in the bushes. Fin nocked an arrow in his bow, and Devon and Teto drew their swords with a start. The cloaked person ran to Tara and grabbed her around the neck, holding her scythe at her throat. Unlike when Chase had threatened to choke her earlier, this was not playful. Barely daring to breathe, Tara froze with the others, everyone waiting to see what the attacker would do. Fin's arrow had swiveled to point at the girl, but it also pointed now at Tara's head. He could hardly fire, and her throat would be slit before Teto, Devon, or Grace could ever reach her.

Chase, to her utmost shock, just stood there with crossed arms, smiling as though he'd been expecting this. Tara realized with a start that he probably had been. Was it possible that Chase had led them to an ambush? No. He would never do something like that. Yet Tara couldn't understand why he hadn't said anything before, because now they were in danger. Chase was usually smarter than this.

To her shock, though, he stepped forward and spoke. "Put your weapon down, Logan. You deserve death more than anybody here, but we won't harm you." The red-haired boy broke into a grin, his dagger somehow disappearing into his many layers of clothing. The blade at Tara's throat faltered in surprise as Tara and all her companions frowned in confusion.

Setting his lantern on the ground, the boy named Logan came forward and embraced Chase. "Where've you been, you lousy sneak? I've been sitting around for years, just waiting for you to creep up behind me!"

Chase smirked. "And you've clearly lost your touch. I thought you'd know not to speak out loud in the woods while you're trying to surprise somebody. I'd recognize your voice anywhere."

Logan side-eyed him. "I thought you might have forgotten me over the years. Daydreaming about the sound of my voice all this time, hmm? You hopeless romantic. Do you hear me calling out to you at night? Do you cry out my name in your sleep?"

Chase grinned. "Never in a million years would I forget to watch my back for some ugly street cat to jump on it. Besides, the last time we saw each other, I was the one pulling a heist on you, so I've been waiting for you to come to me. What are you doing all the way out here, anyways?"

"We were in the same town as you yesterday. I saw you on the street from an upstairs window and decided to follow you. We got really lost for a while, but then I finally heard you—whoa! What happened?" He stared at Chase's bandages.

"Derinium."

Logan stared at Chase with big eyes. "No way."

Chase grinned crookedly. "It's not nearly as fun as it looks."

Logan seemed impressed. "Not bad for a Jisarian thief. You've made your way in the world, you filthy gutter rat. And hey, I got lost for good reason! I missed that battle."

Chase folded his arms with a smile. "Coward," he muttered, then looked over the redhead's shoulder. His gaze fell on the cloaked figure at Tara's throat, then flitted back to Logan. "You mind?"

This entire time, everyone else had been standing in awkward, disbelieving silence. Nobody quite knew what to make of it, but Tara did not appreciate the blade pressed against her neck.

Now, Logan smiled sheepishly. "Sorry. Let her go."

Tara waited for the girl to let her free, but she didn't move. For several moments, there was no movement, and Tara felt panic start rising. "He said you could let go," she said, working hard to keep the fear out of her voice. Miraculously, it worked, and she ended up sounding fairly hostile. Everyone watched expectantly, and Chase's hand drifted subconsciously towards his sword despite the easy smile that remained on his face.

When the girl still did not pull her weapon away, Logan rolled his eyes in his lantern light. "Quit," he told his companion carelessly. Finally, she stepped away reluctantly, and Tara turned to her with a frown. She felt strangely irritated by this girl, and even more strangely confident in that feeling. "You could've done that a lot earlier," she snapped, drawing startled looks from her friends.

Chase whistled. "Haven't heard that tone in a while," he commented. "Sort of missed it." Tara bit her lip immediately after the words were out. She knew she shouldn't have said that, but her life had been threatened far too many times in the past several hours for her to tolerate yet another weapon at her throat. She was sick of being so scared.

The girl's posture tightened at Tara's words, and she lifted her scythe to point it at her. "Do not test me," she warned softly, barely loud enough for the others to hear. Tara stared at the darkness over her face, determined not to let any fear show. She did not want this girl to think she was weak. If Logan happened to stay with them for a while, Tara didn't want this newcomer thinking she could push her around. There were no words for several moments, and then Chase spoke with a very slight change in his tone.

"Come here, Tara." He still sounded fairly lighthearted, but everyone saw the tension in that moment. Even though she couldn't see them, Tara felt the girl's eyes on her as she finally broke their standoff and walked to Chase's side. He silently wrapped his hand protectively around her wrist, undoubtedly feeling the pounding of her pulse that belied what she hoped was a stoic outward appearance.

Tara noticed that Logan lifted an eyebrow at her, to which Chase rolled his eyes and mouthed, *no.* He tilted his head at the girl who'd threatened Tara. "Who is she?"

Logan glanced behind him. "Oh, her? She's my, uh… cousin. Yeah, my cousin from… from, uh…"

The figure spoke for the first time, in what was definitely a feminine voice. "From Soldriz."

Logan snapped his fingers. "Yes, that's it! Soldriz! She is my cousin from Soldriz."

"Does she have a name?" Chase asked patiently.

The girl didn't move. Logan nodded and spoke for her. "Yes. Emma. Her name is Emma. My cousin Emma from… uh…"

Emma intervened again, sounding mildly irritated. "Soldriz."

Logan nodded. "Yeah, that."

Chase nodded a greeting to her, but Tara was far from willing to be friendly with that girl. Besides, the fact that she and Logan weren't related was plain as day, even to her.

"So, who's all *this?*" Logan asked, gesturing to Fin, Tetoviran, Devon, and Grace. Chase introduced each of them, and each of them in turn put away their weapon and greeted each other cordially.

"How do you two know each other?" Fin asked.

"We were both thieves in Jisara," Chase explained. "We became…friends…I suppose, by some absurd chain of events, and we started a game where, at random times and places, we'd try to sneak up on each other or scare each other. Rat broke my arm once jumping on me from a tree." Logan laughed at the memory, and Tara found herself observing him closely. She hadn't known Chase had had any friends before her, but Logan was so like him that their friendship was unsurprising. Then again, most real friends didn't break each other's arms, so it may have been much more of a love-hate acquaintance type of thing.

"Logan left Jisara a few years ago," Chase continued, "but every once in a while, we'd cross paths and try to sneak up on each other again like we used to. So that's what Logan was doing. I was calm because I recognized his voice in the woods."

"Funny that we were okay with each other," Logan mused. "We stole from each other just as much as everyone else, and both of us knew it, too."

Chase laughed. "I beat you up the first time I found out, but after that there was no grief."

Logan nodded grimly. "Believe me, my ribs still remember that day. You broke three."

Emma stepped forward and looked at Logan. "Enough of this. You told me we were going to attack a group of travelers and steal provisions. You mentioned nothing of knowing anyone or playing games."

"Of course not, because you hate games and you take everything too seriously. You wouldn't have participated if you'd known it was a game." Logan turned back to Chase, completely ignoring whatever else Emma had to say. "Oh, and there's been some straggler following us since we left the town. Thinks we don't know he's there, but we lost him a few hours before sunset."

Just as he spoke, a teenage boy with curly brown hair came crashing through the underbrush, got his foot caught on a tree root, and somersaulted into the middle of the group, tumbling head over heels before stopping in front of everyone.

Chase snorted. "You really lost him."

Logan scowled at the ratty boy getting to his feet before him. "Man, this guy's annoying. He just won't give up!"

The boy took one look at everyone around him, scrambled to his feet, and turned to run. Devon grabbed him by the back of his shirt and dragged him back, causing him to put up a frantic struggle until Logan told him to relax. "What's your name?"

The boy dusted himself off and gave Devon a wary look as he let him go. "Oliver Minehart." His voice shook slightly.

Grace frowned. "We're meeting a lot of new people tonight, and I only like one of them." She looked pointedly at Logan, who shifted his feet and reddened.

Chase smothered a laugh. "Look who's found himself a girlfriend." Logan punched him in the gut. Despite his earlier beating there, Chase didn't show so much as a hint of unordinary pain.

Tetoviran rolled his eyes. "I don't like a single one of 'em. We need to keep moving. We don't have time for holding hands around the campfire with olives and cloaky people. We need to go."

Oliver and Emma spoke simultaneously. "Um, it's Oliver." "I have a name, you know."

Tetoviran folded his arms across his chest. "I'm going to call you Olive and Cloaky Person."

Logan grinned. "Hey, I like you." A beat passed. "Who are you?"

"I make fun of everyone and take care of Tara," Tetoviran proclaimed shortly.

Chase shrugged. "About as accurate as that's going to get."

"You didn't make fun of me," Logan pointed out.

Tetoviran sniffed. "Just for that, I'm going to make fun of you the most, Tomato Head. Now shut up or I'll start calling you some other names you *really* won't like." Logan looked delighted.

Tara cleared her throat, trying not to smile. "Sorry to break up this… moment… but Tetoviran's right. We really have to keep moving. We've lost a lot of time already."

Chase nodded reluctantly. "Yeah, she's right. Sorry, Logan."

His friend began to reply, but Oliver—the stranger—interrupted. "Where are you going?"

Chase turned to him with a judgmental sneer, one so rude that it made Tara want to smack him. "Why do you want to know?" Oliver was just barely shorter than Chase, but now he cowered back nervously.

"I was wondering. That's all. My… my parents died, not too long ago. I've been searching for… well, I suppose for a new… something. Family? Community? Uh, of a sort. To travel with. Maybe."

Tara saw pity flash momentarily through Chase's eyes, but it quickly faded, replaced by enmity. "We're going to the Sumadine Woods."

He didn't offer to let Oliver come, though, and he shrank back a little more. "Oh. Well, uh, good luck, then." He turned as if to leave, then turned back hesitantly. "Do you… um, I hate to be so imposing, but do you happen to have anything to eat?"

Tara felt a pang of sympathy in her heart. She hadn't known Oliver more than a few minutes, but there was no way she would let Chase send him away without food. If he'd really been following Logan and Emma for so long, he hadn't eaten much in a while. "Of course," she answered before Chase could, reaching into her knapsack and handing him a small meal she had wrapped in cloth earlier.

Oliver took it with an air of reverence, nearly trembling with gratitude. Her heart warmed as he grinned. "Thank you," he breathed. "Thank you so, so much!" She would have thought she'd handed him a diamond.

Fin tilted his head at Oliver curiously as he began to eat. "You don't seem in any rush to be someplace," he noted. The stranger was barely breathing between ravaging bites. He was obviously starved. "Mm," he agreed around a full mouth.

Fin studied him for a moment longer, then spoke again. "Would you like to come with us?"

Chase let out a noise of protest. "Hold on a minute"—he began, but Fin cut him off, having seemingly prepared an entire argument already. "Think about it, Chase. He'll be all on his own out here if we leave him. Nobody can survive that."

Chase folded his arms. "Then maybe we can leave the two of you to help each other out. This isn't smart. How can we trust him?" he asked impatiently.

"You're a thief," Fin pointed out. "How could you expect us to trust you, but not him?"

"We don't know anything about him."

Oliver's head was turning back and forth from Chase to Fin as he ate, watching the argument as though it wasn't a matter of his life at all.

"Chase, listen. You and Tara didn't know me at all, either, but you let me come along. We all trusted Devon, and Grace likewise, without really knowing either of them. That's how you make friends. If he acts out of line, then it's in our hands to throw him out. It would be six against one, Chase. What have you to lose?"

In the meantime, Devon had been talking to Logan, and he now brought Chase, Fin, Tara, Tetoviran, and Grace into a huddle. "Logan wants to know if he and Emma can come with us to the Sumadine Woods. They said they've got nothing else to do with themselves, and at this point they're just wandering. What do you think?" Tara ground her teeth together slightly at the prospect of travelling with Emma.

"Well, Oliver wants to come, too," Fin said.

Grace wrinkled her nose. "Do any of you realize that we just met these people? We can't just say, *oh, yeah, sure, just come on in* and risk them ambushing us."

"Why not?" Tara asked. "That's what we did with you, Grace."

Grace turned red. "Yes, but…"

"But what? Why can't we give them a chance?"

Tetoviran sniffed. "They all seem extremely stupid, so they'd certainly fit right in." Everyone rolled their eyes.

"Well, I think it's risky."

"I think we should give them a chance."

"I think all of you kids need to shut your chicken holes."

Chase spoke for the first time in the conversation. "I trust Logan. The others can be handled. So either we take them or leave them, because we need to get going."

Everyone turned to look at the three people who stood behind them, then turned back to their group. "Well?" Fin prodded. And they all came to an unspoken agreement.

Tara turned to Logan, Emma, and Oliver. "You can come."

Oliver only stared. For a moment, Tara thought he might cry, but then he smiled and exhaled in relief. Logan gave Chase a happy, playful shove. Chase responded by sweeping his leg through Logan's ankles in a swift arc, bowling the skinny boy off his feet. Emma didn't react at all.

Tara looked around. Their group had certainly gotten larger. They were now traveling to Destiny and Fate with nine people and a baby *tesko.* She just hoped Logan, Emma, and Oliver could fight, because they'd tarried for a long time and made a lot of noise. If the *deriniums* didn't know where they were before, they did now. Soon enough, they were off again.

As they walked, Chase and Tara took turns explaining the situation from the very beginning to the present, which took them forever to accomplish. By the time the newcomers were filled in, the sky was lightening in the east, and one by one the stars began to wink out on the horizon.

The air took on a slight warmth, and birds chirped their wake-up calls through the treetops. The group was trekking up a steep, wooded hill as the sky continued to lighten. Sighs of exhaustion and fatigue surrounded Tara. Her feet ached and her eyelids drooped, and just when she thought she would collapse and fall asleep right there where she stood, the group crested a hill.

The sight that met their eyes was glorious. Just about four leagues ahead, laid out on a flat area below them, was a glittering blue creek, flowing with life and brilliance. The sun stretched its arms over the horizon, painting the sky a breathtaking gold, then orange, and finally an astounding shade of gorgeous pink as it crested the skyline in all its bold and glowing glory. All around them, life stirred as the world woke up. A soft, warm breeze rustled the branches of trees and blades of grass all around them. Birds sang their early-morning songs, and countless blossoms seemed to glow in the youth of the rising sun. Just beyond the flowing creek lay a sea of green—trees as far as the eye could see, stretched out forever. The Sumadine Woods.

Tara's breath caught. "We made it." Chase grinned. "Yes, we did."

CHAPTER 24

Fin broke the awe-struck silence with a whoop of joy. "We found it! Come on, let's get closer!" The others eagerly voiced their approval—all except Emma, who stayed silent and came down the hill after everyone else with a purposeful stride rather than the galloping skip the others took.

Chase couldn't figure out Emma's problem. She certainly acted far, far beyond her years, and Logan was the worst liar Chase knew. She was definitely not his cousin.

Yet he couldn't help but wonder why she always seemed so hostile and serious. Logan seemed affectionate with her—he dismissed her stony façade with a smile and wasn't even remotely affected by her coldness—so she had to be hiding some sort of personality. She still hadn't taken that hood down. No one had even gotten a glimpse of her face yet.

Chase was growing more and more curious and found himself developing a determination to see past Emma's guards. Even if Logan saw something in her that he didn't, he wasn't ready to trust someone whose face he couldn't see.

As they ran toward the woods, his heart lightened. They were getting closer to his mother and father with each step. He could feel it, as though their spirits had somehow whispered to him through the leaves and winds around him. The group was only a few leagues from the trees, and hope was building by the second, when suddenly Grace screamed.

Chase's sword began to move from his sheath as he skidded to a halt. Everyone turned to see what was happening, but
Emma acted faster than anyone could think. She leapt through
the air as quickly as Chase ever could have managed, slicing at
what appeared to be nothing with her scythe. Slowly, a dead rider
and his horse materialized on the ground. A dark, twisted knife
was planted in the earth mere inches from Grace's ankle. Chase's
breathing was shallow. Grace had almost been stabbed, and staring at that bleeding *derinium* was like being attacked by one all
over again. He flexed his injured shoulder fearfully, trying to rid
himself of the memory of that cold, dead hand clenched around
his ankle.

Grace was staring at Emma in astonishment. "Wow." Emma
tugged her hood further down. "That was amazing. I… I owe you
everything. Thank you." Emma didn't move. Grace tried again,
pronouncing her words more insistently. *"Thank you."*

Chase could almost feel Emma roll her eyes. When she spoke,
her voice was sharp and clear. "They almost never travel alone.
Keep your eyes open." She gripped her scythe tightly. "There are
more. I can sense it."

Everyone except Chase just stared at her. He immediately
moved, stepping up to take a place next to her with his sword at
the ready. His hands trembled, and he had a white-knuckled grip
on his handle but kept his expression calm. If there was a *derinium*
to be killed, he wanted to be the one to do it.

Emma turned to regard him. He couldn't see her face, and
when she spoke, her voice betrayed no emotion or opinions. "Are
you all but worthless fools? I warn you of danger, yet you all do
nothing—save for him. Watch now." She turned and narrowed
her eyes at the land before her. Chase caught sight of the slightest
motion to his far left, but before he could take action, Emma was

moving into an attack. With sudden movement, she jumped forward and sliced her scythe through the air again, and again a dead *derinium* solidified on the ground. She returned to her stance as though nothing had happened.

"That was only two of the many to come. Now will you all take heed of what I am telling you and draw your weapons? Or can you even fight?"

Grace immediately drew her dagger and stepped up next to Emma. "I can fight." Emma turned and nodded with curt respect to Grace. "And so, you shall." She turned to Tara. "Can I be so bold as to expect the same courage of you?"

Tara blinked. "I…" She glanced at Chase, their eyes meeting briefly. With some surprise, Chase saw hostility there—not for him, but for Emma. Tara wasn't fond of the cloaked girl in front of her.

"Why me?" she asked haltingly.

The shadow over Emma's face seemed to darken as she stared at Tara. "You are a child of Earth, are you not?"

Her eyes narrowed warily. "Yes. How do you know that?" Emma laced her pale fingers delicately on the pommel of her scythe. "I have followed you. I have seen your fear make nature bow to you."

Tara flushed with embarrassment, but Emma cocked her head ever so slightly. "Fear is not a thing to be ashamed of. It is a source of strength. Those who don't fear are ignorant. It is those who fear who become warriors, as they are smart enough to realize that impressing those around you with bravery is never worth walking reckless and unprepared into a fight. That is how the brave die out."

She whirled suddenly, stabbing her scythe at the air, and everyone stared on as she killed yet another *derinium.* Emma was an amazingly skilled fighter, but Chase simply couldn't figure her out. He cast a glance at Logan and mouthed, '*What is up with her?*' His friend just smiled, looking massively entertained.

Emma turned back to Tara casually, studying her, then walked to her. Tara shied away a bit, frowning, but Emma sheathed her scythe and put a surprisingly gentle hand on Tara's. "You are stronger than you know. You simply have yet to discover your power."

Tara wrinkled her nose ever so slightly. "I *have* discovered my power."

Emma shook her head somewhat disappointedly, then turned to Chase. "You're naked," she stated shortly.

He blinked at her. The subject change had been a little too drastic for him to follow. "Being shirtless isn't being naked," he answered after a moment.

Emma only made a noise of disgust in response to that. "Showing off your muscles does not mean you are strong."

Chase frowned, taken aback once more. "Well, firstly, I'm not showing anything off. I was wounded and my shirt got ruined. Secondly, it flatters me that you think I'm muscular. It must get dreary for a girl to look at Logan's scrawny arms all the time." This earned him a kick from his friend, but Chase merely spread his arms and gave Emma a devious grin. "Stare all you want, darling."

Emma seemed ready to reply—or maybe to slap him—but her voice was drowned out by an ear-splitting war cry thundering over the hill. A conch shell of some sort was blown directly afterwards, followed by several more that rang out in unison. Chase felt a chill run from the base of his head down to his heels, his body trembling slightly. Whatever he might have been about to say gushed from his mind as only one thought consumed him: *deriniums.*

With their hair-raising warning came the beating of hoofs on earth that sounded like thousands of beating drums. It began as a dull rumble, then grew into a thundering roar as the source came rushing down the hills—an army of *deriniums* on horseback, every one of them visible. Chase was frozen where he stood. The riders were clad in identical black cloaks, their red eyes visible even from a distance. Some brandished blades; others carried flags emblazoned with a strange symbol that was unfamiliar to Chase. Their dark steeds seemed to glide forward, their manes and tails trailing behind them like black smoke. Chase couldn't count the *deriniums* in the army. He felt a hand clench around his bare biceps and lurched away in alarm, but it was Tara who held him. Her face was ashen. "What do we do?" she asked, her voice cracking. "This," Tetoviran answered, then turned immediately and began to sprint towards the trees. Chase wetted his lips as terror began to grip him. "Yeah, I like his idea." His sword still in hand, he sprinted after Teto. The *deriniums* would not follow them into the Sumadine Woods. There, they would be safe. It was only a matter of making it on time. The others all followed one by one. Emma was the last to make up her mind, but finally conceded and ran with them. The group was close to the woods now. The *deriniums* weren't going to be able to catch them. They would be safe. But breaking this line of thought came a high-pitched shriek from behind Chase, and he turned to see Emma, standing with a dismounted *derinium* on top of her and wrestling with her. The phantom's knife laid on the ground with fresh blood on the blade. Emma's cloak was torn at the hem, and Chase could see the wound on her leg. Somehow, this *derinium* had snuck up on her. He couldn't imagine how a fully visible monster had surprised her when she'd easily struck down three invisible ones, but now wasn't the time for that. Everyone had stopped just before the woods, and

Devon now rushed forward and hacked at the *derinium* with his sword until death took it and it fell off Emma's back. However, the army was now so close, that three riders in front leapt straight off their moving horses and piled onto Devon and Emma, both of whom began to lash out wildly. Another, bearing the foreign flag of their army, remained on horseback and led his horse in galloping circles around the small fight, attempting to close Devon and Emma in. Chase leapt into the circle when the horse was on the other side of a rotation, joining Devon and Emma as more and more *deriniums* dismounted. The horses fled as their riders left them, and those *deriniums* who remained on horseback were struggling to control the aggression of their animals. Soon, Chase and his friends were faced with countless *deriniums* surrounding them. For a split second everything was still as everyone took in the situation. And then the real fighting broke out.

Chase attacked viciously, his arms moving faster than his brain could function. His muscles acted on pure instinct as he deflected one attack after another at a speed beyond compare. He'd fought this way before, but never with so many opponents. He caught glimpses from the corner of his eyes of his friends struggling against the phantoms. Tara was standing alone and being circled by three armed *deriniums* on horseback. Fin, whose bow was useless in close quarters, was holding a knife that looked awkward in his hand. Chase's shoulder ached with pain, but he did his best to ignore it. Each time he lifted his arm, a searing jolt shot down his back. *Just keep going,* he reminded himself. *This pain is temporary. Death isn't.*

He spun his blade in a wide, powerful arc, slashing three *deriniums* clear in half. The dead bodies piled around him and began creating a sort of fortress to help him foresee the attacks. His body began to work on its own, his muscles no longer needing permission from his brain. Slash, parry, turn, block. He had never killed so much in his life, but he was starting to remember what it felt like to feel good in combat. Things were starting to look better and better.

Devon and Tetoviran were abominable forces, forming piles of dead bodies similar to Chase's. Fin seemed to be getting used to his knife, and Grace was small and quick enough to dart through the fighting and open the sides of every remaining ghost horse. Rebel was biting the legs off of dozens of *deriniums,* and Emma—despite having slowed from her leg wound—was still a whirlwind of destruction.

Tara's powers had awoken, and she fought with sword and earth at her command. If a large group of *deriniums* charged any of her friends, the ground rolled beneath them to throw them off balance, opening plenty of opportunity for her companions to slay them. Two *deriniums,* recognizing her power, charged her together. Tara slashed at one with her sword while crushing the other beneath a towering wave of dirt and burying him alive. Chase, in a short period where he could catch his breath, stared at her with awe. She had never looked so powerful. He also noticed more than one phantom being covered with crawling black spiders, rising from the blood-drenched grass to cover the *derinium* from head to toe with their poisonous bites. His heart lifted with thrill as he slayed another phantom. They were winning. This battle might actually be theirs.

A sudden howl broke the din of clashing weapons and shouts of effort, long and low. Not a human howl, but an animal's howl. Wolves. The slightest pause swept over the battlefield, and at least a dozen other howls answered the first. How Tara had suddenly acquired this ability to control her magic, Chase couldn't imagine, but she had summoned help. Racing towards the fighting was a large pack of dark grey wolves, howling and barking and snarling. With fresh strength, they leapt into the battle and began to ravage the remaining *deriniums*, using groups of two or three packmates to take down monster after monster. Their vicious teeth tore into one body after the next, ripping into the enemy. The army's numbers were dwindling.

A new power surged through Chase as he clambered over dead phantoms and leapt into a huge pile of *deriniums* that had jumped on Logan. Together, they pushed the phantoms away, then stood back-to-back and killed them off. Logan was grabbed by another *derinium* and pulled away, and Chase turned to follow and help him, his sword at the ready.

But then, just when things had been looking so optimistic, he felt a blade cut against his old shoulder wound. It just barely grazed his shoulder, but it came with slicing accuracy, running exactly along his original cut and breaking through both the bandages and the stitches. There was no muted pressure like he had felt before; this was simple agony. Chase yelled wordlessly, then turned and killed the *derinium* without any thought, anger and pain fueling him. Another attacked, and he stabbed it easily.

Rage now powered him, giving a quick burst of angry energy before it fizzled out and he was reminded of his new cut. Throbbing, stinging, burning pain seared his shoulder. The wound had been fully reopened, and he felt warm blood trickling down his bare back. As he continued to fight, the pain grew worse. His vision blurred and everything became fuzzy as his eyes swam with pain. He was losing way too much blood now. Dizziness swept over him as his movements slowed, dragging out like his muscles had liquefied. His motions grew slower. The world spun wildly as the pain incinerated his shoulder. It was worsening by the second, and Chase felt his mind go numb as he swayed with the pain.

He didn't feel himself fall, didn't feel himself hit the ground. All he saw were the fuzzy outlines of moving feet at eye level with him. *We're winning,* he thought brainlessly. *We're winning.*

He heard someone cry his name and saw a shadow looming over him. Saw a blade come down on him. There were figures racing in his direction—wolves, people—but nothing could save him now. *We're winning.*

In utter pain and complete helplessness, Chase let his sword slip from his fingers in defeat as the blade punctured his chest, driven by the blurry silhouette of a dark figure with red eyes.

～

Chase awoke to find himself surrounded in crisp, pure white. There were no shadows, not even his own, and he appeared to be in a huge room with whiter-than-milk walls and no doors or windows.

He dimly remembered what had happened before he'd gone unconscious, and upon moving his shoulder, he felt no pain. He saw the wound clearly and knew immediately that it was far worse than the first cut had been. Blood gushed freely, staining his still-bare chest and back. He brushed his fingers over the wound, and his fingers came away dripping red. The gash ran deep and was an angry, ugly red-brown color beneath the ripped layers of flesh. But somehow, he felt nothing at all.

He shouted, and his voice echoed back to him with such force that he practically stumbled. That was when he noticed the hole. Also gushing blood, a gap pierced his chest right where his heart should be. He remembered getting stabbed. Oddly, he felt no shock or panic at such thoughts. Instead, he felt eerily relaxed and carefree, like he was extremely intoxicated. Nothing, nothing at all, pained him in the slightest.

When he'd been alive, he hadn't even noticed how much his feet hurt or his back ached with tension. Now, he didn't really even think about getting back to his life. He wanted to stay here. He wanted to remain where he was, free of all pain or stress or any real mental state of being. He'd been stabbed in the heart— so what? He was dead now. He'd expected something worse for death. Much more pain and gore and struggle. This was peaceful.

He walked around the empty room, running his hands over cool, smooth walls. He tapped a finger against one wall, and a hollow noise bounced back through the room. He assumed the walls weren't very thick, but then again, he had no idea where he even was. He couldn't possibly know anything about this strange room, and he didn't dare make assumptions.

With a sigh, he sat down, which resounded back to him with a thump. He ran a hand through his hair, and only then did he notice that instead of his black boots, he was barefoot. Although his shirt was still missing, he now wore a white skirt of some sort around his waist. It was so light that he hadn't even noticed it before. It was apparently made of creamy silk and flowed over his legs like a river.

His hand, for some reason, drifted to his hip, though he couldn't quite remember why. Upon finding it bare except for the tunic, his heart skipped a beat in his chest; again, he was unsure why. What was this feeling? He recognized it, but couldn't name it. It didn't belong here, where he was.

"Anxiety." A deep, cheery voice boomed through the room. Chase looked up calmly, distantly wondering who might have said that. "Nervousness," the voice continued. "Worry. Concern. Unease. Fretfulness. Apprehension. Angst. Discomfort. Trepidation. Dread. Hesitation. Misgiving. Alarm. Agitation. A number of accurate words and synonyms to fully describe your unspecified feeling."

In front of Chase, a man materialized. He had a curled black moustache and a neatly trimmed goatee. His hair was slicked back carefully, and he held a feather pen and a seemingly never-ending roll of parchment that tumbled all throughout the room. He smiled merrily.

"Hello. I am Speech, son of Sound and Hearing. You haven't even the slightest idea how delighted I am to meet you, Chase Onaj. My great-great-great-great-great-great aunts, Destiny and Fate, have chosen you. So elated and honored I am to be in the pious presence of such an intrepid, youthful gentleman."

Chase frowned after a moment, then spoke slowly. "Destiny? Fate? Those are just words." Speech smiled and held up a finger. "On the contrary, dear boy. 'Man' and 'woman' are also but mere words. Alas, they exist as living organisms in this world, just beside you and me. In fact, 'chase' is a word as well! Your parents have simply employed it in the form of a proper noun to transform it into to a name."

"Chase? Who's that?"

Speech blinked. "It's you, lad."

Chase frowned again. "Me? My name isn't Chase. It's… uh…" He shook his head. "I… um, I…" Why couldn't he remember his own name? It definitely wasn't Chase. What was wrong with this man? Then again, what was wrong with *him?* Why couldn't he remember his name?

"Where am I? How did I get here?" he asked.

Speech scribbled something on his parchment. "You are in the waiting room!"

"Waiting room?" he asked slowly. "What am I waiting for?"

Speech barely even glanced up from his furiously moving pen. "Well, for the verification and determination of your bereavement and decease, of course!"

Chase stared at the man blankly. "Come again?"

Speech mumbled his response from behind his scroll. "The verification and determination of your bereavement and decease. This is what happens when you die, but the Creators are still debating whether or not to bring you back to life. Now please do excuse me, I'm writing out a new language."

"What?" Chase asked, his words still flowing from him like molasses. "The *who* are debating? And you can't be brought back to life after you're dead. It's impossible."

Irritated, Speech glared at Chase over his parchment before continuing his writings. "Again, lad, you're wrong. The Creators can do anything. Let me see… Heaven, Hell, Death, and Earth want you to die. But Life, Sky, Destiny, and Fate want you to live. It is a tie. So, you are waiting for one of the Creators to switch sides. This will result in the verification and determination of your bereavement and decease."

Chase looked down at his body. "I'm dead?" He gasped softly, without even the slightest air of panic. "How did that wound get there?" he asked emotionlessly. "And… and my shoulder. Why is my shoulder hurt?"

Speech finally looked up from his writings. "Oh, dear. They've begun the obliterating. Your memory is removing itself."

Chase's head hurt as he tried to slowly sort out his thoughts. "The Creators are erasing my memory? Why?"

"Simple. If you die, you won't grieve for what you lost. It is, of course, also to keep you from panicking or resisting. People tend to get worried when they remember the people they left behind.

You will remember later, when you become one of the dead and look down at your former life with happiness."

Chase frowned in concentration. "And if I live…?" "Then your memory will be restored of everything that occurred before this. You will have no recollection of me or of the waiting room."

Suddenly, a loud alarm blared through the room. "Ah! The Creators have decided!" Speech turned cheerily to Chase, who looked back with confusion.

"Who are the Creators?"

"Good day, Chase Onaj!" And he dissipated, his long parchment disappearing with him.

"Wait!" Chase called. "Am I living or dying?" But his lungs suddenly filled with sour gas and he couldn't breathe. He coughed and retched, but couldn't find air. Thrown into a sudden panic, which startled him after such a period of calm, Chase gasped desperately for a breath, which he finally got.

He collapsed on the floor, assured that the one breath would be his last. The pain of his mysterious wounds rushed back, and Chase fell into a dark, hopelessly sorrowful despair. Death had found him at long last.

CHAPTER 25

Tears spilled messily down Tara's grime-smeared cheeks, her whole body shaking violently as she sobbed, coughing and hacking, into Devon's chest. His mouth was tight, clean tears leaving trails in the dirt and blood on his face. Even Oliver, who had known Chase for less than a day, was crying as he helped Tetoviran, Fin, and Logan scoop dirt over the pit they'd dug in the ground. Tara had tried to use her powers to open a grave, but she was such a mess that nothing was under her control anymore. Grace sat a short distance away with her back to them, shoulders shaking.

Tara just couldn't wrap her mind around what'd happened. She hadn't been fast enough. She'd tried to get there in time, but she hadn't. It was an inescapable horror that she'd witnessed, one that had made her retch and vomit before she cried. Blood had spurted over the grass in rivers of red, dying the ground a dark, dark crimson-black. She had never watched a human being bleed like that before. He'd died with open eyes, empty and afraid. The body they'd buried had been so, so broken, his face so devoid of every smirk and scowl and childish grin that had made him who he was.

Tara simply couldn't believe what had happened. It seemed so unfair that the strongest of them would be taken, especially when they were winning. Now, more than ever, Tara hated Destiny and Fate. She finally knew true, raging, fiery hatred. She never thought she'd know vengeance, but she did. She wanted revenge for what they'd done to her. She wanted them to pay for the pain they'd caused her and millions of other people around the world for millennia. Mothers and fathers and sisters and brothers… countless people put to grief because of two Creators. Tara wanted them to feel the pain that their cruelty had caused. She wanted them to die slowly and painfully as payment for the lives they'd taken and the lives they'd ruined by taking others. Tara had never felt such anger, and it scared her to be thinking this way.

Her eyes were alive with power, her necklace burning her throat as the plants around her leaned into her, hugging her ankles sympathetically. Animals had gathered in tribute, as well, and they looked on in solemn silence. The pack of wolves that had come to her service when she called sat together, licking their wounds with lowered heads. To Tara's utmost relief, nothing around her was dying the way it had after the *tesko* attack. She didn't understand or care why.

Fin came to her, gently placing a hand on her shoulder. "We filled it," he whispered, his voice cracking.

Logan, Oliver, Tetoviran, and Rebel all stood behind him crying—even Tetoviran, who didn't even try to make an excuse. Devon squeezed Tara into a tighter hug, then let her go. "It's time, then."

Tara sniffled and tried to calm herself, but she shook with hiccups and kept right on crying. She managed a nod, and Grace joined them. Tara stared straight ahead at the tightly packed dirt in a small, rectangular uplift in the ground. She tried to take a breath, but it shook with sobs and she choked up.

Finally, with one hand clutching her necklace and the other squeezing Grace's hand, she began to walk. Slowly, in step with the others. Logan, who was crying the hardest out of all the boys, put his arm around Tara's shoulder. Tara appreciated this, since she hardly knew him, and she let her hand leave her necklace to grip Logan's forearm.

Everyone moved as one—Tetoviran, Tara, Rebel, Fin, Oliver, Logan, Grace, the wolves, the plants, the insects… all except Emma, who hung back and walked behind everyone else, her head bowed low.

When they finally reached the dirt mound, Fin stood and took a large, flat stone. He dug a small ditch behind the grave with his fingers and lodged the stone inside, packing it into place with the leftover dirt. Then, one by one, everyone took a flower from the plants growing nearby and laid it beside the stone.

When it came Tara's turn, she placed a single white lily, with shaking hands, on the very top of the stone. After her, only Emma was left. She went along respectfully, laying three young daisies beside the stone. When she was finished, Tara felt a sudden sharp, painful tugging in her chest. Words sprang to mind as if placed there by someone else, her necklace burning hotter against her skin. Tara didn't know what those words were for or what they would do, but she spoke them. "Earth," she began hesitantly, "bless this land, that this dust of your realm should forever hold in place the tribute to our beloved. May this stone stand, forever and always, on this holy ground. Never let it fall, until the day its inhabitant should breathe the air of the sky again." Her necklace glowed golden, and her eyes burned as a fresh onslaught of tears filled them. One, glowing the color of her pendant, fell upon the tombstone and vanished immediately into the rock. How Tara understood this blessing, she didn't know, but she was assured that it would stand forever. He would always be honored here.

She then returned to stand with her friends, and together they mourned. They cried for what was lost and for what they'd seen as their friend fell dead. After he was stabbed, the rest of the *derinium* army had been killed almost immediately. Their side had already been at an advantage, and the people and animals fighting beside Tara had become the most ruthless, barbarous warriors she had ever seen. None of it meant anything, though. Nothing mattered except the one human being who'd fallen in battle, who'd done something Tara had never seen him do. He'd dropped his sword and surrendered.

Tetoviran took the initiative and knelt, bowing his head and crying. The others all followed suit, until Tara was the only one left standing. "No." she mumbled numbly. "No. It isn't fair." But nothing was fair. Her knees buckled as she stared at the gravestone. "It can't happen," she whispered hoarsely. "I can't live without him. I need him back." She fell to the ground in despair, pounding the dirt with her fist over and over again. She laid there and cried, filled with complete anger and ruin. They all laid there sobbing for an amount of time that no one kept track of or cared about, weeping over the grave of Chase Onaj.

My best friend, Tara thought. *Gone. Just like that.* She'd stayed with Devon when they buried the body. She just couldn't bear to watch. Now she thought back to that day with Grace, when she had gossiped about him to her. *All he ever does is pick fights. He doesn't care about my feelings at all and doesn't seem to care that I'm a human being, not a rug to be walked all over. He's nothing but a lowlife, conceited criminal.* She never thought she would regret something so, so much. She cried for what she'd said, begging Chase to somehow, somewhere, forgive her.

She thought about the fights they'd had, first in his barn, then after the *tesko* attack, then in the cave after Grace took his sword. His sword… Tara had put it in a tree after the battle ended. She now willed the branches to bring it back to her. They laid it softly on the ground in front of her, and she stared at it through blurry, wet eyes. Chase's precious sword.

She thought also about the time when Chase had been so mad at her but hadn't said a single word in anger. That had been worse than any fight they'd ever had. And yet, he'd still risked his life to save her directly after that.

She thought about how he'd trained with her before others had joined them, how he'd had endless patience with her no matter what. She thought about all the times he'd teased or taunted or mocked her, when he'd scare her and threaten her, try to entrance her with his smile. She thought about the time he'd given her his blanket when she was cold, and that night when he'd lovingly kissed her cheek before she slept. She thought of his smile. Not his smirk or his mockery, but his real, genuine, purely happy smile. With a bit of a shock, Tara realized that she may have been the first person Chase had ever truly cared for—the first person to truly make him smile. Logan was one thing, she supposed, but Chase had seemed so unaccustomed to being affectionate that it was impossible for him to have been as close to Logan as he was to her.

She picked up his sword, cradled it in her lap, and wept over it. She cried for her dear, golden-hearted best friend. There, she made him a promise.

She sat up on her knees, took his sword and stuck it into the dirt. Grasping the handle, she whispered into its familiar hilt, "I promise that I will find your parents, Chase. No matter what it takes. I will find them, and I will bring them home. I promise you that." She pulled his sword from the earth and looked up to find all her friends standing and looking down at her, all red-eyed and puffy from crying.

"We can't stay here, Tara. If we're going to find Chase's parents, then we need to go now. He will rest peacefully here. He's with nature now," Devon said.

Oliver nodded. "Yeah. Which means he'll always be with you, Tara. Nature. He's where he's happiest."

Tara's lower lip trembled, and she threw herself forward, hugging Oliver tightly and crying into his shoulder. He didn't even hesitate in hugging her in return, which she loved him for. He felt so like Chase, and for a moment, she could close her eyes and imagine that it was him she was hugging. That he was right there, holding her in his arms, telling her everything would be fine. She could almost hear his voice, whispering softly in her ear. *"Shhh, Princess. It's okay. I'm here. I'll always be here for you."* And she would look up and see him smiling down at her. Not smirking. *Smiling.*

But she looked up and saw Oliver instead, and she was reminded harshly of how cruel this world could be. She rested her head against Oliver's shoulder again. A stranger. This complete stranger was offering her comfort. A complete stranger had cried over her friend. "Chase is gone," she whispered. "And there's no way to get him back."

Tetoviran sniffled. "We can't get him back, but he wouldn't want us sitting here crying over it. He'd want us to go after his parents, and that's exactly what I intend to do. I am going to honor him, even if he *did* have the ugliest jacket known to man and needed a serious haircut." Everybody smiled a little.

Fin put his hand on Tara's shoulder. "You ready?"

Tara took a breath and nodded. "Yes." Slowly, one by one, the group started walking towards the woods. The wolves' pack leader approached Tara slowly and dipped his head to the ground, then let out a sharp yip that drew his pack to him as they ran off together. But Tara waited until they had all begun walking to go back to the grave. She knelt next to the stone and smiled a tiny bit through her tears.

"Just you and me now. Forever." She laid her shaking hand gently on the dirt covering his body, then willed flowers to grow. They sprouted from the dirt in all sorts of beautiful colors and shapes and sizes. "Eternal flowers. So that I'll always be with you." She touched her forehead to the grave, then kissed the stone marking its place. "Rest in peace. I love you, Prince Charming."

And she stood to follow the others, Chase's sword in her hand and a thorn in her heart.

They stood a good many horse-lengths from the borders of the Sumadine Woods, watching the stillness. Fin squinted. "The trees seem okay from the outside, but look *into* the woods. It's so dark and foreboding…" Emma nodded. "We need to be constantly alert. Do not listen to the winds. If you feel yourself giving into them, find another one of us and they will help."

"Don't we need to stay in the sunlight as much as possible, too?" Tetoviran asked, sounding miserable. Devon nodded. "Yes. The *Aljenez Zijer* feed on happiness. Try not to stray into the shadows."

Tara was barely listening to the conversation. She didn't care about it. How could they all just be back to normal already, acting like nothing had changed? The lack of leadership was vividly noticeable, and the absence of that one, assuring voice made everything seem so empty. *She* felt empty. There was an indescribable hole in her heart, one that would never be filled again.

She looked around at all her friends, wondering how they could have a clean conscience, just forgetting their friend's death so easily. But as she examined each of them more closely, she could see the pain behind their eyes. She could hear the huskiness of grief that tainted their voices. Grace was staring at the forest with an empty gaze, and Logan turned aside occasionally to swipe at his eyes.

She felt a bit guilty then, for thinking that they would ever forget Chase so easily. Even thinking his name made a lump rise in Tara's throat. She tried to block the memory of his limp, lifeless body, stained with blood, his face slack and his eyes frozen open in the stillness of death. She felt tears rising again and tried to remember the good times she'd had with him, instead of that one terrible time. She bit her lip to hold back the tears, taking a deep breath. Suddenly, Fin nudged Tara's shoulder, making her jump out of her thoughts.

"What's wrong?" he asked quietly.

She tried to play innocent, pasting on a stoic look. She had to tilt her head all the way back to look at him. If possible, he'd gotten even taller since she'd met him. "Nothing. Why?"

He cocked an eyebrow. "You look troubled. What's wrong?" he asked again. "I mean, besides the obvious?"

Tara opened her mouth, ready to reply with 'nothing' again, but he stopped her. "If it's something the rest of us should know, you need to tell us. If it's about Chase or anything like that, then you don't have to say a thing."

Tara stopped and looked at Fin. His eyes were soft and gentle, and she knew, in that moment, that he was going to hurt her for the rest of her life. He had blonde hair and green eyes, sure. But he looked so much like Chase through his smile and his kind eyes and his smirks… it would always hurt to look at Fin and remember Chase. "It's him," she whispered, and Fin squeezed her shoulder with damp eyes. "I know," he replied. She swallowed and faced the others, trying to forget about it for the time being.

"Well then, I guess we don't have anything to wait around for," Tetoviran was saying when the pair tuned back in to the conversation. "Are we ready?"

But before anyone could say anything else, a sprawling figure fell from the sky, landing directly on Tara and crushing her into the dirt.

CHAPTER 26

Chase gasped for air as his whole body filled with a shocking pain on the impact of falling. He wasn't sure exactly where he'd fallen from or to, but he felt himself shaking violently after his landing. Frankly, he was rather shocked that he hadn't broken every bone in his body on impact.

He opened his eyes slowly to find seven blurry figures standing over him, along with a smudgy animal-shaped thing. His vision cleared slowly, the fuzz fading, and he saw that the seven people standing over him looked shocked into silence. His ears rang loudly, and he gritted his teeth until it stopped. No one said anything, just stared at him with their mouths hanging open.

He looked around in confusion. He was laying on the ground with a huge forest in front of him and a bunch of green hills behind him. Fuzzy memories danced in the back of his mind, tickling his brain, but none were clear. He couldn't grasp onto anything.

He felt something moving underneath him and rolled over in surprise. He jumped when he found that he'd apparently fallen on a girl. She had curly blonde hair and sharp blue eyes, but she looked dazed and dizzy. She was holding her elbow and groaning through a mouthful of dirt. There was an imprint of her body in the ground where he'd crushed her.

"Oh, sorry," he said stupidly. Two of the many people that stood around him—one buff and blonde, the other skinny and red-haired—pulled the girl to her feet and held her close to them as she spat her tongue clean.

They all stood there, just watching him, staring with looks of terror as he slowly sat up and shook his head. He was surprised to find dirt falling from his thick, black hair, and he looked down to discover that his whole body was covered in dust. He was bare-chested and cold. He stood shakily, stumbling once, and dusted himself off, feeling a little weak. He was vaguely aware of the people still watching him, and he became self-conscious and annoyed.

He turned impatiently to them. "What? I didn't *mean* to fall on your friend. Stop staring at me like a bunch of hungry owls!"

He spun on his heel with an irritated huff and began to walk away, then suddenly stopped dead in his tracks. He frowned in concentration at the biting ache pushing at the back of his skull. He knew them somehow. He turned slowly to look at the people again.

His eyes went wide, and he swayed with a sudden rushing flood of memories. He'd been stabbed. His hand flew to his heart, then jerked away in alarm. There was no blood. No pain. No wound. He touched his shoulder, and found that it, too, had healed completely.

His hands began to shake uncontrollably. What had happened? Why was he better? He should have died.

One of the people standing before him cried out and pointed at something behind him. He whirled around to see what was there, expecting something dangerous, but found a small pile of… things…that had not been there just moments ago. He walked to the small mound and saw that the "things" were clothes. His clothes. Folded neatly together were his shirt, jacket, gloves, and crossbody leather strap with all of its hidden pouches, all of them clean and in better condition than they'd been in years. He stared at the clothes with amazement. He had left these behind when his shoulder got hurt.

"I've gone mad," he whispered incredulously.

He looked up at the people in front of him again, and he suddenly remembered that they were not just people. "Tetoviran?" he whispered. "Fin? Devon, Oliver, Logan, Grace, Emma… Tara?" They all just stared at him with fearful eyes. He frowned slightly. "What?"

Fin opened his mouth, then clamped it shut again. Emma spoke, and her voice shook as she did. "We buried you."

"What are you talking about?"

Logan's hands were trembling. "We buried you. I helped dig your grave, I placed your body in the ground. You died."

Chase didn't understand what he was hearing. "But that's impossible. How could I have died and come back to life?" Everyone just stared at him. Clearly, they didn't understand any more than he did. He had *died?* How?

Suddenly, Grace cried out, "Look! The tombstone!" Everyone turned, and Chase caught sight of a shoddy, makeshift grave atop the hill behind them. They all rushed up the hillside to it, and Chase stumbled numbly after them.

Before it, there was a mound of crumbled stone, broken down as if it had been crushed by a massive fist. There were flowers on the dirt of the grave, but they immediately wilted and died as the group approached.

"Tara's blessing," Tetoviran mumbled. "She blessed that this stone should never fall. Not until the day that Chase came back to life."

Everyone turned to Tara, who was staring at the grave with huge eyes. "Did you know this was going to happen?" Oliver asked breathlessly.

She shook her head numbly. "No."

"But then how did Chase"—

"IT IS DONE."

Oliver was interrupted by a huge, thunderous voice that came at them from every direction. Tara screamed, Fin drew an arrow into his bow, and Logan leapt a foot, landing somehow in Tetoviran's arms like a baby. Teto immediately dropped him.

"THE CREATORS DECIDED. WE RETURN CHASE ONAJ NOW TO YOUR WORLD. DO NOT FEAR HIM; HE IS JUST AS HE WAS BEFORE. LIFE HAS SPOKEN TO YOU ALL ON THIS DAY. THIS PLACE WILL BE FOREVER MARKED AS A PLACE OF REBRITH."

The grave suddenly vanished, along with the stone, replaced with plants and flowers and flourishing fruit trees that sprang from the earth all around them. The air stilled, and birds slowly came and sang in the trees as though they'd been there all along. Devon turned to a newly grown tree and plucked a perfectly ripe fruit from its boughs, staring at it in amazement.

Emma looked at Chase. "The Creators brought you back to life." Her voice was filled with awe.

Chase looked at all the nature growing around him. "But… why?"

"They must have known it wasn't your time. You were needed for more beyond this day."

For a moment, everyone was silent, looking at Chase, trying to understand what had just happened. They had all heard stories of the Creators' power, but never had they seen such vivid proof. Tentatively, Oliver reached out with one hand, stepping cautiously toward Chase as if afraid he might bite. He rested his fingers hesitantly on Chase's shoulder, then pulled back in wonder. "They actually resurrected you."

After another long period of fearful, awe-struck silence, Logan grinned. "Well, no use in sitting here gawking all day; we might as well just take it. Life said so herself. You're back!" He ran to Chase and slammed into him with a hug. Dazed by what'd happened and rather taken aback, he embraced his old friend hesitantly. But, as one by one his friends began coming up to him with smiles on their faces, he began to grin, too. It was strange and impossible to believe, but he would take a miracle.

Tetoviran picked him up off the ground and squeezed him tightly, which was a little weird until he started hitting Chase in the gut, yelling at him for scaring everyone so badly. "How dare you die, kid? I can't believe your nerve! Just walking off and getting stabbed like that! I can't believe I'm even lowering myself to the standard of *speaking* to such a terrible person! Take that! And that! And some of these! Not so dead now, huh, kid?"

Chase started laughing—which felt so good and yet so strange, for it had been so long since he'd really laughed—and when Teto finally dropped him, he gave Chase one final kick, just for good measure. It felt good to be rejoiced over, and different, too. All his life he'd always thought death could be taken lightly, because no one would miss him. But now… everyone had missed him now, and Chase knew instantly that he liked this better. Knowing he was loved was a wonderful feeling.

Then Emma approached him. She stopped in front of him and he stood up, trying to see through the shadow of her hood. She shook her head and tugged the hood farther down. "Don't even try." There was a short pause, and then a pale hand was extended to him. "I'm glad you're okay." Her voice was softer than usual, if not quite friendly, and Chase was taken by surprise. Hesitantly, he took her hand and shook it. Nearly the moment he released his grip, she turned and was gone, standing near Logan without so much as a word more. Logan proceeded to dance a jig around her like a drunk man and toss flower petals over her head. Chase shook his head in bewilderment. They were quite possibly the most bizarre pair he had ever seen.

Everyone was talking over one another with excitement at this point, joyfully embracing Chase and each other. "It's a miracle!" Oliver cried.

Yet Chase was only looking for one person; the one person he couldn't seem to find in this mess of joy. He turned slowly, searching for her face, and finally saw her. Her hair was a mess, her eyes carrying so much doubt and fear. They stood for several moments, just looking at each other, neither one moving.

Slowly, Chase lifted the corner of his mouth. "Miss me?"

In an instant, Tara stormed up to him and slapped his cheek. He yelped and turned his face away. She hadn't hit him hard at all, so the slap was painless, but it startled him into silence. He had not expected that reaction.

"You idiot!" she whimpered, her voice thick and trembling. He could tell she'd been crying recently. "You left me here, all alone! How could you do that to me? I thought I'd never see you again, you… you think I could've *lived* without you? You swore you would stay with me, swore you would protect me!"

Regaining his wits, Chase smiled. "Well, pardon me. Getting stabbed was wonderful on my behalf, and I did it on purpose, just to see the look on your face. Just as priceless as I expected, though all the dirt and…"—he gestured with an air of disgust at her face— "…ah, tear streaks don't flatter you at all." He frowned with false concern. "It would appear you've been somewhat… mm, distraught without me. I always suspected you were madly in love with me, you know. This is your most ardent truth laid bare, my darling, and that elopement offer remains open if you've changed your mind. I hope you do realize that I may die on purpose again at any moment, so you may want to hurry up with that. Fallen angels don't come hurtling out of the sky to crush you flat every day."

Tara's eyes flashed furiously, and for a moment Chase thought she would hit him again. But instead, she rushed into him and hugged him fiercely, crying into his chest. He smiled and returned the embrace, picking her up off the ground and spinning his best friend in his arms. Tears of joy rolled down Tara's face, and she rose onto her tiptoes to kiss his cheek, nestling her hands in his hair.

"I told you a thousand times, Princess," he said softly, smiling as she pressed her face against his chest. Her cheeks were warm against his skin. "I'm invincible."

After a long time, she pulled away, looking him up and down and running her fingers over the place where he'd been stabbed.

Chase allowed this for a short while, then sighed as if exasperated. "If you'd wanted to run your hands all over my bare body, you could have just asked. It would have been far more streamlined than losing my shirt to a fight and being stabbed to death so you had an excuse."

Tara barely seemed to hear him. "You're alive," she whispered. "I can't believe you're alive."

Chase felt himself go warm from his toes up. He knew Tara had cared about him for a long time, but seeing it expressed this way made him feel so loved, so alienly cared for, that he thought he might cry. He hastened to erase that feeling before it happened. "I had to die and come back for you to realize my muscles are flawless and you can't keep your hands off me?" he asked, flexing his pectoral muscles beneath her small hands.

She looked up at him, familiar annoyance spreading over her features—along with something of a flush. He realized in the back of his mind that someone of her upbringing would find such an accusation scandalous.

Her hands finally slid away from him as he remarked, "You have the highest standards of any girl I've ever romanced in my life."

She crinkled her nose at that and poked him in the belly. "You have not *romanced* me," she said. He considered this.

"Well, that's unfortunate. Perhaps I should try harder." Tara shook her head at him, taking his face in her hands. Her fingers were trembling slightly as she brushed a thumb across his cheek. "You're an arrogant idiot, you know that?" Chase grinned and pulled her into a stifling hug. "A devilishly tempting arrogant idiot," he corrected, messing her hair up even worse than it already was and allowing himself to revel in her warmth for a moment. He felt his hand brush something on her hip and pushed her gently away.

"What's that?"

She looked at him with confusion. "What's what?"

"My sword," he noted now that he could see it properly.

She looked at her hip, where his sheath had been wrapped into a makeshift cloth belt. "Yeah. I kept it after they buried you."

"Did you?" "Yes. Why?"

"Well, because I'll be wanting that back, thief."

Tara smiled and tugged the sword out of its scabbard. Holding it with two hands, she offered it to him. Chase took it from her, turning it in his hands, twirling it a few times. He took a deep breath as he handled his blade, then looked at Tara as she was placing Rebel in her knapsack. "Well, no use sitting here. Who's ready to go find Destiny and Fate?"

Chase had always known that incredible things happened. Now he realized that the impossible could be made reality with the flick of a finger. He had died. He had forgotten everything, only to find it after his heart began pumping again, starting over in the wonderful, terrifying, extraordinary cycle of life. As Chase walked, flanked by his friends, toward the Sumadine Woods, everything seemed to happen in slow motion.

He saw the first of the new, bigger army of *deriniums* come over the bluff of the hill. The air was dull. His vision was fuzzy. His ears seemed to fill will fluff, his mouth with water. He heard the shouts rise up behind him, saw his friends turn to find the source of the noise. There were no conch shells this time, no war cries or flags. No warning. He felt the adrenaline and panic rise around him. He felt it rise within his own chest. And then everything rushed to him in a frenzy.

"What do we do?"

"We have to run."

"No! We must stand our ground."

"Fighting didn't go very well last time, now did it?"

"He's right. That's double the amount there were before, and before, one of us was killed."

Chase stared at the onrushing army of *deriniums* with nothing less than pure terror. He made no attempt to hide it this time. More had been summoned, and their numbers were indeed significantly larger than last time.

It took him a moment to realize that these things had *killed* him. Fear was the only thing in his mind, a fear that he'd never felt before. It numbed his senses entirely, and he could only think of one thing: RUN.

He looked from the oncoming army to the woods. In seconds, they would be caught exactly in between the two. He grabbed

Tara by her belt and untied his scabbard hastily, attaching it to his own and jamming his sword into it. "Get to the woods, now! They won't follow us there!" He turned without another word and began sprinting towards the Sumadine Woods. Without so much as a moment's hesitation, he heard the others follow.

He glanced over his shoulder, his heart pounding. The woods were so close. But the *deriniums* had unnaturally fast horses, and the army was steadily filling the yawning gap between them and their targets: the people who had killed hundreds of their brethren. *Nothing like vengeful monsters,* Chase thought bitterly as he ran.

The land flew by him in a blur, and he wished in that moment for a horse that could help him go faster. He was feeling every ache and bruise and pulled muscle from travelling so long on foot, all of it coming over him now. He pushed himself as hard as he could, directing all his energy and focus on taking one rushing step after the next. The *deriniums* were right on their tails now, almost close enough to touch them. The woods were two horse-lengths away. One.

"Jump!" Tetoviran screamed.

As Chase hurtled forward into the trees, he felt the atmosphere change as his body entered the woods. The air became denser and everything seemed to move a little slower. The noise and battle cries and deafening beating of hoofs stopped abruptly. His body flew through the air a little slower behind the borders.

He landed with a smooth thud and rolled a few times before coming to a stop. His body felt light and his eyes felt foggy, even though he could see fine. Everything looked the same as it had from the outside, but the air felt thicker, and Chase found it harder to breathe in the woods. Gravity's pull seemed less intense and more forceful at the same time.

Chase stood up slowly, brushing off his already filthy clothes and looking around, his hands still trembling a little. They were safe now. He had to remind himself of that. The *deriniums* would not follow them here, but that was hardly a comforting thought. This forest was certainly not the ideal safe haven. The enormous trees loomed over him, their branches creating a filter of sunlight that made large golden patches on the forest floor. There was no wind; not even a breeze. The ground was bare of any insects or woodland animals, and Chase couldn't see or hear any birds. It was eerily quiet, but otherwise nothing seemed different. He heard a soft groan behind him and stepped around a thick tree to find Oliver sprawled on the ground, looking up at the trees.

Chase offered his hand, and Oliver accepted it. "Where are the others?" Chase asked, looking around.

Oliver shrugged. "Don't know. They can't have gone far. Let's look around."

Chase nodded, and they began crawling through the bushes and tall grasses. Chase found the border of the woods and, upon looking out, saw a frustrated army of *deriniums* screaming and brandishing their weapons in anger, eventually retreating back the way they'd come. He shuddered and tried to think of something else, not embarrassed in the least to say that the mere thought of the ghost riders made him quake.

He stepped over a large rock and tripped on a dark shape that moved and jerked on the ground. He looked closer and found that it was Emma, struggling with a root that had snagged her cloak. Chase bent to help her tear it free and noticed a thick gash crusted with dried blood on her leg. Suddenly, he remembered when she'd been injured before he'd died. She noticed his concern and swept her cloak over the cut. "I'm fine."

Chase decided not to press. Using his foot for leverage, he grabbed the root and yanked it in two. Her cloak snapped free, and she stood with a curt nod. "Thank you."

Chase didn't respond. He was busy helping Devon up a few feet away. He, too, bore wounds from the battle that Chase hadn't noticed before. His face was bloodied from a thin cut on his forehead. Some sort of weapon had just barely grazed him there, leaving him lucky to be alive.

As the three of them stood together, Oliver appeared from the left side of the border with Logan, Fin, and Tara behind him. Logan had been cut on his left arm, and Fin wore a great many more bruises and cuts than most of them. *He fought with a knife,* Chase remembered of the battle. He wasn't very skilled with that weapon. Tara, of course, was unharmed. Her powers had protected her.

Logan looked around. "Where're Grace and Tetoviran?"

A high-pitched shriek answered his question. Everyone walked carefully in the direction of the sound, peering around a tree trunk to find Grace scrambling back from a dark, lumpy shadow in the nook of some tree roots. Upon seeing them, she scurried to their sides, practically throwing herself on Chase.

"It's Tetoviran," she nearly whimpered, clutching his arms. "He's… he's gone mad. Talking about suicide and sadness… I-I was just getting up off the ground and he reached out and grabbed my ankle, and…"

Chase gave her arm a soothing squeeze, then turned warily to the shadow. Sure enough, mumbling could be heard from it. If he squinted, he could make out Teto's shape huddled in the darkness.

"Shadow Monsters," Fin whispered. "The *Aljenez Zijer.* They're feeding off him. He must have landed in the shadows when he jumped."

"Well, we can't just sit here. We have to get him out," Emma reasoned. Tara was chewing her lip so hard, Chase worried she might bite it off.

His brow knit and he stepped carefully around a couple of smaller shadows and approached the large one where Teto was hunched. He reached out cautiously. "Tetoviran?"

He heard hollow moaning that sounded nothing like Teto. "Death," he muttered. "Come for me, my lord, Death. Take away the light. Blood… Suffering… Pain… so wonderful. Give me pain. Darkness…"

Chase called his name again, but the man just continued his low, empty rambling. Chase took a deep breath, pushing his sword behind his hip, and plunged his hand into the shadow.

Immediately, Chase felt some sort of slimy, finger-like coils wrap themselves around his fingers, holding onto him and seeming to feed like leeches. He could see his hand clearly; nothing was touching it. The shadow itself was clinging to him. The little feelers crawled up his arm as he reached deeper into the darkness. He shivered in disgust, trying to shake the vile sensation and being careful to keep his head well out of the shadow. His arm was in up to his shoulder now, and the slimy snakelike things slid up toward his neck as the light shifted just the tiniest bit.

He pulled away, glancing back at his friends, who were watching nervously. Chase inhaled slowly, then reached in further and let the coils slither up his neck. They reached his ear, and he felt it. A horrid sadness, like nothing he'd ever felt before. He tried to think of happy memories, but he couldn't find any. His mind swirled with ugly, gruesome, awful pictures and mournful thoughts. *Deriniums* cackled in his head, Raka died five times over, Destiny and Fate ripped their quilt again and again. The whole world was darkness. He felt ready to burst into tears.

He tried to shake it off, focusing on his job. He felt around a bit and felt his fingertips brush another slime-covered shape. Tetoviran.

Desperately fighting to ignore the growing heaviness in his heart, Chase reached in again. He was just feeling for Teto's hand when he felt an iron grip clench his wrist. He jumped, squinting through the shadow at Tetoviran's empty, lonely eyes. His face held the expression of a madman, gone crazy with grief. Chase yanked away, but Teto held tight, just staring at Chase.

"You attacked my brother," he whispered hoarsely. "You tricked me into betraying my own brother. You died. I buried you."

Only bad memories. Tetoviran was only remembering the bad memories he held with Chase. Chase tried again to drag Teto free, but it was impossible. The man was brutishly strong, and Chase was still much younger than him, after all. He tugged again, then turned to his friends. "He's too heavy! It's hopeless. We're all going to die!" He could hear the despair in his own voice—and apparently his friends could too, judging by the looks on their faces. Soon, he would be just as bad as Tetoviran.

Logan rushed forward, tugging on Chase around the middle while Chase continued to yank on Teto's hand. Then Devon came up to help, and together the three of them finally managed to drag Tetoviran out of the shadow.

The large man landed with a thump on his back, staring up through the trees with a blank expression. He glanced around, then slowly sat up. He looked back at the shadow in the nook of the tree trunk. "What in the name of Heaven was *that?*"

"Shadow Monsters." Chase offered his hand to help Tetoviran up, but the man slapped his arm away and stood on his own.

"Warning you kids. Don't ever, *ever* do what I just did," Teto grumbled. "Shadows. I got beat up by a shadow!" He shuffled a few feet away, muttering to himself.

The others stood together, staring into the forest. "What now?" Grace asked.

Devon grimaced. "We go through."

"Night will be upon us very soon," Emma said. "We need to move."

Nodding in agreement, Chase took a breath and began walking. But just one step later, he paused, raising his eyes to the treetops. High above the forest, on the very tips of the evergreens, the leaves rustled. Wind.

CHAPTER 27

Tara watched as the gust traveled like a wave through the treetops. The wind was chilly, and she shivered as the breeze blew past. Everyone was silent otherwise, subconsciously holding their breaths in anticipation of what was to come. Tara watched as the leaves gradually quieted, then stilled. Surprised, she looked around. No one else seemed to have heard anything either.

After a moment of bewilderment, Fin barked a laugh. "Stupid myths. It was all a joke!"

Teto rolled his eyes. "Hey, great!" he said sarcastically. "Now we can meet those death ladies even faster!"

Devon was smiling. "Come on, let's go! Just stay away from the shadows and we'll be there in no time."

Everyone began after him, but Tara noticed that Chase held back, looking suspiciously at the sky as if waiting for it to come down and punch him in the face.

Tara rolled her eyes and walked back to him. "Can't you ever let your guard down, Prince Charming? Just accept that for once, something's going our way. Enjoy it."

Chase didn't look at her, continuing to stare at the treetops. "Chase?" She prodded. "Hello?" Chase still didn't look at her. He was watching the holey patches of visible sky far above them, never even glancing at Tara when she spoke. She tugged on his arm. "Chase? Chase, answer me." Nothing. "Chase, come on! You're not being funny, you're scaring me. Would you please stop?"

Finally, he looked down at her. "It's not a myth," he mumbled.

"What?"

"It's not a myth," he repeated, more loudly. "It's true." He turned and ran after the others. "Guys!"

Tara rushed to catch up with him before the rest of their friends heard him and grabbed him by the sleeve of his jacket. "Chase, what happened? Did you hear something?" Chase didn't look at her, only twisted uncomfortably in a weak effort to escape her grasp. "Chase?" she asked, more tentatively now. "Chase, why aren't you talking to me? What exactly did you hear?" No response. "Chase, what is wrong with you?"

He still refused to look at her, and in that scared moment of being unable to think of anything else to do, Tara slapped Chase across the face as if to wake him up. Her hand left a red mark across his cheek, and she gasped in shock at herself, staring at her hand like she couldn't believe what it had done.

Chase jumped back, wrenching himself from her grip. His hand went to his cheek, and he finally met her eyes. "You… you slapped me."

Tara put her hands over her mouth, her eyes huge. She was horrified with herself. She'd slapped him *really* hard. *And you liked it.*

Tara jumped at the snake-like whisper that hissed in her ears. She turned, searching for the voice's source, but saw no one. All of a sudden, she noticed the wind blowing through her hair. "Chase, did you hear…" she trailed off nervously.

He caused you pain many times before. Revenge is so wonderful. When you tortured him with your power, was it a lack of control? Or did you secretly want it to happen?

"I didn't"—

Isn't it delicious, child of Earth, to have a human being at your mercy? You liked slapping him and seeing the pain it inflicted. Imagine the taste of your torture upon his soul. You want to hit him again.

Tara shook her head. "No, I don't," she argued.

Yes. Do it again. Hit him again! Harder!

The scary part was how tempting the voices were. Tara felt the physical struggle of saying "no" aloud, then looked up to find Chase staring at her.

"You hear it, too?" he asked quietly.

Tara's eyes widened. Could Chase hear what the winds were saying to her? No. Everyone hears something different, she remembered. "Yeah," she said. "I hear it."

Chase nodded slowly. "Sorry. For what I just did," he mumbled. "The wind was telling me things, and I was afraid… I was scared that if I looked at you, I would try to hurt you." There was a moment of silence which Chase filled by clearing his throat. "They were tempting me to kill you."

Tara's mouth dropped with the shock of this. These winds only told complete truths. Chase wanted to kill her? But why? Even if it was subconscious, how could that even be possible?

Chase shrugged helplessly at her expression. "I don't understand it any more that you do. I've never had that urge before."

"What happened?" Oliver's voice made them both jump. They turned and saw everyone standing directly in front of them.

"You didn't hear it?" Chase asked.

Logan frowned slightly. "Hear what? The voices? They're just old stories."

Tara shook her head. "No. I heard them. Chase did, too. They're not fake."

Grace laughed a little, but it appeared forced. "That's ridiculous. Of course they're fake."

Chase looked up at the treetops and waited. Everyone was silent, and there was almost no sound until they all heard it—the leaves rustling overhead. Chase pointed upwards and then looked at Grace. She looked scared now. "You did hear it, didn't you? You heard it the first time, at the same time as me."

Grace looked at her feet. "I did."

Suddenly, Devon spoke aloud in an aggressive, defensive voice, making Logan jump away from him in surprise. "No! I would never betray him! Shut up!"

Everyone watched in bewilderment as Devon yelled at what appeared to be nothing.

Tetoviran spoke, too, more quietly. His voice was full of regret and pain, sounding sadder than Tara had ever heard him. "I never meant for her to be left alone. I never wanted to hurt her."

Logan turned in a slow circle, watching people's expressions and listening to them, and he finally came around to look at Chase and Tara. "It's true, isn't it? The winds really do speak."

Tara nodded grimly, even though she herself had heard nothing this time.

The gust of wind slowly died, and everyone grew silent. Chewing his lower lip anxiously, Fin fingered his bow.

"Well, there that went," Logan muttered. "I guess we have to deal with these voices after all."

Chase nodded and pulled out his compass and studied it for a moment, then pointed through the woods. "This way," he determined, and they began on their way.

Fallen pine needles and thin twigs rustled and snapped as Tara walked. Branches seemed to be reaching out to her, except now it was against her command. Tara was beginning to realize that these trees did not belong to her mother. Their spirits felt different around her—unfamiliar somehow. They belonged to Destiny and Fate, and therefore Tara had no control over them. This made her nervous. Clutching her necklace worriedly, she stepped over a fallen log and scurried to catch up with the others.

The sunlight that poked through the trees overhead dimmed slowly, giving a gentle shade over the entirety of the woods that was welcomed with relief. This also meant, however, that the shadows grew longer. Oliver tripped in the front of the group, and Devon was almost barely able to catch him before he went sprawling into a deep area of darkness. Wind came again.

So, Earth's child, what has become of your life? A mere instrument of a great Creator? Your own mother burdened you with this. You want her to stay in Paroaff. You want the griffins to find her and slowly tear at her from within, the same way that this terrible power of yours did to your friend. You want her to know the pain she has caused you.

"No," Tara whispered in horror. "I… I would never think that."

Perhaps, but you are happy Jisara has been invaded. You are hopeful of your Aunt Beatrice's death. Just imagine what a sweet, easy target her lonely house is for a monster.

Tara honestly hadn't realized it before, but as she heard the words, she saw that, deep, deep down, she really did want Aunt Bea to be punished for the way she'd treated Tara. It was unfair, the way she'd had to grow up all those years.

It is also unfair how your parents left you with her. If they had denied their king the assignment, you would never have been left alone. They could still be with you now, and you would have never been involved in this dangerous excursion. Should any righteous parent choose wealth and duty over their own daughter?

"They shouldn't," Tara mumbled as she continued to move forward.

She could see her friends around her, moving at the same slowing pace as her as they all listened to the retellings of their souls' secret diaries.

I see you have come to your senses at last. No good mother would choose money over the wellbeing of their child. She abandoned you, left you alone with your power and your aunt. She must have known you would run at some point. This was all part of her evil plan. You have finally left her life in exactly the manner she had hoped you would. She freed herself from that necklace by giving it to you and forcing you out of Jisara. She knew that no sane person would remain in her sister's home. She took advantage of you.

"You're absolutely right," Tara murmured.

So, you see. What does this tell you?

Tara didn't want to listen, but she knew the words were from her; even if she didn't think they were, they were coming from her heart. These were the truths of the ways she truly felt. "She is not a good mother."

The winds died down, and Tara saw her vision—which she hadn't even noticed to have been glazed—turn clear again. Her friends had been muttering things as well, and now, in this moment of refuge, they looked at each other, everyone greatly shaken.

"We can't listen. We can't let it get into our heads," Grace said.

Chase's jaw tightened. "It's out of our hands. We have no power over this. The only thing we can do now is move as quickly as possible."

He shoved his scabbard a little further back on his hip. "And I think we can all move pretty quickly, right?" Everyone nodded in reply. "Good. Then let's"—

"Wait." They all looked at Emma. She looked down, her voice quiet. "I... I can't."

Chase opened his mouth to ask questions, but she beat him to it. "I'm hurt."

Logan suddenly gasped in realization. "I forgot! She got cut. Before Chase died, a *derinium* hurt her leg pretty badly."

Everyone crowded around for a look at the wound. It was deep and inflamed. Tara knew the dangers of infection. If the gash wasn't properly treated soon, Emma's leg might have to be removed to keep her alive. She cursed herself for not having thought to bring some extra leaves with her when she treated Chase's wound. Not only would Emma be unable to run, she must have been in terrible pain with every step she'd taken up to now.

"Destiny and Fate will heal you," Oliver breathed fearfully. "They have to." Nobody was willing to say a word about the infection.

Fin rubbed his jaw in frustration. "We can't keep up at this pace. We'll never get there before nightfall if we go on this slowly."

Emma huffed. "I know that. I didn't *ask* to get hurt!"

His eyes softened. "I know. I'm sorry."

"We need to figure something out before the next wind comes," Devon said.

"I could carry her," Teto suggested.

Everyone cried, "Yes!" simultaneously with Emma's wail of "No!"

There was brief laughter, and then Tetoviran picked Emma gently up off the ground—she held her hood down the whole time—and they all broke into a run, jumping over fallen branches and pushing aside large boughs in their path. Breath was scarce, but no one dared slow down. They sprinted as one through the underbrush and the woods for several minutes without halting before, finally, the next gust blew past. Everyone slowed to a jog as the winds spoke again, and Tara braced herself for the words.

You are in love.

Tara blinked in complete confusion, and she forced her muscles to move faster. "What?"

You are in love.

Again, she was baffled. "With whom?"

The voices were silent for a long period of time, and for a moment Tara thought they were gone for the time being. She felt an odd pang of disappointment. She wanted to know who she—supposedly—was 'in love' with. The idea seemed ridiculous. She was too young to be in love, and besides, she felt no real… what was the word? Feelings. She felt no feelings of love for anyone that she was aware of. "Who is it?" she asked again.

There was another pause before she got her response. *Devon.*

Tara tripped and fell to her knees. Chase, muttering to himself, reached back and yanked her to her feet without even glancing at her. He did so roughly, too—any hint of the usual gentleness he used towards her was absent. Brushing herself off, she tried to comprehend what she'd heard. She could not possibly love Devon. She didn't even like Devon—at least, not in that way.

The day you fell in the river with him. You felt it. Tara tried to remember. *After you were both back to safety. You remember. When you fell upon him while regaining your wits, you felt tickling in your stomach.*

Tara cringed as she realized that she did remember that. She also remembered having wondered what that feeling was.

It was love. And it still lingers for him. When Chase died, the one you hold dearest, he held you. You felt the warmth of being in his arms. You love him far more than you love Chase.

"No," Tara whispered. "That can't be. Can it?"

But the wind had left. Still jogging with the others, she looked up ahead at the back of Devon's head. His brown hair had grown longer and shaggier over the course of their travel, and his face had shadowed with stubble since he'd last shaved. He looked weathered in a beautiful way.

As the group ran together, Tara thought about what the wind had said. Tara hated to admit it, but she remembered that day when she'd felt that strange sensation in her gut. She'd also felt herself flush when around him several other times, felt her heart pound when he said or did random things that she somehow found attractive.

But still—love? She could see the possibility of liking him, but *love?* Love was a big word. Four letters long, perhaps, but limitless in meaning. It seemed so impossible. *It is impossible,* Tara told herself.

But one little tiny voice in the back of her mind whispered that it was, in fact, very possible. Tara grew annoyed with that voice, and even more so when she realized that that little voice was right. It *was* possible, but she couldn't be thinking of such things now. Now was not the time.

But if not now, when? When will it truly ever be the right time? The answer is simple. It won't. You have to live in the present. Waiting for the future to spell your life out for you letter by letter will never get you anywhere. Even if it is the wrong time, know that it's okay to act right now.

Tara hadn't even noticed that the wind had blown again until she heard it speaking. "How can I act right now? I don't even know what I want."

You want a future with Devon, don't you?

Tara frowned. "I suppose, at the moment. But that could change as I get older, meeting new people or feeling differently. For the time being, though, I… I think so. "

Then answer only one question.

Tara was quiet, waiting for the wind to continue. After a moment's pause, it did.

Would you give your life to save his? Would you die for the one you love?

Tara flinched again at that word. Love. Such a powerful word. Such a strong, binding one. And Tara knew, in that instant, that she did not want to be in love. She did not want to be bound to anything else. Her necklace was imprisoning enough. "I would not."

No? You think you do not love him? The winds seemed to giggle as Devon suddenly collapsed to the ground in front of Tara, wailing. *Let us test that.*

CHAPTER 28

"What's wrong with him? What happened?" Oliver cried as everyone leaned over Devon.

The winds had quieted for the time being, and Chase sent a quick prayer to the Creators, thanking them for this one moment of sanctuary. "Devon? Devon, what happened? Can you hear me?"

Devon's eyes were wide and glazed over, his body twitching jerkily. He scratched wildly at his own face, leaving white marks where his nails dug into his skin.

"Get him under control!" Fin yelled, dropping to his knees and grabbing his wrists. Devon fought him savagely, snarling and clawing at the older boy's hands. Fin wrestled him for a long time, his muscles rippling visibly as he tried to hold Devon down without hurting him.

Finally, Devon seemed to give up, letting his body go limp under Fin's grip. He began kicking, though, and now Chase leapt upon his legs and held him down. Devon sucked in ragged, raw breaths of air, his exhales heavy and spittle forming at the corners of his lips. He looked around wildly, his gaze never settling on one person.

Everyone stared at him with fear. Chase had never seen anything like this before. Devon wasn't in a shadow. Dimming sunlight shone on the area where he lay, yet he was acting like a wild animal. His eyes still darted around desperately, landing finally on Fin's quiver full of arrows on his back.

"Weapons," Devon growled, his eyes filled with sick hunger. "Give me them. Let me rip. Tear. *Kill!*" He lunged at Fin, and Logan had to help hold him back.

Again, Devon fought until his body seemed to give out. His eyes were lightless. "If you won't let me do it, then do it yourselves! Kill me!"

Tetoviran looked on with a fear that Chase had never seen from him before, Emma still cradled in his arms. Although her face was still out of sight, she was clutching Teto's shirt with white knuckles.

"He's a madman," she whispered.

"I'm not going to kill you, Devon," Fin said slowly.

"Do it!" Devon screamed, foaming saliva flying from his lips.

Fin yelled back at him, his eyes reading fear alone but his voice filled with anger. "What's in your head? I'm not killing you, idiot!"

"Just do it! Death be damned, do it!"

Chase's chest rose and fell heavily. What on earth was the matter with him? Gone suicidal, screaming at his friends. Emma was right. He was completely mad.

"Devon." They all turned at the sound of Grace's voice. It was shaky, but much calmer than anyone else's would be. "Why do you want us to kill you?"

Devon stared at her with crazed eyes. "Why?" he whispered.

Grace nodded. "Yes. Why do you want to be killed so badly?"

Anger filled Devon's face again. "Well, isn't it obvious? My fate! They're telling me everything! All of it! I am not going to live to see the day when their plan is fulfilled. I'm not going to die that way! I'm going to die right here, peacefully! They're telling me to end it, well guess what? *I'm going to end it!*" His voice was rough and scratchy with phlegm as he screamed.

Fin struggled to hold him down as Devon fought against him. "Devon, calm down," Grace said. "The winds are talking to you. Do you remember why we're here?"

Devon nodded aggressively. "Yeah. We're here to ask about Chase's parents, to save the world or some garbage. Well, let me tell you something, Onaj. While you're off living your happy little ending, I'll be suffering! Tortured for years and years, barely alive before they finally kill me!"

Chase didn't understand any of this. The winds never lied, but how could this be true? Suddenly, something struck him. It wasn't. None of it was true.

"Devon," Chase said, hearing the waver in his voice as he spoke. "Listen to me."

"No! I'm done listening! *Especially* to you! You're the one who dragged everyone into danger!"

Chase continued as calmly as he could. "You remember the Shadow Monsters?"

Devon growled in his throat. "What? You going to feed me to them now?"

"No. You must have been traveling in shadows for a long time before this. You probably just didn't realize it because you were distracted by the winds."

Devon stared at Chase with hatred, glowering behind eyes that grew farther and farther from sanity with every passing second. "You expect me to trust you? It was the winds! The winds don't lie, and they showed me what's going to happen to me! They showed me everything! Now do what I'm asking you. KILL ME!"

Chase swallowed his fear, knowing he had to remain calm. "You aren't going to suffer, Devon."

"How would you know?!"

Chase rose his voice. "Who would you rather trust? Say it *was* the wind talking to you. Would you rather rely on some enchanted air or on your friend who's fought by your side countless times, who *died* in a battle beside you, who's trying to save your life right now? Who would you pick?"

Devon stilled, looking at Chase. "I care about you, Devon," Chase said, more softly now. "I'm your friend. Don't let these magics get in your head. You need to control it, Devon. Don't let them take you." Devon's breathing steadied a little more. "Just remember," Chase murmured soothingly.

Devon's eyes grew brighter. "I... I remember."

There was a sob from behind them, and Chase turned and saw Tara crying with her hand over her mouth and her eyes wide.

Devon's eyes rested on her, slowly filling with care. "Tara..." He turned back to Fin. "I... oh, I'm so stupid."

Fin nodded carefully. Devon looked rather traumatized now. "I went crazy."

Tetoviran snorted. "You don't say."

Devon shook his head slowly. "I'm so sorry." He looked up. "You saved me. All of you." He sat up, and Fin let him. "Thank you." He stood shakily and brushed himself off, wiping his face and mouth. "Thank you," he whispered again.

A breath that Chase hadn't even realized he'd been holding in escaped his lungs in relief. Just knowing that Devon had grasped onto his last remaining bit of sanity and climbed that thread until it turned back into a rope filled him with hope. Perhaps, if Devon could go from having been so despairingly mad to normal again, there was a chance that they could make it through this evil place.

Devon was trying to calm Tara down, for she was still crying. "Look, Tara. I'm okay, see? Hey, look at me."

Tara met his eyes, and something strange passed over her face. Devon didn't seem to notice it, but Chase saw her expression change briefly. He couldn't name it exactly, but it seemed like either confusion or… well, he wasn't really sure what else it could be. He'd never seen her that way before.

Finally, Devon wrapped Tara in a hug, and her smile, over his shoulder, was the most readable expression Chase had ever seen. Her entire face lit up. Just for a split second, she stopped crying and her cheeks grew rosy. And suddenly, she straightened her face and closed her eyes for a second, as if scolding herself.

Devon pulled away soon after and went on to talk to Fin about travel direction, for they were fairly turned around, but Tara stood silently, watching him and then shaking her head and holding her face in her hands.

She glanced up, and her gaze landed on Chase. Her eyes widened slowly, and she tensed, just watching him. A short staring contest transpired between them, each waiting for the other to do something. Slowly, and ever so slightly, Chase lifted one corner of his mouth in a lopsided smirk. He glanced at Devon, then back at Tara, lifting his eyebrows.

At that moment, Chase saw Tara realize that he knew. Her face filled with dread, and Chase pushed himself up off the ground. He strolled casually over to Tara. She cowered a little more with each step he took, and he finally came and stood beside her, not saying a thing for a long while. Tara stared up at him, completely paralyzed and watching him like he was wielding the blade that would kill her.

Finally, Chase lifted his chin and said quietly, "Well, isn't that something?" She just looked at him silently, her eyes huge. "What, you're not going to try to deny it?"

She didn't react for a moment, but then she finally shook her head in defeat. "It'd be a waste of time." And the winds blew again.

Jealous, are we? "No," Chase scoffed. "Why would I be?"

Because she has never looked up to anyone else like that before. It has always been you. Although you feel no love for her in that manner, you are jealous that she feels that sort of love for him.

"No, I'm not. I think it's fine."

She has always been yours. You have shared everything with one another. You are not only jealous, but afraid, as well.

"Of what?"

Of the possibility that she might turn to him now for advice rather than you. She might go to him when she is sad now, or tell him her troubles instead. Love is a fickle thing. People's entire lives change when they find it. You are afraid that you might find yourself being left behind.

Chase hadn't even had time to think about any of these things, but he supposed it was possible that the ideas had been already forming in the back of his mind.

Would she really leave him behind for Devon? For love? Love. Love was something with many facets to it. There was a love of family and a love of friends, but then there was that type of love that had always baffled Chase. The kind that influenced people so much that they were willing—eager, even—to give everything to one person, even their lives. Chase had never understood such a strong passion for another person that one would so willingly do anything for them.

Yet as he thought about it, he realized that he would give his life for his parents, or Tara, or any of his friends, as well. Love was a scary thing—constantly sugar-coated and romanticized, but such a malicious imprisoner. It was a strong word, one that was feared to speak, though no one really ever seemed to think about it that way. People are always afraid to confess that they are in love, yet it seems so simple to say that they like someone. Chase believed that people feared to speak the name of love because it was binding. Tara definitely *liked* Devon. But love?

Funny.

"What is?"

She said the exact same thing.

Chase was silent for a moment, waiting. Yet the winds did not speak to him again, and he was left feeling resentful not towards Tara or Devon, but towards what they shared now that he wasn't a part of.

~

Chase hopped over a root and helped Logan past a particularly large shadow. The light was dimming fast, and they were already beginning to hear faint whispers of despair and sadness. What had happened to Devon had clearly rattled him greatly, and they were all struggling against the shadow voices.

The winds weren't particularly helpful, either. Every time a gust blew through the trees, Chase learned something about himself that made him think until his head hurt. Some made him angry; others very, very sad. Most didn't make sense to him. Several times, he had to focus on repressing tears.

In addition to all of these secrets Chase apparently had, however, the winds kept saying one thing over and over to him: *You hate him.* No further explanation, no hint as to who 'he' might be. Just those three words and nothing else. Every time he heard that phrase, he would ask who it referred to. Every time, the wind would change the subject. It grew very annoying for Chase, and he found himself hitting his own head several times.

As they all ran along together, and the evening drew nearer, he kept wondering who it could be. Araknan, the former lion king, was the first name that came to mind, obviously. However, Chase felt that that wasn't the right person. It was too obvious. Chase already knew that he hated him, and it was the wind's job to reveal secret truths about oneself—not something as well-known as that.

Another worry, much more urgent than that, was also creeping up on him: night. The sky above the treetops was darkening, and they were deep into the woods now. If they couldn't find Destiny and Fate before nightfall, all of them were dead.

Interrupting his positive thoughts was a sudden roar of rage from Fin. Chase jumped out of his skin, turning to see the blonde prince pointing a trembling finger at Tara. "You," he growled in a voice that sounded nothing like Fin whatsoever. His face was so contorted with anger that even Chase's heart did a backflip. You would've thought he was staring down the person who'd killed his mother.

Tara's eyes filled with hate when she saw him glaring at her. That was scary as well, because Tara hated very few people.

"The winds," Grace cried. "We have to stop them before"— But it was too late.

Fin leapt angrily on Tara and tackled her to the ground, where they rolled several times together before finally coming to a stop. Tara's wrists were already pinned when the dust rose, and Fin was breathing heavily on her face. "Witch," he hissed at her. Tara snarled like a savage dog and kicked his shins. He winced, then reared back his fist.

Everyone cried out simultaneously, but Fin ignored them. Chase cringed as his forceful punch collided resoundingly with Tara's jaw. She screamed and shoved Fin's body away from her. She punched him back, and soon they were wrestling viciously, rolling in the dirt and yelling at each other. Somewhere in the brawl, Rebel wiggled out of Tara's knapsack and watched with wide, scared brown eyes, his ears flat on his head. Fin and Tara were throwing punches so fast that their arms tangled with their legs and became a blur. For a moment no one could do anything but stare on with open mouths.

"This is madness," Oliver whispered.

Finally, Tetoviran got to work and set Emma gently on the ground, coming up around the fight. He jumped forward and seized Tara around the middle as soon as the opportunity opened. She fought him wildly, kicking and screaming, but he didn't release her. He talked to her soothingly, and after a few minutes, her eyes filled with light again and she stopped struggling. He let go of her tentatively, and she was fine again.

Fin, however, was not so easily fixed. It took all four of the other boys and Grace to hold him. He was using all of his strength (and that was a lot) to fight them. "Let me at her!" he screamed. "Let me kill the witch!"

Tara's eyes were wide as she watched him: a boy perhaps three times her size who wanted to kill her.

Somewhere in the chaos, Chase's arm got bitten, and he jumped back with a yelp. Fin took that opportunity to kick back into Devon's stomach, sending him flying into a thorny bush. Blood was drawn immediately, and Devon cursed as the thorns poked him. Grace went to go help him, leaving only Logan and Oliver to restrain Fin. Chase and Tetoviran saw this mistake at the same time and rushed to help, but they collided midway and fell in a heap, cursing each other angrily. Fin easily pushed Oliver and Logan away, and Tara started forward nervously to stop him herself. But Fin whipped out his bow, drawing an arrow faster than anyone could think.

Everyone froze immediately where they stood, barely daring to move. Fin trained his arrow steadily at Tara's chest, fiery hatred glowing in his eyes. Pure terror overtook Tara's face. Everyone knew what would happen if he let that arrow fly. She moved a few steps to the left, and his aim moved fluently with her.

"Fin," she whispered. "Fin, stop. It's okay." Chase could barely breathe. Fin never, never missed. The entire forest went silent as everyone waited to see what he would do.

Slowly, in that moment, something in his eyes changed, and he looked at his bow as if confused by its presence. "What just…" Realization struck him, and he quickly dropped the weapon and ran to Tara. She lifted her arms to protect herself, starting to back away, but he wrapped her in a hug that dwarfed her body. After Tara realized that he wasn't trying to kill her anymore, she hugged him back, both of them stumbling over themselves in a hurry to apologize.

"I'm sorry, I didn't mean to"— "Well, it was my fault"— "If I hadn't"— "The stupid *wind*"—

They returned to friendship very quickly, but a very apologetic Fin confessed that he'd probably punched the air from Tara more than once in their scuffle. She'd suffered much harder blows than he had, and once they began on their way again, they had to stop more often so Tara could catch her breath. Rebel walked with them to take weight off of her back, clinging close to her ankle for safety. A dark bruise purpled her jaw where he had struck her. Fin couldn't have felt worse about the incident, and after a while, Chase got so sick of Fin telling Tara he was sorry that he threatened to gag him if he didn't stop.

Finally, after a long while of jogging, Logan, who had been leading the group, skidded to a halt so quickly that he slipped on a stick and sat down hard. Sitting up with a small groan, he pointed forward through the trees. "Do mirages work in forests? Because I think I saw the… place."

As Fin and Devon helped Logan to his feet, everyone squinted through the trees. Sure enough, in the distance, a wooden door was just barely visible through the falling dusk. There was a long, long time of silence as all nine of them stared at that one little entry through the trees.

Then Tara squealed and jumped up and down. "We're here! We got here, we're finally here!"

Fin whooped and pumped his fist into the air. "Take that, you stupid forest! Stupid plant spirits and phantoms and monsters! We're invincible!"

Chase couldn't remember a time he'd been so excited, so proud of a journey or conquest. All that time spent traveling, fighting, laughing, crying, with the ups and downs and the fear and the peril… the death… it had all been leading up to this. They were finally here. They were really, truly here.

They began to run as one, whooping and screaming with joy, towards the door. Tara even woke Rebel, who'd fallen asleep again a while ago, and she carried him as they ran. His little ears flapped back as the last gust of that cursed wind blew past. Chase would never have to hear it again.

You have arrived at last, the wind whispered.

"Yes," Chase said breathlessly as he ran. And then, just because he couldn't resist: "Eat my dust, you sanity thief." The wind ignored this, much to his disappointment.

You must be very proud. Yet I must ask you… do you wish to know who it is I have been telling you about before you depart for good?

Chase slowed his pace a tiny bit.

Ah. I thought so.

He slowed even more with the rest of the group as they neared the door. He waited anxiously for the wind to continue, but it stayed quiet. Chase sighed in frustration but chose to let it go. So what? Who cared what the wind thought?

As he came to a stop in front of the door, he found himself standing in front of a little stone hut. It was impossibly tiny— a round, one-room cottage with a stone chimney and a rotting wooden door. A small, wilting flower bed laid in a box beneath the front window. The roof's molding shingles were crumbling off, the hinges on the door were red with rust, and the windows looked as though they hadn't been opened in years.

Fin took one look at the place and kicked a tree so hard, the whole thing shuddered and leaves rained down around him. Tetoviran cursed loudly. "It's the wrong place," Grace howled.

Chase shook his head and raked a hand through his hair. "It can't be. That's not fair, they can't *do* that. It's practically dark out!"

Devon clenched his fists. "I swear, when I find those two, I am going to strangle them with my bare hands. I'm not dying here tonight."

Chase noticed, however, that Tara was examining the hut very closely. "What?" he asked her, and she started.

"Well, don't you hear it?"

"Hear what?"

"Just listen."

Sure enough, when Chase concentrated, he could hear two voices exchanging conversation. He couldn't make out the words, but he could tell the voices were female. Youthfully so.

"That can't be right," Emma said. "I thought Chase said they were old."

Devon lifted an eyebrow. "They can appear in different forms. They simply chose to come to Chase in the forms of elderly women. So that could very well be them."

Grace gaped. "We *are* at the right place." Everyone looked at the cottage again, this time with new eyes.

"That's a little pathetic, if you ask me," Oliver mumbled.

Tara shrugged, picked up Rebel and tucked him into her knapsack, and then stepped forward with quick, short strides toward the door. Chase wanted to stop her, but for some reason, he didn't. He knew someone would have to do it, so why not her?

Tara climbed each of the three front steps slowly, taking her time and being cautious of the creaks. Some sort of long grass poked out from the spaces beneath each stair. A tiny, tiny breeze blew past, and no one paid it much mind, as it was probably too small to speak, anyhow. But as it drifted away and Tara raised her fist to knock, Chase heard a whisper.

It was Devon. And then it was gone.

Chase barely got the chance to think before Tara sent two strong pounds to the thick wooden door. The conversation within stopped abruptly, and footsteps were heard coming closer to the door—two pairs of them moving exactly in sync.

Tara froze suddenly, and Chase rushed up the steps, grabbed her by the arms, and pulled her off the stairs to stand down with the rest of them.

A voice came through the door, high-pitched and silvery. "Now, who could that be at this hour?"

With a horrid, rustic screech, the door ground open.

CHAPTER 29

The first thing that Tara noticed about the woman who opened the door was her beauty. Glossy, chestnut-brown hair, thick lips, and long, luscious eyelashes that carpeted gorgeous violet eyes were her central features. She was tall and slim, dressed in a flowing white dress of silk that rippled with her every movement. A band of gold laid round her neck, a silver pendant resting daintily in its hollow.

The woman pushed the door open effortlessly despite its obvious need for oiling. She peered out at them and frowned slightly. "Well, that's odd."

She turned and pushed the door open wider to reveal another woman of the exact same height and structure, with the exact same facial features, as well. The only difference was that her hair was a flowing gold, rather than a rich brown.

The second woman peeked curiously at the visitors. Her eyebrows shot up when she saw them. "Goodness! We thought you wouldn't come." Her voice was just as melodious as her companion's. No one dared respond. "Well, don't just stand there! Come now, night is falling. You don't want to be out there in the dark, now do you?" They all shook their heads.

The first woman smiled, revealing her perfectly straight, white teeth. "Then come in, won't you? We have much to discuss." No one moved. The brunette woman came down the steps—floated, it rather seemed—and reached out for Emma. Emma stepped away, one hand on her scythe. The woman paused and smiled. "I am not going to harm you, Emma Ro"—

"It's Emma!" Emma interrupted. "Just Emma." Suddenly, Tara realized that she didn't know Emma's last name. For that matter, she wasn't sure if anyone did—that is, besides Logan, perhaps.

The woman cocked her head ever so slightly. "Just so."

Emma shifted uncomfortably and tugged her hood further down. "So, which one are you?" she asked, and Tara cringed at her tone.

Unfazed, the woman responded, "I am Fate. Now, if you would like, do come inside." Emma tugged on her hood again and walked stiffly after Fate towards the house.

As they went, Chase leaned over to Tara. "I can't believe that's really them. I know them by such different faces."

"I just can't believe it's them because… well, they're Creators! And they're down here, talking to us, like normal people."

Chase snorted. "Normal people aren't that flawless. These two seem to be made from a mold. They're literally perfect."

Tara lifted an eyebrow. "You realize that they're not up for grabs, right? Not only are they pledged maidens, remember that they're also grandmas when they want to be."

Chase gave her a disgusted face. "I know that. I'm creeped out by how pretty they are. It isn't natural. Besides, I hate them. You know that."

Tara smiled. "I know that. But you're so superficial that you usually go running after anything that looks pretty with outstretched arms." Chase looked like he was about to hit her, so she quickly stepped ahead of him and followed the others. Only when she entered did her smile fade.

One by one, the group walked into the little cottage. The room they entered looked nothing on the inside like it did from the outside. The cottage itself was a one-story round building. Yet upon walking in, Tara found herself standing in a long hallway with several doors, staircases, and other halls leading away from it. The hall she stood in had polished floors lined with a spotless red carpet and a grand, spiraling staircase leading to an upper level. Glass and diamond chandeliers hung from the high ceilings, and golden candelabras perched on the walls at intervals. In between each candleholder, several quilts, tapestries, embroideries, and textiles hung, each depicting a different scene. Some were very gruesome and graphic; others were pleasant and peaceful. Each was incredibly life-like and realistic, done with perfect precision. Some, however, had tears down their centers or in between two figures, separating someone from the rest of the picture. Tara swallowed. That couldn't be good.

The blonde woman, whom Tara assumed was Destiny, led them down a long corridor, one that definitely couldn't fit in the little cottage they'd stood outside mere moments before.

Tara turned and cringed at how muddy and grimy she and her friends were in contrast to this perfectly spotless… house. She couldn't really even call it that. It was more like a castle. Still, each of them left filthy footprints on the perfectly cleaned floors and carpets, and they looked so dirty in this environment.

Fate followed Tara's gaze and waved it carelessly away. "Don't worry about that. We have human servants specifically for this reason."

She snapped her fingers, and four men appeared from a corridor and stood in a crooked line facing them. All of them were so skinny that they looked like skeletons. They held mops and buckets and wore nothing but loincloths on their bony frames. Destiny stopped their procession and pointed to the dirt trail the group had made.

"Clean it," she snapped to the servants. The men cowered and said nothing, fear making their knees knock together. Small bursts of purple fire erupted in the Creators' eyes.

"You dare disobey?" Fate growled, which sounded strange coming from that beautiful voice. It reminded Tara horribly of Aunt Beatrice. Instantly, in Destiny and Fate's hands appeared two thin leather whips. The straps were not just made to hurt. They were made to cut. The Creators lifted them.

"No," Oliver whispered. "They wouldn't."

Yet the whips flew. Once. Twice.

Emma's hands flew to cover her mouth as the men screamed in pain.

Three times.

Tara forced herself to look away, the sound of leather hitting flesh burning into her skull. Destiny and Fate sent six lashes to each man before stopping. Chase watched expressionlessly, but his jaw tightened with pain at the image. He was used to seeing gruesome scenes, Tara knew, but nothing so cruel.

Just as quickly as they'd appeared, the whips vanished, leaving the men bloody and trembling. Two of them were crying.

"DO IT!" the Creators shouted in sync, and the poor pathetic people tripped over each other, unable to begin cleaning fast enough.

Tara felt like she would be sick. Who would dare treat anyone that way? Those poor men were trapped here, living in fear and hopelessness. There was nothing left of them. Tara's friends were barely moving, but Destiny and Fate just stepped more quickly. No one followed them, and they turned together and regarded them with that same purple flame that danced in their eye sockets.

"Come along, children," Fate said, with a voice as sweet as honey. "Or you'll join them." No one protested after that.

Destiny led them up one staircase and down another, through two rooms and another long hall, and she finally stopped and opened the door to a beautiful reclining room. Plush, embroidered chairs and sofas were arranged perfectly and matched all of the carefully crafted wall-hangings that decorated the room. A window on the east side of the large room was cracked open, and a fresh morning breeze blew through the pale curtains. Upon peering outside, Tara saw sprawling meadows of daffodils rolling as far as the eye could see.

But that can't be right, she thought.

"On the contrary, Miss Florreson," Destiny said. "It is magic."

Tara jumped. Had she said that aloud?

"No, you did not say that out loud. As Creators, we have the ability to read minds."

"Please, sit," Fate prompted.

No one sat. Destiny sighed and snapped her fingers, and all ten of them suddenly found themselves sitting. Tara tried not to think very much, for she now knew these two could read her thoughts, but she distantly realized that the Creators had just controlled her body. What would stop them from forcing Tara to kill herself, or kill one of her friends? What would stop them from forcing any of her friends to beat her to death, to break her spine in two and savor the sound of it cracking? Tara blinked in alarm at the thought, shocked that her imagination had grown so wicked, and then realized that there was a massive possibility that those weren't even her own thoughts. That they were Destiny or Fate's instead, disguising themselves as her own as they disguised themselves as young women.

"Well, goodness, you must be famished!" Destiny said cheerily. She snapped her fingers again, and suddenly, a table materialized before them. More bone-thin men appeared, bringing with them a china pot and cups with saucers, each painted in detail and so fragile-looking, it seemed as though they would break at the touch of a feather.

On another table, a variety of gourmet cheeses and fruits were laid out by servant women that looked equally horrible, alongside breads, scones, muffins, meats, and garden vegetables that were set out by children.

Tara felt bile rise in her throat when the children turned to leave. Their backs were scarred with whip marks, their eyes empty and permanently reddened from crying. She felt fiery hatred rise in her chest. Children were being kept in this place.

Chase nudged her with his elbow, meeting her eyes. "You can't do anything about it," he whispered, then nodded to the food. "Look at that."

Despite the terrible things she'd seen, Tara heard her stomach grumble. She hadn't eaten well in a long time. Everyone else looked just as famished. Fin was practically drooling.

Destiny and Fate smiled knowingly. "Help yourselves," they said as one, and Tara was later ashamed to say that she completely forgot the children as she ate.

The entire group devoured plateful after plateful of food, hardly stopping for a breath in between bites. Tara had never tasted anything so delicious, and for the time being, nothing else mattered to her.

She felt a bit self-conscious as Destiny and Fate sat quietly, watching them all as they shoveled food into their mouths. The two Creators didn't utter a single word until everyone had eaten.

When they were all full, they sipped tea as Destiny crossed one long leg over the other and laced her slender fingers on her knee. "So, you have come for answers."

Everyone nodded.

"Well, I must confess, I'm quite impressed. Very few ever work up enough courage to come looking for us, and even fewer actually make it. We thought you would not be coming. After the Shadow Monsters took hold of Devon, we were almost certain you would be too afraid to go on. Besides, you were already extremely late. We stopped keeping track of your progress soon after he was returned to sanity. We must say, we were surprised at your arrival here."

No one responded. Destiny frowned ever so slightly, then leaned forward simultaneously with Fate. "Well, then. Let's get straight to the point, shall we? What exactly is it that you want?"

Chase spoke up before anyone else could. "Several things, but mostly to find Ukrasen and my parents. I'm assuming you already know everything, so I don't really need to explain. I just want to get them back before it's too late."

"We have clearly foreseen that this would be your request."

Chase's eyes were as big as his tea saucer as Destiny and Fate spoke to him simultaneously. "Do you rehearse that?"

The Creators laughed in exact sync. "No. We have the ability to read minds, remember? That includes each other. We could speak in unison with any of you if we wished. Of course, we wouldn't want to scare you, so we won't do that."

Chase curled his lip a little at that and set his tea down on the table, barely hard enough to make liquid slosh over the sides. "Perhaps if you want to scare people, you can decide to rip their happiness into a million little pieces and send them a prophecy of death. That might work."

Tara put a hand on Chase's leg. Fate lifted her chin coolly, but anger flashed in her eyes. "Perhaps if *you* want to scare people, we can turn you into a hideous monster with poisonous breath and force you to kill your friends."

Tara drew in a breath, but Chase just cocked his head, an arrogant tilt to his mouth. "How would I save the world if I was a hideous poison-breathing monster?" The Creators didn't respond, and Chase smiled a little, his voice soft. "No, I think you need me alive, just as I am now. Otherwise, your sick little plan won't work too well, will it?"

"Bite your words, child."

He smiled pleasantly and didn't say anything more as he leaned back to recline lazily on the couch, one leg thrown over Tara's lap and the other dangling to the floor. Now that he had sufficiently irritated the Creators, he seemed perfectly content to relax and watch things play out.

After a moment, Destiny spoke. "So, you understand, of course, that your parents can only be brought back if Ukrasen is restored to Jisara."

Chase nodded, and she snapped her fingers. A thick, leather-bound book with golden depictions decorating the cover appeared in her lap.

Chase stared at it. "That's going to help me?"

Destiny shook her head. "No. That is going to help *us* help you."

"Is there anything else you need from us?" they questioned together before Chase could say anything.

Tara began to speak up, but Chase unintentionally beat her to it. "How come I can use a sword?" he asked, sounding more interested in the answer than he had ever sounded in anything before. Despite his careless posture, his eyes sparked. "Nobody ever taught me. Everyone I know who's a great swordsman has been trained for years. Why did I just have to pick one up?"

"We foresaw that you would need the skill in order to survive to your current age, so we bestowed the ability upon you. You have used it many times to save your life already," they chorused simultaneously. "Any other questions?"

Tara spoke now, refusing to be cut off again. "Yes." Her heart thumped as the Creators' eyes turned on her, but she continued. "I have a lot of questions about my powers. Why is it that when I got angry that time after the *teskos* attacked, everything around me died and I couldn't control it? Why did I hurt Chase the way I did without wanting to? And why can't I call on my powers whenever my emotions are strong? Why do they only come around occasionally?"

Destiny used a single finger to dab at a perfectly plump, tinted lip. "Simple answers to all those questions. You are still learning this skill. It is like… how to make you understand? It is like sewing, Tara. In the beginning, your stitches are crooked and sloppy, and there are large gaps in between them. But as you advance and practice and grow more skillful, you gain more control over your seams, and your stitches become tight and straight, with no gaps in between. Soon enough, there will be no more gaps in your abilities. It simply takes time and patience. I know you have much of both."

Tara blinked. "Oh. Th-thank you." Destiny nodded curtly. She'd gone over this day countless times in her head, imagining all the horrible things Destiny and Fate might say to her. That was hardly what she'd expected.

"And… the torture power?" she asked tentatively, drawing looks of confusion from her friends. She had nearly forgotten that Chase had never told anyone about what'd happened.

Destiny smiled. "Well, I believe you figured that out yourself. Your power extends over men."

"How is that possible? Plants and animals are always affected when my powers are awake. Before Chase, no human beings were ever touched directly by my powers. Why don't they feel the same urge to serve me that plants and animals do?"

"Because Man was never grateful to Earth for the things she gave him. He never respected her and therefore is unaffected by you. The only reason you affected Chase so much that day was that you were very angry with him. Your power is designed so that you have control over men, but only in a negative way."

"Nice," Chase said.

Tara stared at Destiny in silence for a moment before speaking again. *"What?"* she shrieked at last. "I'm… I'm some sort of murder machine?"

Fate shook her head. "Of course not. You can torture and kill men because they are the ones who took Earth for granted, but that, too, can be controlled with some instruction. It may sound like a terrible thing, but you must remember that this is far from the end of your journey, and you will face many bad men. Such a power will be very useful."

Tara could barely wrap her mind around this. Wasn't Earth a representative of Life? How could Tara have such a horrifying power? "Instruction from whom?" she managed.

"Time will show you," the Creators said in unison. "He will come to you, a teacher most unexpected who knows the ways of the old magics."

Tara stared at them. "And… and what, until I meet him, my powers are just doing whatever they want? How will I refrain from killing someone? Or, if I'm in a fight, how can I call on them?"

Destiny shrugged. "Until you meet him, things will be, for the most part, out of your control. In some emotional scenarios, they will awaken; in others, nothing will happen. You have wielded your power to your will before, though, Tara. Remember that."

"Yes," she said desperately, "but I don't know how I did. Can't you help me a little bit right now?"

"No" was the simple answer from both of their mouths, and that was final.

Tara felt as though she was crumbling in despair. All this time, she had been depending on Destiny and Fate to explain her power to her. Instead, they told her she had to wait even longer for somebody who could teach her. How could Tara be certain that this person wouldn't show up when she was an old woman?

"Who are all those poor people working here?" Grace asked suddenly. "Why are they treated so badly?"

Destiny and Fate shrugged together. "They are the more unfortunate folk that we pluck from your world to serve us."

"Have they done anything wrong?"

"Not necessarily."

Grace scowled. "Then why are they treated like that when you could just snap your fingers and do all the work those people are forced to do?"

Destiny smiled. "It's very amusing to see how vulnerable you mortals are. We are Creators, dear Grace, you mustn't forget. We need a taste of power each day, so we do not forget that you are lesser beings."

No one said anything more on the matter, but quiet anger was heavy in the room.

Finally, Emma spoke up. "Can you heal my leg?" A beat. "Please?" The word seemed to grind out of her mouth with force, but there was fear in Emma's voice. If the Creators denied her, she would probably die from the infection. Already, she looked feverishly pale.

Fate nodded grimly. "Speaking of which, you could all use a cleaning up." She raised her hand, and Devon sighed.

"I'm getting tired of all the snapping."

Fate paused and smiled at him. "Oh, you'll like this one, Mr. Arani."

She snapped, and everyone gasped in shock and delight to find that their clothing had been mended and cleaned to perfection. Everyone's dirty, greasy hair was washed and combed, and their wounds—from Emma's cut to Tara's bruises—had vanished entirely. Tara felt Rebel shift in her knapsack and then heard him mumble in surprise. "My fur's all smooth," he said sleepily; then he passed out again.

"Wow," Logan breathed. "Thanks."

Destiny nodded. "Not a problem."

"I still have a question," Fin said. "Why are you being…nice? Of course, you're not portraying the ideal host, but you guys are pretty evil to be this nice to us."

Fate smiled wryly. "It all depends on our mood, young Vidovu." Fin flinched at the use of his father's name. "You were lucky to come to us on a particularly cheerful day. Lots of drama floating about on the Thrones and plenty of opportunities for us to meddle in other Creators' arguments. It's fun, you know."

"You like to meddle with everything, don't you?" Logan asked rudely, drawing a snort of amusement from Chase. "Ever take a few minutes off, or do you always have to stick those fake noses into other peoples' lives?" Chase lifted his brows in agreement, bumping Logan's fist with his over Tara's head.

Each Creator fixed them both with a glare. "I think," Fate said coldly, "that you have outstayed your welcome, young rake-fires."

She flipped open that big book and started leafing through the yellowing, crumbled pages. Finally, she stopped as a piece of paper fell from the book. Destiny handed it to Chase, who naturally started to unfold it.

However, Fate stopped him. "Wait until you arrive."

Chase frowned. "Arrive where? Where are we going?"

The Creators simply smiled and shook their heads, lifting their right hands in unison. They snapped their fingers, and the world flipped upside-down.

CHAPTER 30

One second, they were standing in the posh, fancy foyer in Destiny's and Fate's house, and the next, they were standing on a crowded fisherman's dock. The salty spray of the sea hit them in the face along with the smell of fresh-caught fish. Fishermen all along the dock were pulling in their catches, separating pink and white fishes of all sizes. Ship bells rang in the sharp air. Small boats were tied up along the harbor, and larger ones' crews were pulling up their nets from the sea, their sails footloose in the buffeting wind. The worn wooden planks of the dock were dank and encrusted with algae.

Chase did a quick headcount. "Everyone's here. Good."

"We went all that way, struggled so much, and we only saw the witches for a half hour!" Tara's voice was getting dangerously close to a whine. She was tired.

Fin looked around, his mouth pruned up in disgust. "They sent us to some sailors' town."

Devon stepped towards the sea. He frowned and scanned the harbor. "There must be something here that we need. They wouldn't be cruel enough to just send us someplace random."

"Mm, I wouldn't be surprised," Emma muttered.

Chase reached for the parchment they had given him, puzzled, when all of a sudden, a rough hand came down on his shoulder. He turned and saw a withered old man with gray hair and a wild beard that frizzed in several directions, with a single braid down its center. His skin was browned, and he smelled of salt and blood. His hands were blotched and sea-weathered. "It'll be costing you two coppers to tie up here, lad."

"We don't have a boat, sir."

The man turned and examined the dock through sharp old eyes, the creases around them deepening as he did so. He looked back at Chase. "No. So you don't. How'd you get to be standing there on that there dock, then, eh?"

Chase smiled coyly, fully prepared to run his mouth until the man left them alone, but he was cut off before he could start. "No excuses, here, lad. You pay, just the same as everyone else." "Well, just listen for a"— "Where be your captain, boy?"

Chase shook his head. "I told you before, sir, I don't have a boat or a"—

"I am the captain," Tetoviran said, stepping forward. He spoke in a ridiculous sailor's accent as he shoved two coppers into the man's hand. "There's my boat," Teto said, motioning to a small sailboat moored at the dock, "and here's my money. Good day." Without another word, Teto strode past the man, leaving the others to follow.

The group walked through the sea-worn town, passing shops and saloons and fisheries. It was a quaint little place with dozens of seafood vendors and a pub on nearly every corner. Drunken old fishermen smoked pipes drowsily outside the bars, and plump women chatted while children played together, tossing a small ball or drawing in the dusty sand on the streets. The whole town smelled of ocean air and salty fish.

Grace shook her head in bewilderment. "What could possibly be here that will help lead us to Ukrasen?"

No one could answer her question; they were all wondering the same thing.

Chase pointed to a small, rickety building with a sloppily painted sign that read *Helmsman Inn.* "We can start by getting some rest. Nobody's slept in over a day."

The others agreed immediately, and they stepped through the wooden door of the inn. Immediately, they found themselves practically running straight into a tall, skinny man with close-cropped hair and a long, pointed nose. He peered at them from behind his spectacles, then smiled to reveal yellowed, crooked teeth. "Good morning!" he said chirpily. "Welcome to the Helmsman Inn! What can I get for you?"

Chase looked flatly at the man through half-lidded eyes. He was not in the mood for that level of enthusiasm. "A room," he said shortly.

"Only one?" came the bright reply. "There are three available at the moment. Lucky day for you, I'd say. Usually a full house."

"We'll take all three," Chase answered.

The man's smile, which Chase thought couldn't have widened, grew. "Splendid! I'll get them ready right away. I'm Carlton Wills, by the way. The innkeeper here. Truly a pleasure!"

As he scampered off to prepare their rooms, Logan made a halfhearted rude gesture to his back. "He has more energy than a drunk child," he grumbled softly.

Despite everyone's renewed appearances, Destiny and Fate hadn't restored their strength. Exhausted, the group collapsed in the lobby's various chairs and sofas, each shabby and wearing away. No one spoke throughout the entire wait.

A short while later, their rooms were ready, and Carlton escorted them to the third floor. "Is there anything more I can do for you today before I leave you off?" he asked, his energy still overflowing.

Fin nodded. "Yes. What time is it, and what is the name of this town?"

Carlton seemed a bit baffled by these questions, probably wondering why Fin didn't know the answers to either of them, but he responded quickly. "It is midmorning, young man, and you are currently residing in the seaside town of Weather-helm. This town is very special, I'd say. Talked about up and down the coast, got all the maids and housewives gossiping."

Chase put up a hand to signal that they didn't care and wanted to sleep, then sighed as Tara asked curiously, "Why?"

"Well, because of the treasure, of course!" Chase rubbed his eyes in exasperation. He did not want to stand here and listen to some stupid sailors' myth.

"What treasure?" Grace asked with an air of interest.

"You haven't heard the stories?" Carlton leaned forward excitedly. "We've got a hidden treasure somewhere in this town. The first mayor of Weather-helm hid it somewhere that no man has ever been able to find. It was originally meant for emergency provisions, but it's never really been necessary. Not that it would really matter anyhow; we can't find the darn thing. Supposedly, it's worth more than a king's entire treasury!"

The man glanced down the hall and lowered his voice. "Only bad thing about that, I suppose, is the pirates. Those vile men love to sail their ships into our harbor at night and raid the town. They've been searching us for decades, but nothing's ever been found. They never seem to give up, though. Greedy creatures, pirates. Come here and loot everything, so often it's become a normal thing. Set things aflame, steal whatever they can find. They'll take a wench alive once in a while, too. Always come back, though, always searching for the same exact thing."

A voice called up from the lobby below. "Oi, Carl, where be you? Come down, I need a quick word!"

The innkeeper smiled apologetically. "Friend of mine visiting from the north. I'll have to be leaving you for now, but if you happen to need anything more throughout the day, just let me know."

Carlton retreated down the hall and down the staircase, leaving the nine people—and one *tesko*—alone in the hallway.

Chase took a deep breath. "Let's rest in a moment. For now, we need to have a meeting."

He pushed the door to one of their three rooms open, and they all stepped inside. It was a bit compact for the amount of people they'd squeezed in there, but they all managed to sit down, whether it was on the bed or the floor. Chase folded his legs and sat down in the center of everyone, pulling the parchment Destiny had given him from his hidden pouches. It was a map.

The others crowded around him, examining the parchment. "Well, there's Weather-helm," Fin pointed, drawing exhalations of relief from everyone. "So, we're not in a random place."

Grace frowned, examining the map. "I don't think we're even anywhere near the Sixteen Kingdoms anymore, though. I don't recognize any of these places."

"We're not," Emma mumbled. "How far away do think we are?"

"We'd have to be quite a distance away by now," Logan said. "The map covers an entire ocean, but the Sixteen Kingdoms aren't on here."

Chase blinked. He had never ventured so far in his life. He hadn't really imagined the world could be so big.

Devon pointed to a spot in the center of the ocean, where a star was depicted. "There it is."

Written underneath it in swirling calligraphy were the words, *Here Lies Thy Sword Ukrasen*. There was no island shown, however, which Tara asked about.

Chase shrugged. "There's got to be some sort of landform there. They marked where Ukrasen is, so there must be an island where the star is located."

"Unless it's underwater," Grace added. "That would definitely be a good hiding place."

Chase winced. He didn't want to think about that possibility. If the sword was at the bottom of the sea, it would be impossible to retrieve.

"Okay, look," Logan said, "we can't jump to conclusions like that. We have what we need now. We need to get ourselves out there." He traced the route from Weather-helm to the marking of Ukrasen. "That should be easy enough; we landed in a sailor's town. We can just steal ourselves a boat."

Emma shook her head thoughtfully. "It can't be right," she murmured. "Destiny and Fate wouldn't make things that easy for us. There's another reason why we're here. There are millions of these towns all along the coast, and it isn't nearly a straight route to Ukrasen from Weather-helm. Why would they choose this specific one if there was no real reason for it?"

A steady, thoughtful silence followed her statement. "She has a valid point," Devon said, crossing his arms and leaning his back up against the wall. "Destiny and Fate don't tend to mess around."

"Mess around?" Chase said. "All they ever do is mess around, trying to screw up people's lives. We're all just like puppets to them. They love that sort of thing."

Oliver nodded. "I agree. Those two don't care what happens to us. Knowing them, they'd probably drop us in the middle of the ocean without a boat and watch us drown. We should be thankful they set us down in such a convenient place."

"Well, what about that guy Tara was supposed to meet?" Devon suggested. "Maybe he lives here."

Fin sighed. "So, what are we going to do, go to every door looking for him? Whatever's waiting for us here will find us on its own. I say we rest for a few hours, then split up into two groups. One of us goes and tries to take a boat; the other tries to make one. If one fails, we have the other to rely on."

"Make a boat," Grace said incredulously. "Make a—how in the world do you propose we should go about making a *boat?* None of us have ever even sailed before, much less crafted our own ship!"

"It doesn't need to be a ship; it can just be a rowboat. That's simple enough to make, isn't it?" Nobody answered. Nobody knew. They were all from places far away from the coast.

Grace began to protest, but Logan interrupted her. "It's an okay plan. If it doesn't work out, we'll try something else. Nothing to lose at this point."

"Nothing but time," Emma muttered darkly. "With every passing day, Jisara comes closer to destruction. Soon enough, more and more monsters will flood in. They'll move on and take the entirety of the Sixteen Kingdoms, and after that, the rest of the world. We certainly can't dawdle along."

"What a darling ray of sunshine you are," Chase said in sarcastic adoration.

"Let's just try it," Tara said. "Stealing a boat was the original… unfortunate plan. We might as well have a backup. Making a boat isn't a bad idea."

Chase felt his eyelids drooping. "Sleep," he murmured. "Sleep, and then we'll talk about it later. None of us are in the condition for this now."

Thankfully, no one argued. Everyone began dividing themselves between the three rooms, separating and trudging sluggishly to the beds. Chase remained where he was, not even bothering to remove his boots or sword before crawling exhaustedly to the bed. He collapsed on the quilt with a sigh, and his eyes fell closed at once. He felt the mattress shift beside him, and he knew that someone else also laid on the bed. Someone plopped himself down at his feet as well, but he never opened his eyes to see who slept next to him. He didn't open his eyes at all for the next several hours. It had been a long, long couple of days.

When Chase finally woke again, there was soft snoring beside him, and bright sunlight streamed through the center crack in the curtains, hitting him directly in the eyes. He cringed and turned his face away to find himself staring at the slumbering face of Fin Vidovu. At Chase's feet, sleeping with one hand brushing the floor, was Devon.

Deciding not to wake them just yet, Chase stared intently at Devon's face. He slept silently, with his mouth closed and his eyelids still.

Chase couldn't wrap his mind around what the wind had told him. Was he worried about being replaced by Devon? He didn't care if Tara liked Devon better. *Don't lie to yourself,* the voice in his head chided him. And Chase knew it was right. He cared. He cared a lot.

True, he didn't like Tara in a romantic way, but she was his best friend. She was the first one he would go to about anything, and he played the same role for her. He didn't want that to change—not ever. Especially not for something as ridiculous as… love. The winds must've been exaggerating. Of course, Tara *liked* Devon. Chase could plainly see it. But she couldn't love him. Not yet. For her to love him would mean that Chase would get forgotten and left behind. Again.

It all made Chase feel strange—almost protective. He had always taken care of Tara, from the day they met. He didn't want her getting whisked off by some boy. The thought made him chuckle softly to himself. He was beginning to sound more like her father then her friend.

Despite all this, however, these feelings were all rather muted. None were tugging furiously at him, demanding attention like his anger towards Araknan or grief towards his destroyed childhood. These feelings and opinions were far in the back of his mind, and even from these he couldn't see the possibility of hating Devon. He was a good friend. So, what was it, then, that made the winds whisper in his ears that hatred existed between him and Devon Arani?

He heard a knock on the door of their room and called softly as the others began to stir. "Come in."

The door creaked open an inch, and Logan's unmistakable green eye peeked through the tiny gap. He began to crack the door open a bit further when suddenly a thick, muscled arm lodged itself behind the door and slammed it open so hard that it banged into the wall behind it.

Fin and Devon leapt awake, cussing like horses while Tetoviran marched himself inside. "Wake up," he announced gruffly. "We've got work to do."

CHAPTER 31

A short time after she'd been rudely awakened by Chase, Tara was walking through Weather-helm with Fin, looking for a place to buy wood. They had, indeed, gone along with Fin's plan and divided themselves into two groups. Tara was with Fin, Chase, Logan, and Tetoviran, and their job was to build a boat. Oliver, Emma, Devon, Grace, and Rebel were out to steal one. If one failed, they fell back on the other.

"How are you?" Fin asked as they walked.

"Fine. Why?"

He shrugged, looking at the ground for a moment. Tara waited, sensing he had more to say. Sure enough, he rubbed a hand over his face and spoke more. "I… I know I beat you up fairly bad in the woods. You were really bruised afterwards."

She almost felt like laughing. 'Fairly bad' did not even begin to cover how he'd beaten her. Since Destiny and Fate had healed her, there had been no pain, but before that, it had been a desperate struggle to even keep moving. Every step had been torture.

"I'm okay now," she responded truthfully. "It was only during and directly after the fight that there was really bad pain."

He scrubbed his blonde hair in agitation. "But… to think I almost shot you." Her own stomach turned at the memory. "I still feel so terrible, Tara."

"Don't," she said simply. "I know you would never attack me like that in any other situation."

"Yeah, but those winds are honest. I attacked you with anger from my own head."

She shrugged. "So? I attacked you right back. The only difference is your strength."

Fin threw up his hands. "How can you act like it's no big deal? We basically hate each other. We just pretend not to all the time."

Tara stared at him in shock as they walked. There was a lengthy period of silence during which he scanned the streets tensely.

"Fin…" she began after a moment, "…it doesn't work like that. You know that. It's all subconscious."

"Yes, but it's there," he said softly. He seemed to hesitate, then went on, "I apparently hate you because you're so powerful. I feel threatened by you and all your magic."

Tara looked at him in surprise. "Really?" He nodded.

"That's kind of funny," she smiled after a moment.

Fin threw her a dirty look, to which she responded with an innocent shrug.

"Think about it. You? Afraid of me? You're literally two of me." He still frowned at her. "Come on. It's a little funny."

Relenting, he loosened and shook his head at her. "Fine. Maybe a little. But you attacked me, too. Why did you hate me?"

"Apparently because you barged in on our journey and sort of ruined the closeness Chase and I had. I don't really understand that, because Tetoviran joined us first, and Chase and I are still close. I also feel threatened by your size and strength, according to the stupid wind, because you make me feel small and inferior, or something. It all seems ridiculous, but the winds don't lie, I guess."

Fin rubbed his fingers over his belt. Coastal sun shone down on him brilliantly, and he had taken off his jacket in the heat. Now, his bare forearms were laced with a web of veins from the tenseness of his hands.

"I guess not. I'm still sorry, though."

"I know, but you don't"—

Tara trailed off as Tetoviran ran up to them through the crowd, pushing people breathlessly out of the way. "We found a shipyard with tons of wood there. The kid's getting ready."

Fin's face lit up, his muscles loosening as he seemed to completely forget his concern. "Oh, that's great! Wait… which kid, and ready for what?"

Tetoviran grunted and looked at Fin for the first time. "Oh, yuck! You're here, too, Blondie?"

"Yeah."

"Once more—yuck! Now, where was I? Ah, yes. The Onaj kid, of course. He's getting ready to steal some wood."

Tara's eyebrows shot up. "Steal wood? But the planks must be huge! How is he going to do that?"

Teto snickered. "That's exactly the point. He gets caught, then we're all home free! No more kid, no more sneaky charm, no more shaggy hair. Destiny and Fate cut everyone's hair except for the only kid who really needs it. It looks like a deformed raven."

"Teto!" Tara scolded. "He won't ever be able to pull that off."

"I know, I've been telling him since we met, the hair isn't going to work out for you. Kept arguing, kept arguing. Like you said, he just can't pull it off."

"Not his hair, the theft! He'll get caught! When is he going to…?"

"Right about now, I'd say. Tomato Head's there, too."

"Take us there. We have to stop Chase, or they'll catch him."

Tetoviran whined. "No. Let him do it. Please?" Tara glared again, and his mouth drooped in disappointment. "Fine."

Tara and Fin followed Tetoviran at a jog through the crowded market area of Weather-helm. Tara saw a shipyard up ahead and began to speed up, but Tetoviran motioned her and Fin behind the fence that surrounded the yard.

They crouched there and peeked through the gaps in the poorly-built fence. Tara saw stacks of planks and logs and beams, each piled high in disorganized mounds. Ropes, netting, and sailcloth were messily strewn about. A wood seller was shaping planks while men milled around. Small boats were undergoing maintenance checks while larger vessels were being cleaned and repaired. There did not appear to be a single boat in the process of construction, and none were for sale. Chase was nowhere to be seen.

"Is he in there yet?" Fin whispered.

Tetoviran shrugged. "Probably. He was heading in when I left, and it took me a good while to find you."

Tara clenched her teeth. She knew Chase was good at this, but... wood? Wood was large, and heavy, and anything but stealthy.

"Teto," she said suddenly. "You paid the man at the dock. How? Do you have money left over?"

The big man smiled. "Nabbed it from a sailor walking past me. And no."

Tara frowned, feeling a pang of indignity. Why did it seem like everyone could do things like that and she was the only one who just couldn't seem to do anything for herself? Emma, Grace, Oliver, and Devon could fight like demons, Chase, Logan, and Tetoviran could steal anything without being noticed *and* fight, Fin could shoot a sprinting mouse from a league away... even Rebel could hold his own better than her. All she had was her stupid power, and even that didn't work most of the time. She really, really wished she could fight. It was embarrassing to be surrounded by people who could do such amazing things when she couldn't do a single thing to defend herself. If her powers didn't happen to cooperate, she became weight. Someone else would always have to be there, saving her. On the other hand, did she really want to be off stealing and slashing swords through the air? Not particularly.

Suddenly, with timing that was almost too perfect after that thought, hands landed roughly on her shoulders, one of them clutching a knife. She cried out and turned, grabbing for her sword, but stopped with surprise. Logan looked down at her, his mischievous features upturned. "Easy there. Come with me. Chase has everything ready."

As Logan led them back through the streets again, Fin interrogated him relentlessly. "Where have you two been? What happened? How did you get the wood? Where are you hiding it? What happened to the men working there? *Why won't you tell me anything?*"

"Because you aren't giving any of us a chance to breathe in between questions," Logan replied. "We've got the wood just around this corner here. I guess the people around here build stuff a lot in public, so we won't have to hide."

A woman with nearly a dozen children in tow moved across their path, and everyone stopped as the little ones ran past.

"The shipyard workers seemed sort of surprised that we were building a boat, though," Logan continued. "They kept trying to get us to use a different type of wood that was more expensive. Said it was 'ship wood' or some garbage like that. Obviously, we didn't fall for it. You can build a boat with anything you want."

Tara wasn't so sure about that, but she didn't know the first thing about boats, so she couldn't very well tell Logan he was wrong.

When the children had passed by, he held up what looked like a small pastry and had seemingly appeared out of thin air. "Kids around here aren't too sharp," he commented as he popped it in his mouth.

Tara stared at him openmouthed. "You took food from a child? What kind of monster are you?"

Logan grinned and waggled his eyebrows. "A hungry one."

Tara's mouth folded in disgust. She could see why he and Chase got along so well.

As the four of them rounded the block, they saw a grassy area on an outcrop overlooking the sea. A single tree stood tall and proud on the edge of the cliff, shading the entire area. Standing in its shadow was Chase, talking to two men. They were just topping off a stack of smoothed wooden boards. The men seemed friendly enough, despite being unshaven and strapped with muscle down to their toes. Chase looked like a child next to them.

They hefted up the last of the wood and waved to Chase as they walked away.

The four hurried to meet him. "What happened?" Tara demanded.

"I bought some wood."

"Right. More like you *stole* some wood. Who were those men that helped you? Weather-helm's own little band of thieves?"

"Tara, relax. I actually did buy that wood."

"Do enlighten us," Fin said flatly, leaning against the tree's thick trunk with his muscular arms folded. "How did you get the money? Or rather, from whom did you take it?"

Chase shrugged. "A couple different people. I just figured that stealing money would be a lot easier than stealing wood."

Tara wasn't sure whether to chastise him or hug him. She had been so worried he'd get caught, but she supposed she should have realized he would be smart enough not to.

"So those guys were shipyard workers?" Fin asked.

"Wait…" Tara mumbled. "Why couldn't we just buy a boat?"

Chase's eyes got big. "You wouldn't believe how stupidly hard it is to find a boat for sale in this place! I haven't seen a ship or raft with a price on it. It's insane. It seems like everybody here has one; where do they buy them?"

Tara sighed. "This is going to be impossible. We don't know the first thing about making a boat. Can't we hire someone to help us?"

Fin shrugged. "Let's just try it ourselves and see what happens."

So try they did. For what seemed like years but was only hours in reality, the five of them slaved over wood and nails, hammering until their muscles were trembling. Tara's hair grew unruly from her own sweat, the hot sun beating down on them as afternoon fell into early evening. Still, they worked on.

Tara tried to remain optimistic whenever she looked at their progress, but their little boat was looking less and less like the ones they'd already seen with every added piece of wood. There were unignorable holes in the sides that Teto tried to cover with smaller pieces of wood, but that resulted in uneven surfaces. One side rose up higher than the other.

Tara's back was aching when the sun began to sink, its light reflecting blindingly off the ocean. As they were putting the finishing touches on their shabby excuse for a boat, sweat glistening on everyone's faces, an evening breeze swept over their outcrop.

Panting, Logan stepped away from the boat. "I think we're done," he breathed. "I can't do any more of this."

Tara nodded, dropping the hammer Chase had "borrowed" from a man in the shipyard in exhaustion. The others followed suit, and another gust of wind blew in from the ocean. Almost without realizing it, Tara braced herself before she realized that this wind wouldn't talk to her.

Chase lifted his face to it with relief. "Wind smells different here," he sighed as he sat down in the grass. "Salty."

"That would be the ocean, stupid," Tetoviran muttered, taking a spot next to him. Chase threw a hammer at him, which he swiftly dodged.

Fin wiped a freshly-tanned arm across his face, shaking his head and sending droplets of sweat flying from his blond hair. "I hate to say this after we worked so hard," he said, "but I get the feeling we did this wrong."

"Of course we did. None of us are from the coast," Tara reasoned.

"No, but we need to find a way to leave it," Chase pointed out. His skin was darker than it had been that morning, and Logan's was red from sunburn.

She nodded. "Just… rest for a minute first."

They all sat beneath the shade of a tree and tilted their faces up to receive the last light of day as winds blew in on them from the sea. The days were getting longer.

CHAPTER 32

"I really, really hope the others managed to steal—or buy—a boat," Logan was saying. "Ours is…nice… but it'll be really cramped. I don't know if we can all fit."

The group had been resting for some time now, and Chase, while still tired from the strangeness of the time change they'd undergone, felt much better.

Teto sighed. "We don't have an anchor, either. Or steering."

Tara frowned. "Then it'll be impossible to use."

Fin shook his head. "Not if we get some oars. This town may not sell boats, but they must sell those. We could use them for speed and steering."

Teto sighed. "I really don't want to do that right now."

"The others will be back soon, though. We'll have to get them pretty soon if we're to be ready in time to meet them," Logan pointed out.

Tara stood somewhat reluctantly. "I can go." No one protested. She hesitated, almost as if she hoped someone would, then nodded shortly and turned to leave. She took one step, then turned back around. "Um, money will be an issue."

Teto, Logan, and Fin all turned simultaneously to look at Chase, who groaned. "Make Logan do it."

"No," the redhead said instantly, in a tone that made it clear he was not willing to debate on the matter.

Chase gave him a sour look, debating whether or not it would be worth his energy to clobber him, then turned back to Tara.

"Why don't you try to do it yourself? You've got legs. Somebody sees you, you run."

"Short legs," she corrected. "Everyone here knows I'd get caught."

He put his arms over his face for a moment, then stood up with a grunt and a sigh. "All right. Come on, Princess."

The thinning crowds closed around them, the hustle and bustle merry and light. They walked next to each other in silence for a time, and Tara kept looking at him. Finally, he smiled. "What are you watching for?"

She lifted her eyebrows as though it should be obvious. "Well, aren't you going to…" she glanced around and lowered her voice. "Do it?"

Chase scanned the area. "I'm waiting for an opportunity." "Why?"

"Because that makes it easier."

"Yes, I understand that, but you never waited before. You just picked a person and dove into it."

He nodded. "Yes. But I just built a boat in the hot sun, so I'm tired. I don't want to do the work today."

As they continued on, a drunken boy, looking no older than sixteen, staggered across their path. Spotting Tara, he grinned and swayed closer to her. She stumbled away from him in surprise, pressing against Chase. "Hey, darlin'," he slurred, running his calloused, sea-worn fingers over her lips. The young drunk held up a dark brown bottle, waving it under her nose with a lopsided grin. "Want some?"

She pulled further away from him in disgust, crinkling her nose. "No, thanks." He shrugged, stumbling onwards and throwing a suggestive whistle after them that made Tara's face flush. Chase smiled slightly, only having to wait about two heartbeats for the idiot to cry out in shock as his pants fell to his ankles. He lifted the drunk's belt and waved it in Tara's face as he pulled her into a saunter.

Once they were past, she shook her head. "That's vile. No one should be drinking that much at his age." She looked at Chase for approval and saw his growing smile. "What?"

He grinned. "Don't hit me."

She frowned. "Why would I need to"—

"I've been drunk like that before."

She stopped dead in her tracks and stared at him. "You're joking."

He shook his head and shoved his hands in his pockets. The crowds parted around them. "It was with Logan, some years ago. I hadn't seen him for a while, so we got together, went to a neighboring town, and drank. It was kind of fun until he passed out. I left him unconscious in the street and didn't see him again for a year."

Tara's mouth hung open. "Are—are you serious?"

Chase shook his head in bewilderment. "That was my reaction. I mean, I know he's kind of skinny, so drinks hit harder, but who knew three glasses would affect him so"— "Not *that!*" Tara interrupted. "I meant, who would give two kids alcohol?"

"We stole it."

Her mouth opened and closed repeatedly for a moment, then she took a deep breath. "You stole alcohol and got drunk." "Yup."

She nodded slowly. "Ah. WHY WOULD YOU DO THAT?"

He smiled crookedly. "We didn't have any rules to follow. Besides, it's not like we did it a lot. Just once." He paused. "With Logan."

Tara stepped away from him. "There were *other* times?"

"Maybe."

She glared at him. "The devils will be eyeing you from the darkest depths of Hell, Chase."

"They already were long before I drank." "At least ask forgiveness."

"From the devils? I don't want their pardon. It's the saints I'm worried about. Heaven must be cursing me with every breath she exhales."

"And who is there to blame but yourself? Drinking isn't good for you, and it doesn't make you somebody."

She began to walk again, and he followed at a slow, lanky pace. He'd been almost afraid to share this with Tara, but she wasn't half as angry as Chase had expected her to be. As they walked for a long moment in silence, he wondered why. Perhaps she was finally learning that he would never be tamed, as so many had before her. Chastisement was pointless, because he'd never listen. Out of pure spite, he usually made a point not to.

Yet maybe it wasn't just that. He had a feeling that perhaps she was a bit curious, too. She'd never known such things as drinking and doing things that she knew to be wrong.

Proving him right, she tugged on her shirt nervously and spoke. "What did you even do? While you were drunk, I mean?"

He shrugged, smiling at the memory. "Got annoying and loud. Made a lot of older men angry. Flirted. Not much different than what we did sober, I'd reckon. It was sort of fun. Not really all that it's made out to be, though. I've had better times."

Tara shook her head in exasperation. "I just can't believe you did that. Don't you know better?"

"Of course."

When he didn't elaborate, she sighed. "You're hopeless, you know that?"

Chase grinned and put an arm around her as they continued through the streets. "I know that."

A short time later, he stopped and took an abrupt left turn down an alleyway. "Why are we here?" Tara asked.

"Because this is where you're staying until I'm… finished."

Tara nodded like they shared an inside secret—which, Chase supposed, they kind of did. The man on the rooftop overhead that'd been watching them all day didn't know what he was about to do.

Chase had taken careful note of him throughout the day. He was strange-looking. Long, sleek gray beard, but pitch-black long hair, meaning that he dyed one or the other somehow. Bulbous nose, but narrow face, and knowing eyes. Thin and tall, and dressed in a shepherd's robes. He'd been prowling around all afternoon, keeping a steady watch as they built their boat.

Now, Chase felt worried about leaving Tara alone. Chase didn't look up to the rooftops, for he didn't want the man to know that he was aware of him. Yet aware of him he was, and he didn't like the thought of leaving Tara alone with this strange man so close if she didn't know he was there.

He took her hand and yanked her out of the alley and away from the buildings. He caught a glimpse of the man disappearing over the rooftop as they went, no doubt coming to watch him in the street. Chase would have to be fast.

"Why am I out here now?" Tara asked obliviously.

Chase put his arm on her shoulder, covering her face discreetly with his forearm, and nudged her head in the direction of the roof on which the man had been standing. "Up there," he said, "there was a man. Watching us. He's been keeping a sharp eye all afternoon, the whole time we were building. I saw him sitting in the lobby of Helmsman Inn, too. He was there when we arrived and when we left.

While I'm doing… the thing… I want you to stay very aware of your surroundings, Tara. He hasn't shown any signs of threat, but when someone's watching you like that, it's never good."

Tara's eyes were full of fear. "I never even noticed him. What does he look like?"

"He looks," Chase said, tugging her to the other side of the street, "exactly like that." He pushed her to sit on the bench right next to the man who'd been stalking them all day long.

Tara's jaw clenched and her eyes grew huge. She glared murderously at Chase, and he simply smiled and announced loudly, "Wait here. I'll be back in no time. Just going to run an errand or two."

Tara pressed her lips together tightly as Chase turned away, trying to keep a smile from his face. She'd be fine. It was much better to be right next to—and fully aware of—your enemy, than to be paranoid and always wondering where he could be hiding. Besides, the street was bustling with people. If the man did, by some rare chance, try to do anything to Tara, other people would surely step in. And in any case, Chase was not going far.

He followed a fat old man down the street, walking slowly and pretending to be enjoying a nice leisure walk. A fishing cap seemed tiny atop the head of such a massive person.

As he passed the man, Chase bumped into him roughly. The man jerked sideways from the impact, knocking a woman's purse from her hands. The bag slid over the cobbled street and stopped a few steps away. While the man was feverishly apologizing to the woman, Chase ducked away from the exchange, picked up the woman's purse, and emptied its contents into one of his pouches. He then set the purse down again as it had fallen and slid back into the crowds. By this time, the fat man had turned to see who had jostled him and was now yelling at a random sailor who had

had nothing to do with the situation but seemed in the right position to have shoved him. Chase walked away with heavy pockets and without detection.

Coming back to the bench, he found Tara sitting alone, twisting a stand of her hair. He smirked and walked up to her.

"What happened to your little friend?"

Tara shrugged. "I don't know." Her voice was quivering a little. "He left shortly after I sat down. Did you take care of your errand?"

"Yes, it's all done. We can go shopping soon. But by Death, does it feel good to relax a bit first," he sighed with exaggerated exhaustion and sat down with a huff, throwing his arm around Tara in an extra wide arc.

His hand promptly collided with a face. *Bull's eye.*

Chase whirled around with mock surprise. "Oh, my goodness! Are you all right? I am so sorry, let me help you!" Tara's eyes were huge as that very same man who'd been following them crawled out from behind the bench.

"No, no, it was entirely my fault," he muttered stiffly.

Chase frowned slightly. He recognized that voice. He'd heard it before. But where? "If you don't mind my asking… what exactly does one hide behind a bench for?" Chase inquired with thick curiosity.

The man smiled wryly and shook his head. "No need to ask such things, lad. You know why. But enlighten me. I *don't* know why you've been building yourselves a boat."

Chase nodded slowly. Most people didn't admit to suspicious behavior so easily. "You're right. You don't know. And you never will." He tipped an imaginary hat. "Good evening."

He linked his arm in Tara's in a gentlemanly fashion and pulled her along with him. Her hands were trembling and her nails dug into the leather covering his knuckles.

"Calm down," he whispered.

"Have I told you recently that I hate you?" she growled. "How could you make me *sit* next to him?"

"I love you so dearly that I thought I would let someone other than myself have the pleasure of murdering you."

Tara glanced over her shoulder, then turned back around and pressed closer to Chase as they walked. He didn't need to look back to know that the man hadn't given up yet. "You don't know very much about seafaring, do you, lad?"

Chase did not answer him.

"I suppose you're quite the landlubber, seeing how you thought you could actually craft a boat. You also don't seem to understand that a raft cannot carry you over the ocean. Had you ever been on a real boat before, you would know that your contraption will never float."

Still, no response. Secretly, Chase got the feeling he was right, but he would not give this man the satisfaction of a response. The man changed tactics.

"Might I make a deal with you, boy?"

"No, you may not."

"Oh, come now." The man was struggling to keep up as Chase continuously quickened his pace. "There's no need to be so unfriendly, lad. I don't bite."

Tara was all but running to allow her short legs to keep up, but the man finally caught up with them. "Why can't you tell me why such young people need to be out on the sea alone?"

"Because it is none of your business. You don't know anything about us, so I would appreciate it if you would leave us to our evening now."

"Apologies, dear boy, but I cannot."

Chase turned around, stopping in the center of the street, and regarded the man calmly. "You are a stranger. You have no right to be following us, and what we are doing has absolutely nothing to do with you, so please stay out of it. If you don't leave us alone, the night watch will become involved, and I will see to it that you are put on trial."

"Let us not be so hasty. I wish to bargain."

"I will not make deals with someone I don't know."

"Oh, you most certainly will, lad."

"What makes you think that?" Chase asked, his tone still cool.

The man smiled thinly and tilted his head. "Persuasion."

Chase stared darkly at him at him for several moments before speaking.

"What exactly do you want?" he asked quietly.

"I want to know what your boat is for."

"Why?" "You'll discover the answer to that question if you bargain."

Chase lifted an eyebrow. "Name your terms. Quickly."

The man nodded. "You put your little boat in the water. If she proves to be seaworthy, then you and your friends can be on your way. If not, then you have to tell me why you want to go out to sea."

Why on earth would a stranger care so much about this? Chase shook his head. "I'm not an idiot. You'll sabotage it."

The man chuckled. "I don't think sabotage will be necessary with that so-called boat."

Chase drew in a breath. He was becoming extremely irritated. He shook his head and waved the man away. "My answer is no. It's not going to change, so leave us alone."

He began to walk away, giving Tara's arm a hard pinch to remind her to breathe.

"I think," the man called after them, "that you will regret walking away from me."

"Uh-huh."

"Forget the deal, then. I just need a quick word."

Chase stopped suddenly, his memory jogging. "That's it!" he whispered.

Tara clutched his shirt in fear. "What?"

"That voice…" He remembered now. When they'd first arrived at the Helmsman Inn earlier that day, Carlton had been called down to the lobby by a friend visiting from the north. It was him! The man had been at the inn before and after their stay there, and the voice was definitely his.

"How's Carlton Wills been doing lately?" Chase called smugly, resuming his quick pace.

"Oh, just fine, Chase, thank you for asking. How's Tetoviran been?"

Both Chase and Tara stopped dead in their tracks at this. Chase turned and studied the man that stood before him through narrowed eyes. "You were never nearly close enough to hear names. Who are you?"

The man lifted his index finger triumphantly. "That will come, my boy, with the deal. Should your little contraption sink—or prove unseaworthy in any way—then we will all sit down and have a little talk. I have much to discuss with you. *All* of you."

Chase curled his lip. He was annoyed now, because he wanted answers—and the man knew it. "Fine," he muttered forcefully. "But if you try anything funny in the meantime…" "I can assure you, I will not."

"Just come on." Chase walked fast, staying well ahead of the man.

"Have you been drinking again, or are you truly this foolish? What on earth is in your head?" Tara hissed, gripping his upper arm.

Chase shrugged. "Not sure myself. But he was never close enough to hear our names. There was never a time when he was out of my sight, and all day, he was too far away to hear anything."

Tara slowed uncomfortably, but Chase yanked her forward again. "Let's hurry. Night is coming. Again," he muttered with contempt.

They finally reached the small grassy outcrop. Tetoviran, Logan, and Fin still laid on the ground, but they were now joined by the very exhausted-looking Devon, Emma, Grace, Oliver, and Rebel. Devon and Oliver had damp hair.

Chase jogged up to them, still arm-in-arm with Tara. As he did so, he noticed Devon glance at their locked elbows and frown. He also noticed that Tara saw it, too, and dropped her arm from Chase's as soon as she did. This made Chase frown. First of all, everyone knew that he and Tara were just friends, and secondly, he didn't like how willingly Tara gave him up to please Devon. He knew it was a small action and one he shouldn't dwell on, but it bothered him nonetheless.

"So, what happened with you guys?" Chase asked the other group.

Oliver shook his head in exhaustion. "We stood on that dock for hours, waiting for an opportunity. That same old sailor who asked us for money earlier sits out there at the end of the dock. All. Day. Long. He watches everyone and everything that happens there. A fisherman told us that he sits there from sunrise to sunset, and there's another guy who takes the night shift. Boats are life around here. Families eat and breathe on their vessels, so they want to make absolutely sure nobody takes one."

Devon nodded. "There's constantly someone there, watching. Hawk eyes, he has. It's impossible to do anything without being seen, and nothing is for sale. Nobody would even let us borrow a boat or take a ride."

Chase frowned. "You couldn't distract him?"

"We tried," Grace grumbled. Chase noticed that she was cradling her knee. "He realized what we were doing right away and didn't take anything from anyone. He shoved Devon and Oliver into the water when they tried to untie a boat and kicked me off the dock when I tried to divert his attention."

Chase winced. "He literally kicked you off?"

She nodded and moved her hand away from her knee, revealing a nasty bruise. "He has one sturdy pair of boots," she said with distaste.

Chase whistled through his teeth, blowing the injury a mocking kiss. "Well, by this time, I'm sure you know how *our* afternoon went."

They all nodded, glancing at the boat in polite silence. Nobody wanted to say it, but everyone knew the vessel looked pathetic.

Rebel scampered up to Tara, grunting and snorting, and licked her hand. Tara smiled and picked him up, responding in *tesko* tongue.

"So, stealing a boat was a failure," Teto said pointedly. "We'd better pray this useless slab of wood works." Everyone eyed the rickety, crooked boat doubtfully.

"Oh, yeah," Chase said suddenly. "Speaking of which."

He turned around and grabbed the man out from behind a bush. Everyone yelped.

"Who's that?"

"I didn't even see him there!"

"How long has he been there?"

"This man," Chase announced, shoving him forward roughly, "has been watching us all afternoon. He was Carlton Wills' friend in the lobby. He watched while we made the boat and followed me and Tara through town."

Tetoviran stood immediately, and several others reached for their weapons.

"What do you want with us?" Fin growled, his fingers creeping towards his bow.

The man smiled. "I struck a bargain with Chase Onaj."

Everyone's eyebrows shot up at once. "You told him your name?" Oliver cried.

"No," Tara said. "He didn't, and this man was never close enough to hear us talking." Everyone glared suspiciously at the man.

"However," Tara continued, "he has agreed to tell us about himself and what he wants from us under one condition. If our boat proves seaworthy, we can go off on our journey. If not, we need to talk to him. He says he has lots to tell us."

Collective cries of protest arose.

"No way!"

"We don't even know him."

"He'll probably sabotage the boat!"

Chase silenced them. "I, personally, would like to know what this guy wants with us. Besides, talking can't hurt anything. Either the boat works, or it doesn't."

The others were silent. "Fine, then," Emma said quietly. "Let's test the boat."

A short time and plenty of complaints later, the tired group had hauled their boat down to the shore. Everyone stood up to their thighs in the ocean, the slow tide lapping gently against their legs.

"How much farther?" Logan moaned. The poor, thin boy's arms were trembling from weight he wasn't used to bearing. Logan relied on cleverness and speed to get him out of trouble, not strength.

"The water can't be too shallow," Tetoviran responded from the other side of the boat.

All of them were holding the boat above the water's surface, wading it out deep enough so that nothing would interfere with the boat's abilities. The sunset was pale, shrouded deeply by fog and tinting the water a faint orange.

They waded out until they were well past the breaking waves— which had battered some of them into the sand—and entering into deeper water. Chase felt the cold seeping up into his shirt as the water level reached his waist and then his chest. Tara, being the shortest one by far, was tilting her head back to keep it above the water.

Finally, Teto, who was holding up the front of the boat, stopped. "It's deep enough now," he announced.

Chase took a deep breath. "Okay," he whispered.

They prepared to set it on the water but were stopped by the sound of the man's voice faintly echoing from the beach. "It doesn't count unless it floats with at least one person in it!"

Logan made a gagging face.

"I hate him," Devon muttered. "We're listening to him why?"

"Because he knows things," Grace said.

"Well, no arguing with the beard," Fin said. "Who's getting in?"

"Whoever's the lightest," Oliver said matter-of-factly. All eyes turned to Tara. She groaned and walked carefully up to the boat. She couldn't possibly reach it from that height, so Chase braced his knee underwater.

"Climb aboard," Teto said drily.

She took a deep breath and stepped up onto Chase's knee while he supported her balance with an arm encircling her hips. She hoisted herself carefully and slowly into the boat and sat down. The whole thing creaked under her weight, and everyone winced.

"That can't be good," Logan mumbled.

"Okay, let's just get it over with. On my count," Fin said. "One... two... three!"

They all set the boat down on the water and backed away. For one heart-lifting moment, it floated on the surface.

"Ha!" Tetoviran yelled. "Works perfectly!"

And then the whole thing promptly sank.

CHAPTER 33

Tara's entire body was plunged instantly into a piercing, icy cold. In less than an instant, the entire boat was underwater, taking her down with it. The water closed over her head, and for a moment, time seemed to slow. Suddenly, she was back in the river, thrashing helplessly against the current before the world went dark and her body was swept away. Panic was muted but present.

Yet this water was much stronger than the river. This water was wild and violent. This was Sea, and it did not welcome her. Here, panic was vivid and blinding.

Tara felt her lungs begin to ache, and she frantically tried to push herself to the surface. It felt as though the ocean was pushing down on her, every thrashing movement making it stronger. It was swallowing her.

And then, strong hands grabbed her clothes and yanked her upwards. Her head broke through the surface, and she gasped for air with relief.

She was completely soaked in freezing cold water, down to her last layer of clothing. Her legs felt numb as Fin—who'd pulled her from the water—wrapped his arms around her to give her his body heat before she caught a chill. She found her footing and stood in silence, staring at the spot where the boat had gone under. Fin's hard, strong arms and chest pressed into Tara somewhat uncomfortably, his grip tighter than necessary. He was angry, and Tara was indescribably grateful that he wasn't angry at her. No one spoke for a long time.

Tara shivered in the rapidly cooling evening air, attempting to wring the water from her hair. Her mouth tasted salty.

Finally, Emma spoke. "I don't know much about boats, but I don't think they ever sink quite that fast."

Chase shook his head, his jaw clenched. "They don't." He glanced back at Tara. "Are you okay?"

She nodded through chattering teeth. "J-just c-c-cold."

He nodded. "Let's go ashore. I want to hit somebody." Together, they waded to the beach.

Chase marched right up to that man and, contrary to his spoken desires, spat in his face. "What was that?" he demanded.

"Your boat sank," he replied coolly, wiping spit off his cheek.

Chase gripped his sword hilt like he was ready to decapitate the man. "Yes, I understand *that*. How? Nothing can sink that quickly. It didn't even fill with water, first of all, and secondly, it was made of wood. That thing sank faster than an anvil." "Are you implying, Mr. Onaj, that I had something to do with this?" Chase opened his mouth angrily to respond, but the man didn't give him time. "Even though I was standing a quarter league away?"

Chase's mouth slowly slid shut, his jaw set forward. It *was* impossible. He'd sound crazy if he kept persisting. But Tara also knew that it was impossible for a wooden boat—however rickety or flimsy it may be—to sink that quickly. It hadn't even had time to fill with water. It just went under.

"Time for our chat, I suppose," the man said lightly, turning to walk away. "Come along."

There was a slow, metallic drawl as one of Teto's swords slid menacingly from its sheath. "All right, Your Grayness, the boat's gone, you got your way. Who are you?"

The man turned around and reached out a single finger. Teto stared at it. "What's that supposed to—gah!"

At the flick of the man's finger, Teto's sword flew from his hand and danced around his head in midair. Everyone backed away from the floating blade warily.

"Are you a Creator?" Fin asked in terrified awe.

The man smiled and flicked his finger again. The sword flew, with rapid speed, back down towards Tetoviran, agilely dodging his flailing limbs and sinking smoothly into his sheath.

"No," the man said chirpily. "I am a sorcerer. Blessed by Creators with power, but not a Creator myself, no. My name is Wedlem, and I am one of the greatest sorcerers and seers of beyond that has ever walked this earth," he proclaimed with a flourish.

Everyone just stared at him.

"What's up with the raccoon's nest hanging from your chin?" Teto asked. Wedlem scowled at him.

"Wait a minute!" Chase yelled suddenly. "It *was* you! You *did* sink our boat!"

He smiled, looking pleased with himself. "Yes. I did."

Fin clenched his fists. "Do you have any idea how long it took us to make that?"

"Yes, I was there, Fin Vidovu. I watched the entire pathetic process unfold. Oh, and in case any of you were wondering, I don't know anything about this one's powers," he said, gesturing to Tara dismissively and making it clear that he knew far more about their journey than he had let on so far. "It will be long before this child can make a leaf bend on command, so I suggest she begin learning to swing that stick on her back before someone cuts her open with it."

Chase lunged forward, and Logan had to wrestle his arms to keep him back.

Emma stepped up. "Hang on. There must be a reason for all this. *Why* did you sink our boat?"

Wedlem turned to her with mild surprise, looking at her with great interest but not seeming to hear her question. "My, you've grown. How interesting your life has become, Emma Ro"—

"It's just Emma!" she said through clenched teeth, for the second time on this journey. For the second time, Tara wondered why she didn't want them to know her last name.

Wedlem studied her for a moment, then nodded. "I see. I know what you want, Emma. And I will not disrupt that. But you will play a big role in the future of this quest."

Tara shivered harder as a gust of wind blew in from the coast. Wedlem's gaze fell upon her. "Forgive me. You must not want to stand out here and listen to me prattle on. So very sorry about this, my dear," he said, stepping toward her with his arm outstretched. "Here, come along now."

She took a step back, but her legs were failing. She was freezing, and could no longer feel her feet. "Cold," she mumbled, because that was the only word in her vocabulary at the moment.

Chase stepped in front of her. "Keep away from her," he said stonily. "I don't care what you've got to say. What you've done is not—and never will be—appreciated. So, for the millionth time, would you please just do your talking and leave?"

Wedlem frowned ever so slightly, as if looking upon a pesky fly that wouldn't leave him alone. "Ah. This one does not like me. We can't have that, can we?" He flicked his hand, and Chase flew through the air, pushed by an invisible force, and he fell on his back hard in the sand nearby with a grunt. A collective gasp of shock rose. Chase shook sand out of his hair and swore at Wedlem, who frowned with distaste.

"Mind your tongue, boy. There are less respectable men than myself who would kill you for those words."

Devon and Logan rushed to help him up, and Oliver scowled at the man before them. "No one here likes you. If you insist on being here, quit stalling and say what you bloody came to say!" Tara blinked at the harshness of his words. It was the most aggressive thing she'd ever heard Oliver say.

"Yes, I suppose I should try to be quick about it. No sense in wasting time." He snapped his fingers, and everyone found themselves sitting suddenly in a warm room with dim lights overhead and people laughing and eating all around them. They were seated at a round dining table.

"Hey," Grace said, looking around once they'd recovered from the shock. "This is Helmsman Inn."

Wedlem nodded, then reached out and tapped Tara's shoulder before anyone could stop him. Immediately, she felt dry and warm, and the change was so vast that she sighed in comfort before she could stop herself. Her clothes and hair showed no signs of her former soaked condition. She glanced at Wedlem nervously, and he just shook his head slightly. "No appreciation. How typical for children," he muttered.

"Just get on with it," Devon snarled.

"Well, I'll start at the beginning. I am a seer of beyond. This means that I often receive pieces of the future, and have clear visions of the past. When I arrived this morning in Weather-helm, I saw flashes of nine people and one *tesko* traveling together. I saw pictures of your future, and that is why I sunk your boat. I saw that your boat needed to fail in order for your mission to succeed.

"I have seen a way for you to get out on the open sea. It is the way you must take."

He swirled his hands, and a glass orb appeared in the air, hovering over their table. Tara's eyes widened, then darted around the room. People were watching.

Wedlem smiled. "Don't mind the others, Tara. I am here quite often. They all know me by now."

Tara focused nervously on the floating ball. Wedlem waved his hand in front of the orb, and an image appeared in it. It was dark and difficult to make out, but a huge ship was visible, docked beside a town. It was night, and people were screaming and crying out. Explosions sounded, and then the image faded, replaced with swirling black smoke.

"Tonight," Wedlem said darkly, "there will be an attack. A ship will come, and pirates will come ashore and loot this town. As I'm sure you know, this is unfortunately common. But this is also *your* ticket to sea."

He waved his hand again, and the image changed. It showed blurred figures climbing aboard the empty ship, the vessel sailing off into the night. "You must board this ship while the pirates are gone. You must hide and wait until they return. Once the ship leaves the harbor, you will be on your way." He waved his hand again, and the orb vanished. "It is the *only* way."

There was silence. Tetoviran leaned back in his chair. "So how do we know you're not playing with us, the way you were with the boat?"

Wedlem flicked his hand, and a mug of foamy liquid appeared on the table before him. He took a long swig, then wiped his lips and leaned forward, his eyes dark and foreboding.

"See for yourself, if you believe me not. A ship will come, a ghost ship that vanishes in the night and disappears into the mist. A ship with a merciless crew and a captain with a greed so immense that no amount of treasure can ever slake his wanting for more. Kidnapping, thieving, murdering pirates, and nasty ones, too."

Grace laughed harshly. "And you want us to climb on a ship with them? No thanks."

Wedlem drank again, slamming his mug back to the table with a bang. Grace jumped a little. "You will stay here, you know. You will never succeed in building nor stealing a boat in Weatherhelm, or anywhere else, for that matter."

"What, you've *seen beyond* about that, too?" Logan asked.

"I have."

Chase closed his eyes and pinched the bridge of his nose. When he looked up again, his eyes were uncharacteristically tired. "So, in order to get where we want to go, we have to sneak onto a ship full of bloodthirsty murderous pirates. And you actually expect us to listen to you?"

"Well, of course I"—

"We're not stupid, Wedlem," Chase interrupted him brashly. "We've come a long, long way, and not to go on a suicide mission because some old stalker tells us to."

Wedlem shrugged and downed the last of his mug. "Suit yourselves. You'll see. Choosing not to do as I have told you would be very, very foolish." And with a wave of his hand, he was gone, his cup with him, and the group was left in the Helmsman Inn with their thoughts.

"What a psycho," Logan muttered.

"What a phony," Emma corrected. "He's mad if he thinks we're actually stupid enough to believe his ghost stories."

"Yeah, but what now?" Devon asked. "The boat was a bust. How are we really going to get out there?"

Fin shook his head. "Sleep now, talk tomorrow. Destiny and Fate had to mess up our time schedule, on top of everything else they'd screwed with. Chase, did you manage to steal some money while you were out there for oars?"

Chase nodded and emptied the pouch that he'd filled with the contents of the woman's purse earlier. Looking at the items in his palm for the first time, he frowned. There was only a small quantity of coins; the rest of his hand was filled with small trinkets and hair ribbons. He took everything but the money from his hand and threw it carelessly on the ground. "Not much, though. Not nearly enough for three rooms again."

Tetoviran leaned over the money. "That's barely enough for one, kid! Hurry up and go steal some more before we fall asleep on the table." Chase shook his head. "I'm too tired. I'll screw something up."

Suddenly, Tara thought of something she'd never asked before. "Chase?" she asked.

"Hm?"

"What's the penalty if you're caught stealing?"

Chase yawned and rolled his shoulders. "Hanging." He threw it out casually, but Tara sat bolt upright.

"What?" He smiled a little. "You've been stealing things your entire life when you knew the punishment for being caught was *death?* What is the matter with you? And why was I never aware of this?"

"Because of *that,*" Chase said, gesturing towards her miniature heart attack. Logan shared a look of amusement with him.

"Chase, you could be dead by now! Both you and Logan! Do you have any idea how"—

"Which is why," he interrupted, "I'm careful. For instance. Right now, I'm not going to attempt to steal anything because I know myself, and I know that when I'm tired, I get careless. I've been doing this a long time, Princess. Don't worry."

Tara stared at him with a gaping mouth. Don't worry? How in the world could he expect her to not worry after that? She would be worried for the rest of her life now.

Fin smiled a bit, but it was strained from exhaustion. "All right, then. We'll have to make do with one room. Let's find Carlton. We all need sleep."

About fifteen minutes later, the group was dragging itself up the stairs. As they finally trudged up to their room, Carlton Wills unlocked it for them and eyed them carefully. "No messing around in here. I mean it," he said. "I've got a reputation to uphold, you know, and I wouldn't normally let men and women into the same room together."

"Fill a hole in the ground," Chase grumbled, pushing past him gruffly.

Carlton frowned slightly, almost looking hurt, and Tara smiled tiredly at him. "Thanks for your hospitality," she said apologetically. He nodded, much of his former energy gone, and moved along down the hall.

Everyone else practically crawled into the room, dropping on whatever surface they could. Four people squished into the bed and everyone else collapsed on the floor. The door slid shut, and Tara's eyes did, too. She slept deeply. Dreamless.

The screaming came first. There were cries from outside the window and beneath them in the lobby. People hollered in panic in the hallway, and Tara stirred out of her slumber as the others rustled awake, as well.

"What's going on?" she mumbled drowsily. Suddenly, there was a loud bang and a crashing sound outside the window. More screaming followed.

Tara and Emma got to their feet and rushed to the window, where Chase already stood. Upon looking out, they found it difficult to see. The entire town was shrouded in a thick, dark mist. Judging by the darkness of the sky, it was very late—still the middle of the night.

Squinting through the darkness, Tara saw a house on the streets below, splintered and collapsed in on itself. "What happened?" she breathed.

There was another bang, and down the street another house exploded, bursting into flame that spread and burned so quickly that the building was completely penetrated in moments.

"What is it?" Devon called from the bed, still half asleep.

Chase shook his head. "I can't believe it," he muttered. Then he turned into the room and grabbed his sword, attaching it immediately to his belt. "Get up, come on, we have to go. We need to get out." People mumbled and began to move sluggishly. Chase swore and tore the sheets away from the bed aggressively. "Get up!" he shouted, beginning to hit people to awaken them fully. He punched into Fin and grabbed Grace's face. "Get out of bed, you lazy animals! We're under attack!"

Everyone rose worriedly, wide awake now, and chaotic, fearful voices filled the room.

"Kid!" Teto's voice rose over them all. "What is it?"

Chase glanced at the window again, then tackled as many of them as he could to the ground. "Catapults!" he shouted. "Get down!"

Without hesitation, everyone hit the floor as the room exploded with a deafening crash. Tara screamed as wood splintered and fell all around her, debris littering the floor. A lamp hit the floor and broke, sending glass shards flying. A section of the ceiling above her caved and fell, and she barely rolled out of the way in time.

Scrambling to her feet as the ceiling continued to fall in around her, she ran for the door, jumping over wood and fallen beams from the bed. Her friends followed and she shoved debris away from the door, pushing it open with Devon's help and racing out into the hall.

Barely able to think of anything except escape, she sprinted for the stairs. She felt a sudden wave of heat hit her as she began to round a corner, and Chase stuck his arm out and pushed her back. "Stop!" he ordered.

Her chest rose and fell heavily. Chase's face was cut and bleeding beneath his eye. "Fire," he whispered. Sure enough, smoke was coming from just around the corner.

"Fire?" Emma shrieked, her voice just on the verge of terror. She let out a shockingly uncharacteristic scream of fear as the noise of the flames became audible.

The heat was already making Tara sweat, and Chase turned and shoved everyone in the other direction. "Go, go, go! The building's on fire, we have to get out!"

As they ran, the fire crackled around the corner and started spreading down their hall. Emma was hyperventilating, screaming and trembling frantically, and her fingers were folded in a strange gesture over her heart.

"Mercy, mercy," she kept gasping, far more upset than any of them. Her screams were far from calming in the face of an emergency. The heat was unbearable as the polluted air surrounded them, covering their clothes in ash.

"Get down!" Fin gasped, and they all dropped to their knees, crawling down the hall with their shirts over their noses. Emma was sobbing and struggling to inhale, having a complete panic attack.

Tetoviran, who was leading the group, stopped at the end of the hall. "Dead end!" he shouted.

Emma's wails grew louder and more despairing. For her—the most emotionless and collected of all of them—to be screaming so agonizingly terrified Tara. She felt her necklace begin to burn but didn't care. She was so afraid that she didn't even consider using it to her advantage.

"Use Rebel!" Fin screamed as the fire drew nearer. Instantly, the *tesko* wriggled out of Tara's knapsack and opened his mouth but only managed to inhale a small bit of flame before the smoke overpowered him and he began hacking in choked fits. His kind knew the outdoors. The wild. There was nothing they could do about a fire that closed smoke in on them.

"He can't!" Tara yelled back, and there wasn't enough time for them to try and make it work.

Devon pushed past everyone to the wall. "It's already damaged," he yelled. "Help me kick it down! Hurry!"

Everyone started ramming their bodies into the wobbling wall. Emma was sobbing horribly. With every hit, it gave a little more. With every second, the fire got a little closer. Rebel bit through the wall in sections, opening a gap in it and letting cracks branch out from the hole to the ceiling. Tara's eyes burned from the smoke and heat, but she refused to give up.

She slammed her weight into the wall once more and closed her eyes as she felt the wall give way. She felt herself begin to fall, felt someone's hand grip hers. The world was sliding out from under her feet. She was falling, falling, falling… until she wasn't. She hit the ground and rolled down a grassy hill, tangled with whoever held her hand as they tumbled down a gentle slope into a cool pool of water.

Tara laid for several moments before finally opening her eyes. Chase was lying on top of her, groaning. His fingers went limp, dropping her hand as he gasped for clean air. Devon, Tetoviran, and Rebel laid next to them in the pond behind the inn. Their other friends were visible atop the hill.

Tara lowered her shirt from over her nose and breathed, inhaling deeply despite the crushing weight of Chase's body on top of hers. The air still reeked of smoke, but it wasn't as strong down here. Her necklace's heat had fizzled to abrupt coolness as soon as she'd landed in the water. Being in the water seemed to extinguish her powers completely.

She took ragged breaths, hacking and coughing until her lungs felt clear again, then took a deep breath and tried to calm herself down. No one moved for some time. She finally looked at Chase, who still laid breathlessly on top of her. His face was completely black all over from soot and ash, and she knew hers must be too. The front of his shirt had been slashed open down the middle, his chest gray with ashes and sweaty. He lifted a shaky hand and brushed a piece of her now-wet hair from her face.

"Are you... okay?" he asked. His voice was deep and raspy. She nodded rather numbly and found that swallowing had now begun to hurt. Chase smiled, despite everything, and pressed his parched lips to her forehead. "Good."

He finally stood, hopelessly trying to brush the soot from his clothes, and helped Devon and Teto to their feet. Their clothes, hair, and faces were blackened with ash as well.

"Let's get to the others," Chase said. "We have to make sure everyone's okay." He reached down and pulled Tara up, and with Rebel in tow, they made their way up the hill to find the rest of their friends unharmed and waiting for them.

"Everyone here? You're all okay?" Tetoviran asked. Everyone nodded. Emma showed no signs whatsoever of her former breakdown.

Together, they looked up at the burning building. Flames licked the sky, and people yelled orders and rushed around with buckets of water. The entire building gave off an orange light that shone over all of Weather-helm as destruction ravaged the town.

"Life bless it all." Fin said the words fearfully, wetting his dry, cracked lips. "Don't tell me there's actually a"—

"Ship," Emma finished with horror. She stood a short distance away, staring in the direction of the harbor. Everyone hurried to join her and saw a humongous, looming vessel, dark and foreboding in the night. It was tied down at the beach, the tide lapping gently at its base.

"I don't believe it. That sword-floating smoky-ball-creating grog-drinking toad was actually right," Tetoviran whispered. Tara swallowed, then winced. Her throat was so dry.

All of a sudden, Chase turned and ran toward the street. "Chase!" Tara screamed coarsely. Everyone sprinted after him.

When they came to the road, though, Tara pulled to a stop as a horrible sight met her eyes. Filthy, grimy men with thick-bladed cutlasses were lighting houses on fire, stabbing people, stealing things, grabbing animals and women and children… Tara's mouth hung open. She couldn't believe the things she was seeing. A house collapsed in on an elderly woman, a pirate slit a man's throat and took his things, another man ran wildly through the streets and sliced his sword through one body after the next. Women were being harassed terribly, children were slain right along with adults, and all those disgusting pirates seemed to care about was how much money the person they killed had on their body.

Tara turned to the bushes simultaneously with Grace and vomited. The sight was so horrifying that she had to look away. She and Grace clutched each other's hands as they retched. Tara couldn't bring herself to watch what those wretched men were doing.

Suddenly, she felt rough hands grab her around the waist from behind and lift her off her feet. Her heart felt like it had jumped into her throat. The arms around her were thick and roped with tattoos. She screamed and kicked, reaching for her sword. She managed to draw it by some miracle and ram the pommel into the chest of her attacker.

He dropped her in surprise, and Tara whirled to see a disgusting, filthy man with bugs crawling through his beard and a gold-toothed, wolfish grin.

Her friends helped her immediately to her feet and moved to protect her, but the pirate recovered and leapt at her again.

Fin tried to get in his way, but he shoved the boy out of his path like he was no bigger than a kitten.

"You're mine, lass!" the pirate snarled, his hungry gaze sweeping over her greedily and clearly suggesting his sick intentions.

Tara glanced in a panic at Chase, who drew his sword as another pirate lunged at him and yelled one command: "RUN!"

Tara didn't need to be told twice. She turned and sprinted down the street, dodging a flying child and stepping over a dead body. Her stomach was rolling in disgust, her eyes overflowing with tears that she continually swiped away in order to see. It was one thing to watch phantoms and monsters be slaughtered, but human beings were an entirely different scenario. Tara had never seen so much blood in her life, nor had she hated her stupid powers more. Where were they when all these people were in danger?

She ran around another pirate who tried to block her path and jumped out of the way as a tall building came down behind her. The fallen remains had separated her from the pirate. He stood fuming on the other side, spitting on the ground and cursing. Bending over on her knees to catch her breath, Tara wiped her palms on her pants to regain a good grip on her sword.

In that moment, she heard something behind her; not so much an audible sound as it was a change of pressure in the air, and she turned just in time to parry a swing from another pirate.

Their swords met, and his strength was so overpowering that she was pushed several steps backward. "Hello, lass," he said softly, his eyes dancing with the same light as the one before him. When his gaze absorbed her body, clad in tighter clothes around the legs and hips than was customary for a girl, his face became anything but stoic. She kicked at him from beneath their locked blades, making it clear that she would be everything but cooperative. "So, that's how you want it to be?" he hissed.

He whirled his sword in an agile circle to free it from their locked stance and attacked. Tara barely had time to raise her sword against him. *It's not all about defense,* Chase's voice echoed in her ears. She struck at the pirate, but left her right side exposed. He kicked her hip while taking a parry and she fell, scraping her side on some broken glass. She bit her lip in pain as she got to her feet, keeping one hand over the stinging cut.

The pirate smiled triumphantly, and Tara took that opportunity to leap at him and take a swing. He reacted incredibly quickly. Although she wasn't sure how, in mere seconds, Tara was weaponless and back on the ground, pinned down by the pirate's blade on her throat. In his other hand, he raised her own sword.

"You tried, girlie. But you sure aren't good enough. Now, be a good girl and do as I tell you," he grinned, his eyes sweeping over her once more. Leaning close to her face and breathing his hot, sour breath all over her, he murmured, "or else one of these blades might just slip."

Tara's eyes widened, and the pirate had just begun to issue a command when a dark figure jumped from the shadows behind her and knocked Tara's sword from the pirate's hands—Chase.

Her weapon clattered to the ground a short distance away while he was still in midair, and he now landed protectively with his feet on either side of Tara's head, his own sword at the ready. "Touch her," Chase snarled, "and I will kill you."

The pirate squinted up at him, then smiled. "We'll see about that." Removing his sword from Tara's throat, he took a swing at Chase's legs. After that, everything was a blur. The two exchanged blows so rapidly that Tara couldn't even see their blades. She tried to get away but stumbled, and before she could even get to her feet, the pirate's grimy body fell on top of her.

Tara panicked, the first thought in her mind being that something had happened to Chase and the pirate was now trying to kill or rape her. Yet as she twisted over, she realized that the man was not moving. In fact, he was not even breathing. Tara's first instinct was to throw up as she stared at the dead, bleeding man that laid atop her, crushing her under his weight.

Chase shoved the body off of her and crouched beside her. He dropped his sword and cupped her face in his dirty hands. "Are you okay? Are you fine, are you sure?"

Tara didn't respond. She had been shocked and sickened into silence, paralyzed with her mouth open in terror. The dead man's blood was all over her. So dark. For her. Dark. So, so dark.

"Tara!" Chase yelled, gripping her chin in one hand. Suddenly, she breathed again. She stared at him, then at the pirate beside her. Quickly, she regretted that and averted her gaze. She was still crying, but now she no longer bothered to wipe her face. "Y-you… you killed him," she gasped finally.

Chase helped her into a sitting position. "It was him or you. I didn't have a choice."

Her jaw was still slack. Her best friend, a murderer. And she knew that there truly hadn't been an alternative, but she would never forget the image of that dead man's body falling down on her. That pirate… he might have had a family somewhere. A mother, a brother, someone who loved him. And he had been a child once.

Chase helped her slowly to her feet, rolled her shirt up to her waist, and examined the cut in her side. "Flesh wound," he said, readjusting her clothes roughly enough to make her stumble. "Nothing embedded. You'll be fine."

He picked up his sword and handed Tara hers. His expression was taut and rigid. He would not be offering her comfort right now. "Come on. We have to find the others. Don't let go of me."

He grabbed her wrist and raced down the street, striking a pirate that grabbed at Tara's knapsack and dodging a huge mob of them on his way. He slipped a knife from someone's boot as he passed him and hurled it at a group of three men trying to intercept them. Tara did not stop to see whether it hit someone, but she knew the men had cleared a path.

"Chase!" Tara yelled. "What are we doing?"

Instead of answering, he pulled her behind a thick shrub, grabbed her by the back of her jacket, and shoved her forcefully onto the ground. She landed on warm bodies and screamed when arms grabbed her. She whirled and punched someone right in the nose, then heard a yelp and realized it was Logan. She turned and saw her friends, crouching behind the bushes. All of them were there, and all were okay. She took a gasp of air, barely able to think.

Logan scowled and gave her hair a quick, hard yank. "Thanks a lot, Tara." She apologized sheepishly, and he shrugged. "I'll get even."

That was definitely not what she wanted hear right then. Rebel was whimpering, and she gently set him in her knapsack.

"We," Chase said sinisterly, "are getting on that ship."

CHAPTER 34

It was insanity. It was pure insanity, Chase knew. They had all seen what these men did to people, but they would all be out in the town, looting and pillaging and so forth, so the ship would be practically empty. Any vessel that large had to have lots of storage room in which they could hide themselves until they reached open ocean. As the group snuck along the side roads and back alleys of Weather-helm, making their way to the dock, no one spoke. The fear and trepidation made the silence heavy and loud. Everyone knew what they had to do, but not a single one of them wanted to do it.

They crept up behind a building. The dock was right there, standing in the mist in front of them. Sure enough, sitting stubborn as a mule on the wooden plank, was the night guard. Not reacting at all to the destruction and devastation that raged through the town, he sat, still and stiff as a rock.

"You have got to be kidding me," Grace muttered when she saw him. "What is so important about that bloody slab of wood?"

Chase shrugged. "No matter, anyhow. All we need to do right now is get to the beach, and to get there, we need to go right past the dock."

Fin frowned. "Well, there're people everywhere. Why can't we just walk on past?"

"We can," Oliver said. "But we'd run the risk of getting caught in the fray."

Emma drew her scythe. "We'll run. Run as fast as we can through there and get to the beach. Everyone holds someone else's hand. We'll go in pairs. If something goes wrong, we meet by the ship. Understood?"

Everyone nodded and reached for one another. Chase grabbed Logan's hand. Emma paired with Grace, Tara with Tetoviran, and Oliver with Fin and Devon, since they had odd numbers. With weapons in their open hands, they all waited for Emma's signal. A fighting mob rolled past, and there was a brief open space.

"Now!" she yelled. Together, they all sprinted as fast as they could through the opening. Fin let go of Devon's hand and shot down two men who tried to block their paths. Tara turned her face away as the men fell.

They came to the cliffside and scrambled down to the beach as quickly as they could, pressing themselves against the rocks until any pursuers moved on.

Chase sagged against the cliff, then opened his hand and gazed at the golden coins in his palm. Devon took one look at them and burst out laughing.

"What?" Chase demanded.

"We're running for our lives through a crowd of murderous pirates, and you still find an opportunity to steal something," Devon guffawed.

Chase shrugged, the closest thing to a smile he'd worn all night passing over his face. "The pirates did all the dirty work for me." He turned to face the giant ship that loomed above them in the sand.

"So, this is our ride," Logan said.

"Pretty impressive," Emma commented in awe. The ship was beautiful and sleek, towering high above the beach. It was a city all on its own.

Fin put his bow over his shoulder and motioned the others forward. "We need to hurry. They'll be coming back soon."

Chase nodded. "Let's go."

Everyone sheathed their weapons and crept up behind the ship. They snuck around it, heading for the mooring lines and keeping close to the sides. Chase pointed at the mooring, quietly grabbed hold, locked his ankles around it, and began shinnying up the rope towards the deck. One by one, the others followed suit. Chase pulled himself up onto the deck, then turned to help the others up. When the last of them was on board, he put a finger to his lips and waved them on.

They tiptoed to a hatch where stairs descended to the first-floor compartment. Chase crouched and listened. He heard the raspy breathing of one person and nothing else. The breath was coming from the left side of the stairs, so Chase motioned for the others to wait where they were. He crept down the stairs, quietly drawing his sword. He saw the pirate right away. He was a thin man, sitting at a table with his back to Chase and holding an empty bottle.

Careful of creaking, Chase made his way slowly down the stairs. He reached the bottom and silently advanced on the man. He waited until he was mere steps away from him. Then, in one motion, he jumped forward and clubbed the man on the head with the pommel of his sword. He promptly fell unconscious, and Chase dragged him into the shadows of the hold's corners.

He ran back up the steps to his friends. "One man," he said. "Knocked him out from behind before he could get a glimpse of me. We're all set."

Together, they all ventured into the ship, passing rooms full of treasure and loot, and countless others loaded with food and supplies. They passed the kitchen and several storage rooms, then finally they came to a spot where Devon tripped on a metal ring sticking out of the ground.

Chase bent and saw that it was a rusty old handle to a trap door of some sort. Tugging on it, the hatch groaned open with a shower of dust. Chase coughed and waved at the air, then peered inside. "Couple of treasures. Some liquor. Not too much else, and plenty of room."

Tetoviran pushed him aside and stuck his face down there, examining the compartment. He straightened with a grim smile. "Ladies and idiots? I think we've found our hiding place."

Slowly, they lowered themselves into the room, helping one another until only Logan was left, standing above them.

He took a deep breath and glanced around anxiously. "Are you guys sure about this? Because once this door closes, the decision is final."

Chase snorted. "None of us want to do it, Logan. There's no turning back now. Just come down."

Logan clenched his jaw. "Here goes nothing," he said, and he plunged everyone into darkness. The door thudded shut with a heavy bang.

For a moment, no one said anything. It was impossibly dark and very musty. Someone coughed in the dank air. Some sort of rodent—a rat, no doubt—squealed from the far corner. Oliver shrieked suddenly, and everyone was thrown into a momentary panic until he told them it'd just been a spider.

With a huff, Chase plopped himself down on the hard floor. "Well, we might as well get comfortable. We're going to be here a long time."

Chase wasn't sure when he fell asleep or how long he slept for. He woke up, however, to someone shaking his shoulder. He squinted and waited a few minutes, letting his eyes adjust to the darkness. As everything came into visibility, he saw that Oliver had been shaking him.

"What?" he whispered, and the boy immediately clamped his hand over Chase's mouth. On his other side, Emma pointed silently upward. He looked at the trap door above them. He heard footsteps and voices, and dust rained down from the hatch's cracks as people walked over it.

And then, he realized something else: the boat was rocking. It was rocking from side to side, moving for sure. Chase wanted to cry in relief. His face was cut and covered in ash and grime, his hair was dusty and his clothes were charred, his hands were covered with blood that wasn't his. But he had never felt so very, very happy. They were on the ocean. They were on their way at last. They were going to find Ukrasen. They were going to save the world.

His triumphant line of thought broke off when he heard clomping footsteps stop right above the trap door. Everyone froze, tensed.

"I'm getting the rum now, so shut yer trap, ya lazy drunk!" The voice called from directly over them.

Another voice, further away, responded, "Aye, Cap'n."

The door began to shift, and Chase held his breath. No. No, no, no, no, no, *please* no! Not now! Not when they'd come this far! Especially not the *captain!*

The trap door swung open, and everyone shielded their faces from the ray of light that streamed in on them. When his eyes were finally used to the brightness, Chase squinted up in horror at the pirate staring coldly back at him. He had nasty, jagged scars running up and down his face and wore a royal blue and gold long-coat. He sneered cruelly, laughing a horrible, gravelly laugh.

"Well, now," he rumbled. "Stowaways, have we?" No one dared so much as to breathe. Chase felt like he was going to throw up his heart. Terror was so thick in the air that he could've choked on it.

"Well, then," the captain said quietly, "ye can all find out what happens to stowaways on my ship."

ACKNOWLEDGEMENTS

Wow, okay, first book. It literally still doesn't feel real. This was so much fun to write, but getting this off the ground as a teenager would have been impossible to do by myself. First and foremost, I want to thank God for the gifts He has given me and for all of the beautiful people He has brought into my life. Every opportunity I have received has been His doing, and every stroke of inspiration has been His brush. To Mom, for reading me picture books practically since birth and inspiring a love of stories in me. You never stopped supporting my successes. To Daddy, who is always full of cool ideas and constructive feedback, and who never doubted that I could do it for one second. I love you both with my whole heart. To Jess-Jess, for telling stories to me with our dolls in the basement as kids and teaching me how to use my imagination, for illustrating the picture book I wrote when I was five, and for buying me Starbucks practically every week during quarantine. You're literally my best friend. To Auntie, Uncle Pete, and Aunt Sandra: you guys are the best cheerleaders ever. I love you so much. To Ms. Thomas and all of the wonderful people at AcuteByDesign who worked so hard to make this happen: I will never forget the moment that I saw your acceptance email. Ginormous hug to you guys. To all of my teachers, from preschool to sophomore year, for teaching me how to write and encouraging me to do so. To Mr. Cosgriff, who was the only adult other than my family members to tell me I could do it. To Mary, who met with me multiple times and taught me everything I needed to know about the world of publishing. You, Bruce, and Riley never lost faith in me. To Sammie, for being the best hype-woman on the planet and for bringing the Sixteen Kingdoms to life on a map: you're the most talented person I know. To Ruby, who supported me from start to finish with this book and who I cannot go a single day without talking to. You inspire me infinitely. To Olivia, for taking the time to read and edit my entire manuscript before it ever saw a publishing house. To my astronomically supportive friends at Mercy, who changed my life for the better and never fail to make me laugh. To all of my peers at the Stanford Precollegiate Summer Institutes, for teaching and supporting and inspiring me endlessly. To every author, teacher, friend, or adult who told me I should wait, that a kid couldn't get published, that I was too young or too inexperienced, and to every publishing house that sent me a letter of rejection in the mail: you are the reason I kept trying. And lastly, to the readers, because I never dreamed that I would have some. I love you all so much.

AcuteByDesign, Publisher

Printed in the United States of America

Michele Thomas
Executive Publisher